Prince

S.J.A. Turney is an author of Roman and medieval historical fiction, gritty historical fantasy and rollicking Roman children's books. He lives with his family and extended menagerie of pets in rural North Yorkshire.

Also by S.J.A. Turney

The Ottoman Cycle

The Thief's Tale
The Priest's Tale
The Assassin's Tale
The Pasha's Tale

The Knights Templar

Daughter of War
The Last Emir
City of God
The Winter Knight
The Crescent and the Cross
The Last Crusade

Wolves of Odin

Blood Feud
The Bear of Byzantium
Iron and Gold
Wolves Around the Throne
Loki Unbound

The Damned Emperors series

Caligula
Commodus
Domitian
Caracalla

Last Emperor of Rome

Prince

S.J.A. TURNEY

PRINCE

canelo

First published in the United Kingdom in 2026 by

Canelo, an imprint of
Canelo Digital Publishing Limited,
20 Vauxhall Bridge Road,
London SW1V 2SA
United Kingdom

A Penguin Random House Company
The authorised representative in the EEA is Dorling Kindersley Verlag GmbH. Arnulfstr. 124,
80636 Munich, Germany

A CIP catalogue record for this book is available from the British Library.

ISBN 9 781 804 36952 4

Cover design by Henry Steadman

Cover images © Shutterstock.com

Printed and bound in Great Britain by Clays Ltd, Elcograf S.p.A.

Look for more great books at
www.canelo.co | www.dk.com

For Kerim Altug, Byzantine scholar extraordinaire and all-round superb human being

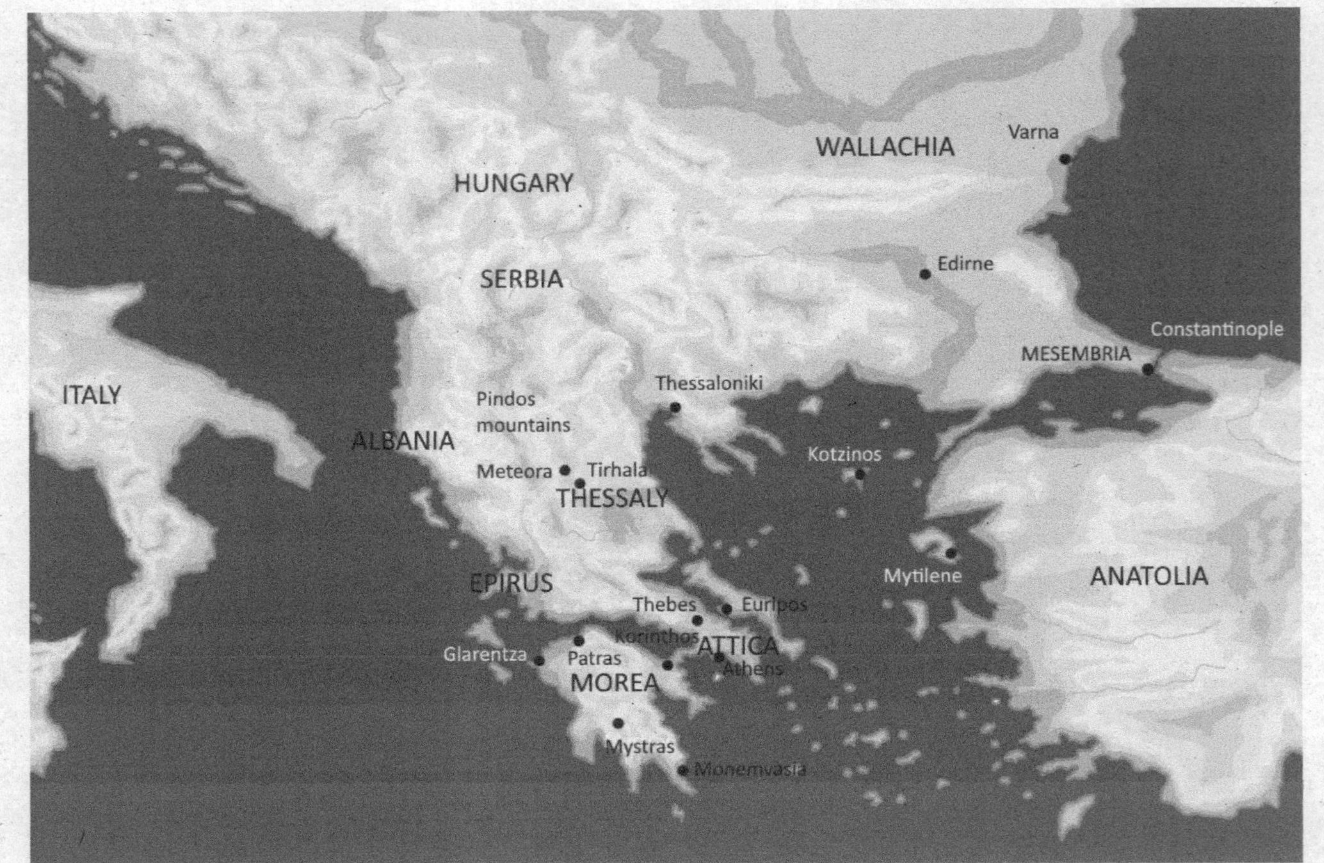
WALLACHIA
Varna
Edirne
Constantinople
MESEMBRIA
HUNGARY
SERBIA
Thessaloniki
ITALY
Pindos
mountains
ALBANIA
Kotzinos
Meteora
Tirhala
THESSALY
Mytilene
ANATOLIA
EPIRUS
Thebes
Euripos
Korinthos
ATTICA
Glarentza
Patras
Athens
MOREA
Mystras
Monemvasia

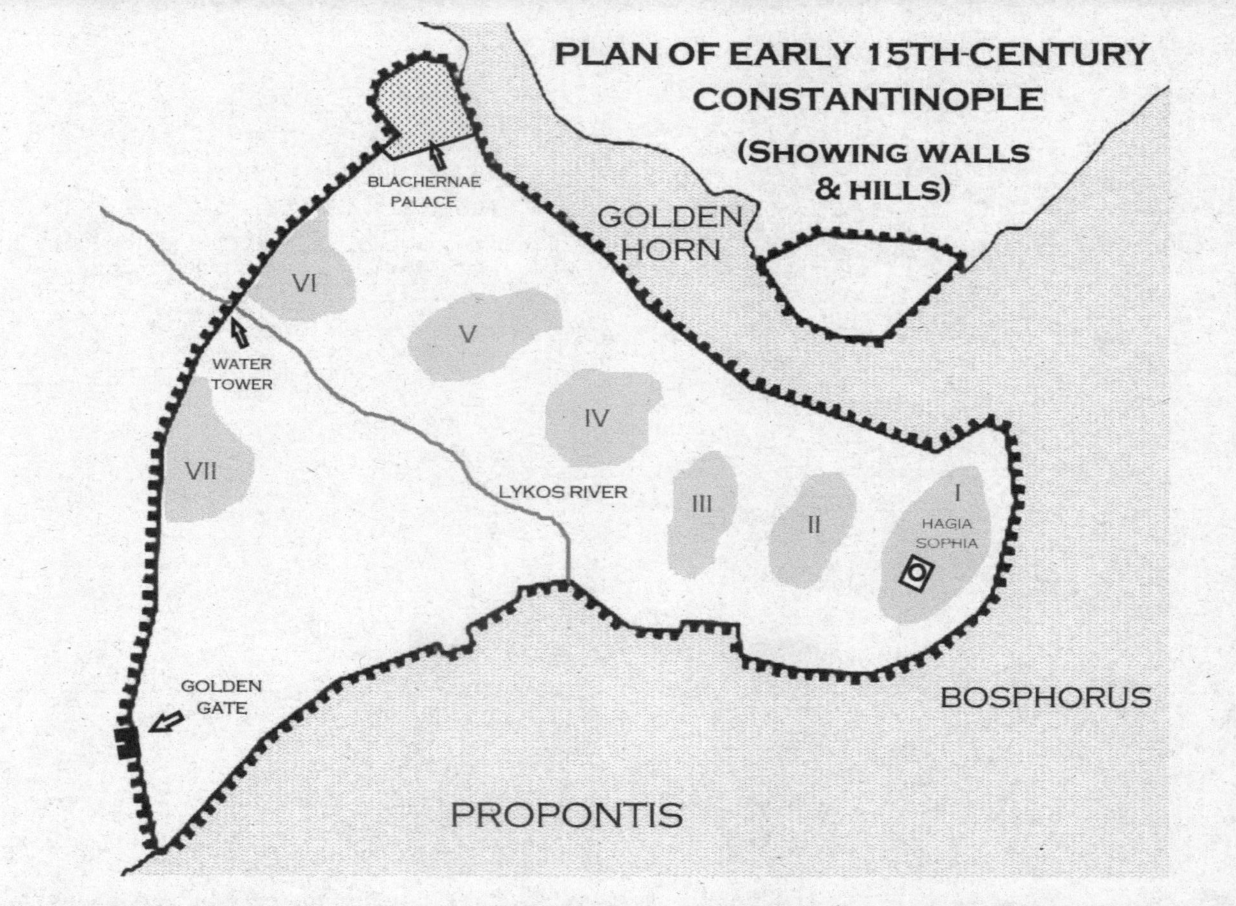

PLAN OF EARLY 15TH-CENTURY CONSTANTINOPLE
(SHOWING WALLS & HILLS)
GOLDEN HORN
BLACHERNAE PALACE
WATER TOWER
VI
V
IV
VII
LYKOS RIVER
III
II
I
HAGIA SOPHIA
GOLDEN GATE
BOSPHORUS
PROPONTIS

Glossary

Allagatōr – imperial officer, commander of an allagion

Allagion (pl. allaghia) – unit of the imperial standing army, numbering 200–500 men

Appanage – a grant of land or title to the non-inheriting offspring of a ruler

Aula – Latin for 'hall', with the 'aula regia' denoting an imperial audience chamber

Azab – irregular conscript infantry in the Turkish army

Başı – Turkish officer with a rank similar to captain

Bertha Palace – part of the Blachernae complex in Constantinople

Bey – Ottoman title denoting a provincial governor or high-ranking official

Blachernae – imperial palace in Constantinople, a vast complex beside the city walls

Catalan – native of Catalunya in the north-east of the Iberian peninsula

Chalke – great gate to the Byzantine imperial palace, later used to refer to the imperial court

Consilium – an emperor's close council

Danubios Palace – part of the Blachernae complex in Constantinople

Despot – an imperial regional governor

Devşirme – Turkish system of forced recruitment from among Christian subjects

Doux – high-ranking imperial military position, from which we derive 'duke'

Epirot – inhabitant of the region of Epirus in northern Greece

Forum Tauri – the 'forum of the bull' in Constantinople

Frank – medieval term for the French

Galley – a ship with a sail, but largely propelled by oars

Golden Gate – triumphal arch in Constantinople, later converted to a gate in the city walls

Golden Horn – inlet from the Bosphorus that protected Constantinople's northern side

Gorget – armoured throat protector

Hebdomon – suburban imperial palace and harbour outside the walls of Constantinople

Hexamilion – six-mile defensive wall across the isthmus at Korinthos

Hodegetria – icon of the Virgin Mary and child

Ianitzaroi – late Byzantine imperial bodyguard, after which Janissaries were named

Kadirga – Turkish galley

Kontostaulos – late imperial high military rank

Lepanto, Gulf of – body of Greek water now known as the Gulf of Corinth

Lykos – small seasonal river that flowed through Constantinople from the west

Mangonel – a traction-powered catapult

Megas Doux – high imperial rank, literally 'Grand Duke'

Merlon – the raised defensive sections of battlements

Mesembria – Byzantine city on the Black Sea coast, now known as Nesebar in Bulgaria

Milion – structure at the heart of Constantinople from which distances were measured

Morea – medieval term for the Peloponnese peninsula in Greece

Mutesellim – Ottoman title for a local governor

Mystras – fortified city, the Byzantine capital of the Morea

Ourghos – lesser Byzantine military rank, similar to a corporal

Palaiologoi – the last ruling dynasty of Byzantium

Pasha – mid- to high-ranking Turkish official

Propontis – now the Sea of Marmara, separating Europe and Anatolia

Pteruges – protective leather straps attached to a military tunic

Sanjak – a smaller provincial division of the Turkish empire

Sipahi – cavalry of the regular Turkish army

Stavraton – late Byzantine silver coin

Strategos – title denoting a general in the Byzantine army

Sublime Porte – grand title for the Turkish court

Terreplein – a revetted mound, constructed as a base for artillery

Theotokos – Greek term for the Mother of God

Tırhala – capital of Turkish Thessaly, now the city of Trikala

Tonsure – monkish hairstyle involving shaving the centre of the head

Trebizond – former Byzantine city in eastern Anatolia, later a separate breakaway empire

Introductory Note

In antiquity, the Roman Empire became too difficult for one emperor to administrate alone and gradually came to be split into Eastern and Western empires. Rome remained the spiritual capital of the West, even when administrative and palatial capitals devolved to other cities, while Constantinople, now Istanbul, was founded by Constantine the Great to be the 'New Rome' of the East. As the Western Empire fell to invaders in the fifth century, the focus shifted entirely to the East, with Constantinople as the successor of Rome, in some ways becoming the cradle of Western civilisation.

Though modern scholars refer to the Eastern Roman Empire as the 'Byzantine Empire', this is more a modern academic term than a name used by the people of the time. It may seem strange to the modern reader to see the empire's population referred to as Romans, and referring to themselves and to each other as Roman. However, this is as accurate as any treatment in English could be. The language used throughout by the characters would be Greek, despite their own belief that they were still the Roman Empire, but while I have used Greek terms where required (for instance, for titles, and for cases where there is no adequate translation into English), other words I have anglicised for the reader's ease (sic: Constantinople rather than Constantinopolis). At times I have referred to the city as Byzantium, a name that has always been usable, named for an ancient Greek hero by the name of Byzas, and the city's name before the age of Constantine, and I have in places substituted 'Byzantine' for 'Roman' – largely for the reader's ease (it can be a little headache-inducing to portray Romans vs Italians). As always, with historical fiction based in non-English-speaking lands, there is a play-off between authenticity and readability, and so I have striven for the best available balance. The novel contains a glossary and maps of the region and the city of Constantinople at the start, all of which may be worth referring to throughout.

The world of the eastern Mediterranean in the early fifteenth century is extremely complex. The Byzantine Empire, having shrunk more than three centuries earlier, was ruined by Christians during the Fourth Crusade of 1204, when they sacked Constantinople. From that moment on, it could never truly claim any cohesive empire, much of its territory was carved up and controlled by the various Italian states involved in the crusade, a situation still reflected by the time of this work. By 1422, Byzantium consisted of the great city itself, a narrow strip of land to the north and west, now part of European Turkey, centred on the city of Mesembria (modern-day Nesebar in Bulgaria), and a large part of the Peloponnese in Greece. The empire clung to the hope of expansion and rebirth, even though it was financially broke and largely powerless. One notion that was repeatedly raised was a reconciliation of the Byzantine Church with the Church of Rome, though that was never popular with the citizens of Constantinople, whose memory of their city being sacked and burned during a papal crusade never dulled.

Apart from Venetian holdings and other Italian states, the great power in the East was, of course, the Ottoman Empire (the Turks). Having emerged from the Caucasus Mountains, related to the many Turkik groups there and of the Eurasian Steppe, the Turks rapidly built an empire centred on the lands of ancient Persia, expanding across the Middle East and the Levant and ever pressing back the borders of Byzantium. The Turks were ruled by a sultan, along with his court (known as the Sublime Porte), and he was assisted by nobles in the form of *beys* and *pashas*. The political and military balance in the East was always difficult, a great game played for high stakes. The Byzantines could only hope to expand with the support of Western Europe, and the Turks could only expand when Western Europe did not care enough about the lands they were attempting to annex. Constantinople stood at the meeting point of these worlds, and was crucial, even with diminished power. As such, the Turks and Byzantines had one of the most fascinating political relationships in history, sometimes allies, sometimes enemies, sometimes with Byzantium paying lip service as vassals while retaining a tenuous hold on independence. It was an incredible balancing act in a very tense and changeable world, and onto this stage came a young prince, the fourth son of the Byzantine emperor: Constantine.

[illegible] he [illegible] place it on Europe also its [illegible]
[illegible] to [illegible] Watson [illegible]
[illegible] spread out with the support of Watson this [illegible]
[illegible] stacks could [illegible] report which Watson E page b [illegible] not
[illegible] enough [illegible] build they [illegible] newspaper in a tree [illegible]
[illegible] paper [illegible] a thing world is
[illegible] really even will stimulated power [illegible] there the
[illegible] power had one [illegible] because [illegible] portant
[illegible] communications requires [illegible]
[illegible] Byzantine page liberty [illegible] with liberty
[illegible] observance [illegible] it was to him, that
[illegible] liberty [illegible] the last essay of the [illegible]
[illegible] Catherine power [illegible]

Prologue

Constantinople

4 September 1422

A voice cut through the distant din of the fighting.

'Who are you?'

Gabriel turned, looking up at the wall-walk and tower from the courtyard below. The man was an officer of the regular army, judging by his ornate uniform and silk sash. He had a big nose. Odd that this was the first thing Gabriel noticed, and once he'd realised that, it became quite hard not to look at the nose.

'Catalan company – *Ianitzaroi*, as you call us.'

The man gave him an odd look – hard to do round that massive nose – and then turned away without another word, writing Gabriel and his men off as unimportant, but also wanting to be away from him as fast as possible. Nothing new there. He jogged away, shouting for another unit to fall in.

Gabriel *was* disconcerting, and he knew it. He liked it that way. When people were immediately put off by your presence, it put them on the back foot, made them unsure, which was always the best way to deal with them. Like all the Ianitzaroi, Gabriel had a darker skin tone than most in the city – darker even than the Turks; it was the legacy of his Berber heritage, albeit several generations ago. But it was not his swarthiness that put people off. What did that was his appearance, partly the result of an old injury, partly the work of nature. A sword wound that had nearly done for him four years ago had left a scar across his pate that divided his hairline and a white line diagonally across his nose; it had also taken away the corner of his lip, which meant that unless he compressed his lips, his rear teeth showed even with his mouth closed. Perhaps odder than that, though, he had been born without irises, which left his eyes a very disconcerting black on white with no colour. Children tended to stare, but it did mean that tedious Byzantine noblemen generally avoided him where possible.

The two men at his back did little to encourage visitors, either. His second in command, Gaspar, was a veritable mountain of a man with arms and shoulders like a hairless bear, but his left arm from halfway to the elbow was missing. And then there was Manuel, who would actually appear fairly normal, were it not for the monk's tonsure shaved into his hair, which always left people oddly uncertain how to act around him. The Catalan company was not popular with the regular army, generally considered little better than mercenaries despite their sixty-odd years of service as an imperial guard unit for the emperors.

As the officer hurried away, a second figure came into sight behind him, emerging from the doorway in the tower out into the open, where men were mustered and equipment and ammunition was gathered in bundles, piles and buckets. The man stopped, turned, and looked across at the Catalans. He frowned.

'You are equipped for war and clearly ready. Why are you not helping?'

Gabriel shrugged at the seventeen-year-old prince Constantine Palaiologos, fourth son of the emperor. 'Your brother, the emperor, told us to protect your father, the emperor, *sir*. Then your father, the emperor, told us to go away and look after your *brother*, the emperor. We are at an impasse. Too many emperors, too few Ianitzaroi…'

Constantine's frown deepened. 'So you do nothing?'

'We have our orders, conflicting as they are, *sir*.' In truth, Gabriel was irritated by it, but he had long since learned that emperors tended to think in straight lines and would simply dismiss any confusion or concern. Better the Catalan company obey both orders… and do nothing.

'Your orders are nonsensical,' Constantine snapped. 'Come with me.' And with that, the man started for the wall stair.

That made Gabriel blink. Habitually, the rich and important tried to get *away* from him, not drag him *along*. 'Sir, your brother, the emperor—'

'Is a little busy commanding the city's defence,' Constantine finished for him. 'I am the ranking officer on this section of the walls, so get off that bony, dusty backside, rouse your men, and get up on the walls, now.'

It occurred to Gabriel to argue. It was not that he disagreed. At a time like this every man counted, but he might be disciplined later for disobeying an imperial order… Yet, oddly, he found himself gesturing to his *ourghos*, Gaspar, to have the men fall in.

'What about the horses?' the giant rumbled.

'We're going to the walls. Have you ever ridden a horse on the city wall?'

'Twice. Your point?'

Gabriel gave a rough chuckle. 'Leave the horses.'

With that, Gaspar turned and bellowed the order to fall in. Manuel grasped the banner of the company – a gold wyvern on a red field, a carry-over of their Catalan-Aragonese heritage – and raised it so that the twenty-four riders of the unit could form up. Gabriel turned back to the young nobleman, brother and son to the current co-emperors of Byzantium. Constantine was waiting, seemingly calm, at the bottom of the stairs, but Gabriel recognised the subtle signs of impatience.

The young man was clearly going to be a surprise. During the years of serving his father, and then his brother too, the Catalan company had often been away from the city, and so Gabriel had only encountered Constantine sporadically, sometimes in visits years apart. He'd seemed the usual indolent middle son of an aristocratic house, not senior enough to have much responsibility, but not so junior as to be overlooked and forgotten. He'd spent much of his time hunting, reading and journeying around the somewhat reduced territory of the empire, and Gabriel had presumed him to be marginally intelligent but fundamentally lazy.

The man before him did not seem to fit that description. Constantine stood on the steps, waiting for him, sword belted at his side and eyes sharp with fierce intelligence, his strong jaw set in grim determination. He wore a simple gold diadem, patterned elegantly, but without the gaudy hangings and jewels that adorned the imperial crowns. There was a saying among the Byzantines that hard times made hard men, and perhaps that was what was happening to the prince, for there could be no denying that these were hard times.

They had been particularly hard since the start of June, Gabriel reflected as he climbed the stairs behind Constantine. The Turks, who had been pressing on the shrunken borders of the Byzantine Empire these past decades, had rarely reached the city itself. That had changed this summer.

Gabriel stepped out onto the wall-walk behind the prince, his men hurrying up the steps behind him. His gaze strayed out across the defences and beyond, to the west. Thank the Lord God for the holy city's great walls, the strongest in the world, for the Turkish army was immense, and truly powerful.

But to enter the city, the Turks would have to break through those defences, and that was no easy task. Two sides of the city were defended by water: the Propontine Sea to one side, and the channel known as the Golden Horn on the other. A great anti-ship chain stretched across the mouth of the Horn, denying entry by sea. Rising from the waters were the sea walls, strong white ramparts spotted with artillery. On the landward approach, the walls were all the more impressive. First, an enemy would encounter a moat, then a low rampart, then a bare, open killing ground before the powerful outer walls. Only once they had crossed all these barriers would they reach the massive inner walls.

Of course, there were weak spots, and one of those was right here, where the Catalan company waited, outside the complex in which the ageing seventy-two-year-old senior emperor rested. This region, Blachernae, had become the principal residence of the emperors, and had been fortified periodically over the years with a succession of mismatched walls, some of better quality than others. It was only the powerful towers and the additional strengthened walls within that stopped the area being an obvious target. What it lacked in the ordered grace of the walls' southern section, it made up for in sheer bulk and clutter.

Gabriel was still looking at the enemy. The Turks seethed across the landscape out of artillery shot beyond the moats, a camp of military tents so numerous and closely packed that they resembled the white peaks of a mountain range.

'There are more now, I think,' he noted as he looked out.

The first army had come on the eighth of July under a Turkish bey, a regional governor, by the name of Mihaloğlu Mehmet Bey. That army alone had outnumbered the rather small garrison of the great city, but they had only finished the investment of Constantinople, surrounding it on the landward approaches, and not launched any great attack when that number more than doubled on the fifteenth with the arrival of the sultan, Murad bin Mehemmed Han, with their main force. Then the fighting had begun.

As with all sieges, action was sporadic. Sometimes days passed with as little activity as a few optimistic bowshots or cavalry riding the length of the ramparts, while at other times, the walls would be battered for days at a time, supported by infantry and archers. With the arrival of August and the hottest months, infantry activity had tailed off in favour of artillery. The Turks had built a *terreplein* in the shallow valley between the sixth and seventh hills, a great platform fronted by ramparts of timber and packed earth, upon which they sat their cannons. Facing them, above the channel of the Lykos stream that ran through gratings in the base of the walls, behind one short section where the moat had silted up and all but turfed over, stood the Water Tower, the weakest structure in the line of the walls. It had been damaged a few years earlier in one of the regular tremors endured by the city, and it was this cracked tower upon which the Turkish artillery concentrated.

Throughout the sizzling days of August, the cannons had kept up their barrage – in particular, the great beast of a bombard Murad had brought with him. It was so large that a particularly thin child would be sent down the barrel with a cloth to keep it clean. That beast struck the damaged tower no fewer than seventy times over the summer, and yet the defences held, a few new cracks opening up, but nothing that suggested the tower was about to fall.

Towards the end of the month, the Turks had started to seem irritated with their failure, and never more so than when the ammunition for the great gun ran out. Murad had seemingly never considered it likely that the walls would survive seventy shots, and it would take a great deal of time to manufacture new ammunition. The Turks needed to push for a quick victory, then, for as the winter months began to loom on the horizon, no one would relish the thought of carrying on the siege over a time of snow and rain. Rumour also had it that Murad was facing a usurper back in Asia, and would need to turn his attention there as soon as possible.

And so, this latest assault bore all the hallmarks of this urgency. Siege towers had been brought up, though few were of use, thanks to the moats and low outer walls, and Murad's men began to try and undermine the defences, again with little success, or to dig in search of aqueduct channels they might be able to use to gain entry, which they never found. The engines they created were ingenious and fabulous, the stuff of nightmare for the defenders, yet all came to naught over the August days.

But there were definitely more men out there than Gabriel remembered the last time he'd looked out. And though the

Turks remained solidly shut out of Constantinople, the sheer weight of numbers made it likely that a breach, and the city's fall, were only a matter of time.

'They've received reinforcements,' he said, noting a new area of tents.

'Yes,' Constantine confirmed. 'Their patriarch – a prophet, apparently – arrived a few days ago with half a thousand wild Turkish monks and various hangers-on. Militarily, it is believed he and his men are of little direct value, but the sense of purpose they have instilled in the sultan's army is troubling. It is said he has announced that he knows the date the city will fall, and from the look of the way they're moving, he might mean today.'

Behind them, the Ianitzaroi were now emerging on the wall-top. There were barely more than a score of them, but it said much about the dwindled numbers of Byzantium's armies that they almost doubled the number of men visible on this stretch of the defences. Even as the Ianitzaroi fell into position, horns blew and calls rang out across the open ground before the walls. Here there was no moat to stop them, for the walls descended the slope to the waters of the Golden Horn, and the gradient was too steep. The defenders had managed to dig a narrow trench during the days before the Turks arrived, but it would not stop them for long.

Gabriel turned to the prince. 'Give the command, sir.'

'Consider it given. Fight the fight, and no quarter. Here they come.'

A roar arose from beyond the walls as the Turks flooded towards the city, and Gabriel readied his sword.

–

'This is getting exhausting,' Manuel grumbled as he jabbed out with the forked wooden staff, levering the siege ladder away from the walls and tipping it outwards, half a dozen Turks crying out in panic as they fell into the seething mass of men below.

Gabriel nodded. He was too breathless to reply as he ducked, an arrow whirring through the air above his head to disappear into the gloom behind him. Evening was fast approaching now, the sun almost gone beyond the hills, and darkness encroaching from behind them. He turned to look back into the city. Since they'd been brought up onto the walls, the open street and grassland behind them had changed drastically. Now, it held a massive awning being used as a hospital, half the staff just ordinary citizens with no skill or experience, drafted in to do the grunt work, and there was plenty of it. A pile of severed limbs lay mouldering outside, the grim result of the surgeons' constant labour.

Close by, citizens were readying themselves to join the fray, the latest batch who'd been equipped with whatever they could find. Some carried wooden shields that were far too heavy, made from tabletops; others held spears formed from carving knives and broom handles tightly lashed together. They were untrained levies, yet each was determined to defend the city to the last. Nearby, a gathering of women, children and the elderly – those who could not take part in the defence – had created a workshop, where such ingenious weapons and armour were being created from everyday household items. And despite the seeming impropriety, there had been no regard for gender in the matter of volunteers. Housewives and serving girls stood beside soldiers and workmen on the wall-tops, each doing what they could to hold back the tide.

Gabriel turned once more, in time to see a young man with a hatchet felled by a Turk at the parapet, one hand grasping the stonework even as the other pulled his sword free of the Roman defender. As the defender fell away, Gabriel took a step to the side and brought his own sword down on the hand gripping the stone, even as the Turk tried to vault over onto the wall-top. The attacker's hand smashed and almost came free, so deep was the wound, and with a scream, he disappeared into the mass below.

A sharp cry of pain suddenly drew Gabriel's attention, and his head snapped round to see the prince reach up to grip his throat. Blood spattered his neck and shoulder, and burbled out between the gripping fingers. Gabriel's breath caught. Such a wound was a given fatality, and yet when the prince took his hand away to look at it, the blood simply gouted rather than spraying. So close a call. A Palaiologos had almost died in that moment.

The prince, hand going back to his neck wound, scanned the army below, looking for the source of the missile that had almost ended him, and Gabriel spotted it at the same time: a man in Western armour, a surcoat of blue and white stripes, stood among the sultan's favoured, lowering a crossbow, gaze locked on his victim.

'Are you all right?' Gabriel asked the prince as he peered at the would-be killer. The man had the colouring of an Italian, and his face was hard, eyes narrowed, as Turks clapped him on the shoulder, either congratulating him on the shot, or commiserating that it had not killed the target.

'A little bloody and a lot bloody angry,' the prince snapped in reply. 'Isn't it bad enough to be fighting for survival against the Turks without having our *allies* shooting at us?'

Gabriel frowned. He didn't know the nobleman, but there were plenty of Westerners whose sons spent time at the Turkish court. Whoever he was, he had clearly singled out the Palaiologos prince as a target and had almost succeeded. From the look on the crossbowman's face, he had relished the opportunity, which was odd, given that capturing a nobleman for ransom was the done thing, not attempting his death from a distance. Perhaps the man had something to prove to his Turkish masters?

A hissing noise gave them sufficient warning for the entire wall section's defenders to drop behind the stonework as the hail of arrows passed over them. Behind them, down in the work area and hospital, figures with hastily constructed shields of wooden planks bound together carried them over any area in danger as the arrows fell to earth.

Gabriel looked this way and that. Gaspar suddenly lurched back from the wall with a stream of very unchristian language, reaching up with his sword hand to brush away the blood from a wound on his cheek. His other arm, such as it was, had a small shield bound to it, making use of the stump. Gabriel took a breath for a moment.

'How many have we lost?'

Gaspar grunted. 'Four at the last count.'

'That's little short of a miracle in this.'

'They're being careful, and rightly so. This could go on for a while yet. I think the sultan has decided it's all or nothing this time.'

Gabriel snorted. 'I suspect it's their prophet driving them. Still, it looks as though we'll get a little divine inspiration ourselves now,' he added, pointing off to the south, along the walls. Gaspar turned to look up the slope, blinking away more blood, and grinned at what he saw. A procession was making its way along the ramparts, and wherever it went, it was like a tidal wave of hope. Leading the way was a familiar figure: John Palaiologos, emperor of Byzantium by the grace of God and the Virgin. This morning, when Gabriel had seen him, the emperor had been dressed in riding clothes and without even a coronet, looking more like a commoner than the master of all Romans, but now he was a sight to bring heart to every man on the walls. Clad in purple that was largely covered over with gleaming steel, he wore the red boots of the emperor and the great imperial crown, its pendants hanging down from the temples. The ensemble, part imperial regalia, part warrior's armour, was completed by a crimson cloak that brushed the dusty walkway at his heel. But it was what followed the young emperor that truly brought hope and joy to the hearts of the warriors on the walls.

The *Hodegetria*, the great icon of the Holy Mother in robes of purple, indicating Jesus as the source of hope for all mankind.

A delicate, sacred painting on boards of cedar brought from the Holy Land many centuries ago; the most sacred thing in the whole city... in the whole empire. The priest who bore the image aloft for all to see was clad head to toe in crimson, even his gloves, hood and veil, as were the other nineteen priests who followed him in a line, chanting a paean to the Mother. Even as the soldiers watched this miracle traversing the walls, a strange last stray beam of sunlight from between the peaks and trees of the west caught the holy icon and lit it like the brilliant fires of Heaven, raising a gasp of reverence from every Christian soul on the wall, and from those down below within the city. The Turkish forces let out a low moan of despair at the sight, for though they did not follow the Gospel, they knew it when they saw it, just as they knew the power of God.

The attack on the wall faltered, and slowed. It did not stop, and among the enemy, officers and priests bellowed the orders to press home the attack and to take the walls, but the sight of the Virgin and child, bathed in the holy light of God, had robbed them of much of their valour.

Gabriel instinctively turned to the emperor's brother, standing not far away, sprayed with the blood of friend and enemy alike, gore-coated sword in hand, scarf wrapped around his neck, soaked in his own blood. There was an emperor close by, and several officers of senior rank, and yet in that moment, without realising why, Gabriel looked to Constantine for the word. And the young prince seemed to understand, locking eyes with him, and not even flinching from the sight of those black-on-white eyes.

Constantine Palaiologos thrust his sword into the air, and then swept it down towards the enemy. 'Children of the holy city, now is the time to take the fight to the enemy and drive the Turks from the walls. God and the emperor!'

'God and the emperor,' roared a hundred voices in time.

–

In the end, the fight did not press on into the hours of darkness. The sight of the glory of God in the hands of the Romans had pulled the teeth of the rabid Turks, and even their officers could not make them fight on.

As the light came up the next morning, though, it made clear to the beleaguered defenders of the greatest city in the world that the siege was not over. Despite everything, the sultan and his officers had managed to marshal their army for another push. Though they had seen the Virgin bathed in sacred light giving power to the Romans, their great seer, the dreaded Mersaita, gave them hope, claiming Constantinople was destined to fall on *this* day.

Gabriel had counted his men at nightfall, and they had lost only six – a small miracle – and so he had thanked God. By rights, once that clash was over, he should have led his men back to one of the emperors, whose guard they were, but the old man had not yet emerged from his chamber in the palace, and if the walls fell, the Ianitzaroi would be of little use protecting a bedroom. And as for John, the eldest son… He had taken to his horse and now led the defence of that endangered section in the Lykos valley, and was surrounded by the most heavily armoured men in the empire. By rights, Gabriel and his men should be there but, again, they would make little difference, a score of light cavalry lost among the heavy. Instead, it seemed natural and right to stay in the company of the emperor's younger brother. Constantine had valiantly led the defence of the Blachernae walls the previous day, and seemed determined to do the same again as the sun rose. Besides, he had so narrowly escaped death once, that perhaps he needed the Ianitzaroi more than his brothers.

The Turks came on once more, with every manner of weapon, and every manner of siege machine. The Catalan company found themselves mixed in with every manner of defender, from regular infantry to palace guards, alongside farmers, carpenters and bakers all armed with makeshift equipment – shields from barrel lids, butchers' cleavers, and so on. Scattered among them were the valiant women of Constantinople, ready to hurl fist-sized rocks into the press of Turkish attackers. Twice, Gabriel saw the blue and white of that nobleman, whom he had learned bore the colours of the Tocco, lords of Epirus, and both times the man had been singling out Constantine, though fortunately not with a crossbow in hand these times.

The morning wore on, defenders falling in a slow but worry-ingly steady stream. The woman beside Gabriel had taken an arrow to her right shoulder but had vociferously refused to be removed from the walls, as she kept that arm clamped by her side and used her left to throw stones. Another of the Ianitzaroi had fallen, and a second man had retreated to the medical tent down below to have a wound stitched.

Gabriel was no wilting flower, and his sword found flesh and muscle with every fourth heartbeat throughout that bloody morning, as the Turks flowed up ladders and siege towers and fought to gain a foothold on the walls. Three times, the enemy managed to get small pockets of men over the parapet, and each time the defenders had found it a little harder to push them back. It felt as though the defence was slipping away from them bit by bit. Sooner or later, surely, there would come a moment when the enemy gained ground and held it.

A Turk came even now, tumbling over the parapet and rolling to his feet in a clatter of steel plates and a shushing of chain, both hands coming up with his sword, ready to strike. Gabriel swung, his own blade catching the Turk in the armpit of that raised arm, smashing bones and tearing a lung. The Turk fell, and Gabriel suddenly realised that the man had not been alone. A second interloper had been off to his left, and was coming straight for him. But as the man's sword stroke was falling, suddenly Gaspar was there, his buckler turning the blade even as his own axe bit deep into the Turk.

Gabriel nodded his thanks to his ourghos, then turned and once more launched into his own fight. As he dispatched another hopeful, who went tumbling back from the wall with a scream, the commander of the Ianitzaroi leaned forward and took in the scene. There were still too many Turks down there even to count with a lazy guess, and they swarmed up the walls like an army of ants, endless and single-minded. Once again, he spotted the blue and white of Tocco, this time straining to make for one of the siege ladders, but being held back by the sultan's guards. A noble hostage was too valuable to risk on the walls of the city today, after all.

Gabriel looked up. The sun was high, probably past noon now. They had fought hard all morning, and it looked as though the rest of the day would be much the same.

'To the left,' Constantine bellowed. 'Look to the left. Quick.'

Men surged that way, where the wall was endangered, too many of the defenders injured to stem the tide. With the reinforcements they managed, and the wall held, but the defenders were spread too thin now. Disaster was just a matter of time.

Gabriel marvelled for a moment at Constantine – definitely not the pampered and lazy princeling he had initially thought. Indeed, Constantine had proved himself a match for his brother John these past hours, fighting like a lion, and forcing heart into a failing defence. He was fighting too hard, really, putting himself in personal danger, facing the Turks with bloodied sword in hand. His brother was too busy to admonish him, and his father too weak, and so he continued to fight, although two messages had already come from his mother, the empress, commanding him to leave the defences and return to the safety of the palace. He had politely refused, both times.

And that was why it was less of a surprise to Gabriel than it might have been when shouting drew his attention, and he turned to see the figure of Helene Dragaš Palaiologoina, empress of Byzantium, striding along the walls of the city with a fierce gait and an even fiercer expression, marching towards her fourth son, delivering her third ultimatum in person.

And that was when the miracle happened.

The danger disappeared. The threat melted away. Those Turks at the wall-top stared, their weapons falling from open palms. Others removed their feet from ladder rungs and slid down the sides, fleeing the walls. All across the open ground outside, men were turning, running, fleeing, a roar of panic arising from them.

Gabriel turned to see the mass rout in astonishment, then turned back, and realised in that moment what it was. The holy empress herself was clad in violet robes, as was her wont, and the Turks, already shaken the previous evening by the sight of the Virgin Mary's image giving heart to the Romans, were thinking they saw her now in person, the very Mother of God herself, bathed in bright sunlight atop the walls of the sacred city.

Moaning and cries of panic were spreading throughout that huge force outside the walls like ripples from a stone cast into a pond. Everywhere Gabriel looked, the Turks were fleeing, doing everything they could to get away from these walls and the divine presence that moved along them in the midst of violent battle as though impervious, armoured by faith.

Gabriel could not stop staring.

He stood, wide-eyed, as the empress swept towards them, and only had the presence of mind to drop respectfully to a knee at the last moment as she came to a halt in front of her son.

'It seems I have saved you, Constantine, when what I had planned was a thrashing for disobeying your mother.'

The scion of the imperial house gave an odd chuckle.

'Try not to say such things too loud, Mother. The Turks should not hear the *Theotokos* scolding a boy.'

She rolled her eyes for a moment, then turned to look out across the rout. Here and there, a few small pockets of men had paused in their flight, looking back up at the wall.

'Begone,' she bellowed, her imperious tone cutting through the din.

Even the last stragglers fled at that, one of the last to leave a Westerner, staring up at the walls with a sour expression, before turning away.

'Would that you were ever able to stand atop these walls and terrify the Turks,' Constantine laughed.

'Would that I had a son with more sense than to leap into the fray,' she countered, reaching out and gently pulling at the bandage around her son's neck and examining the wound within. She huffed, and with that, turned and swept away.

Gabriel waited until she was safely distant, and then rose to his feet, turning to lean on the wall. He was startled when, a moment later, Constantine joined him.

'It is a reprieve, you understand,' the imperial scion sighed. 'Not a victory. Nothing has really changed, and in time they will return.'

'Can they ever be truly stopped?'

Constantine took a deep breath and exhaled slowly. 'Perhaps. But the solution to that is not in defences. We have the best walls in the world. But walls are no good without armies, and armies cannot be raised without money, and money cannot be taxed without lands. Once, our empire covered half the Earth, and now we can all but see its borders from the walls of the city. My brother believes the Pope in Rome can be persuaded to heal the rift between our Churches, and that together we can drive the Turks back forever, perhaps even retake the Holy Land.'

Gabriel frowned. 'But you are of a different opinion, sir?'

'The rift is too wide. Once, perhaps, it could have been done, but the Italians sacked and burned our city, remember, and the memory of our people is long. No. The rift will not be healed, and the Italian states will never come to our aid. If we are to hold the West, to be a bulwark against the Turks, we must rebuild what once we had.'

'Can *that* be done?'

Constantine slapped him on the back. 'Perhaps. Perhaps not. But I know this: if it cannot be done by men like us, then it cannot be done by *anyone*.'

PART ONE – MOREA

While he was in control of all these places, and having no wish to remain quiet, he [Tocco] showed ingratitude to his benefactors. Three years had passed and it was already the middle of the winter; he seized all the herds of the Peloponnesian Illyrians; there were many horses, many oxen, many sheep, and many pigs. Even though he had agreed to a treaty, he did not hesitate to violate its terms and he took away the herds.

Cardinal Isidore

Morea is the contemporary name for the Peloponnese peninsula of southern Greece. The land is controlled partly by the Byzantine despot Theodore, brother of John and Constantine, from his capital at Mystras, but with large swathes owned by various Italian city states, and with the Ottoman Empire pressing upon its borders from the rest of the Greek mainland, barely held back by the Hexamilion, a six-mile defensive wall at the Isthmus of Korinthos. The Morea is a land in peril at all times.

The town of Glarentza, an important port in the northwest of the Morea, has changed hands several times between Western powers, most recently coming into the possession of Carlo Tocco, Count Palatine of Kephalonia and Zakynthos. The expansionist count has recently engaged in raids, seizing herds within adjacent Byzantine territory, and the fear that Tocco intends to continue annexing lands has driven the empire to action.

Though the Morea has its own Byzantine despot, Theodore, he is an intensely religious man more concerned with a monkish life than with warfare and politics. Consequently, the emperor John has led forth an army from Constantinople, accompanied by several senior generals and courtiers, including his brother Constantine, to launch an attack on Carlo Tocco at Glarentza.

The emperor and his force arrive at Mystras, the capital of the Byzantine Despotate, on 26 December 1427, collecting Theodore and his forces, and then march on Glarentza, arriving the following March, and investing the city, settling in for a siege. The news that Tocco has gathered another army in Epirus and plans to ship them to Glarentza has driven the emperor to send his own fleet out to intercept them.

While John VIII, along with Theodore and the brilliant nobleman George Sphrantzes, maintain the siege of the city, veteran commander Demetrios Laskaris Leontares has been made Megas Doux in command of the navy, and has taken them north towards the Echinades islands, to meet the fleet of the Epirot count Carlo Tocco, under the command of his infamous son Torno. Constantine, now twenty-four years of age, serves as an admiral with Laskaris in the fleet, bound for war.

1

To Command the Seas

Six years later: spring 1428

Gabriel stood at the prow of the ship, his tattered hair whipping around in the wind. His fingers were white with such a tight grip on the rail, but then he would have been the first to admit that he was no great sailor. It was not that he was afraid of the sea, and certainly no seasickness plagued him, but as a horseman, he'd never had much use for ships, and had not spent a lot of time aboard them. They felt oddly unnatural.

He turned. Most of the Ianitzaroi had much the same look plastered across their faces, though, regardless of any discomfort, they were determined and ready for war. His gaze slowly returned to the fore, passing across the ships of the Byzantine fleet on the way. It was, from what he'd heard, the largest fleet gathered by the empire for a single action in centuries. Ten war galleys, each with two oar banks, had been hastily constructed at Monemvasia, and those numbers had been bulked out with thirty more vessels of varying designs, hired at significant cost from Rhodes and Genoa. They ploughed through the water like a maritime stampede, and at the fore of each stood artillery of various types. Before reaching the prow once more, his gaze fell upon the cannon close by, on a raised platform in order to aim over the rails, anchored with timber wedges and many ropes. He'd heard horror stories of accidents with gunpowder aboard ships, and the presence of the cannon, already primed and ready, was doing little to make him comfortable.

But it was their job to be here. Constantine might not be an emperor like his elder brother, but he was an admiral and a member of the imperial family, and since the death of the old emperor and John's accession as sole ruler of the empire, the Ianitzaroi had been permanently assigned to their lord.

Gabriel's eyes swept to the fore again, blinking in the salty spray.

The fleet of the Epirot count was every bit as impressive as their own. Fewer ships, but generally a little larger, designed to carry an army to their beleaguered master, rather than just the usual complements of marines. The two fleets raced towards each other, both clearly with no intention of stopping or turning aside. The Epirots needed to break through the Byzantines and deliver their loads, and the Byzantines had to stop them. No quarter would be given.

All across the imperial fleet, the noise was immense: paeans were being sung to the accompaniment of horns and drums, though in truth they were hard enough to hear even in the adjacent ships over the crash of waves, the thunder of oars, the crack of sails and the creaking and groaning of timbers. Certainly the Epirots would not be able to hear it. It mattered not. It was about giving heart and strength to the Byzantines, after all.

The gold-on-crimson double-headed eagle banner of the Palaiologos family snapped in the wind at the head of the warship, denoting its important commander, and three ships over, Gabriel could see the black-on-gold variant marking Laskaris' flagship.

'See the big enemy ship?' Constantine bellowed to his officers. 'The one with the blue-and-white flag? That carries their admiral, Torno. I *want* that ship. Leave the others to the rest of the fleet, but take us alongside that one.'

The ship's master frowned at the prince's tone – the spite and urgency in it – and well he might. A sea battle was an odd place to find an imperial prince, but then the sailors did not know who the enemy admiral was, and Constantine had a score to settle, enough to have made him seek a place here. Not only had that man on the flagship stood among the Turks outside the walls of the great city and tried to put a crossbow bolt through the prince's neck, but to add insult to injury, at the time, his family had been imperial vassals, his uncle the despot of Arta, acknowledged by the court at Mystra.

'Haul in the oars as we close,' he continued, 'and we'll smash their outriggers. Cannon, fire as soon as you're sure of a shot. Aim for their mast if you can. Disable them. Everyone else, I want archers clearing the rails of men, and then spears and swords, ready for boarding.'

Impressive, really. As far as Gabriel knew, the prince had no experience of naval matters, yet he had taken command of the ship and part of the fleet as though born to it, just as he had that day when the Turks pressed the walls of the great city. Of the various sons of the former emperor, few could claim a true calling for war, but it seemed the emperor John and his brother Constantine had been born with more skill than most.

'Why is the admiral so important?' a sailor murmured nearby.

Gabriel glanced around at the prince, but Constantine was intent on his prey and had not heard. Gabriel turned to the sailor. 'Torno put that nice scar on the prince's neck, and Constantine feels the need to return the favour.'

The sailor blinked, stared, but Gabriel had already turned away again.

The ship raced towards that large, powerful vessel of the enemy commander. Its pilot and master bellowed out instructions to their flanking ships that were passed along the line, and the Byzantine fleet widened their spacing as they closed, allowing Constantine's flagship the space to turn first left, then right, adjusting its approach to come alongside that enemy hulk. Gabriel almost soiled himself as the cannon fired just six feet from him, the boom and crack of the discharge followed by a cacophony of timbers, ropes and shouts, as the recoil threatened to buck the cannon back across the deck.

Gabriel, ears ringing, shivering with shock, turned back to the enemy. The shot had not been quite good enough to take the mast, which was, of course, an extremely difficult target, but the damage it had done was horrifying. The shot had hit the rail close to the bow, tearing through the timbers in its passage, then turning half a dozen men into red mist and bone shards before smashing into the deck and disappearing from sight. But that was not where the real damage came from, and Gabriel found himself fervently hoping that ship did not have a cannon to reply with. The shot had turned the timber through which it passed into clouds of foot-long splinters that burst outwards at speed, peppering the crew and marines in a truly shocking manner.

The cannon was reloading, though Gabriel doubted they would manage in time to shoot again before the ships met, for which he was actually quite grateful. His hearing had become overlain with a constant whine from the proximity of the explosion.

'He's turning, Admiral,' one of the officers shouted, and indeed, Gabriel could see the enemy ship veering suddenly. The oars were pulled in, the sails adjusted, and the enemy was suddenly not directly ahead.

'What's he doing?' Gabriel breathed.

'I think he's just trying to avoid us,' Gaspar replied.

'That cannon shot ruined his ship,' Manuel added, 'and a lot of his rowers. I think he knows he's doomed if he stays.'

'Bring us back in line,' Constantine bellowed. Gabriel watched, tense, as the enemy vessel turned once more, changing its alignment. Once again, it was aiming for the Byzantine fleet, but now it was making for one of the gaps that had opened up as Constantine's ships spaced out. At least the delay in their meeting had allowed the cannon to reload, and this time Gabriel braced himself and covered his ears. Still, the explosion was deafening, and he watched as the shot tore into more timber and flesh aboard the enemy flagship.

Manuel was right. She was a powerful ship, but the initial cannon shot had ruined her. Even as they closed, Gabriel could see the immense damage, the bodies all across the deck. Even the catapult on the ship's prow was mangled.

'Slow her,' the master called to his men.

'No,' Constantine countermanded. 'Catch that ship.'

'Sir, if we do not slow, we will either shoot straight past her or hit one of our own amidships as we turn.'

Constantine's lip wrinkled, but he nodded his assent, trusting the expertise of his men. Gabriel watched as the manoeuvres were carried out. The enemy ship was almost alongside now, the oars not deployed, since it would be possible for Constantine's ship to smash them in passing. Though the cannon was currently of no use, the men were reloading it anyway. As their ship slowed, the master risking putting the oars out to back water and aid the slowing. Archers flocked to the port rail and began to loose, peppering the enemy ship with arrows as it passed. For just a moment, Gabriel spotted the ship's commanders, a burst of bright colours amid the brown, before they disappeared back into cover, arrows clouding towards them.

The enemy galley ploughed past them, taking more and more arrow damage, not only from Constantine's ship, but also the one on the far side. Then they were past. Their own ship had slowed so rapidly that it almost threw Gabriel from his feet, and he realised then that the master had not only adjusted the sails and back-oared, but had dropped the anchor, for they were in relatively shallow waters, around the Echinades islands. The anchor dragged along the sea bed, slowing them, and as they did so, they turned, the sharpest turn Gabriel had ever seen in a ship, so tight that the deck began to lean worryingly, and small piles of equipment slid and tumbled across the timbers, men holding on or staggering across the deck. They were pivoting round the anchor, and now the oars on the starboard side were back to normal, turning them ever faster, even as the sails were moved once more and filled with an audible crack.

The Catalan was astounded at the speed with which they'd changed course, and now they were coming round to follow the enemy flagship. Even as they finished the turn, Gabriel looked across at the action, for all along the line, the Byzantine ships had engaged the Epirots, and it was immediately clear that Laskaris had got the better of them. Enemy ships were reeling, some on fire; the air was black with the exchange of arrows and javelins, and here and there already Epirot ships were attempting to turn and flee.

'Get me that ship,' Constantine bellowed to his sailors, and the galley now moved once more to full speed, sails full, oars whirling at an impressive rate on both sides, the anchor already being raised and coming up through the water to be hauled aboard once more.

Gabriel was no sailor, but as far as he could see there was too much distance between them. It would take the hand of God himself to help them catch their prey now, for the Tocco ship had not needed to slow at all, while it was taking time for the Byzantines to build up their speed once more.

Or perhaps not the hand of God.

He turned at shouts to see the cannon being adjusted in an attempt to slow or halt the fleeing ship. With another blast that sent all nearby staggering into the rails and holding their ears, the weapon discharged, and the shot sailed out across the open water. To Gabriel's dismay, it disappeared into the sea a full ship-length short of the Epirots. Still, it did not seem to deter the artillerists, who immediately went about adjusting their shot once more.

Gabriel watched with interest as the small wedges under the gun's carriage, used to raise its elevation, were removed and replaced with larger versions, significantly raising the mouth of the barrel. Meanwhile, even as men used wet cloths to cool the beast, one of the artillerists seemed to be mixing the powder from two shots, forming a larger charge than the ones they had been using. There was a heated exchange between two of the men, and Gabriel caught the heart-stopping word 'dangerous' in there, but still the extra charge was inserted and packed down into the raised barrel.

He found himself edging away from the thing along the rail as best he could as its loading was finished, and then covered his ears once more as his gaze returned to the vessel ahead of them. There was argument, adjustment, and then another enormous blast. Gabriel, ears ringing more than ever, was thrown against the rail and almost tipped over it; he grabbed it hard and leaned back desperately. Screams and shouts suggested that something had gone wrong with the cannon, but despite that, Gabriel could see the shot arcing out over the water. The aim was good, and the thing slammed into the rear of the Epirot ship, sending out a cloud of dust and timber that obscured the vessel itself for a moment.

Gabriel took the opportunity then to turn.

The cannon had indeed suffered a calamity. The rear of the barrel had shattered in the detonation, and though it had thrown the ammunition first, the iron had cracked badly, and two of the crew were clearly sorely injured. The ropes that held the beast in place were on fire as another man desperately tried to extinguish them with his bucket of water.

Turning back, he could see that the cloud was dissipating. The cannon damage was impressive, but apparently not enough to slow the Epirots, let alone stop them.

'They've lost their rudder,' someone shouted. 'Look. They can't turn.'

Gabriel peered into the distance ahead. They were certainly moving in a straight line, and there was a lot of damage to the aft, though he was no expert and couldn't identify the individual ruinations. But they seemed to be ploughing at full speed towards the open sea, to the west, away from the Greek coastline. 'Where will they pitch up if they can't turn?' he demanded of the nearest sailor. The man frowned, peering off into the distance.

'Perhaps Arkoudi? Or Atokos? Or if they're lucky, Lefkas, where they can get onto the mainland easily. If they miss all three? Italy.'

Gabriel whistled through his teeth. Hopefully not that. He wasn't sure Constantine could risk chasing them down that far, and more Italian states were opposed to the empire than considered it a friend. He turned, as someone shouted, 'Your orders, sir?' but the question had been directed at Constantine.

The prince turned and looked back at the battle. The imperial fleet was triumphant already. Clearly the battle was far from over, but enough of the enemy ships had been ruined or sunk, or had turned and fled, to make the result a foregone conclusion. Their presence back there would no longer make a difference. Gabriel recognised the look that fell across the man's face, and he knew what it meant.

'Chase them down. I will have Torno alive, or just his head, but I'll have him one way or another.' The prince's hand reflexively went to the raised ridge of the scar that ran around the right side of his neck, as it often did when he spoke of the man who'd tried to kill him.

They would no longer be able to damage the ship. Without the cannon they had no weapon that could reach their prey, and they were moving at roughly similar speeds, so it seemed extremely unlikely they would ever catch up with Torno, barring an act of God. All they could do, then, would be to follow the enemy and hope to take them when they finally hit land, unless somehow they managed to turn.

A thought occurred to Gabriel. 'Why don't they use the oars to turn?' he asked.

The sailor shrugged. 'They could only turn very slowly like that, and at the speed they're already going, it would be troublesome. Plus, if they slowed enough to turn, we might catch up.'

He nodded. Yes, Torno would be more concerned with getting away from the Byzantine ship than with where he was actually going to end up. Speed over manoeuvrability, right now. He glanced back at the cannon, where the ship's surgeon was tending to the two men, and the rest of the gun crew had put out the fire and removed the danger.

A shout drew him, and he ran over to Constantine, who was calling his officers to him.

'If he slows to turn, we will have him. We'll be able to get close enough for the archers to kill everything that moves. So he won't slow. The master tells me that if he stays on his course, he will hit Lefkas in about twenty miles, which will take around three hours of sailing. It is my belief that he will not deviate. From Lefkas, he can easily cross the strait to the mainland, and there he has allies and family. We will not catch him at sea now, so we must pursue doggedly. When we reach Lefkas, he will beach his ship, probably still at full speed, and do what he can to flee us ashore. I want every ounce of speed to the very last moment. We too will beach at full speed, and the moment the sand flies, I want every man here disembarking at a run and chasing them down. No escapes.'

One of the ship's officers had the courage to raise a question. 'Majesty, why is he so important?'

Constantine took a deep breath. 'He is a demon in a man's skin, trained by the Turks and steeped in the blood of a dozen nations. But more than that, he is Count Carlo Tocco's illegitimate son, and that makes him a powerful bargaining tool in the siege back at Glarentza. He will make a lot of difference. Perhaps even end the war for us.'

And because he had eschewed all the standard rules of war and tried for the prince's murder that day on the walls, Gabriel added, silently.

That was why the ship swept on at immense speed, in the wake of the Epirot flagship. Gabriel returned to his place at the rail, giving the instructions to Gaspar and Manuel. Then they leaned on the timber and watched, as the sea swept past them. Such was the coastline in this region that the sea was never bare and entirely open, and sailors named the islands as they passed:

Kastos, Atokos, Kalamos, Kithros, Meganisi, and then Arkoudi, and finally, as a narrow line of white and grey appeared atop the waves: Lefkas.

In fact, Lefkas, as they came ever closer, was so large it might as well be the mainland. Far from being a flat and welcoming land, the island rose as huge peaks and deep valleys, presenting a tough face to the approaching ships. Now, as they closed on it, hours into their pursuit, Gabriel could see them start to turn, the move slowing them, and realised that much of Lefkas consisted of rocky cliffs and inlets, rather than beaches. Should the Epirot ship make land in the wrong place, far from being saved, it would be utterly destroyed and many would drown. Indeed, though it meant they lost a little speed themselves, Constantine's own ship slowed and followed suit, continuing the pursuit as Torno aimed for a narrow strip of beach in an inlet.

Gabriel found himself silently urging them on, now. They were so close.

The beach came nearer and nearer. Beyond the white sands, he could see a stretch of green field before the slopes rose, wooded and dark, offering sanctuary to the desperate. If Torno reached the woods and the hills, there was a good chance that Constantine's men would never find him, and this whole pursuit would have been wasted. Now, as details resolved, Gabriel could see a farm set back from the beach. No village, and it seemed unlikely a farm could supply much support for the man. He watched, heart in mouth, as Torno's ship ploughed through the shallows, making for that beach at speed.

When the Epirot ship hit the land, it was impressive. There was a crunch that was audible even this far back and out to sea, and the whole vessel bucked, as though it might cycle end over end and land upside down. Then, however, it crashed back into the water and sagged over to port, leaning precariously.

The Byzantine vessel was not far behind, and as men aboard shouted and prayed, Gabriel watched small figures leaping from the stricken ship and flooding across the beach. Then the prince's ship was too close, their own danger too much to pay attention to those they followed. Despite Constantine's earlier order, the ship's master did slow them as they approached, enough to allow them to beach hard but without damaging the galley. As they hit, every man aboard obeyed the bellowed instruction to brace, clinging on for dear life. When the ship slammed to a halt, its keel wedged into the sand, even braced as he was, Gabriel was thrown into the rail so hard that as he lurched and staggered back, he quickly tested and prodded to make sure he hadn't broken or sprung a rib.

He was the fourth man to leave the ship, leaping down the drop – the height of two men – to land in the giving sand with a thud. His sword was out in a heartbeat as he spent a few moments recovering from the impact, his ribs still painful from the beaching. Then he was off, others of the Ianitzaroi with him, Manuel raising the standard as they ran.

It was immediately, irritatingly, clear that they were going to fail to catch all of their foes. The crew of the Epirot ship had sufficient head start that some were already halfway to the trees, and with no horses on board, the Byzantine force was unlikely to catch them. Still, officers were directing their men to pursue the various fleeing Epirots. Gabriel slowed.

'Are *we* not chasing them?' Gaspar rumbled in surprise.

Gabriel turned to him. 'We are the imperial bodyguard. Our duty is to protect the prince. Imagine that every man with a sword races for those woods, and then a few enemies break out of hiding and come for the ship?'

The ourghos nodded at the sense of this, and apparently Constantine understood, for, as he too dropped the long distance to the sand, he walked over to the Ianitzaroi and nodded at them. 'It appears not everyone ran.'

Gabriel followed the prince's pointing finger and realised that a small group of men were gathered on the sand not far from the broken ship and, best of all, the Tocco colours fluttered from the pole there.

Constantine marched in their direction, his bodyguard clustering around him. Those with shields made sure to be close by, in case the enemy still had archers with them and the will to fight. Neither Constantine nor the Ianitzaroi wore armour. There were plenty of horror stories of men who'd fallen into the water from a ship and been pulled to the depths before anyone could help them. Still, they were armed, and determined, and the small clutch of Epirots did not seem inclined to rise and put up a resistance.

As they neared, they could see why. Each and every man there was injured. Some had broken limbs, likely caused during the hard beaching, while others sported a wide variety of nasty wounds, many caused by arrows or flying splinters. Among the men, a standard-bearer gripped the Tocco banner, using the pole more for support than anything. Close by his feet, a man in shining steel armour and the Tocco colours, with perfectly oiled and curled hair that was now coated liberally with white sand, lay groaning. He did not appear at first to be badly injured, but then Gabriel noted that one of his legs was not quite pointing the right way, and must have been broken, any wound hidden by the plates of the leg armour.

'Torno,' Constantine demanded as they came to a halt close by. The wounded man did not look quite how Gabriel remembered, but five years had passed, and they'd only seen him in snatches from a distance then.

The nobleman looked up, wincing at the movement that disturbed his leg, and nodded.

But Gabriel knew something was wrong. He instinctively turned to look at the more active men around them, peering at their faces during the exchange. His eyes narrowed as he watched the standard-bearer. The man was sweating slightly, but it had been his shifty expression in that moment that had drawn Gabriel's attention. He took a step towards the man, who suddenly looked extremely worried, and took a step back in response, and that, Gabriel felt certain, was not just because of his disconcerting appearance. There was untruth at work here.

He turned back to the man on the ground.

'You are not Torno.'

Constantine frowned, turning to him. 'What?'

'I *thought* he looked different, but then I saw his bannerman's face and that confirmed it. He's lying.'

The young prince held Gabriel's gaze for a moment, then nodded and turned back to the man with the broken leg. Whoever he was, he was still important, for there had not been time to put a man in Torno's armour and livery in the short time before they were found.

'Who are you?'

There was a long pause, and finally the stricken man sighed. 'I am Ciolo Venier, of Negroponte.'

'Yet you wear Tocco colours,' Gabriel noted.

Constantine nodded. 'Nicola Venier is the brother-in-law of Carlo Tocco. I would wager that makes Ciolo here a nephew.' He straightened. 'I fear we have lost Torno, but perhaps his cousin might at least help press the old man into submission.' Turning, he gestured to Gabriel. 'Secure him and his people. Have them brought aboard. As soon as any survivors have been rounded up, I want us back in the water and making for the fleet. They must have seen us leave, and Laskaris will not depart without us. I do believe we can end the siege of Glarentza now, speedily and without further bloodshed.'

Gabriel nodded, though his gaze rose to the treeline beyond the farm. Torno had got away. With luck, he would perish before he could find help. But somehow, he felt this was not the last they would see of the Epirot admiral.

2

The Archbishop's Might

Patras

One year after the Echinades victory: late March 1429

'Why is this place so damned important anyway?' Manuel grunted.

'What?'

'Well, the empire's centred on Constantinople, and the Turks are sitting on the other side of the water there, even on the same side in places. If the prince is so set on starting wars, wouldn't he be better pushing back the Turks than fucking around in the Morea and fighting other Christians?'

Gabriel nodded sadly. It was a question that often arose among the various mercenary forces fighting for Byzantium. And the answer was as saddening as it was simple.

'They have a saying in the city, and I'm surprised you've not heard it – "better the Turk's turban than the Pope's crown." They have a long memory. Four hundred years long, in fact, and they'll never forget the crusaders who sacked and burned the city.'

'Doesn't explain his fascination with the Morea.'

'Constantine believes that to become strong once more, we need to reforge the empire, and he can't face the Turks until he's achieved that strength. So the empire has to be here, away from the Turks. He can push the Italian states back out of the Morea and take control, and the Turks might even support him

35

in doing it. They've no love of the Pope or his peoples, after all.'

'I thought his *brother* was despot of the Morea,' Gaspar put in.

'He is, but Constantine has been promised the position. Don't forget, Theodore is more monk than master. The Morea needs a strong hand. Now that the north-west is back under Byzantine control, it's time to seize the north.'

Not that Theodore was altogether pleased with the move.

It had been a strange few months. They had sailed back victorious from the island with the Byzantine fleet, to raucous applause at Glarentza. Count Carlo Tocco had suddenly found himself in an unenviable position. He was trapped in the city he'd taken, besieged by the most powerful Byzantine army raised in some years, and had been reliant upon his reinforcements from Epirus. But they had not come. Indeed, they had been thrashed in the seas to the north, by Laskaris and his fleet, and now Tocco was trapped and outnumbered. Moreover, his son had been forced to flee the battle and his nephew had been taken prisoner.

The terms Tocco offered showed that generosity born of utter desperation. He would return to Epirus and withdraw all his forces from the Morea. He would cede Glarentza to the empire without argument or delay. He offered his niece Maddalena in wedlock to Constantine as surety for the peace, and the deal had been agreed. In one fell swoop, the Byzantines had retaken Glarentza, made a nominal ally of an enemy, and put him safely back outside their boundaries. Not all of the count's people were supportive, though. Rumour had it that his refugee son, Torno, had taken offence at his father's deal with the empire. He had not turned himself in, nor returned to his father, and his current whereabouts and situation were unknown, other than he had made it plain to his father that as long as Constantine was married to his cousin, Torno would shun his family.

The joy and adrenaline of the victory had been infectious. That next night, Constantine, over too much wine, had put to his brother the emperor the idea of reconquering all Italian possessions in the Morea, leaving it in imperial hands, with only the Turks hovering at the border. By the time the brothers had retired for the night, John slept with a mind filled with dreams of conquest and a new strength for Byzantium.

The next day, the arguments had begun. John and Constantine both knew that the sensible next step in any war of reconquest had to be control of Patras, that great northern trading port, currently owned and garrisoned by the papist archbishop Pandolfo Malatesta. The problem came with the intensely religious Theodore, who was married to the archbishop's sister, and was therefore not hugely enthusiastic about going to war with his brother-in-law. The argument exploded to such an extent that Theodore turned his back on them and returned to Mystras with his army, flagrantly refusing an imperial command from his brother. Constantine and John were left alone, though still with the lion's share of the army.

They were undaunted. Within the month they were marching the army for Patras. Indeed, the wedding of Constantine to his new bride was celebrated in the camps of the army outside the walls of the great port city. Oddly, the striking Tocco woman seemed to be rather pleased with how things turned out, and Constantine in turn was gracious and good to her. Gabriel had swiftly formed the impression that there was no love lost between Maddalena Tocco and her family, and that she was somewhat relieved to be out of the viper's nest. Certainly she had voiced her relief that neither her father nor her cousins had deigned to join them for the wedding.

Dropping from the saddle and leaving Uri with his men, Gabriel strode into the prince's command chamber, nodding to other Ianitzaroi in passing.

'How can they delay so?' Constantine was saying, swatting yet another letter away irritably.

Gabriel came to a halt near the door and made rumbling noises until Constantine looked across at him. 'Yes?'

'I have a piece of news for you, sir. We just did another tour of the city's walls, and spotted something we'd not seen before.'

'Don't be cryptic, Gabriel. I'm too tired for guessing games.'

'One section of the walls, close to the castle hill, is flying colours that are not Malatesta's. Colours that are blue and white.'

Constantine straightened. 'Tocco?'

'For sure. Of course, we cannot say for certain which of the Tocco, but I'd wager a small fortune on one certain bastard.'

The prince sagged back again. 'Well, we'd wondered more than once where he'd gone when his father and sister came to us. Makes sense that he would find another Italian to side with. He might have picked the wrong one, though. Gives me a second chance to winkle him out and spear the villain.'

'It may be, my prince, that it is Torno who's commanding the defence, since the archbishop himself is not there. Rumour places Malatesta out at sea, beyond the pickets of our navy and bound for Italy, seeking reinforcements.'

'All the more reason to press the siege, then.'

Their arrival on Palm Sunday had not had the impact they had hoped. Despite Malatesta's absence, and the celebrations in the city's cathedral and churches, the defending army seemed to have taken it all in their stride, even when Constantine's men laid palm branches along the way to the city gates in emulation of the famed event in the life of their blessed Lord. Constantine fumed, baffled how the defenders could be so confident and defiant, despite it all, and Gabriel had suspected that while the archbishop was away, some new lord was behind those walls, directing events. Now, he had an idea who.

The Byzantine high command had expected the city to surrender. The defenders were outnumbered, supplies would be difficult to acquire with more and more Byzantine ships patrolling the Gulf of Lepanto, the army investing the city on land and the voice of power himself, Malatesta, gone. Given the number of important men who had secretly pledged their support to Constantine, it was a surprise that resistance held so firm. Or a surprise to most, anyway.

Torno…

'I am sorely vexed by this,' Constantine grumbled. 'By rights they should have crumbled by now without the archbishop. I recognise that perhaps Torno is directing things, but the city folk have little reason to pay attention to him. He's a foreigner, not even kin to the archbishop. And none of our signals seem to have borne fruit, either. Not once have any of our potential allies answered our call. Where are they, now they are needed?'

An urgent knocking at the door interrupted both conversation and train of thought, and all three of them turned to the sound. One of Gabriel's men, standing by the door, waited for Constantine's nod, and then opened it to admit the visitor.

A *kontostaulos* of Constantine's army was standing outside in his ornate uniform, and hurried in, bowing deep and with a flourish.

'Highness and great lord, you need to see what is happening.'

Constantine was on his feet in a heartbeat, followed swiftly by Gabriel and Sphrantzes, running out after the officer. The headquarters had been sited, on Constantine's orders, near three ancient churches close to the Zeugolation Gate, with a clear view of the city walls, actually worryingly close to the action for a man so eminent as the prince. As such, the moment the three men emerged into the bright sunlight, the view was clear, and all saw what it was that had so grabbed the officer's attention.

Five bodies dangled from the city wall to one side of the gate, the ropes around their throats enough to choke them, if not break their necks. Their identities could not be determined from this distance, but what was clear was that they were noblemen in rich attire. Even as the three Byzantines peered at the grisly sight, a sixth body dropped from the wall–top, the rope snapping tight, its doomed load dancing a merry jig of death for a few moments before falling still.

'I think we all know who they are,' Sphrantzes noted, 'and the curs have the temerity not only to murder our allies in the city and display them to us, but they even came out to watch their work.'

His pointing finger drew the attention of the other two, and now they saw that the city gate was open, and a small group of colourfully attired horsemen had come out and were sitting there, looking back up at their handiwork on the walls. Colourful indeed, in their blue-and-white-striped surcoats.

'My horse,' Constantine growled, snapping his fingers as he began to move. Gabriel had just enough time to frown his surprise and worry at the command before he nodded to one of the company, who was looking after the horses nearby.

'Wait?' Gabriel urged.

'No,' Constantine replied. 'No. Not with that happening. Not with Torno murdering our people and taunting us with their bodies.' The prince snarled angrily as he pushed his way between the men to his horse.

'What do you mean to do?' Sphrantzes demanded as Constantine grabbed the reins and started to pull himself up into the saddle.

'We have armed men with us, and I will not *countenance* such actions from the swine. Let us chastise the villain.'

And with that, he was kicking the horse's flanks, and riding hard. Gabriel stared in shock. What was the lunatic doing? He could quite understand the prince's fury at Torno, which was nothing new – and whose fires had been stoked afresh by the Italian's actions – but to charge forth like that was little more than suicide. It was only shouts of concern that shook him from his thoughts, as he turned to see that Sphrantzes had pushed through the Ianitzaroi to his own horse and was mounting hurriedly.

'To horse,' Gabriel bellowed now, sending his men to their own mounts. As his was brought over, he peered out towards the city walls. Those enemy riders were far enough from the gate, and this headquarters close enough, that it might be just about possible to catch them before they fled. But why would they flee? One man rode out alone ahead, intent on teaching them a lesson. Gabriel's blood ran cold. This had all the cold unpleasantness of a trap. Sphrantzes was close behind the prince, and the Ianitzaroi were now in pursuit, but still Constantine was alone ahead, and dangerously angry. Gabriel had his horse moving before he was even in the saddle, and then was racing to catch up.

What is the prince thinking, charging off without waiting for support? The fool.

And yet the most astounding thing was happening. Even as those colourful horsemen realised what was happening and began to move, the city's Zeugolation Gate slammed closed. The riders were trapped outside, and though Constantine was alone out front, the Ianitzaroi were coming behind him, and the result could be a bloodbath. The dozen or so enemy riders turned and raced their horses to the north, parallel with the city wall.

Constantine was on them, and Sphrantzes close behind; Gabriel kicked his animal into the fastest gallop he could manage, desperately trying to catch the two idiots. As he raced towards them, he saw what the enemy riders were making for. The city's next gate along, the Agialos Gate, had opened to receive them, a small force of the defenders spilling out to cover their approach.

Gabriel's heart was pounding in his throat as they followed. Constantine was riding directly into the worst kind of peril, and he seemed to be doing so without an ounce of fear, or even common sense. Sphrantzes looked panicked, and well he might.

They were never going to catch up. Gabriel watched in horror as the prince of Constantinople closed on the city gate and its gathered defenders. He'd already seen it coming in his mind's eye, and now he watched it all happen for real. The enemy horsemen stopped close to the gate, and turned, now backed by infantry. Archers appeared on the walls. It had all been a lure, designed to draw them close enough to pick off. Perhaps the defenders had thought to catch the attentive kontostaulos, or perhaps just hoped to draw a senior officer, so close to the headquarters. They surely had not expected to lure Constantine himself, especially more or less alone and unprotected. They would not be able to believe their luck.

Constantine seemed to have finally realised his peril, and reined in sharply, but it was too late. Arrows were arcing out from the walls of Patras, falling sporadically around the prince, for he was at maximum range. The Theotokos Maria seemed to be protecting him within her folded divine arms, for every shot went wide or fell short as Sphrantzes now closed on him, and Constantine wheeled his horse desperately, ready to ride away. That was when a stray shot struck home. The shaft plunged into the horse's rump, and it bucked wildly in pain.

Gabriel watched in fear as the prince was thrown clear of the horse, and that fear turned to panic as the wounded horse dropped to the ground and rolled onto its rider. Two more arrows thudded into the beast, and one was true, for it killed the animal, which lay still, atop Constantine. Sphrantzes was there a moment later, and Gabriel was impressed, once again, at the ease with which the academic slipped into the mode of a soldier. The enemy horsemen were racing out again now, desperate to kill or capture the emperor's brother, and the arrows stopped coming, for fear of the archers killing their own men. But Sphrantzes rode his own horse around the fallen one of his friend and master, and there drew his sword, yanking his shield from its place on the horse.

As Gabriel now pulled out ahead of his Ianitzaroi, bearing down on the scene, he could only hope he was in time, and that the horse had not crushed their master.

'Go. Help the general,' he shouted to his riders, pointing at Sphrantzes, but even as they reached the site of the disaster, the prince's friend shook his head. 'No. Protect the *prince*!'

With that, Sphrantzes kicked his horse and, like some doomed hero from an ancient epic, raced directly towards the dozen enemy horsemen to head them off, sword out and roaring like a madman. Gabriel lost sight of him then, for he reached the downed prince and leapt from his horse desperately, crouching close to Constantine. His men were arriving now, many of them moving to form a wall around the prince and his fallen horse, shields up in case the arrows started once more. Three of them dismounted and joined Gabriel.

'My lord?' he asked, voice laden with concern.

Constantine, whose legs were beneath the animal, had been grunting and growling, head thrashing this way and that, but now his gaze fell upon Gabriel and he stopped. 'Get this fucking thing off me.'

The four of them began to heave, pushing the dead weight of the animal off its rider. Gaspar's impressive muscles counted for much of their strength, and yet still it took quite some effort, all of them heaving in breaths as the horse finally rolled away.

'Can you move your legs?' Gabriel asked urgently.

Constantine gingerly tried, and it was a great relief all round when both limbs seemed to react properly. They helped him to his feet, and he managed a shaky step or two, but was clearly not going to be up to anything much more. Gaspar snorted and reached down, grasping the prince and throwing him over a shoulder. They carried him to one of the horses and hauled him up into the saddle, and Gabriel mounted his own beast close by. Constantine was still groggy and in pain, and so the commander of the Ianitzaroi took hold of his master's reins. He turned, then, taking a moment to work out what was happening. His men were gathering with him once more, and even as they pulled back, the arrows started falling, mostly short, but the odd one thudding into a shield. Past them, Gabriel could see the shape of George Sphrantzes being dragged away towards the city gate by triumphant men, protected by those riders. He'd not fallen easily, though. Two of the enemy horsemen lay dead at the site of their clash.

Swiftly they pulled back, out of the range of the defenders, and Gabriel kept glancing back at the city gate until he finally lost sight of the heroic nobleman, dragged inside and out of view. If only they'd had time to do something to save Sphrantzes as well. Then, safely out of immediate danger, he turned to Constantine, who wore an expression of impotent fury.

'I have ever spoken my mind to you, Constantine Palaiologos, and I shall not stop now. What in the good God's world could have made you do such a foolish thing? That was a trap set to catch a commander, and it did just that.'

Constantine slumped a little, ire still written on his features. 'Torno. Like a serpent sent from the Devil himself, the villain takes charge of the enemy city against us, murders our supporters in the city, displaying their corpses to us, and all of that a trap set to catch me? The man vexes me, Gabriel. We came to Patras, which should have surrendered but did not, because Torno is there. Theodora warned me that he would find ways to set himself against me. She believes he is driven to fury more than ever by the ignominy of his defeat at our hands. I am the kill he cannot make, the job unfinished.'

'It is undoubtedly he who is keeping our allies in the city from delivering the city to us,' Gabriel sighed. 'He executes those who advocate surrender, to deter others from even thinking about it.'

'Despite how frustrating that is, it could perhaps be made to work to our advantage,' Constantine said, wincing at his pained leg muscles.

'Oh?'

'Those others of our supporters in there will be all the more desperate to be free of him.'

'Which is only so much use if Torno has the place in his gauntlet.'

When the messenger came it was not entirely a surprise. Something had been happening in the city over the past few days, and it spoke heavily of changes inside. For a while, more hangings had been carried out on the city walls, but they had petered out as Torno ran out of confirmed enemies, and to Constantine's clear relief, they had not all been executed, for there were a number of luminaries from Patras who had earlier sent letters promising peace, but who had not yet fallen with a snap to bounce against the ancient stonework.

Two nights ago, there had been an uproar within the city. It had almost sounded like a civil war from outside, yet the soldiers had not moved from the walls, and nothing had burned. But the next morning, it had taken some time for observers to note one key fact. All the banners connected with Torno, which had been seen here and there, involved in the defence and the killings, were now concentrated in the citadel atop the hill.

'Perhaps the archbishop has returned?' one of the courtiers had mused, but a little querying had revealed that the only ships that had been seen entering the city by the picket vessels out in the bay had been small traders, not the huge ship that would bear a man like Malatesta.

'Most likely they have tired of being under the thumb of a foreign tyrant and fought back. Torno might now be trapped in the castle,' another wondered.

'He may have withdrawn to the citadel,' Constantine responded, 'but he must still have sway in the city, else likely they would have opened the gate.'

And this morning the messenger had come from outside the Agialos Gate – one of the officers of the regular patrols. He had ridden to say that there was some commotion at the gate, and that then it had opened, though no one had yet appeared.

In moments, Constantine, along with a small entourage and his bodyguard, had mounted and ridden for the gate a little further along the walls. Sure enough, as the messenger had noted, the gate stood open; men had gathered in crowds on the walls. As if the arrival of Constantine, along with his banners and entourage, had triggered a reaction, in a matter of moments the open maw of Patras disgorged a figure on horseback. The Byzantine command party looked to one another for answers, but no face held one, and they turned back to watch that single rider in peasant's clothing, on a horse that was more mule than charger, riding out alone from the city towards them.

Gabriel's eyes may have been eerie and colourless to behold, but from within they were as sharp as could be, and so he was the first to see, or at least the first to voice it.

'Sphrantzes.'

There were murmurs of disbelief and of curiosity, but as the figure came closer, no one could deny it. He might be dressed like a nobody and on a poor nag, and his hair had grown wild and untamed, his beard longer, like a Turk's, but it was definitely him. Gabriel heard the exhalation of sheer relief from the prince, and responded readily when Constantine ordered them to mount up and ride to meet him.

Sphrantzes came to a halt roughly halfway between the city gate and the nearest pickets of the Byzantine force. Gabriel was one of the first to reach him, carefully judging arrow range from the walls. The man looked tired and dishevelled, but he was whole, though marked with ground-in dirt and healing injuries. Indeed, his left arm sported the scar of a recently healed wound which looked to Gabriel a great deal like the mark left by a sword cutting through the corner of a shield and drawing a line across the flesh in the process. They had not looked after him well, though his wounds had seemingly healed over the forty days they'd had him.

Constantine was the first to speak, reining in before the nobleman.

'I had thought you gone, old friend.'

Sphrantzes flicked him a look that could have been mistaken for ire, though Gabriel saw a dark humour in it. 'Are you sure?' the weary man answered. 'Because I was under the impression that if I died, you would roar the world's end and tear Patras apart brick by brick in your grief.'

There was an oddly stilted silence, and then Constantine burst out laughing. 'I have missed your wit, you know? But quick, tell us, what has led to this miracle?'

Sphrantzes shrugged his shoulders, wincing at the discomfort this brought, and breathed out slowly. 'It seems the presence of our friend the Tocco scion is not greatly desired by the majority of Patras, and there is something of an uneasy truce in the city at the moment. Torno is too strong to be easily overcome from within, and since he is a guest of the archbishop and an important heir of the Count Palatine of Kefalonia, they are loath to remove him. As such, he has retreated to the hilltop citadel and left the city to itself, though I noted a few of his key men in place as I departed, so I suspect he is still able to clamp down upon Patras if he truly needs to.'

'And what of our allies, then?'

'Hard to say. But there has apparently been a conference between the archbishop's advisors, and they tasked me with delivering an offer to you. Malatesta's continuing absence seems to be eroding the loyalty of his people in the face of your assault. He is still in Italy at the moment, but his council proposes a cut-off point of the end of this month. If Malatesta returns by then and retakes control of his city, it will be up to him to fight on, surrender, or come to terms with you. If he has *not* returned by the end of May, the council will take on his authority and hand over the keys of Patras to you. This is their offer. I suspect it is the best you will get, for if Torno hears of this, he will undoubtedly move to prevent such a thing.'

Constantine nodded, slowly, at every point.

'Of course, if the archbishop returns, it will likely be at the head of a sizeable Italian army, which will render any terms moot. Essentially, they are gambling that he will return by the end of May with sufficient forces to save the city, but if not, they have a backup plan of surrender, likely with terms beneficial to them. It is highly tempting to refuse the offer, I have to say. They are hardly in a position to dictate such terms.'

There was a long silence again, and finally Constantine sighed and relaxed back in the saddle. 'However, you are probably correct in that this is the best we will get. I am willing to give them a single month. The army will remain in place, of course.' He turned and gestured to one of his attendants. 'Take this down in your neatest handwriting.' There was another pause as the man located pen and paper among his bags, then searched for something to lean on, and ended up with one of the Ianitzaroi's shields.

'Constantine Palaiologos, Despot of the northern Morea, on behalf of his Imperial Majesty John, emperor of the Romans, accepts your terms. The besieging force will remain in position during the proposed period, but will launch neither missile nor assault, excepting in retaliation to such from within the walls.' He waved a hand. 'Seal it with my seal and have it delivered to the city's defenders.'

He now focused on Sphrantzes. 'How are you, George? Really?'

'I live, though I have no great wish to repeat my stay, I shall admit. I was hustled inside with grievous wounds, but they were not inclined to treat me well. Perhaps those civil noblemen we have dealt with might have seen me cared for in a monastery, but it was Torno's men who took me, and they had taken exception to my killing two of their number. I was dragged to a dingy and stinking tower by a granary, and there clamped in irons in the gloom, with only weevils and mice for company. Fortunately they left my brooch and attire with me for a time, and I used the pin from it and a loose thread from my tunic hem to stitch up the wounds that threatened my survival, and I am eternally grateful to God and the Theotokos that none of my wounds succumbed to rot. But here I am forty days later, hungry, creaky, achy, but still intact. It will take more than an Italian prison to break me, my lord.'

'Hmm. Well, since we have the better part of a month with no fighting looming, perhaps we should return to Glarentza and comfort. There I have the best physicians in the Morea, and they can look you over and put you on the path to strength. Glarentza is sort of my unofficial seat as a despot.'

'A rather *unofficial* despot,' Sphrantzes said with a glint of humour in his eye. 'Don't forget that your brother Theodore is currently officially the Despot of the Morea.'

'Theodore couldn't rule a classroom, let alone a country,' Constantine laughed. 'He is a good man, but he is too philosophical and wrapped up in what God thinks about everything he does. No, the Morea needs a *new* despot, and the despot it needs –' he fixed his old friend with a grin – 'is me.'

Glarentza

28 May 1429

'It was only a matter of time.' Constantine nodded, leaning back in his chair. 'Show them in, Gabriel.'

The Catalan nodded and turned, striding back over to the door. He opened it and left the room, crossing to the small gathering standing and looking bored in the centre of the large antechamber.

Turks.

It was to be expected, really. The Ottoman Empire encroached on the Romans from almost every side these days, and their nearest bey, commanding Thessaly, sat just across the Gulf of Lepanto from Patras. Watching Constantine and his brothers retaking the Morea and consolidating their hold there would be concerning to the Turks, to say the least. And though it was not something a wise man said out loud, everyone knew that these days an emperor only maintained his strength by not provoking the Turks.

Of course, Constantine was prepared for the visit. It had been expected for some time. The ambassadors regarded Gabriel coldly. There was a little flinching at his face, but they had seen him several times since their arrival half an hour ago, and the initial shock of his appearance was wearing off.

'My lords, the Despot Constantine Palaiologos, Prince of the Romans, will see you now.'

Gabriel noted the twitch among the facial muscles of the visitors at this rather grandiose title, given Constantine's tenuous hold in the Morea and the oppressive power of the Turks. They nodded curtly, and Gabriel led them to the door, opened it, and stepped to one side.

'Imperial Highness, the emissaries of Turahan Bey, governor of Thessaly.'

The Turks swept past him without a glance and came to an imperious halt insultingly close to Constantine. The Ianitzaroi moved in a little closer in response, but not enough to provoke an incident.

'Well met, my lords,' Constantine said calmly, without rising. 'You know my companion here?'

The head of the embassy glanced only momentarily at Sphrantzes, then gave a slight nod.

'And my wife, Theodora?'

Again, a brief acknowledgement, though with a touch more appreciation, before the ambassador turned back to Constantine.

'I shall come to the point directly, Prince of Romans. The great bey is incensed by your activity. He allowed your war against Glarentza and the Tocco –' a momentary guarded glance at the princess there – 'against his better judgement, for it is known to us that your campaign was in response to raids on the part of the count's people. This is just and acceptable. Your move to take Patras from Archbishop Malatesta, however, is not acceptable. You risk upsetting the balance of power in the region. Turahan Bey has an understanding with the archbishop that supersedes any agreement with your despotate. You will therefore cease and desist all attempts to conquer Patras, lest you incur the bey's wrath, and force intervention. You understand?'

Constantine reacted very calmly, simply arching one eyebrow and waiting for the monologue to end. He let the silence sit for a moment, then steepled his fingers and sat forward.

'Are you versed in the politics and agreements of the region, Ambassador?'

The Turk frowned. 'Of course I am.'

'Then you will be aware that the emperor, through his lawful despot in the Morea, has a standing agreement with the sultan and his bey to maintain the status quo, applicable to both the Romans and the Turks. This agreement has kept war in the Morea from our door for years, and can only be considered beneficial, yes?'

'Of course. And it is this agreement you shatter, threatening the status quo.'

'I fear you are mistaken, Ambassador. You are aware that the archbishop is not in Patras at this time?'

'He has embarked upon a mission to the Italian homeland.'

'Quite. You are clearly unaware of his purpose. He seeks to increase his military might and his power through the acquisition of Venetian armies, fleets and artillery, and Catalan mercenaries, from his allies in Italy. Should he be allowed to fortify with such forces, he will outnumber not only our forces in the Morea, but also those of Tocco in Epirus, and of the Duchy of Athens. There can be no other reason for such an escalation than the expansion of territory. Having been informed early of the archbishop's strategy, we moved to prevent this growth, to limit the strength Malatesta can bring to bear, to uphold the status quo, and to maintain the peace.' He glared daggers into the face of the ambassador, who suddenly looked shaken and rather unsure. 'I suggest that you return to your bey with the facts, and that you try to make sure you are fully educated on the subject before levelling threats and accusations at your allies. You may go.'

It was bold. It was provocative. It was also a command. Gabriel and his men began to move forward, and the Turkish embassy backed away without another word, turned, and then marched out. Gabriel saw them as far as the door, and then let Gaspar take it from there. He closed the door, then, and there they paused in silence until they were content that the Turks were long gone from earshot. Finally, Constantine leaned forward.

'Once again, we need to take advantage of uncertainty and confusion. In a matter of days, our ultimatum to the city will come to a head. As things stand, we have a tacit excuse to continue our campaign. If Turahan Bey is given time to receive tidings and consider matters, perhaps even send to the sultan, he may decide that we have hoodwinked him. We must move on Patras and seize it. Once we have control, we can decide how to appease the Turks, but that is currently my secondary concern, after the siege itself.'

Sphrantzes nodded. 'It may be possible to persuade Turahan Bey that we are acting in Turkish interests, even perhaps on behalf of the Turks.'

'I would say,' Theodora added, 'that it matters not who holds the deeds to a castle if you have your archers on its walls.'

Even Gabriel had to nod at this. Possession was what mattered, and men like Sphrantzes would always be able to argue the minutiae.

'Good,' Constantine announced. 'Then send word. We ride for Patras in the morning. I want to be inside the city there before Turahan's ambassador even reaches home.'

Malatesta had yet to return, and the deadline had arrived. The night before, as the commanders had settled in with the besieging army once more, there had been a commotion in the city. Tocco banners had been seen on the walls, but this morning, things were quiet once more, and the blue and white snapped in the breeze only atop the towers and ramparts of the hilltop citadel. Whatever trouble Torno had started during the night seemed to have been subdued.

The great church of Hagios Andreas sat sizzling in the summer heat, the bricks shimmering and almost glowing, the sky a featureless blue canopy. Constantine had chosen his wardrobe very carefully that morning. He was not the ruler of the Romans, and could not wear the crown or the crimson boots of the emperor, and so had opted partly for the dress of a despot, including the purple and white boots and red hose. However, he had forgone the ornate, pearl-encrusted *skiadion* hat of that rank, opting instead for a diadem that marked his membership of the emperor's close family. But despite the nods to his despotate and to his imperial blood, he had augmented the heavy robes with a gleaming breastplate and gauntlets, a plain soldier's sword buckled at his side. He represented everything he felt was important: imperial authority, granted by God; rulership of the Morea through his despotate; and his martial nature as commander of an army at war.

Even Sphrantzes had gone for armour today.

Most of the court were in their finery, while the officers of the military present, from the lowliest *allagatōr* to the loftiest *doux* wore their colourful dress uniforms, augmented with armour in much the same manner as their commander. Only the Princess Theodora failed to gleam with armour, yet her stately dress in the Byzantine style fitted with the crowd.

By contrast, the opposing party showed not a glimmer of steel in the bright summer sunshine as they made their stately way from the city gate towards the church and the waiting imperial high command. They were colourful and richly attired, and rode proud destriers, but there was no doubt from even a glance that they were a civic deputation rather than military. The only swords among them would be ornate variants with little military value. As Gabriel registered this, he couldn't help sweeping his gaze up to that fortress on the hill, where the real military power in the city still lay. There, the costumery would be less ornate and colourful, but there would be a great deal more steel.

Which led him back to the approaching party of horsemen, his keen gaze trying to pick out every rider among them individually and check their colours. Nowhere could he see the blue and white jagged stripes of the Tocco, and the only sign of the chequered red and white stripes of the Malatesta was on the banner being carried at the fore. The archbishop himself was absent, along with any of his kin. What was left, then – the group now approaching – represented the nobles of the city, including those few remaining who had pledged their support for Constantine.

All was hopeful.

Because if the leaders of Patras lived up to their end of the bargain, the city was now Constantine's. Of course, there were Italians involved, and when Italians were involved there was always the possibility of duplicity, but with Malatesta gone and Torno shut up in the fortress, it seemed likely the deal would go through.

Still, Constantine's men, Gabriel included, were poised, ready to burst into action should there be any sign of betrayal. The army fair twitched as they stood ready.

When the riders came close enough for an exchange, they reined in, horribly conscious of several hundred heavily armed men within striking distance, the Ianitzaroi close enough to cut a throat before an order could issue from it. Three of the men rode a few steps further, then, facing Constantine, Sphrantzes and John Rhosatsas, the prince's senior *strategos*. The central one was clearly the leader and spokesperson, while at his right side rode the man carrying the banner of Malatesta, and to his left, a man with a rich leather satchel over his shoulder.

'The day has come,' Constantine announced, his voice ringing out across the land, over the faint snap of banners in the feeble breeze, the calls of wheeling birds and the buzz of insects, the creak of leather, clonk of wood, clatter of steel and snorting of horses that told of the presence of many hundreds of soldiers.

The delegation's leader bowed his head low. 'As agreed, the archbishop has not returned. The leader of the Roman force has made good his promise to hold back his army, and so we abide by our agreed terms. In the absence of our appointed lord, the nobles of Patras, both clergy and laity, hereby grant dominion of the city to the Lord Constantine Palaiologos. The gates are opened and the city's garrison stood down.'

He nodded at the man with the satchel, who rode forth now, rummaging within. Gabriel tensed, ready to move, in case the hand came out with a throwing knife or suchlike, but relaxed a little as he retrieved a huge and ornate key, almost as long as his forearm. This, he placed upon a red cushion also pulled from the bag, and proffered to Constantine. Before the prince could respond, in the name of safety, Gabriel hopped over and collected the cushion, checking it for trouble, then wiped it with the sword-cloth at his belt and passed it to the prince, whose quirky smile at this made the Ianitzaroi roll his eyes.

'The key to the city of Patras, my lord Despot,' the local nobleman announced, loudly. At this, the banner-man by his side lowered his standard, untied the Malatesta banner from it and let that flutter to the dusty ground, then replaced it with a freshly affixed imperial eagle, which he raised, to the mutual cheers of the city's deputation and the men of the Byzantine force around them.

'An investment before God and the notables of Patras has been arranged in the church of Hagios Nikolaos,' the nobleman said. 'If you would accompany us, with your court and your guards, of course, my lord.'

Constantine inclined his head, hands still crossed on the reins of his horse. 'It would be a pleasure. But first, tell me of Lord Torno.'

The nobleman had the grace to look more than a little embarrassed.

'Regrettably, my lord, not every soul in Patras favours our decision. Lord Torno considers it a betrayal, and as such has taken on the mantle of the archbishop's regent in his absence. He, and a number of lords and commanders who refused to change their allegiance, have retreated to the castle and there make their stand until the archbishop can return. I must also warn you that we are still finding their men in position in places around the city. We are slowly rooting them out and clearing them, but it is a work in progress.'

Constantine nodded. 'Of course. And a barrel of good apples cannot be held accountable for a handful of rotten examples at the bottom. I hold no ill will towards any loyal inhabitant of Patras. Let this be a day of joy for all.'

More cheers.

In a matter of moments, they were on the move. The party from Patras led the way now, turning their mounts and riding slowly back to the city gate. Behind them, Gabriel and Gaspar rode with four men, then the imperial party with the inevitable entourage of gilded lackeys, then the rest of the Ianitzaroi, with a couple of riders out to the flanks for additional safety. More soldiers followed, for the strategos Rhosatsas was not about to let the prince ride into an uncertain city without adequate protection.

They reached the gate quickly, and as they approached, Gabriel snapped out a series of orders, his eyes up on the parapet of the city walls. Though there were figures up there, no arrows flew and all remained still. In response to commands, the Ianitzaroi moved swiftly, changing their positions so that Constantine, Theodora and Sphrantzes were each well attended by half a dozen bodyguards, each with shield out and ready and a hand on their sword hilt.

Passing through the gate was a nerve-racking event, for each of them knew that it would be an easy thing to set up an ambush just inside and to fall upon the victorious despot, and it was only as Gabriel emerged into the city and looked about sharply that he felt himself relax a little. A score of men were on duty there, but they were standing at the periphery with their weapons sheathed. Beyond them, the people of Patras lined the narrow, ancient streets. There was an odd silence for a moment, and then Constantine emerged from the shadow of the gate into the bright sunlight, with his glowing wife by his side, and the crowds burst into spontaneous cheers. Gabriel was not quite ready to fully relax. He turned and looked up, confirming that no one was waiting to pick off the conquerors from the gate as they entered.

The reaction of the populace certainly appeared to be genuine, and flowers were being cast into the street in the path of the imperial party.

'Nice,' Manuel drawled. 'Not been welcomed anywhere like this for a long time.'

'*You've* never been welcomed anywhere like this,' Gaspar smirked, 'except at the cock pox infirmary.'

Manuel shot him an irritated look as several of the Ianitzaroi nearby sniggered, and Gabriel cleared his throat. 'As you were. Knock off the jokes with ladies present, and keep your eyes and ears open.'

As they rode through the streets of the labyrinthine city, Gabriel's gaze shot this way and that, all around them, constantly evaluating danger, watching for weapons or unexpected movement among the crowd. Anything unusual could be a hint of danger, even a face not smiling amid the joyful grins. Still, as they rode, he saw nothing, once he dismissed the commonplace gasps of horror at his appearance, and parents hurrying to pull their children away from him.

'I think it's time you started wearing a helmet with a visor,' Manuel quipped, though he fell silent instantly at a glare from his commander.

The attack came without any warning, and Gabriel cursed himself for having overlooked an obvious danger, given that last time he'd been here he'd contemplated the peril of attack from above. The arrow missed Sphrantzes' horse by a hand-width, slamming down into the paving and clattering away harmlessly. By the time the second and third arrow struck, the Ianitzaroi, prepared for this from the start, were beside their wards, covering them with shields, looking up and about for the source of the missiles. Constantine was desperately trying to put himself between the falling missiles and his wife, an impossibility in the press. One of the Ianitzaroi behind the prince was lolling in his saddle, a crossbow bolt in his shoulder – from the angle, one meant for the prince. Gabriel's mind flashed back momentarily to the walls of Constantinople, seven years before: another crossbow bolt, in another city.

The source of the attack was easy enough to spot. Above the roofs of the city, here and there, rose narrow stone towers, the status symbols of Patras' wealthier dynasties, and the one they were just passing was clearly the home of the assault. Even as they rallied, more missiles came raining down. Horses were wounded, rearing, and men shouted in alarm. Gabriel's professional eye shot suspiciously to the deputation who had led them here, but they were as panicked as anyone, arrows falling among them. At least this had not been a betrayal, then, an intentional trap. Which suggested it was part of the sporadic resistance the emissary had already mentioned.

The crowd had erupted into shouts of shock and dismay, and were pressing this way and that in their need to get away, a mob in danger of trampling their own. This sort of event quickly turned into a riot if it was not halted.

The first thing to do was to get Constantine and his wife to safety. Gabriel cantered over to the man who'd led the city's deputation. 'They know your route, and they planned for it. Take the despot and companions. Find another route, and do it *now*.'

He then turned to Gaspar. 'Take half the men and keep him safe. Get him to the church by a different route, and keep your eyes open.'

Then, finally, to the nearest group of Ianitzaroi, who were looking to him for orders.

'I want those archers. Come on.'

The first problem was going to be finding a way into the place. Like most cities in the Morea, Patras had grown organically over two thousand years, and so its plan was a complex web, larger streets crossed, connected and intersected by narrow winding alleys. There were no regimented square blocks, as were to be found in Constantinople, but rather collections of buildings huddled together, sometimes clustered around a dead-end alley, sometimes with houses actually buried within the block with no obvious approach, reached by an arcane system of passages. And worst of all, the towers rose amid the roofs, with no obvious connection to any of the buildings around them. Gabriel sucked on his teeth in irritation, trying to make sense of the place between the panicked throng of people surging this way and that, while arrows continued to fall around him, clacking against the flagged street to either side. There was nothing for it. They'd just have to hope to find the access. He turned and gestured to Manuel.

'Take four men to the right, and use that alley. Try and find the way to the tower. I'll take the others and go left.'

With that, he gestured to four of the horsemen, and they turned and began to push their way through the crowd. The hail of arrows decreased considerably as they moved, partly because the unseen assailants were still trying to pick off Constantine and his companions as they forced their way out of the thoroughfare through screaming citizens and into a side street, and partly because, regardless of any orders, some were probably loath to drop arrows into a crowd of their own citizens.

Indeed, a man who prized civilian lives would even now be unable to move. Gabriel regretted collateral damage, but there was nothing for it. If they wanted to reach the assailants, they needed to force a way through the desperate crowds. He could hear the cries, and even the crashes and crunches as he drove Uri through the press, heedless of the damage he was doing. Behind him one of his men cried out, and he glanced over his shoulder briefly to see an arrow jutting from the shoulder of a rider, though his teeth were clenched and he rode on, his shield hanging limp at his side.

Gabriel turned back and forged on. An arrow brushed his elbow without truly connecting, disappearing among the people he pushed through. It was a considerable relief as they burst out of the crowd at last, pushing into the side alley behind them. The angle of attack here was steeper, and the positioning of the roofs hid the tower-top, making archery impossible, and the hail of arrows had died out. Gabriel noted with frustration a number of doorways into buildings, any of which might connect through to the tower. Logic suggested, though, that the entrance would be considerably more grandiose than these. The tower had to belong to a noble family, and would rise from their principal residence, after all. As such, he ignored the ordinary doorways and moved on hurriedly, looking for the next opportunity to turn right.

When he found it, he knew he was correct immediately.

The narrow alley had an ornate iron gate that should prevent access but for the fact that it stood wide open, leaning against the alley walls, an arch above it holding a carved shield with some unknown coat of arms. Gabriel veered into the alley speedily and raced down it. Ahead, he could see a courtyard enclosed by the block's buildings, and as he made for it, the situation came into view. Perhaps thirty feet across, the yard held a well, a fountain with some stone creature spouting a jet of water, a small garden with three narrow, well-tended trees, and a flight of eight stairs leading up to an ornate carved doorway. Its doors gaped open, a dark maw inviting them into the residence. A quick glance up confirmed that the tower rose above this doorway. Two other aspects of the courtyard caught his attention, though. One was a rail for the tethering of horses, with two already tied there, and the other was another alleyway leading off. It was no use listening to try and learn anything, for even here in the backstreets, the noise of the city in panic was almost all-encompassing.

He rode into the centre of the courtyard, where the view was panoramic, and looked along that second alley. His anger mounted as he spotted a rider at the far end, bursting out into the open, leaving the scene. He wore a coat of jagged white and blue lines and fine armour, face covered by a helmet: either Torno himself or one of his most senior officers, presumably fleeing the scene while he could, leaving his men to face the inevitable, the cur.

Gabriel turned to the others.

'Take the tower. No mercy.'

Leaving the other four, he immediately turned for that second access and kicked Uri into action once more, picking up to a canter and then a heart-stopping gallop along the narrow alleyway. He lost sight of the rider as he turned at the end of the alley, and Gabriel raced on, desperate not to lose him.

He rode out through a second ornate, arched gate and into another backstreet, veering right after his prey, and spotted the white and blue figure instantly, just before he also spotted the two horsemen the man had left to protect his back. The men were well armoured in plated steel, while Gabriel wore only a cuirass of scales over leather, strap-like *pteruges* hanging from shoulders and waist. It was an uneven fight in terms of both numbers and equipment, though Gabriel felt he could almost certainly claim superiority in skill, training and determination.

One held a long and narrow spear, his left hand on the reins with no shield, while the other held a mace and shield, reins gripped behind the board. Clearly neither had expected Gabriel as he turned the corner in the wake of the Tocco rider, and they suddenly burst into activity. That gave Gabriel the moments he needed to change the odds. Shield up, he drove his horse straight at the spearman, barging mount and rider together, and lashing out with the shield, hard. The man was held in place with his feet in stirrups, but his leg came free with the collision, and with a cry of alarm, he was tipped over the far side of the animal. Gabriel ignored him further for now. The other rider was a little more prepared, but his mace was unable to reach Gabriel, the downed rider and his horse in the way. Gabriel, grimacing, drove Uri on, silently apologising to the animal as his horse barged the riderless mount sideways into the mace-man.

The second cavalryman was pushed back, crying out, mace flailing. He was fighting for control, trying to make sure he stayed in the saddle and did not fall away like his companion, and that was his undoing. The moment the riderless horse between them broke free and cantered away, Gabriel was ready, lunging forward and swinging with his sword, hard.

The man wore a helmet of fully enclosed steel, visor down, leaving only a slit for the eyes, the neck protected by a guard that was attached to the visor rather than the main helmet. Gabriel had worn such a helmet before, and had learned a hard lesson. The neck protection was only really good with an extra layer beneath – a metal *gorget*, for preference. And the way this example moved, he'd immediately seen it lacked that essential second layer. His blow was not meant to cut, for there was no real chance of slicing through that steel, just like the rest of the man's armour. Instead, his attack had been delivered with all his might in order to crush.

The blow drove the iron throat protector into the man's neck, hard, ironically delivering just the damage it was designed to protect from. The man made a weird hollow gurgling noise deep within the helmet as his windpipe was flattened by his own steel. As he flailed, he dropped both mace and shield, reaching up to try and unhook his visor, then lift it. Gabriel ignored him. Probably the blow had only hurt and inconvenienced him – even with the heavy weight behind it, the neck-guard would not have done too much damage – but it would certainly put him out of commission for now.

He danced his horse out of the way, looking around for the Tocco rider they'd been protecting. It took him just moments to spot the blue-and-white-clad rider, racing off up the slope towards that massive citadel on the hill. He had removed the helmet as he rode, removing all doubt now that it was Torno himself. Gabriel made a brief mental estimation, and came to the irritating conclusion that he was never going to catch the man before he was within missile range of the castle walls. The pursuit was over.

As Gabriel sat, frustrated, watching the villain escape yet again, Manuel arrived from the far side of the block with his riders. He nodded to his banner-man and pointed at the gateway from which he'd emerged.

'That alley. The others are in the tower. Go and help them.'

As his men raced off to aid in the removal of the threat, Gabriel went about taking out his frustration by administering the *coup de grâce* to the two men he'd incapacitated. On other occasions he might have been tempted to clemency, but this had been another deliberate attempt at assassination, engineered by Torno, and mercy was becoming thin on the ground. The two men dead, Gabriel returned to the courtyard and waited for his men to finish their work.

–

That evening, Constantine leaned back in a comfortable chair, cradling his glass of wine, and looked around his *consilium*. 'I think we can safely say that Patras is ours. Alone, we have done what we could not with John and Thomas present.'

'Not quite,' Gabriel reminded him.

'You mean the castle on the hill? Yes, I'll grant you that is a thorn which remains in our side, and it will be a tough one to pluck out. But for now, we have it monitored and surrounded. Nothing gets in or out. They may be able to hold out for months if they are well supplied, but not forever. Sooner or later it will fall. And for now, I have men all across the city, checking for other small groups holding out like the one you removed from the tower. I must thank you once again for your work there, Gabriel.'

He shrugged. 'It's our job. We'd be poor bodyguards if we let you die. And unemployed, too.'

Constantine laughed aloud at that, then sighed and took a sip before drumming a tattoo on the arm of the chair. 'For now, the greatest threat we face comes neither from Malatesta and his reinforcements, nor from Torno and his defenders. The latter is trapped, and the former absent and likely with insufficient men to retake the city even when he returns.'

He glanced across at his wife but despite the position she was currently in, with her cousin shut up in the castle under siege by her husband, she was unfazed. There was no love lost between them, after all.

'So who is our enemy now?' Gabriel frowned.

It was Sphrantzes who turned with the reply. 'The Ottoman sultan and his beys.'

'Why?'

'The prince bought time by claiming to be working in the best interests of the Turks, as well as our own. It will not take long for Turahan Bey to conclude that we have simply annexed Patras, and not just prevented foreign proliferation.'

'You think the Turks will take exception?'

'I think that is guaranteed,' Constantine put in. 'Turahan Bey may take it upon himself to deal with us appropriately, or he may send to Sultan Murad at Edirne for instructions first, though likely that command would come anyway. And while we must look to potential trouble from the Turks, it is far from unlikely that the Pope will also take exception at his archbishop being driven from the city by those of us who follow the Byzantine rite. We may well face threats from both east and west.'

'Prepare for a siege?' Gabriel mused.

'Hardly worth it. If the Pope called for our destruction, we would not last a month, and against the Turks even less. The future right now lies in wiles, deception, and the political game.'

'And that is where *I* come in,' Sphrantzes said with a smile.

Lepanto

10 June 1429

Gabriel eyed the party trudging up the gentle slope from the port, and once more questioned silently how he'd ended up in this mess. He was the commander of the Ianitzaroi, the personal guard of Constantine Palaiologos, so why was he here, more than twenty miles from his master, across the water, at the side of the irrepressible George Sphrantzes?

The answer, of course, was simple: Constantine valued Sphrantzes more than anyone else in the imperial court, and so was happy to divert part of his own guard to look after his friend. But still, it was wrong. Gabriel had argued, but the prince had been adamant. Rhosatsas had been sent to the West, to reassure the papal court that the capture of Patras was a necessary move to prevent the Malatesta of Rimini from expanding their power in the Morea at the expense of other Christians. While Constantine owed no fealty to the Pope, he hoped the deputation would smooth over the matter, especially since Rhosatsas was armed with a number of rumours concerning Malatesta ambitions, some at the expense of the Church, and some of which were even real. A solid guard had been sent with him, but not from the Ianitzaroi, for Catalan mercenaries were common among the Italians, and even Constantine could see a potential

65

conflict of interest arising there. Thus that guard had been formed from another unit, while Gabriel had been sent with ten men to accompany Sphrantzes north and east, leaving the rest under Gaspar to protect the prince.

And so they had crossed the Gulf of Lepanto on what could prove to be a long journey. First they would embark upon the three-day ride to Tırhala, seat of the Ottoman governor Turahan Bey, whom Sphrantzes was prepared to mollify in any number of ways, neutralising the immediate threat of Turkish invasion from the north. Then, that mission complete, they would travel to the capital via the port of Platamonas, to collect the noted diplomat Markos Palaeologus Iagros, a distant cousin of the emperor and regular visitor to the court of the sultan. From there, they would ride to Edirne, and repeat their attempt at flattery and mollification on the supreme leader of the Turks. If all went well, they would be back at Patras and at the emperor's side before the winter set in, having removed the threat of warfare with the Turks. In truth, even Gabriel had to admit that it was probably more important to stop that war than to stand by the prince's side and wait for it to begin.

They were not a large group. Indeed, apart from Gabriel and his ten riders, there were only Sphrantzes himself and his assistant, a bookish lad named Lukas with a squint and a slight stammer, but the most impressive memory Gabriel had ever come across. They had arrived that morning at Lepanto, a Venetian enclave jammed between Tocco and Turkish lands, aboard a trader from Patras, but had spent the day in the city securing supplies for the journey north. The delay had led to what promised to be an interesting evening.

There was one hostel provided for noble visitors and embassies in the city, high up in the town, below the castle walls, and already they had visited the place and settled in for the night, only to discover that it housed a Turkish deputation. Now, though, a newly arriving party, on top of the imperial delegation and the Turks, could make it a dangerous evening.

Their ship had drawn the attention of the man Gabriel had left on watch at the port, and he'd hurried to warn them. A large galley had arrived in port with the fading evening light, bearing two flags: the red and gold of the Catalans, and the devilish banner of the Malatesta.

Now the newcomers were close enough, climbing the hill, that Gabriel could see them from the hostel balcony. Sure enough, Pandolfo Malatesta himself, Archbishop of Patras, led the way on a destrier, a captain of his soldiers at one shoulder, and a commander of Catalan mercenaries at the other.

Gabriel's lip twitched.

No matter what anyone expected, there was no conflict of interest there. Catalan mercenaries were prevalent even out here in the East, but Gabriel's men had served in the great imperial city for several generations. The current crop of men had been born into the Patriarchal Church of Constantinople, each to a Byzantine mother or father, and in reality celebrated more ties with the Byzantines than with the grasping mercenaries from the West.

Malatesta had clearly not seen Gabriel yet, for he would surely remember him, given his rather striking appearance, and so the Catalan hurried back off the street and inside the hostel to warn Sphrantzes of what was coming.

'Well, well.' The ambassador smiled. 'One wonders what the good archbishop is doing on this side of the water.'

'Well, he can hardly go home,' Gabriel noted.

'True, but he has mercenaries with him, so this enclave is not his intended destination, but a stop along the way. Gabriel, we must be sly and attentive this evening. Give nothing away, but learn what we can. The peace of the region may rely upon our actions tonight.'

Gabriel shrugged. He was a soldier. He would let Sphrantzes deal with the diplomacy and just try not to let the man get himself killed.

One side of the great common room, with its high ceiling and decor of banners to remind all present that this was Venetian land, was formed of booths, lit by candles, and two such booths were already occupied by Gabriel's men. He and Sphrantzes joined them, sending one of the Ianitzaroi for fresh drinks.

Three booths away, a small party of turbaned Turks sat in an insular huddle, watching the room suspiciously and speaking in their own tongue. Another booth was occupied by a bear of a man in rich clothes, with a face that would frighten demons. Even Sphrantzes, laying eyes upon the man, had remarked that it was possible Gabriel had met his match. The big man was generally speaking a mix of Italian and Greek, and was clearly local, a Venetian.

And now, Malatesta and his Catalans arrived – a fourth group, just to add to the difficult game that was about to commence. The archbishop entered the room with a sneer that seemed pinned to his face, his standard expression. His gaze swept the room, taking in the Venetian theme and the ugly man in the rich attire with disdain, then falling upon the next booth. His eyes met Gabriel's and his face broke into a violent twitch. He had no reason to recognise Sphrantzes, of course, but he knew the Ianitzaroi from their earlier meeting, and he would have identified Sphrantzes as a senior Byzantine dignitary just from his mode of dress. The man's gaze lingered for some time before he managed to tear it away, moving on until it found the Turks. There, Gabriel noted with interest, there was no such enmity and, indeed, an air of recognition arose.

Malatesta murmured a brief exchange with his men, and then, with just his captain, left the rest to it and strode straight for the Turks. To Sphrantzes' clear irritation, he was on the wrong side of the booth to see what transpired, and so he whispered across the table.

'Tell me what they do. In detail. Leave out nothing.'

Gabriel watched the archbishop reach the Turkish booth, where he leaned in. Their conversation was too low to catch, but Gabriel murmured a running commentary.

'They're talking. Just quietly. Standing a little apart. No, wait… He's leaning in. They're shaking hands. Not close, but polite, like visitors expecting one another. I think they were waiting for him. Now his captain's close. He waves at the man. The captain's got a bag, and he's getting something from it. What is that?'

Gabriel squinted, trying to see in the dim light.

'For God's sake,' Sphrantzes hissed, 'try not to look so suspicious. Try to be nonchalant.'

'*You're* the diplomat. I'm just your bodyguard.' Gabriel nodded quietly to himself. 'Letters. That's what they are, I reckon. Tied up in leather folders, sealed with waxed ribbons. Looks quite official.'

'Tell me how they take them.'

Gabriel watched. 'Very carefully, as though they're precious.'

'Then they're for someone important. Turahan Bey, perhaps. Maybe even the sultan himself. Malatesta may have lost Patras to our lord, but his game is not over. He plays new moves, bringing the Turks onto the board, just as we try to drive them from it.' He leaned back. 'I need to see those letters.'

Gabriel blinked. 'Impossible.'

'Very few things are impossible, my friend. Making gold from lead, perhaps, or changing a prince's mind, or finding a generous Venetian, but not something like this.'

He stopped suddenly and Gabriel felt a presence looming behind him. He turned to see the ugly great Venetian had approached their table.

'Mind if I join you?' the man asked in reasonable Greek.

Gabriel spotted the look of irritation pass momentarily across Sphrantzes' face. Now was not the best time, but to refuse would draw attention. 'Of course, sir.' The Byzantine smiled.

The Venetian pulled up a seat. 'Allow me to introduce myself. I am Bernardo Marcello, captain of Lepanto. I try to make it my duty to greet all visitors to our fair city. I note, clearly, that you are an imperial personage of some rank.' The man glanced at Gabriel for a moment, shivered, then turned back to Sphrantzes. 'A Byzantine emissary to the Ottoman court interests me, since it might indicate a change in the fortunes of the region. Something to do with the recent war over Patras, perhaps?'

Gabriel frowned. 'What makes you think we're on our way to the Turks?'

Marcello laughed. 'Where else would you be going? If you were here to seek Venetian contact, you would have sought me out. If it were the Tocco you were after, you'd have made for Epirus, and if you were heading to the capital, you'd have sailed for Korinthos, not here. You are clearly a senior diplomat, and so that means a high-ranking visit. Were you come from Constantinople, there would be a hundred of you, in a huge entourage, which tells me you are a private envoy, presumably from Constantine, the new despot. All this is simple. What interests me is the purpose of your embassy.'

There was an odd silence for a moment, then Sphrantzes took a breath. 'You will not expect me to answer that, I'm sure, just as I do not expect you to tell me the stance the local Venetian enclaves are prepared to take in various potential circumstances, following the fall of Patras. I fear, Captain Marcello, that you are destined to learn nothing, just like me.'

The Venetian's eyes narrowed. 'You play the game well, Byzantine, but there is a long evening ahead of us yet. For now, I hear a bottle of rich Vernaccia plaintively calling my name. I shall return.'

With that, he rose and left the table with a bow. Sphrantzes waited until he was gone, then fixed Gabriel with a look. 'What has happened now?'

'The Turks put the two letters in a bag, which sits by their feet. Malatesta spoke a little longer, then he left the table. He went to the stairway, and I presume from there up to his room.'

'Has he left anyone down here, or taken them all with him?'

Gabriel glanced around as casually as he could. 'They've all gone apart from one man, a Catalan, standing by the bar. He looks as though he's just drinking, but I think he is keeping an eye on the room.'

'That is good. It means Malatesta has retired for the night. Just one observer. I need to see those letters, Gabriel. And that means I need the Turks distracted, as well as that man Malatesta left, and Marcello, if he is still around. I shall need privacy with the documents long enough to read them, and preferably make copies.'

Beside him, Lukas leaned in. 'B-b-begging your pardon, my lord, b-b-b-but if I can r-read them, I can m-m-memorise them long enough to r-recite them to you.'

'You're sure?' Sphrantzes asked, and received a nod in reply. 'Well then, that will speed things up. Gabriel, you're a soldier. How's your drinking constitution?'

'I'm hardly a sot, Sphrantzes, but I can hold my own, I suppose. Why?'

'Because Marcello might be a match for you, and your fellow Catalan over there, but the Turks are bred on a mix of wine and raki, and you'll need a good constitution to outlast them.'

'You want me to get them all drunk?'

'Quite. I can give you enough coin to get an *army* drunk, let alone a few men.' He rose from his seat, and spoke loudly enough now to be overheard. 'Too much noise here. I must concentrate. Be sensible. I shall be over there,' he added, pointing to an empty booth on the far side of the Turks. He then shuffled over to Gabriel the bag with the purses in, taking from it his papers, pens and all the accoutrements of the writer, beckoning to his assistant. 'Come, Lukas.'

Gabriel watched him go, chewing on his ruined lip corner in irritation, a habit that was becoming set in. He was a straight-forward man, a gauntlet rather than a glove, and he was not made for such subterfuge. He toyed with the idea of not really trying and then pleading uselessness afterwards, but somehow he knew such an excuse would not wash with Sphrantzes, let alone the prince.

He waited a short while, then looked at the others in the booth. He singled out Aleix and Jordi, as the two had already finished their drinks. Leaning close, he spoke in a low tone. 'Start building to an argument. When you get a bit louder, stand up, and challenge each other to a drinking contest.'

'Sir?'

'Just do it.'

He sat back, listening until he heard them start a discussion – which could blossom into more – over a girl, then left the booth for a moment and strolled over to the bar, carrying a purse. The innkeeper shuffled his way at the sound of clinking coins.

'I would like to run a tab for my men. I am good for the coin, and am staying in room three.' He waited until the man eyed the bag of coins and nodded. 'Five bottles of good wine. Preferably imperial, but Italian or Turkish otherwise. And one of raki, if you have it.'

As the barman nodded again and shuffled off to acquire the drinks, Gabriel waited. Without looking at the Catalan mercenary leaning on the bar a few paces away, he took a breath. 'I don't know about you, but despite my blood and my name, I've never even seen Catalunya.'

There was a pause, during which he could hear Jordi starting to sound angry back at the table. Finally, the man sighed. 'I left at sixteen. I miss the straightforward life of home, where there is only one Christianity, and the Moslem is a distant menace in the south. Here, every man prays a different way, and every corner holds a new enemy.' His sigh deepened. 'But then, it's good for business, I suppose.'

Gabriel smiled, turning to him. 'Gabriel de Vallbona, of the Catalan company in the emperor's service.'

'Call me Bernat.'

'Well, Bernat, it is a sad soldier who drinks alone. Join us.'

'I don't think—'

'Good. You'll fit in perfectly, then,' Gabriel interrupted with a chuckle. As he swept up the tray of bottles and led the uncertain mercenary back across the room, he was rather gratified to notice the Venetian, Marcello, paying him attention and drifting his way. He smiled to himself. The man knew he would get nothing from Sphrantzes, and probably hoped to learn something of use from his bodyguard, especially if he was drunk. Sure enough, as Gabriel returned to his men in the booth, Marcello returned to his own beside them, sitting with his back to them, which was as close as he could get while being unobtrusive. Good. From there he could see none of them, and would be paying attention to everything they said, so he would not be watching Sphrantzes. That left only the Turks.

As Jordi and Aleix gradually got louder and more belligerent, Gabriel kept up the small talk with Bernat the Catalan, all the while dredging his memory. Over the years he had sat in bars with Turks on a number of occasions, and spent time with them elsewhere, too. They had a number of sayings he'd filed away, and there was one he wanted right now. *What was it, again? Ah, yes.* He waited until the two Ianitzaroi were on their feet, faces almost touching, shouting at each other.

'Put your stomach where your mouth is, Jordi,' snapped Aleix, 'if you think you can outdrink me. And then we'll see who deserves a shot at Maria, eh?'

'Fucking right. You're on.'

The two men grabbed a bottle and poured two very full glasses. Gabriel tensed, trying not to smile. He turned to them and waved his hands. 'Come on, you two. Calm down.'

'This dick—' Aleix started, but Gabriel overrode him.

'The Turks have a saying. *Pilaki deve yapmak…* don't make a flea out of a camel. You're both overreacting.'

'*Pireyi,*' called a voice from another booth.

Gabriel turned, to see that one of the Turks had stood and was looking their way. 'What?'

As he turned, the Turk flinched. 'Fuck, Roman, but God did a number on you, didn't he? Did a camel dance on your face?'

'Funny. What were you saying?'

'I said *pireyi*. Pireyi *deve yapmak*. Don't make a flea out of a camel, even if it *did* dance on your face.'

'Isn't that what I said?'

'No. You said "Pilaki *deve yapmak*" – don't make a *stew* out of a camel – which is actually not a bad thing to do at all.' The Turk and his friend laughed together.

Gabriel snorted. 'Unusual to find Turks laughing among Venetians. You bound for Tırhala, by any chance?' He cursed himself silently as the Turks stopped laughing. He'd been too direct. Too soon. He was immensely relieved when the pair looked at each other and smiled.

'We are.'

Good. They'd not been put off by the enquiry, but then again, it was an innocent enough question. He followed it up quickly. 'Perhaps we can try the road together, for we too are bound for the court of Turahan Bey, and roads are safer in numbers.'

There was sufficient truth in this that the two Turks held a silent exchange of looks for a moment, then both nodded. 'There is sense in this, and after all, Romans and Turks are allies, are we not?'

Gabriel bit down rather hard on the automatic reply that threatened to burst free, remembering that dreaded siege seven years earlier. Instead, he forced an easy smile. 'Join us.'

'We… er…'

'We have raki. And what passes in Venice for wine.'

'Ah, Venetian piss?' One of the Turks chuckled. 'But raki I will take.'

'Shuffle up,' Gabriel told his men, then gestured to Jordi and Aleix. 'And you two, piss off to the other booth to make room. Take your drinking contest there.'

The Turks joined them, facing Gabriel, their back to the booth where Sphrantzes sat with Lukas. They brought their bag with them, and it was placed down beside their feet. Gabriel turned and whistled to the barman. 'More raki and wine, over here. *Plenty* more.'

The following two hours tested not only his constitution, but also his patience. It was hard work trying to maintain a veneer of semi-drunken affability with this motley collection of folk, and he felt that he deserved a medal by the time the first of the two Turks leaned forward, head on his crossed hands on the table. His friend was still slamming back raki, now engaged in a competition with one of the Ianitzaroi, where they were trying to name landmarks in the great city, the slowest to respond having to drain his glass.

Time wore on, the conversation bawdy and genial now, even Bernat the Catalan joining the reverie. Not once had Captain Marcello looked their way, his ear occasionally twitching as he eavesdropped carefully. Finally, Gabriel spotted Sphrantzes moving. The man had waited for the barman to be absent in the back, and then slipped from his booth, crept over, observed only by Gabriel and others of the Ianitzaroi, and dipped into the bag by the sleeping Turk's foot. He grabbed the two letters and vanished back to his own secluded booth.

Gabriel made every effort then to keep everyone distracted and busy, though at this point, he could almost leave them all to it. Still, he was immensely grateful when Sphrantzes reappeared, the letters wrapped back up, their seals repaired using the wax from the candles on the tables, and slipped them back into the bag.

For the sake of appearances, Gabriel kept the party going for a while after that, until finally Sphrantzes appeared at their table with Lukas in tow.

'We have an early start, Gabriel. I am for bed. I suggest you and your men retire now, while there is still a faint hope of sobriety tomorrow.'

Gabriel nodded. 'Yes, my lord.' He turned to the others. 'Finish up. Time we all retired.' Then to the Catalan. 'It has been good speaking to you. I pray we meet again, and hopefully not on different sides of a field.'

'It will be as the good God wills it,' slurred Bernat with a smile.

'And I shall look forward to your company on the road,' Gabriel added, addressing the Turks, wondering whether one of them might not even wake up the next morning.

'*Güle güle.*' The one still awake wished him farewell with a smile, and with that the Ianitzaroi rose from the table. Gabriel spent a few moments at the bar, settling the tab, then they followed Sphrantzes to the rooms above. Entering the chamber he was sharing with Sphrantzes and Lukas, and locking the door behind him, he settled onto a cot with a relieved sigh.

'You got what you wanted?'

Sphrantzes grinned. 'Oh yes. Two letters from our archbishop friend, one for Turahan Bey and the other for the sultan himself, both making a case for ongoing Malatesta control of Patras and seeking the Turks' aid in retaking the city. He has a few valid points, and left alone, the letters might just have turned Murad and his bey against us. Fortunately, now that I know what they say, I am already beginning to form my counter-attack. By the time we reach both courts, on the heels of those letters, I will be able to neutralise the damage they could have caused. Gabriel, it is hard to overestimate how lucky we were to intercept this meeting. God truly smiles upon us.'

'Let's hope he continues to do so, then.'

Patras

25 November 1429

The relief Gabriel felt at their return after five months away was immediately overshadowed by the atmosphere in the prince's court.

The missions had been an unqualified success. Turahan Bey had been suspicious, having read the letter from Malatesta, but when he confronted Sphrantzes, the Byzantine ambassador took it all in his stride, with beautiful orations that destroyed every argument in the blink of an eye, all while vilifying the

76

archbishop. By the time they left Tırhala, the bey was ready to back Constantine as the new master of Patras, and to walk across Malatesta's corpse in order to do it. It seemed that Sphrantzes had been quite correct concerning the value of their chance encounter. It had turned what could have been a disaster into a triumph. The visit to the Porte, the sultan's court, was no less successful. By the time they reached the place, Murad had read Malatesta's letter and was ready to order that Patras be abandoned by Byzantium, but a combination of Sphrantzes' ambassadorial skill, and a letter of recommendation Turahan Bey had sent with them, helped sway the sultan away once more. He had in the end pronounced that he would leave the matter in the hands of the bey.

They had returned from their travels joyful, having spent a month in the great city putting a few affairs in order. Then, for speed and ease, they had taken ship from there, travelling with alacrity and comfort through the Propontine and Aegean seas, circling the Morea and putting into port at Patras. They had wondered at the faintly subdued mood that seemed to hang over the city, but it was when they arrived at the palace that it seemed to deepen to a black cloud of gloom.

Indeed, Constantine looked pale and drawn as they were escorted into his presence.

'Dear God in Heaven, my prince,' Sphrantzes breathed, 'what has happened?'

Constantine seemed to be looking actually *through* his friend for a moment, then appeared to focus suddenly and straightened in his chair. 'George, it is a balm to the soul to have you back. Things went well, I presume?'

'I shall tell you about it at length, my lord, but in short, yes, everything has fallen together just as we could have hoped, though I worry that in the process, something here has fallen apart?'

Constantine took a shallow breath, nibbled his lip for a moment. 'No, I think we can say that on balance all is progressing. The fortress on the hill continues to starve, and must be considerably weakened by now, and no reinforcements have come for it. Thomas has Khalandritza under siege, and hopes to bring Baron Zaccaria into the fold, forcing him to accept overlordship. With that, the Morea will more or less be ours. We have already started work on restoring the Hexamilion at Korinthos to seal off the land approach. The only real political blot is that the Catalan mercenaries who came east with our archbishop friend, robbed of their war, have seized Glarentza from us.'

'Glarentza has fallen? That is a problem.'

Constantine shrugged. 'They are Catalan… easily bribed. A little glittering gold and they will leave and cede Glarentza back to us. They just did not want to go home empty-handed.'

Gabriel tried hard not to feel offended at the sweeping appraisal of Catalans, particularly since he would privately admit that in his experience the various mercenary companies from the West fitted that model particularly well.

'So, in fact, all is good,' Constantine concluded, although his grim expression suggested otherwise. 'The Morea is almost Roman once more, our defences rise, we are on good terms with the Turks, Patras castle falters, and Glarentza is a mere hiccup that will cost us a little gold.'

'Then what is this black pall over Patras?' Sphrantzes pressed.

Over *you*, Gabriel corrected in his head.

Constantine sighed, sinking back into his chair once more, where the angle of the light only accentuated the black circles beneath his eyes and the prominent cheekbones of someone having lost more weight than is healthy for them.

'Theodora has passed, a little more than a week ago. She became ill, and weak, and one night she slept and did not awaken. I have known her for such a short time, and yet we had become close. When she died, a small part of me seems to have gone with her. I am… I am bereft, George.'

Gabriel closed his eyes. He did not know what to say. He'd had women in his life, of course, and some even that he'd not paid to be there, but no one who'd ever stayed in his heart. He looked at the prince. The man looked ill. He needed to be brought out of his shell. Gabriel looked then at Sphrantzes. The man was a great diplomat and a clever politician, but he was shooting wide of the mark here. Constantine was wallowing, and Sphrantzes' ready sympathy was only going to deepen the mire of that trouble. Gabriel, however, could see the path. Distraction. Something to focus on.

'So all the Morea is ours, barring a town Lord Thomas besieges, and the castle on the hill above us?'

Constantine nodded. 'And a few meaningless villages in the south that still bow to Venice, though they are of little concern.'

'Then what are we waiting for?'

'What do you mean?'

'Your brother will take his town, and all that will be left is that castle. The sultan and his bey have given their blessing to hold Patras. Nothing stands in our way apart from those walls. Let's take that castle, my lord.'

And for the first time since they arrived, he saw a glint appear in Constantine's eye, a hint of the man he had erstwhile been.

3 May 1430

'Manuel, take three men and get between the prince and the fucking enemy. Edge him back, without him realising it, if you can.'

The standard-bearer nodded, gripping the gold and red wyvern banner with one white-knuckled hand and his sword with the other, used the weapon to gesture to the two nearest Ianitzaroi, and hurried forward. Gabriel ground his teeth as he watched the banner-man and a small party of his men force his way past the prince rather indelicately, Manuel trying – and failing in his usual tactless manner – to talk down the prince and make him see sense.

Constantine seemed desperate to get himself killed, though perhaps without understanding that himself. The prince had ever been a courageous man, unfaltering in his willingness to step into the fray and play his part, but since the day the delegates returned to find the man's wife gone, things had changed subtly. Rather than a willingness to face mortal danger, he seemed now to seek it out.

For five months they had laid siege to the castle, and not a week had passed without Constantine finding some way to put himself in direct danger. Leading an assault against a heavily defended position, riding out to scout in full view of their artillery, countering a sally from one of the gates with dangerously few men around him. It was as if he dared the Devil to take him. Gabriel had seen such behaviour before in men whose will to live had crumbled. Death lost its sting, and danger its fear. Indeed, danger became a lure, drawing that man into its arms. The difference was that Gabriel was convinced Constantine genuinely did not realise he was doing as much, which made it all the harder to stop him.

'It will end today,' Gaspar said, close to his side.

Gabriel nodded. He was of a similar opinion. 'As long as it doesn't end for the prince, too.'

'Ah, he will be good. I am starting to think he's indestructible.' The big man sighed. 'Except from within, perhaps.'

'We have to keep him safe while he mourns, and rides it out. Keep an eye on him, my big friend. Manuel is doing so, but he can get distracted.'

'Usually by women, though. You'd think a man with a monk's tonsure would be less inclined to rut whenever the chance occurred.'

Gabriel gave a light chuckle at that as he watched Constantine being surrounded and protected by men of the Ianitzaroi, who carefully edged him away from the enemy redoubt as arrows whipped through the air around them and clacked against stonework. Leaving the job to Manuel, he took the opportunity to look around and take stock.

The castle of Patras occupied a sizeable hill, with impressive defences, including outer ditches and breastworks. It had taken four months to secure those outer walls, and more casualties than any Roman officer was truly comfortable with. But eventually, a feint against the main gate had drawn the lion's share of the outer ward's strength, allowing the attackers to launch a second, unexpected, assault on the south postern gate, which fell after a bloody hour of bodies piling up, granting them the access they so needed. The army of Byzantium had flooded into that massive complex and taken but a few hours to secure all the outer walls, with their towers and bastions, filling them with men.

As that day ground towards an end, the spring sun sliding into the west, the defenders risked opening the gate to the inner fortress for short bursts, allowing the desperate and beleaguered Italians trapped in the outer ward to flood across the bridge and to the last redoubt of safety. By the time Constantine's army had raised the imperial flag over every tower and rampart, only the dead and the crows that fed on them filled the enclosure and its buildings.

That had been the beginning of the end for the castle. With the Byzantine fleet picking off ships in the gulf, the imperial forces in control of the city, and now their army massed within the walls of the castle itself and pressing on the great keep, there was nowhere for the enemy to go, no hope of relief. The majority of their supplies and equipment had fallen with the outer ward, and even most of their artillery was now in imperial hands.

Of course, there was no sign of surrender. Those men would hold the keep to the bitter end and die in its defence.

But that, at least, was now inevitable.

The morning sun caught the flags atop those high and powerful walls, the jagged stripes of blue and white of the Tocco alongside the red, yellow and white of the Malatesta, all snapping in the breeze, streaming wild, then dropping to hang limp until a fresh gust from the sea caught them once more. Between them, the gleaming helms of the last defenders were visible between the battlements; arrows were launched forth whenever a defending archer saw an opportunity.

There was only one way in.

'The gate is ready to fall,' Constantine announced, striding to stand beside him, Sphrantzes hurrying across to join them.

'Frankly, any of the men could have gone forward to confirm such a thing,' the counsellor grumbled. 'It did not have to be you, putting yourself in danger.'

'I wanted to see for myself,' the prince replied. 'I trust my own judgement, after all.'

And you once more tested whether Satan clawed at you, Gabriel added in the privacy of his head. But the prince was right.

There was only one way in, and it was almost ready.

The great walls of the massive keep, with its mismatched towers, had been built by the Romans in the distant past, enhanced by the Franks and Venetians over the centuries, and rose to an impressive height over rocky approaches, protected by ditches and outworks. Getting a man up onto those walls would be, if not impossible, highly costly, and so the only realistic approach was the straightforward one: the bridge across the inner ditch, which led to a low set of outer walls with a strong gate. Within that set of walls, a wide stair led up to another gate, this one directly into the keep. The attackers would have to cross the bridge, storm the first gate, then climb the stair – under a constant rain of missiles – and take the inner gate, before gaining access to the keep. Only then would Patras truly fall.

For two weeks now, the artillery had been concentrating on those two gates. It was careful work, for they could not allow their shots to accidentally damage the bridge in front of the first gate or the stair that led between them, or they would destroy their own path. Fortunately, the men at the great stone-throwers were good at their job, and their equipment had been enhanced by the capture of the Malatesta artillery.

Mangonels and other catapults had targeted that outer gate, and pounded it throughout the daylight hours, day in and day out, and Gabriel had watched the stonework chip and flake, *merlons* disappearing, mortar flying, cracks gradually appearing. Four days earlier the outer gate had collapsed into rubble, and a few more well-placed shots cleared the creaking remains to produce a useable breach.

The great weapon that Constantine called his 'Hand of God', which had been concentrating on the inner gate, had paused then to allow a probing attack. Men had been sent to test the inner gate. They had endured arrow fire all the way across the bridge, then as they clambered across the rubble of the gate, and again, all the way up that wide stair until they reached an inner gate that was far from open. A lot fewer men had returned, shattered and dispirited, to the attackers' camp.

The last four days had seen a step up in preparations.

At night, men had moved forth in small parties with great wicker shields, and laboured to clear the rubble of the gate, tipping it into the ditch to clear the way for an assault when it came. And then, as the sun rose, they returned to their lines and safety as the Hand of God began its work once more. The great counterweight trebuchet was almost three times the size of the next largest catapult, and had required specialised engineers drawn from the city's Frankish population, whose work it had once been. It had sat for decades down by the port, on a bastion, where it could be used to sink galleys in the event of a sea attack, and it had taken weeks to dismantle, ship all the way up the hill to the castle, and reassemble in view of the inner gate. But now it was there, with sufficient range and power to pound that gate from far enough back to be well out of range of the defenders.

The massive rocks the thing threw every half-hour were large enough that they required teams of men, with mule carts, to collect and load. And every one that hit, which was almost every shot, slammed into the gate and its surroundings with the force that had given the machine its monicker. The cracks around the gate were now yawning things, and the gates themselves had been smashed some time ago, though that had not been the end, for the defenders had shored them up inside with extra timbers, stones, sacks of grain and whatever came to hand, in order to keep them blocked.

A sixth sense made Gabriel look up, and there, on the keep's west tower, he could see Torno in his gleaming armour and blue and white colours, directing his men.

'You will have him,' a voice said, quietly.

Gabriel turned to George Sphrantzes. 'It's not my place. I am Ianitzaroi, the prince's bodyguard. My place is with him.'

'I will persuade him to let you go. It is in all our interests to see Torno fall, and you have almost as much invested in his defeat as Constantine does. He has battled, taunted and outfoxed you repeatedly, and it is clearly not a prince and despot's place to cross swords on the battlefield. Besides, you will not need to be here to protect Constantine when the assault begins, for I will not let him come within arrow-shot of that place again. He cannot fall in the very hour of victory.'

Gabriel nodded his understanding and gratitude. Keeping the prince out of danger was difficult work, but if any man could do it, that man was his friend Sphrantzes. And if Constantine was safely back with the rear echelons watching the battle, the captain of his bodyguard could be spared.

A massive crash drew his gaze once more, and he saw an entire ten-foot section of the gate's surrounding stonework lean out precariously, separate from the walls, and then slowly topple forward to land on the ground with a crunch and a rumble, a cloud of dust filling the sky as the men of the Byzantine army cheered this next step. Another shot or two like that and there would be a breach.

Gabriel looked round. The army was ready. It had been ready for days, in fact, but never more so than now. Sphrantzes and the strategos John Rhosatsas had formed the men up and made sure they were kitted out and ready for action. They had been moved forward as far as was safe, and every man, from general to ditch-digger, had been briefed thoroughly. One of the most eager faces was that of Gaspar, his brutish second, whose massive hands gripped his sword pommel as though wishing it were the enemy so he could crush the life from it. The ourghos was about to be disappointed.

'Gaspar?'

'Sir?'

'Change of plan. Sphrantzes is going to keep the prince here with Rhosatsas, out of danger. I want you and Manuel and sixteen men to stay by his side and to help the governor keep Constantine out of danger.'

Gaspar's face fell at this. He'd anticipated the prince launching into the assault and he getting the chance to break a few Malatesta heads himself, and now he'd been not only taken out of the attack, but turned into a warden, keeping their master safely out of the battle. The ourghos frowned. 'What about you, sir?'

'I'm going to take the other eight and climb that tower, so that I can cut Torno from navel to chops and drop him from the ramparts for all to see.'

The look Gaspar threw him was heavily loaded with jealousy, but the big man nodded regardless.

Another bang drew Gabriel's attention once more, and as the next cloud of dust settled, he could see fragments of daylight between the broken sections of gate. *One more shot.*

Behind him, where the artillerists worked on the Hand of God, alongside their strenuous labours, he could hear an officer directing them to shift their focus ever so slightly to concentrate on the upper section of the gate and the lintel above it. He stood and watched the keep, tense and expectant, along with everyone else, as pieces of stone and showers of mortar and grit continued to fall from the stonework surrounding the gate, portending the coming cataclysm. The sounds of the work behind went on for some time, as the massive counterweight rose into the air, the sling-arm being slowly pulled down with ropes by a team of strong men. Only when it was in position and locked into place did the cart arrive with its load: a two-hundred-pound rock the size of a man's torso, which was then struggled out from the vehicle by two soldiers and heaved into the sling.

Gabriel waited still, while the last preparations were made, and then, finally, they were ready. With a creak and a groan, the weapon was set, and then a series of ear-splitting thuds and crunches signified the counterweight dropping and the arm being ripped up into the air. The sling whipped round with an unearthly noise and sent the boulder flying for the gate. The skilled engineers had aimed true, and Gabriel nibbled the corner of his ruined lip as he watched the missile roar overhead and slam into the gate. The din of its impact was astonishing, though the details were lost in the cloud of splinters, stone and dust, and it was only as that cloud settled, amid a tense silence, that the result came slowly into view.

Then: a roar of cheering.

Though the dust hung in the air as a grey haze, they could all see sufficient blue sky through the gateway to confirm that the breach had been widened sufficiently to allow an assault.

'Go,' Rhosatsas bellowed. 'Make use of the cover.'

Horns blew, and in that moment the army surged forth. Gabriel turned to the eight men of his Ianitzaroi who had not been pulled back to the emperor's position by Gaspar, and waved them on. Swords were drawn and shields lifted, helmets settled into position, ready to protect against flying perils, as they moved in to join an *allagion* of Mesembrian infantry, similarly preparing to fight off missiles. As they moved towards the bridge, Gabriel glanced back and could just make out Constantine, safely far back from the action, surrounded by Sphrantzes and the Ianitzaroi. They would keep him safe.

He turned to his men, all moving on foot now among the infantry, horses of no value in such an assault.

'Don't get distracted. We're not just here to kill them, I want that tower-top, and Torno himself. As soon as we're through, we look for the way up. Try not to engage anyone if you can avoid it, and let these Mesembrian lads do that. Just defend yourself and get to that tower-top. If Torno dies, what heart remains will go out of them.'

There was little chance for much more, for moments later they were on the approach to the bridge, and the arrows were starting to fly. The defenders, well aware that there was little danger from any other approach now, had put all their archers on the parapets facing the assault, and the missiles came thick and fast.

Gabriel gritted his teeth and held his shield over his head, angled to cover falling missiles as he ran with the others. The shield was heavy, for Gabriel and his men had long opted for shields not just of painted wood, but reinforced with iron bands, increasing the weight noticeably, but making them considerably more defensive and durable. As they passed onto the bridge, two of the Mesembrian soldiers, struggling to keep their momentum under the constant barrage and with their mates jostling around them, staggered out in front of Gabriel, and he barged into them, unable to do anything else in the press. The pair turned, expressions angry, and immediately blanched at the disfigured monster they'd been about to bellow at. One turned and pushed his way back in among his friends, though the other was less fortunate, for a falling arrow slammed into the flesh between neck and shoulder as he turned, just missing his armour's neckline. He screamed, but the sound faded as one of the Ianitzaroi simply pushed him over to the left, where he fell from the parapet of the bridge, tumbling down the grassy bank.

Gabriel and his men ploughed on.

Arrows thudded into the shield above him, clanking into the iron bands as often as not and falling away, though one struck hard enough to punch through the boards, the point extending a finger-length within, coming dangerously close to spearing his arm.

The relief he felt as his stumbling feet encountered the debris from the fallen gate, confirming that they had reached the far side of the bridge, was short lived. As Esteve, the man at his side, gave a relieved sigh, an arrow managed to slip beneath the edge of his shield and plunge into his leg in an unarmoured section. Esteve yelped and fell sideways, which sealed his doom. His shield wavered and dropped, and in the following heartbeats two more arrows slammed into him, the first failing to breach his armour, the second taking him full in the face. The young guardsman fell among the rubble, his scream commuted into a dying gurgle. He was replaced a moment later by another of the Ianitzaroi.

Would they get to return to Constantinople after this, Gabriel wondered for a moment? There were always a few Catalan mercenaries in the city looking for work, and he habitually retained them to bolster lost numbers, but recruiting such men was going to be hard out here.

He had no chance to ponder further, the falling missiles increasing in intensity as they closed on the keep. Here and there men tripped and stumbled over the debris, occasionally falling, but most of the mass of armoured, snarling men pounded across the rubble, through the gap where the worst had been removed during the night, passing through the pitiful, shattered remains of the outer gate and hurtling across the short open area to the wide, shallow staircase. Keeping his Ianitzaroi on the left flank of the advance, Gabriel led his men up the stair, close to the wall, reasoning it to be the safest position, more difficult for the defenders to reach. Indeed, the arrows were considerably fewer here, unable to come to bear. Instead his shield resounded to the clongs and thuds of debris, masonry and other makeshift missiles dropped over the edge of the parapet and onto the heads of those advancing below.

Gabriel's left arm was tiring under the combination of the shield's weight and the constant battering of heavy missiles, and it was with considerable relief that he saw the top of the stair approaching and the shattered and broken timber gates awaiting them.

This, he knew, was going to be the most dangerous moment.

He slowed in his advance, allowing the Mesembrians to get ahead, and watched beneath his raised shield and through the falling hail of missiles as they reached the gate. Though the portal was shattered and torn, with sizeable holes, the assorted objects used to bolster it within remained partly in place, providing obstacles. The defenders were ready to hold the ruined entrance to the end, crowding forward into those gaps and jabbing out with spears. The Mesembrians hit the gate like a tide, slamming their own weapons into the breach, trying to fell the defenders and open a path. And as that brutal meat–grinder of a struggle went on, still a barrage of missiles continued to fall on the massed men outside as they pushed.

Gabriel and his men pressed close to the wall, near enough the gate to take advantage when it fell, but not so close as to be involved in the struggle. They moved as close together as they could, interlocking and overlapping their shields to create a makeshift roof against the constant hail.

It seemed to take forever. Every time Gabriel thought he saw progress, the men of the Mesembrian allagion bellowing victoriously and surging forward, they were repulsed, fought back out of the breach. Several dead or viciously wounded men were pushed out of the way by their mates as they battled to be the next victims.

When success finally came, it came suddenly. A push like any of the previous ones was this time not swiftly repulsed, and as the Mesembrians clambered and lurched into the gaps, hacking and stabbing as they went, more came behind, pushing forth, securing the hold.

Gabriel still waited for a few moments, knowing that he and his men were currently in the safest position they could manage, but then, as the allagion began to advance through the gate at a steadier pace, he lunged forward and joined them, his men at his back. As he neared the gate in the press, someone standing painfully on his foot in the process, something particularly heavy struck his shield from above and tilted it. A half-brick scraped on past his arm and bounced from his hip, off into the mass. Before he could set the shield right once more, though, he was into the gate, beneath the wall and momentarily out of danger from above.

The gates were now little more than a few heavy timbers studded with iron, clinging desperately to ruined hinges in broken stones. Several of the men leading the assault had left their mates to the task of pushing the enemy back, in order to devote themselves to removing the last obstacles so that the rest of the army would gain easy access.

Then Gabriel was through, past those labouring soldiers. His shield came up again, for the men on the walls above were just as intent on sending down missiles onto the enemy inside the walls, and debris and arrows began to clatter against it once more. Inside the gate, the wide stair continued to rise between revetted stone walls to reach the level of the keep's courtyard. Defenders had been lined along the sides, stabbing down, though they were now locked in combat with men who'd surged up to take them on.

Ahead, at the end of the stair, a major struggle was underway, a massive melee as the invading Romans attempted to break the lines of the Italian defenders even as they desperately tried to hold until reinforcements reached them from other parts of the keep.

Gabriel, though, had a different goal. He was not interested in breaking the enemy and seizing control of the keep. *His* target stood atop the tower to the left, and as soon as he was far enough up the stair to see over the side walls, he turned towards that tower.

His heart pounded with possibility. That tower was accessed by a doorway one floor up, and in yet another defensive aspect, the steps up led to a wooden drawbridge into the tower.

However, with the defenders still nominally in control of the keep's main courtyard, the bridge was down, and the door open. Moreover, right now there was no one defending the entrance. That would undoubtedly change very soon. Once the main line of defence broke, men would appear, slam shut the door and raise the bridge.

'With me. Fast.'

Trusting his men to follow, Gabriel discarded his shield, which was now battered out of any recognisable shape and so crammed with broken arrow shafts the design was hard to make out. He sheathed his sword for a moment, then reached up and grabbed the wall-top, pulling, hauling himself up and over, onto the flagged ground of the courtyard. As his men followed suit, Gabriel quickly looked this way and that. He could, really, have now tried to flank the defenders and help the Mesembrians break them, but that would give the other defenders time to seal the tower. Instead, he started to run for that next staircase. His Ianitzaroi were with him a moment later as he reached the flight of steps and began to pound up them, now far enough away from the gate to not worry about the falling missiles.

As he reached the top of the steps, there was a hollow, metallic clank and a grinding noise that he recognised as the windlass of the drawbridge. He wasted no time in racing onto it, pounding across the timbers as he drew his sword. Others of his unit were at his heel, doing the same even as the bridge started, slowly and laboriously, to lift.

Gabriel reached the doorway and dived into the darkness within. He turned this way and that, blinking, and finally saw the two men heaving on the windlass, struggling to raise the bridge as men ran across it. His sword came round in a wide arc, smashing the arm of one, and as the man screamed and fell away, Gabriel spun with his momentum, and slammed the sword into the second man, gutting him. The soldier's hands fell away from the windlass, which instantly whirled back at speed, the drawbridge falling back into place. Knowing better than to leave potential enemies behind him, Gabriel wasted a few moments finishing off the two men before turning and looking for the stairs up. They were not hard to find, for his men had passed by, leaving him to his killing, and moved to secure those stairs. He charged over and climbed up in their wake, following the sounds of combat and swearing in accented Greek.

Reaching the upper floor, he staggered out onto the wooden walkway, stepping over two bodies and noting a pair of Ianitzaroi battering at an Italian soldier on the far side of the room. Other Ianitzaroi were already in the next stairwell fighting upwards, clear from the noise, and Gabriel followed the sound once more. As he turned into the stair, he could see blue sky ahead, and ran, sword at the ready.

Bursting out onto the tower-top, he was surprised at how few defenders there were. Three soldiers were busy fighting off three more Ianitzaroi, and two soldiers were at the far side with bows, loosing wildly into the mess below, paying little attention to what was happening behind them on the tower. But Gabriel's attention fell only upon one figure: a villain in full armour, gleaming rich plate, helm sporting a blue-and-white plume complementing the Tocco colours of his surcoat. The man had a sword out ready, but no shield.

Gabriel wasted no further time, and ran at the man.

Torno had been paying attention to the struggle close by and had not noticed Gabriel until the last moment, but danced out of the way just in time, bringing both hands round now to grip his sword.

Gabriel slowed, and the two men circled each other, a duel of Titans against a backdrop of war. All other struggles on the tower and walls were forgotten, the pair leaving the Ianitzaroi and the defenders to fight it out.

'Nowhere to run this time, Torno,' Gabriel said quietly. 'No chance to use a crossbow like a base assassin. You'll have to fight like a man.'

'Be quiet and fight,' came the retort, hollow and metallic from within the helmet.

Gabriel did so, but his words were true. Torno had proved himself villainous time and again now, murdering citizens, attempting to assassinate the prince twice, placing soldiers between himself and danger as he fled the scene. No more. Now he was trapped on a tower-top, and Gabriel had no intention of letting the man go again.

He swung his sword wide, coming round towards Torno's left arm. Even a less than powerful blow could break the arm within plated armour, and it might not be the man's *sword* arm, but any such wound would be a distraction and a handicap regardless. He was surprised when, at the last moment, Torno lifted his arm and caught the blow such that, rather than smashing straight into the steel, it struck a glancing blow with little power, sliding along the vambrace and harmlessly out into the air. The man was good. Better than he'd expected.

With a grunt, Torno retorted, his own sword coming round in a two-handed swing at the side Gabriel had left exposed in his own attack. Only a lifetime's experience of avoiding death on the battlefield allowed him to twist and drop his own blade into the path of the attack, turning away Torno's sword. The two men separated.

'I wonder,' Gabriel said, 'why you are always so keen to escape me, if you are so skilled with a blade.'

Torno made no reply, setting his stance ready to face his opponent once more. Gabriel passed his sword from hand to hand, almost as though juggling, trying to keep the man off balance, and when he struck, it was with his left hand. He was not as good with the left, but he had hoped that the surprise of it would more than counter the lack of strength. The blow landed, hammering into Torno's side, though he had the sense to try and back out of the way, and so as he retreated with the blow, he robbed it of most of its weight. A strike that could have easily broken ribs would have bruised at best. Still, the nobleman danced away, wheezing, letting go of his sword with one hand to reach to his side with the other. There was now a visible dent in his cuirass.

Gabriel steadied himself. He had managed to land both blows so far, while Torno had failed with his only strike, but the man was fast, and bright, and it was only a matter of time before he landed a good blow of his own. This dancing around was only giving the man opportunities. Gabriel needed to end this before they bore fruit.

He swapped his sword again, to his right hand, then poised himself as if ready to lunge, but as Torno changed his stance, ready to sidestep or parry, instead, Gabriel threw himself forward. The Catalan hit the nobleman hard and slammed into him, sending him flying backwards to land with a metallic clang on the stone floor. Torno struggled. One of the few major disadvantages of a full suit of plate was the difficulty of rising from a supine position, and as Torno struggled like a tortoise on its back, Gabriel made his move. It was going to be near impossible to kill him swiftly through that armour, and so he had to lever some of it open, and quick, while the man struggled.

Gabriel dropped onto his opponent, his own knees protected with armour that clanked into the man's breastplate. He nearly slid off, steel on steel not easy to maintain a grip, but he was practised, even an expert at what he did, and he knew every underhanded move in the book. As he dropped, he reversed the grip on his sword and then brought the hilt up hard, slamming the pommel into the chin of the helmet. He both heard and felt the catches that held the visor closed snap, as it jerked upwards. Indeed, his blow, driven partly by fury, was strong enough that the helmet came away, lifting from the man's head. The heavy pommel raked up the man's face in the process, probably breaking his nose. Because of the wash of blood it caused, it was only as Gabriel lifted his fist again, ready to bring down the pommel and cave in that face, that he realised it had to be the *wrong* face.

'Who are you?' he snapped.

The man in the armour, pale and blond, perhaps a German mercenary, was too dazed and in too much pain to answer.

Gabriel rose and stepped back. It was not Torno, though he was clearly wearing the nobleman's panoply. The voice as they'd met had not been Torno's, but Gabriel had not noticed because of the steely echo of the helmet. Gabriel ground his teeth. *Not again.* Twice now, once on a beach and now in a falling castle, Torno had somehow slipped away and left a doppelgänger in his place.

Gabriel lurched back across the tower and leaned on the parapet, looking down on the chaos below as Patras castle finally fell to the Roman force. That was it. Patras was theirs, and that meant almost all the Morea belonged to the empire. Somehow they'd managed to maintain good relations with the Turks even as they began to rebuild imperial power at the expense of these greedy Italian lords. He ought to be elated, but somehow the failure to find Torno robbed him of joy.

'What shall we do with him, sir?'

He looked around to see that his men had secured the tower. The last enemy, one of the archers, was being tipped over the parapet to fall to his death even in that moment. Only the fake Torno remained, lying, agonised and supine, as Ianitzaroi stood over him with swords drawn.

'Secure him. The prince will want to speak to him.'

Four days later

Gabriel washed his hands vigorously, dried them on the slightly pink cloth by the door, and then paused only for a moment to look back at the broken thing in the cellar. He was not proud, but neither was he particularly disturbed by his work. A soldier, by his very nature, could not afford to be squeamish, and a mercenary, by his nature, could not afford to let principles stand in the way of his work.

The German had been brave. Hard to break. Constantine remained where he'd sat for most of the past three days, as the questioning had progressed.

The prince had been no more squeamish than Gabriel.

'We Romans have a long history of extracting information, punishing with pain, and even torturing simply for the enjoyment,' he'd said. Gabriel had winced at that. Yes, the Byzantines were an inventive people when it came to torture, but Constantine had always seemed above such things. It was just another facet of the darkness into which he'd been sliding since his wife's death.

'I will not break,' the German had snapped.

Gabriel had been the one to respond to that. 'Yes you will. All men do. Everyone breaks in the end. It's just a question of how long it takes and how strong you are. In my experience it's better to be a weak coward, for then you break faster and it's over sooner.'

'Of course,' the prince picked up once more, 'most of our traditional methods are of little use here. We don't have a giant bronze bull to roast you in, and if we did, you'd be unlikely to answer with anything but screams. But we'll start small anyway. I suggest you answer my question straight away. We may even let you live. One simple query. What happened to Torno, and where has he gone? I suspect that telling me the answer will make little difference, and I might suggest that you owe little to a man who left you to take the fall while he saved his own skin.'

The German had not replied, just glared, mouth pressed shut as Gabriel stripped him of his remaining clothes and accoutrements, leaving a naked figure, ready for whatever came.

'Very well. We shall start small. Gabriel? Take his eyes, and then start on his knuckles with the hammer, slowly. One at a time.'

That had been three days ago. The man had an impressive pain threshold, and was brave indeed. As Gabriel had said, though, he'd broken in the end.

Leaving the prince to it, he walked up and into the guard chamber atop the stairs, where Gaspar, Manuel and Felip were sitting, playing dice and sipping cheap wine.

'All done, then?' the ourghos asked.

Gabriel nodded.

'Did you snick off his German sausage?' Manuel said with a deeply distressing grin.

'Yesterday,' Gabriel answered quietly.

'Is it a secret, or can you tell us?'

The door to the cellar had been shut throughout the interrogation, and the Ianitzaroi had been here to prevent the unauthorised from getting too close, but Gabriel couldn't really see how the information was of any great secrecy now to anyone, let alone to the prince's own guard.

'Lots of details, some of which consists of gaps we'll have to plug up. There was a network of people still in the city below who answered to Torno. It was over a month ago that he made his escape. While trapped up there, they'd put together a surcoat and arms that closely resembled one of our own units. Torno slipped out of a postern alone in the middle of the night, disguised as an imperial soldier, and managed to slip down the hill in the dark, falling in among our men. Once he was down in the city, his network took over and he was taken to the port, where he boarded a local merchant ship and was spirited away.'

'So there are people in the city who need a hanging for their part in it?' Felip noted.

'Yes. We'll be clearing the place of Torno's informants and agents. Last thing I want is some bastard on a tower-top with a crossbow, watching Constantine riding through the streets.'

'So where is he now?'

'In truth, even his German double wasn't sure, though he'd heard Torno talking more than once about Turahan Bey, the sultan and the Sublime Porte, and so the safe bet is that he's run back into the arms of the Turks.'

'Where we will almost certainly find him soon enough,' Gaspar said, quietly, a statement that rang true with Gabriel, more than most stuff he'd heard the last few days. Sooner or later there would be a reckoning with the interfering assassin.

'Karaca Pasha, emissary of Turahan Bey, of the Sublime Porte and of the Sultan Murad bin Mehemmed Han.'

While most of the court straightened, silent and stately, Gabriel made sure to loom and look grouchy and unaccepting. It was supposedly important to seem at the same time proud but subservient, for there was little doubt that the Turks could crush the empire's hold in the Morea with little difficulty if they decided to do so, but subservience had never sat well with Gabriel, beyond what was required in military contracts.

The Turkish ambassador swept into the room as though he owned it, his robe raising motes of dust where it dragged along the floor, which swirled among the attendants that followed. Karaca Pasha was an imposing man, impossibly tall and thin, yet with wide shoulders that gave him an oddly triangular shape. His beard similarly came to a point at the chin. The man was all angles, and so was his expression. He did not look impressed.

'Karaca Pasha.' Constantine greeted him with a slightly cold tone and without rising from his seat. He gestured around at his court. 'I presume you know my Consilium, including the *pro tem* governor of Patras.'

George Sphrantzes, appointed such in the wake of their victory, also inclined his head.

Karaca Pasha glanced momentarily at the governor, and clearly wrote him out of the meeting in a heartbeat, turning back to Constantine.

'I shall waste no time, prince of the Palaiologoi.' His Greek was smooth and with no trace of a Turkish accent, though his voice was as sharp and angular as everything else about him.

'I would expect no less.'

'Turahan Bey accepts your overlordship of this city as per our earlier agreement, but the Sublime Porte is concerned with the Roman Empire's growing hegemony in the Morea. Your recent acquisition of Glarentza since the seizure of Patras has not gone unnoticed.'

As the man paused, Constantine wagged a finger at him. 'It may be worth my pointing out, Karaca Pasha, that Glarentza was not *freshly* acquired this winter. It had been an imperial possession for some time, granted to the empire as part of the dowry of my late, beloved wife, a city that was rudely stolen from us by rampaging Catalan mercenaries, and which we have retaken from them, as is our right. There was no conquest, just simple recovery.'

Costly recovery, Gabriel silently corrected. The Catalans who had come east with Archbishop Malatesta had given the city up readily, but only upon receipt of more gold than the empire could really spare. Constantine was gambling with what little resources they had to create a source of more.

The Turk's eyes narrowed dangerously. 'Do not attempt to fool me, Prince Palaiologos. Glarentza had been in the hands of the Count Palatine of Kephalonia before you snatched it away from him by feat of arms, only to have it stolen once more by mercenaries. It is part of imperial expansion in the Morea, which goes against your agreements with the Sublime Porte.'

Constantine's eyes flashed angrily for a moment as he shook his head. 'Bear in mind, emissary, that when speaking of the count, you are speaking of my brother-in-law, and that I currently mourn his sister's loss. Have a care, man. And if you study your history a little closer, you will learn that though Glarentza was founded by our Italian neighbours, it was done so in the territory of imperial Andravida, during their wars of conquest. The territory is imperial by tradition. Moreover, the empire is permitted by all agreements with the Porte to defend itself from external aggressors. Putting aside said dowry, our initial acquisition of Glarentza was a direct response to the raiding of imperial territory. We have broken no accords.'

The disagreement hung in the air like a bad smell, as the two most important men in the room glared at each other, locked in some silent contest. Gabriel was impressed when it was Karaca Pasha who looked away and nodded first.

'This we grudgingly accept. You have bent and twisted accords to breaking point, but reined in just in time. Still, Turahan Bey and the sultan himself are concerned with the growing power of the emperor's despots in this region.'

'A threat?' This came, surprisingly, not from Constantine, but from Sphrantzes, who stood at his elbow, dressed in the ornate regalia of the imperial governor.

The Turk's gaze snapped to Sphrantzes, clearly irritated at having to once more acknowledge his presence.

'No threat should be needed. You, and all imperial officers in the Morea, continue to wield power only at the whim of Sultan Murad the Second. You will continue to acknowledge his overlordship, and as such he will continue to suffer your little games. But at times it is fitting that the Sublime Porte should remind you of your place in the world. As such, the army of the sultan has occupied the isthmus, and even now demolishes your crumbling Hexamilion.' He turned back to Constantine, now. 'You may build your territory in the Morea, Prince of Constantinople, but you will not build walls to keep us out.'

Gabriel only realised when the Pasha's guards bristled that he had taken a step forward and his hand had dropped to rest on his sword hilt. He was angry, not just at the Turk's attitude when speaking to the emperor's brother, but particularly at the news that the sultan's men had simply decided to demolish the great isthmus wall of a nominal ally. From Sphrantzes' expression, he was of a similar mind, yet Constantine's face remained serene, if a little threatening around the eyes.

'It would have been preferable to have discussed such activity with us first,' the prince noted. 'The Hexamilion, after all, may seal off the peninsula's only land approach, but you might remember that it protects imperial territory in the Morea from depredations by Acciaioli, Duke of Athens, who, I might add, could consider your military activity on our joint border – with which you have no connection – an act of war.' As the emissary wound himself haughtily to respond, Constantine waved him back down. 'But I concede your point. The Hexamilion will remain a border with Athens, and will continue to be garrisoned, but we agree not to reinstate the wall itself, *unless* provoked to do so by our neighbour. I refer you once more to the point in the accords that allows for the empire to protect itself from aggressors.'

Karaca Pasha twitched silently for a few moments, and then, unable to find fault in the prince's words, nodded curtly. 'Very well. We accept your position, and the point is made. Peace remains, and the accords hold. Please convey my deepest respect to your brother, the emperor and your fellow despots.'

With that, he turned and swept from the room in much the same way he had entered, his entourage filing out behind him. Gabriel gestured to his men at the door, who followed them, escorting them from the palace, and then shut the door behind them.

'That could have gone better,' John Rhosatsas murmured from behind the despot's throne.

'Actually, I don't think it could,' Sphrantzes offered. 'There was always a danger that any move we made to secure power in the Morea would offend the sultan, and to have achieved what we have without provoking disaster is, I think, a notable thing.'

'But they have demolished the wall.'

Constantine nodded. 'That is irksome, but walls can be rebuilt, and this is an issue that can wait. The wall was repaired as a statement to the Duke of Athens, reminding him not to interfere with our affairs, but having the Turks wandering around the area will deter any Athenian moves in that region just as surely as any wall. And when the time comes that we do need the wall again, George here will undoubtedly manufacture a reason that the sultan will accept. For now, we have hegemony. With the exception of a few coastal settlements in the south-east and south-west, we control the Morea. And now that we do, we can concentrate on rebuilding its economy and trade, in order to produce taxes and militia. Strength will come in time, and those few straggling villages will fall to us. The balancing act will go on for a while, but we are managing it with aplomb, gentlemen. Now I must contact my brother, the emperor, and confirm the despotates of the region.'

Four years later: summer 1435

Those words of Constantine's on the day of the Turkish embassy rattled around Gabriel's head as he eyed the enemy across the field. *Confirm the despotates of the region*, indeed. Gabriel could see trouble coming between the brothers, and had foreseen it since that very day at Patras castle. The Morea had been an imperial despotate for a long time, and though it had grown in size with the recent imperial successes, it was still too small a region to be controlled by three men.

Theodore had been the first despot, ruling alone from Mystras, and all had expected him to give up his throne and take holy orders, especially after the death of his Malatesta wife two years before. However, the oldest of the three despot siblings had steadfastly refused to step down, and the emperor back in Constantinople had made it clear that he had no intention of forcing Theodore, who had precedence on his side, to resign. Thus Theodore remained nominally the senior despot in the Morea, still sitting in sacred Mystras. But Thomas and Constantine had each been promised and granted a despotate in the region too, and so now three brothers governed one land.

In Gabriel's private opinion, there would already have been civil war had not fate intervened and given them a common enemy. Ironically, it had been the destruction of the Hexamilion that had been the catalyst.

The Duke of Athens, the very man whose ambitions had caused the wall to be rebuilt, passed away unexpectedly. His widow, aware of the danger of being trapped between the Morea and the Turks, decided to cede her husband's lands to the empire in return for a nice retirement plot somewhere safe.

Sphrantzes had been sent with a small guard to see the job done, but had hurried back early upon the discovery that Turahan Bey had seemingly taken exception to the empire's sudden good fortune, and decided to move in on the duchy himself.

The Turks had swept down across the border into Athenian lands and began seizing frontier territory as far as Thebes. Constantine had mooted the possibility of military action, though he, like all present, must have known that such would have been veritable suicide, and would bring the empire and their nominal ally the Turks into open war. The Turks likely saw Athens as a viable land to annex, after all. Even then, he had considered it. Before he could make any solid decision, however, the prince had received a summons back to the capital from his brother. Taking with him only his Ianitzaroi and a small company of Serbs, he and Sphrantzes had boarded a Venetian ship and set sail. However, they had only reached Euripos in Euboea, on the edge of the Athenian Duchy and just twenty miles from the current seat of Turahan Bey at Thebes, when he changed his mind and decided his brother could wait.

At Euripos they had learned of Turahan's current position, and that various small forces of Turks were rampaging across the duchy, sacking and annexing as they went. With the Hexamilion down and only young and inexperienced Thomas on the far side, how long would it be before Turks began to raid direct imperial territory across the isthmus, all while Constantine merrily sailed home? No, he'd decided. He had to resolve the issue here, first.

The prince had stood on the battlements and watched three galleys across the channel, close to the far end of the bridge, where a small force brooded. 'If something is not done fast, we shall be at war with the Turks anyway,' he sighed.

Sphrantzes had nodded. 'I presume you do not mean to give Athens up to the sultan?'

'No. Since the Italians lost Thessaloniki and Ioannina, the Turks now control the whole mainland north of us. If they take

Athens, the Morea will be alone and isolated, especially without the Hexamilion. No, we need Athens, and it is rightfully ours. But it is a problem. Challenging the Turks over it could very well erupt into a war all across the east. George?'

Sphrantzes had tapped his lip, thoughtfully. 'There may be a case to state that the Turks would be better having us in control of the duchy, as other Italian states will accept that it was bequeathed to us, while Turkish seizure of the land could put them at war with Venice. Turahan Bey is a sensible man. I may be able to persuade him.'

'Then you'd best persuade him fast,' Gabriel had countered, eyeing the Turkish force, where it had split into four, three units embarked for the crossing, while the fourth secured the bridge.

The wily ambassador had taken ship with a small Serbian guard and skipped away across the waves, giving the approaching force a wide berth as they raced for Thebes and the Turkish bey, while Constantine had taken control of the city, sealing the gates and raising the drawbridge across to the mainland in the meantime.

That had been the morning of the previous day.

Since then, the Turkish force had taken up position at the far end of the currently uncrossable bridge, while the vessels had ferried across the rest of the warriors to take position around the city on land. In the morning, at first light, the force's commander had ridden boldly out across the bridge to challenge Constantine. His identity had been clear from the moment he trotted into view, that tall and angular frame identifying the same Karaca Pasha who had delivered the threat to them in Patras a few years earlier.

'In the name of the Sultan Murad and the Sublime Porte, I hereby command you, as vassals of his magnificence, to open the gates, quit this city and return to your lands in the Morea immediately.'

Constantine had graced the man with that same cold smile that had been with him since widowerhood and spoke through gritted teeth. He informed the man that the Duchy of Athens and all associated territories had been ceded to the Morea by the late duke, and that the great and noted ambassador George Sphrantzes was currently at the bey's court clarifying this point.

Gabriel had actually chuckled a little at the Turk's face. He'd had the rug well and truly pulled from beneath him, for he had been sure about his course, and now he would be worried that to continue on said course would unduly annoy Turahan Bey. He had blustered for a few moments, and in the end settled on telling the prince that even if that were the case, nothing had yet been made official, and that he should quit Euripos in the meantime. Constantine, still smiling, still cold, very politely refused.

The day that followed had been exceedingly strange. Time and again there had been small tussles and forays, which had pulled back as soon as they met any resistance. It was almost as if the Turkish soldiers themselves were determined to take the city, and their pasha kept having to haul them back. Gabriel suspected that, more likely, the pasha himself kept chancing his arm and then deciding against it, hoping to push Constantine into leaving without a direct fight.

Two Serbs had been wounded with Turkish arrows a little after noon, but by the time their mates had fetched bowmen, the enemy were far back from the walls. Then, later, one of the Ianitzaroi had taken an arrow in the thigh across the drawbridge in the mid-afternoon. Once again, there had been no chance to retaliate. The fact that Constantine kept standing proud on the battlements making a very tempting target had not escaped Gabriel, either, who had constantly kept his men on the seemingly suicidal prince.

Then had come the *real* reason to worry.

Karaca Pasha could not know the military strength of the city, though he would estimate it as worryingly small from the number of figures visible on the walls. There were, in fact, just over fifty imperial soldiers present, along with the standing ducal garrison of two hundred. The Turks numbered around twice that.

Which made the sudden appearance of a cannon, as the light faded, of more than a little concern. There would be no need for a cannon if there was no intention to fight, and the fact that they also brought forth ammunition and began to stockpile it beside the weapon suggested that its use would begin with the first light of day. Indeed, there was a general massing of the Turks at that position, too, at the south gate of Euripos, inland.

'Does he really mean to fight?' Gabriel pondered, watching as the cannon was prepared.

Constantine, peering out into the growing gloom, pursed his lips. 'He may. This Karaca Pasha is not the careful politician and strategist that his master Turahan Bey can claim to be. He is, I think, hungry for power and victory. He is dangerous, and not above making a deliberate mistake to achieve his goals. And you know how these things work with the Turks.'

Gabriel nodded at that. It was an age-old game among the notables of the sultan's court and army. Perilous gambles. They would launch some campaign that had no backing of the Sublime Porte, if they were at least partly sure of success. If they won, the chances were good that the sultan would forgive their presumption, for they had enhanced his realm. If they failed, there was always a reasonable chance they could blame it on some unfortunate contemporary. In essence, if Karaca Pasha was sufficiently daring to attack the prince, win, and leave no important witnesses, he could claim that he had not heard of the inheritance and was simply following protocol and winkling out an invader.

'I pray that Sphrantzes has persuaded the bey in Thebes,' Constantine murmured, watching the cannon carefully.

'*I* pray that he made it to Thebes at all, and isn't dead in some ditch with a Turkish spear in his back,' Manuel put in, earning a dark look from them all. He was right, though. It *was* a worry. The forces here may be smaller than during that siege in the great city a dozen years earlier, but the odds were somewhat similar. All it would take was for that cannon to make a breach, and the city would almost certainly fall, and with it the prince and his men.

'Whatever the case,' Constantine said, straightening, 'we had best prepare ourselves for trouble.' He turned to the captain of the city garrison, standing nearby. 'Have every man you can round up busy bolstering this gate. Stack anything heavy against it. And anywhere where the walls are a little worn in this section, have timbers braced against the inside, and backed with more heavy goods. I recommend sacks of grain for the job. And leave only pickets on the walls everywhere else. They are concentrating on this gate. Here is where they will come.'

And here, Gabriel noted drily, was where Constantine Palaiologos, prince, despot and widower, would stand and face arrows, swords and cannon in a fierce challenge to death itself. They continued to watch the preparations as the last of the light faded and torches were lit on the walls. The city began to glow, as did the camp out in the open, where the Turks waited. The sky was a deep, clear, dark blue, and moonlight produced a silver blaze across the world. It was almost serene.

Until the first shot.

Despite preparations and extant worry, it still came as a surprise to Gabriel. He'd not truly believed this Karaca Pasha would be brave enough to attack the emperor's brother without at least the nod from his superior. Yet the cannon let out its first shot at around an hour before midnight, slamming into the base of the wall near the gate.

'Is he insane?' Gaspar snapped. '*No one* uses artillery at night.'

Gabriel shrugged. 'He needs victory fast, before Turahan Bey hears about it and has him nailed to a door for his presumption. If he wins, he may be a bey himself before long.'

'God has a way of visiting redemption on men like him,' Manuel grunted. 'Though in his case, I'd like it to come in the form of red-hot pokers up his tight arse.'

Boom.

A section of the city wall only thirty paces from the gate took the shot, which turned a merlon into a cloud of flying stone missiles that injured men for twenty feet in both directions. The walls trembled sufficiently that Gabriel felt it through the soles of his feet even this far away. He looked down. The walls of Euripos had been built in the days before even Rome came here, and had been enhanced and strengthened by every new owner since, but the past century or more had seen a lot of deterioration. They were thick walls, high, and of masterful construction, but they were also crumbling and in need of repair. In Gabriel's own not inconsiderable opinion, they would last a day. Two at the best. And that was without considering the possibility of a lucky shot. If the Turkish gunners were good, this could all be over remarkably quickly. So far they'd fired two shots and hit both times.

The third shot was raised once more, as the gunners constantly tweaked their aim, and struck the parapet only ten paces from Gabriel. The missile hit a merlon, which made a stony creak and sent shrapnel away outside, but remained solid and harmed no one. He glanced momentarily over at the prince, standing proud and seemingly indestructible.

'Pass the word. Have everyone check the wall beside them. If there is crumbling mortar, move to a stronger position.'

That done, preserving the defenders as far as possible, Gabriel checked his own position and then lowered himself to the stonework and pulled his bedroll from his pack.

'What are you *doing*?' a garrison officer gasped, staring, partly at the seemingly calm act in the midst of chaos, and partly at Gabriel's features.

'Going to sleep.'

'With *this* going on? What if they hit?'

'They'll still hit whether I'm awake or not, and if they breach, better to be rested than tired.'

'But *how* can you sleep?'

'Son, you're obviously new to this, so watch me, and I'll show you.'

Gabriel lay down, pulled his blankets over him, mentally blocked out the cannon fire, and eventually slept.

In truth, he only managed four hours, and even then he'd stirred several times and had to drain his bladder once, but he reasoned he'd still be fresher than many. Rising, he checked on the four men he'd assigned to be with the prince at all times, for Constantine was not about to leave the walls in the circumstances, and he was still prey to that irresistible urge to seek out trouble. Satisfied that they were all well, Gabriel ignored the latest blast, rumble and tremor, and went to find his second.

Gaspar was already stirring, so he left the man to it and walked over to Manuel, who was still fast asleep, but wore a curiously boyish smile as his hand probed around at groin height under his blankets.

Gabriel leaned down close to his head. 'Hand off your cock and on your sword, my friend,' he bellowed, grinning as the standard-bearer awoke with a shock and nearly tore off his own manhood in the process.

'Fuck you,' Manuel grunted. 'Fuck you very much.'

As his men found their feet and the first light of dawn began to glow with promise in the east beyond the horizon, Gabriel walked over to Constantine. He reached down to the waterskin at his belt and took a long swig.

'Looks like being a warm one again.'

The prince nodded, almost distractedly. 'I am concerned about Thomas, Gabriel.'

'Oh?'

'Here, we know what we're doing, and though we might be in trouble, we've done everything a man can do to avoid it. We have me, and you, and the silver tongue of my friend George. Thomas might have more men, but he has no experience, no skills and no strong commander or politician upon which to rely. If Turahan Bey refuses, or even if his marauding officers cross the border and make some kind of attack before that? Well, Thomas is unlikely to acquit himself well. Whatever we do here will be entirely moot if Thomas starts a war with the Turks at the Hexamilion.'

'What of Theodore? Will he not come to Thomas's aid?'

It was clearly all Constantine could do not to snort. 'My monk of a brother? He has little more knowledge and experience of war than Thomas, but more likely he would pat Turahan Bey on the back and turn on us.'

'Really?' Though despite his sounding surprised at that, in truth Gabriel had come to a similar conclusion some time before.

'The man was never my greatest supporter, nor that of Thomas, and when we attacked Patras, the city of his father-in-law, we did ourselves no favours. But since his wife died, he has truly lost his way. He is a hollow shadow of his former self, and the man was little more than a shadow in the first place. It has been two years, and he is still in the colour of mourning, where even in my own grief I let the black go after two months. His bitterness and grief could make him do anything. So no, no one can rely upon the support of Theodore, and the time is coming, I fear, when he will be more dangerous to us than the sultan.'

Gabriel sighed. That description of Theodore was almost applicable to Constantine these days, if a little less so. Over the years he had met all the sons of the old emperor. Beside Constantine, John, the oldest, was certainly the best, which was to the good, given that he now ruled as emperor. The second son, Theodore? Well, it was safe to say he had his faults. The third, Andronikos, had retired to a monastery in the capital and passed away a few years earlier. And then, born after Constantine, there were Demetrios and Thomas. The latter was young, excitable, and had the benefit of being the youngest of six brothers, which removed any hope of true power, and therefore also removed the stress and danger that came along with the succession. The same should be true of Demetrios, but that young man was hard and bitter, envying his elders and always with one eye on the throne. There was trouble waiting to happen there. Certainly, if Gabriel were wanting to defend a land, he would seek out John or Constantine, and none of the others.

Boom.

The wall trembled once more, and a ligneous crack suggested that aim had been shifted now, directly to the gate. They did not have long.

Another four shots struck, each with the sounds of ravaged wood and stone, before the first blinding ray of gold crested the horizon and fell upon the ruined features of the prince's bodyguard commander. Gabriel blinked and turned, to see the Turks gathering ready. They knew it was close now. They would wait for the gate to fall and then swarm across the defences, take the city and kill the prince.

Shit.

They were out of time.

The next shot sent half the packing behind the gate scattering in a cloud, almost opening the way. Constantine had no need to give the order. The Serbs were already gathered below, waiting within the gate along with the local garrison to try and hold back the Turkish flood. The Ianitzaroi remained on the parapet with the prince, ever their direct concern.

In fact, Gabriel was so busy mentally preparing for what was to come that it was only when the runner actually reached him and hammered on his back that he turned.

'What?'

'The ambassador, sir?' the breathless runner announced, rearing back as the monstrous face turned to him.

'What? What ambassador?'

'Sphrantzes, sir. He's here.'

Gabriel blinked. 'God in Heaven, man, that's good news. Where?'

'He reached the drawbridge a few moments ago. They are lowering it now so that he can enter the city. He has his guard with him.'

'Thank the Holy Mother for such blessings. Now go. Tell everyone.' He turned to the prince, standing nearby. 'You heard?'

'I did. Come on.'

And with that, they found the nearest wall stairs and pounded down them to the street where the defenders were bracing, ready for the worst. They did not have to wait long. Sphrantzes came galloping round a corner like a racer in the circus, looking dishevelled and tired, and pulled his mount to a stop as he reached them. He vaulted from the horse, and then made a face at the discomfort this caused.

'George,' the prince said, the grin threatening to split his head in half as he hurried over and threw his arms around his friend.

'Careful, Constantine. I slept on a pile of rocks last night on the other side of the bridge and I feel broken.'

'What news, old friend?'

'Good news, my prince. Turahan Bey apologises for his hasty advance. He says he was unaware of the late duke's decree, and had he known, his armies would never have crossed the border. He hopes that his long-standing respect for you will clear the air. Moreover, the late duke's nephew, Nerio, who has been contesting the will and determined to claim Athens, has made an agreement with us. He will claim the ducal throne of Athens, but as an imperial vassal. The best of both worlds, Constantine, for we will control the dukedom, without the headache of having to hang on to it.'

Constantine grinned, and for a moment, all that darkness that had gathered since the death of his wife fell away, leaving only the shining prince of Byzantium. 'I can think of a nasty little pasha who's not going to like this.'

As they jogged across to the stairs and climbed the walls once more, Sphrantzes began to recount his perilous journey across occupied lands, avoiding marauding Turkish armies, and his short, but pleasant and profitable time in Thebes. Reaching the parapet, Constantine had a musician blow his horn while a white flag was raised and waved. After another shot, the cannon fell silent for now, and a small party of officers, including Karaca Pasha himself, rode forth.

'What lies have you for me this time at the cusp of your undoing?' the man snapped.

'The eminent ambassador George Sphrantzes has returned from the court of Turahan Bey,' Constantine replied, and actually laughed at the glimmer of panic that flitted across the man's face. 'The sultan's great bey has confirmed our treaty and the empire's hegemony over the Duchy of Athens. Your armies are being withdrawn. I'm sure your own envoy will be with you within the day. Should you withdraw now and press the attack no further, I am sure I can persuade the ambassador not to lodge a formal complaint with your master.'

Gabriel laughed too, now, as he watched the pasha wrestle with his unpleasant options. In the end, the man bowed, his lip twitching. 'A dreadful mistake has been made. Please accept my apologies as my forces withdraw.'

Constantine continued the exchange for a short while, but Gabriel had already turned his back, noting something dark in Sphrantzes' expression. 'What is it?'

'There were other things to learn at Thebes, Gabriel.'

'Oh?'

'Turahan has already had the borders redrawn. He will not let us simply take all. A portion of the northern reaches of the duchy are already to be considered part of his *beylik*. And I did not think it wise to press our claim. We have very narrowly avoided true disaster here.'

Gabriel nodded. 'Regrettable, but entirely expected. This worries you so?'

'Not as much, Gabriel, as the tidings that the despot Theodore is massing his armies. He has no complaint against the Turks, the Venetians consider him an ally, and Thomas is not worth his effort. That only leaves one potential target for such an army, in my opinion.'

Gabriel nodded. 'Then perhaps it is time that the prince visits his brother in the capital after all.'

3

A Troublesome Brood

Near Kalamata, in the Morea

One year after the siege of Euripos: September 1436

'How is the empire ever supposed to be brought back to its former glory like this?' Gaspar sighed.

Gabriel nodded silently as he eyed the force awaiting them across the parched landscape, below a blue sky whose only resident, a lonely buzzard, circled lazily. The army facing them this time was another Roman army. He snorted at his own thought, then, for though the armies were both led by Palaiologoi despots, there was little truly Roman about them. Constantine had a small core of troops from Mesembria who could claim Roman blood of ancient times, and his brother, down by the beach, had a similar unit drawn from Thessaloniki, before first its donation to Venice and then its fall to the Turks. But the rest of the armies on both sides, the vast bulk of the men, were Serbs, Bulgars, Catalans, Albanians, sundry Italians, and even Turks. A truly multinational force, all accepting much-needed gold to fight for the empire.

And to fight *against* the empire, Gabriel added silently and grimly.

Down towards the shore, the army of Theodore Palaiologos, despot of the Morea and eldest brother of the emperor, directed his officers as the units were deployed in various positions. Gabriel turned and glanced over at Constantine. The younger brother looked confident, strong, every bit the general in the field, and well he might. Theodore's army was larger, drawn partly from recent levies and also from his own force at Mystras, but his experience in war was negligible at best, while Constantine was a man forged in battle.

'It's fucking foolish,' Gaspar grunted, earning a glare from his commander. It was entirely true, but that was not the sort of thing to say within earshot of the prince. Fortunately, it seemed Constantine was not listening, instead watching his brother's forces deploy.

'Have the Bulgars tighten up on the left flank,' the prince said, 'where they can face his Turks. He's failed to deploy anything else of value on that flank, and it should be turned easily. Have the Cuman cavalry brought round to the left, and bring the Serbian archers up in support. Unless he does something unexpected, his right flank will break, and from there, we can rout the rest.'

'Yes, sir,' an officer barked.

'What of your brother, sir?' John Rhosatsas offered.

'What?'

'Should they break and your brother be taken? What then?'

'That depends entirely upon Theodore. After all, it was he who brought this all on, was it not?'

It was. The man was a fool.

Jealousy and suspicion seemed to drive Theodore these days. It had ever been so in a small way, but things had become so much worse recently. When Constantine's brief marriage had ended with the death of his new wife, he had darkened and become edgy, repeatedly putting himself in danger, something he had been doing even as far as that almost-siege at Euripos, but his grief had only ever made him more dangerous to the enemy and to himself. On the other hand, the death of his own wife seemed to have sent Theodore into a dark spiral of distrust and paranoia, to the extent of preparing to make war on a brother he now perceived as a rival, and threatening to tear the empire apart.

Constantine *was* a rival, of course, although a legitimate one, and that was not his fault. After Euripos, Constantine had sailed for the capital, where the emperor had confided in him that he was John's favoured choice for succession if it came to that, rather than one of the older brothers, apparently at the instigation of their saintly mother, the former empress. Whatever John had intended changed immediately, though, when Theodore's ship also landed, having raced from the Morea in Constantine's wake. He had made it clear to the emperor that, as the second oldest brother, the succession should fall to him. He would not accept his younger brother as emperor.

John, ever a force of sense, had settled upon a plan that overturned the original scheme of three despots in the Morea: the older brothers, Theodore and Demetrios, would remain in Constantinople, acting as regents when John was not available, while Constantine and Thomas would return to the Morea and forge the peninsula into the new power centre of the empire. To rule in Constantinople, even as regent, was a powerful honour. In theory it had satisfied all parties, even Demetrios, whom Gabriel considered the bitterest weasel of the brood. Constantine had agreed readily and had taken ship for the Morea once more, dispatching Sphrantzes to follow on after securing the support of Turahan Bey at Tırhala. The prince had returned to the Greek shore and begun to strengthen the imperial position, only for Theodore to race back to the Morea in his wake, messengers sent out to gather his armies.

The desperately penned letter from the emperor warning Constantine of what was coming was forthright to say the least. Theodore, it claimed, had suspected some collusion between Constantine and the emperor, believing that he was being kept in the great city in order to be watched and controlled, while Constantine was to forge a grand new empire in the Morea in order to more easily succeed when the time came. As such, Theodore would not stay, and was determined to return to the Morea and put a stop to what he saw as Constantine's ambitions.

'We could fall back,' John Rhosatsas said. 'Make them pursue us for a few days. Not only would that tire them and stretch their supply line, but it would allow Thomas to reach us with his army, bringing us closer to parity.'

Constantine stroked his neat beard for a moment. 'Perhaps it would be wise, but I have a mind to fight here and now. What we lack in numbers we make up for in skill and in heart.'

Gabriel kept his expression carefully neutral. He was a body-guard, not a general or tactician, and it was not his place to advise the prince in matters of war, but the simple fact was that whichever despot won the battle today the empire still lost, for its own masters threw away in internecine wars gold and men that they might well need against external enemies.

'We might be a little late for pulling back,' one of the generals said, pointing out over the heads of the enemy force. Everyone's gaze rose to follow it, picking out the four ships in the bay, making for the beach behind Theodore.

'Reinforcements,' Rhosatsas sighed. '*Now* will you consider withdrawing?'

'I don't think they're reinforcements,' Gabriel said, peering into the distance and then drawing his gaze back to the enemy in between to confirm what he thought he'd seen.

'Explain?'

'Well, yes, they're Venetian transports flying the imperial banner, but look at your brother's army, sir. They're confused. Men are looking round at the ships, and a small group of their officers has ridden off to the side, watching them. I don't think they know who the ships are. In fact, I think they believe them to be ours.'

'By God, you're right,' Constantine said. 'And it can't be the emperor. John is busy preparing for a synod. Thomas is behind us. Demetrios, perhaps?'

They stood and watched as the four ships slowed, closing on the shallower beach, then dropped anchor. Far from the flotilla of landing craft that would herald the arrival of reinforcements, a single pinnace set forth from the larger vessel, splashing its way towards the shore. It was impossible to identify the occupants at this point, but they were certainly bright and colourful, without the predominant metallic gleam of a fighting force. The leaders and officers waited, tense, as did those of Theodore's force.

The pinnace reached the beach and landed, sailors jumping out to steady it and run down a boarding ramp. As the world watched, fascinated, the new arrivals began to disembark, and Gabriel frowned at the sight.

'Priests?'

'Not just priests, but men of the highest rank. At least two bishops, several senior monks, and someone in quite rich robes.'

They continued to watch as the small party of holy men ascended the beach and moved onto the grass. The army they skirted watched them with interest, no one making a move. Most of the men in both armies were of the Christian faith, and were not likely to pose a threat to priests, no matter their purpose. The party passed the enemy flank, and Theodore and his men began to ride towards them.

'Come with me,' Constantine said, gesturing at Rhosatsas.

'Surely you're not going down there?'

'Hard to speak to whoever they are from here.'

Rhosatsas shook his head. 'They are within easy bowshot of your brother's army. Whatever their purpose, it would only take one signal from Theodore and you'd sprout a dozen arrow shafts. Don't be foolish, my prince.'

Constantine snorted. 'That's why I have a bodyguard. Gabriel? Mount up with your men. Fast.'

In a matter of a hundred heartbeats they were all in the saddle, the Ianitzaroi gathering around the prince and his two advisors, each of them with shield out and ready to protect Constantine. The prince's attitude was changing, Gabriel thought as they rode. Just a few months ago, he was putting himself in deliberate danger, still driven by the death of his wife. Now, though they rode into bowshot of the enemy, it was not simply Constantine daring fate to fell him, but a legitimate need to investigate.

The priests had ridden far enough forward to be out of earshot of most of Theodore's army, and it was there that the older brother and his men caught up with them. As they closed on the meeting, Gabriel frowned. 'I recognise the man at the centre, from back in the capital. Who is he?'

The response came from Constantine. 'That, Gabriel, is Gregory Mammis, one of the cleverest men I ever met. He was among the priests who walked the walls of Constantinople that day we threw back the Turks, blessing the soldiers and occasionally joining them in sticking a knife in a stray attacker. Last I knew he was at court, the emperor's own confessor. What he is doing here is a great question.'

They rode closer, and Gabriel's men started to gather tighter, shields high and ready to catch any missile meant for Constantine. Despite the danger, none came, and they slowed close to the churchmen. On the far side of the group, Theodore Palaiologos glared at Constantine with a look that could bore a hole through rock.

'Gregory, well met,' the prince said with a smile and a bow of the head.

'My lord.'

'Tell your men to lower their shields,' Rhosatsas murmured to Gabriel.

'What if they decide to shoot?'

'They won't. Don't forget that Theodore is a very devout man, almost a monk. He would never dare murder any other Christian in front of Gregory Mammis, let alone his own brother. He is quite safe for now.'

'There must be peace,' Gregory announced. 'There *will* be peace.'

'Not while my brother schemes to leap ahead of me in the succession, there will not,' Theodore spat.

'I have no desire to rule,' Constantine said in an oddly bored tone. 'I am content with a despotate. What I do desire is a strong empire, no matter who sits on the throne, and should John not be able to do so, it will be John who decides his successor, not you, not me, and not even the order of our birth. Should he decide that we are all too fractious and dark for the task and pass it to gentle and pleasant Thomas, then I for one will bow to my youngest brother and help make his throne secure.'

'As you should,' Gregory Mammis nodded.

'I shall not,' Theodore growled. 'This empire needs a true hand on the tiller, a man who follows the path of God and the Theotokos. Not John, who would have a synod with the West and have our churches unified so that we would bow to Rome. And you…' He turned and wagged a finger at Mammis. 'You are almost as bad. Don't think I don't know your mind. You would have us wash the feet of the Pope in Rome. You are all as bad as one another. My whole family and all their advisors are either apostates who would see us join with Rome, or would-be usurpers with their eye on the throne despite the order of precedence. God will see me in the succession and you in the dust, Constantine. Mark my words.'

Before Constantine could reply, Gregory Mammis threw out a finger at Theodore and spoke, his voice sharp and dangerous enough to surprise all present, coming from a pious churchman.

'Theodore Palaiologos, I charge you here and now that among the worst sins in the world stands that of fratricide. If you proceed with this war, with the intent to remove your brother from the succession, I will have no option but to exclude you from communion until such time as you make amends. Do I make myself clear?'

Theodore's face screwed up into a distasteful mask. 'You would not dare. I would speak to the Patriarch and—'

'The Patriarch who currently favours a union of the Churches for the strength and preservation of the empire?' Gregory snorted. 'That same Patriarch Joseph who fled to Mount Athos and took his vows after his half-brother murdered his full brother to keep the bloodline of the Bulgarian tsars pure?

I suspect my good friend the Patriarch might have a thing or two to say to you.'

Theodore glowered, but said nothing, unable to refute any of this.

Gregory took a breath and leaned back, folding his arms. 'The emperor, in his wisdom, is prepared to go to almost any length to prevent his brothers tearing the empire apart and wasting its resources, but he has charged me with attempting a peaceful solution in the first instance. So here it is. Here is the judgement of Gregory Mammis.'

He turned and pointed now to Constantine. 'You will lay down your despotate in the Morea today, and relinquish control of this army. You are hereby summoned to Constantinople, where you will act as regent in the name of the emperor.'

Theodore blustered an angry noise, and the priest turned to him and produced the jabbing finger once more. 'No. No words, Prince of Constantinople. You will remain in the Morea as its senior despot, with Thomas Palaiologos as your partner, running the northern part. You will consolidate the forces and turn this peninsula into the power base that it needs to be. I am led to believe that it was your insistence that Constantine intended to use it for his own ends that led you to bring an army here? Then you have achieved your goal, so seal your lips and stand down. You and Thomas here in the Morea, while Constantine acts as regent in the emperor's absence.'

'Absence?' Constantine asked quietly.

'The emperor prepares to sail for Italy and the synod with the Church there, seeking an agreement between the two faiths. Your brother Demetrios will accompany him.'

He turned and stepped back, rubbing his hands together. 'I trust there will be no objections.'

It was not a question, and Gabriel had to smile at the way a priest had just laid a steely ultimatum before two of the most powerful men in the world. There was a tense silence, and finally both Constantine and Theodore nodded.

'Good. Now, it has been a long trip, and I favour the notion of wine. Perhaps you could have your officers stand these forces down, and someone could find a nice vintage for me?'

–

Two days later came another ship, bearing a familiar figure just as welcome as the priest had been. George Sphrantzes stepped down to the sand and stretched after his cramped journey. He strode up the beach, then, and was met by two of the Ianitzaroi, who escorted him to the prince's tent.

Gabriel stood to one side of Constantine's chair as the ambassador was escorted in.

'A worrying gathering of armies?' Sphrantzes noted.

Constantine nodded. 'We came close to true conflict. Theodore followed me back with intent to remove me from the playing board. We are fortunate that John sent voices of both reason and strength to prevent the outbreak. Gregory Mammis left Theodore standing there with his jaw flapping helplessly. It was all I could do not to laugh.'

'I can imagine. Where is your dark brother now?'

'He has set out for Mystras. Most of the army waits here for Thomas to arrive, and then they will be settled under the command of the pair of them. I was awaiting only your arrival, and now we are bound for the great city itself. I am to serve as regent while John and Demetrios are in the West at the synod.'

'Demetrios is going? That is a mixed blessing, I'd say. Good to have his dangerous influence away from the capital, but even more worrying to have it at such an important council.'

'Well, it is done, for good or ill. And he will be away for many months, for sure. Constantinople will be in our hands.'

'And we had better be prepared to look after it,' Sphrantzes said ominously.

'Explain.'

'I have news from the court of Turahan Bey. There are worrying rumours flying about there. The bey himself was swift in avowing his support for you in the Morea, though I wonder if his tune might change a little when he learns that you are no longer here, and that it is Theodore who commands. Still, Turahan Bey has no intent to set himself against you. However, he has been instructed by the Sublime Porte to demand tribute from the Duchy of Athens. It would appear that the sultan is content to let us rule those lands, but not to tax them for our own benefit.'

Constantine scratched his chin. 'That now will be Theodore's problem to solve, and I wonder how long it will be before he regrets coming here and leaving the capital. There is little he can realistically do but capitulate. Perhaps he can persuade the Porte to accept a small imperial cut from the tribute. But certainly we cannot refuse. Not unless we want to face the full might of the Turks.'

'And that is where the really worrying news comes in, and in two parts,' Sphrantzes said, slumping against the wall. 'Firstly, though I could not confirm the veracity of such reports, while at Tırhala, I heard several rumours of a build-up of Turkish forces at Edirne. What the sultan could be planning to do with a new army just a hundred miles from Constantinople I cannot say, but the news certainly left me uneasy.'

Constantine nodded. 'And Turahan Bey gave away nothing?'

'Neither by word, nor with his eyes, and not even with his gesture or stance. If the bey knows anything of his master's plans, he hid it well. And I can only hope it does not tie in with my other piece of unsettling news.'

'Go on.'

'Word has it that Torno Tocco is now at the sultan's court in Edirne.'

For the first time in the conversation, Gabriel properly paid attention, straightening, his expression dark.

'He does turn up in the most dangerous places, does he not?' Sphrantzes said. 'It seems that after the death of the older count and the fall of Arta, many of the less favoured Tocco sons and nephews have found themselves serving as vassals of the sultan. It is my distinct hope that the perpetual thorn in our side named Torno is now ruling some distant Turkish district, and is not connected to the military build-up at Edirne.' He turned back to Constantine. 'At least with you as regent, the capital will have a firm hand in the face of what might be coming.'

Edirne: the court of Sultan Murad II

October 1436

'*Esther*,' the four-year-old prince said, brow knitted, trying to tie his tongue around the unfamiliar sounds. 'A weird name. Why does no one call you it?'

'Hush now, Mehmet,' the elegant lady in her colourful silks said, kindly but firmly pushing the child back into his bed. 'Time for sleep now.'

'Your name is Hüma,' the boy insisted. 'Hüma Hatun. It's a beautiful name. Esther sounds like dog poo.'

The lady gave a strange chuckle. 'It is from a different tongue, my dove. Esther is a name among the Jews, one of the People of the Book, although my father once told me that Esther is just the Jewish name for Ishtar, one of the oldest goddesses of the world.'

'There is only one God,' Mehmet said grumpily, frown deepening. 'Ahmet Pasha insists on it. He says any other notion is the work of the infidel.'

'Of course, my dear. Of course. But many people give God their own name. You should never be blind to the beliefs of others, for belief is often what drives people to do the most extraordinary things.'

'So why does no one call you Esther?' the child pressed. 'Is it because Jewish are infidels?'

She laughed for a moment, but it passed in a heartbeat, as though the words had been a little too close to the bone for comfort.

125

'I have been a daughter of Islam since I was little older than you.' She smiled. 'My father converted with the arrival of the Turks in our lands, and I was brought up in the court of the sultan. I am privileged that your father singled me out among so many as one of his concubines. And that means that you, Mehmet, are the son of a sultan, and one day you might rule.'

'If snot-face lets me.'

The lady's expression hardened. 'Şehzade Alaeddin Ali is the eldest son, and heir to your father. Never let anyone hear you call him snot-face.'

'He is. He's always snotty. Bogeys hanging down. Who would ever follow him?'

Again, she chuckled.

'So where is Jewland?'

'Well…' She smiled. 'That's a little complicated. They don't really have one.'

'Why?'

'Think of it a bit like carpenters. Do carpenters have their own land?'

'I don't know. Probably not.'

Again, that easy, quiet laugh. 'Well, Mehmet, I am from a place called Bulgaria. Once we were Roman, but then the Turks came and brought Islam to us.'

'What's Roman?'

'My word, but Hundi Hatun warned me that when you turned four you would never stop asking questions. Sleep is clearly going to have to wait until you are five. Rome, my dove, is the oldest empire there is. Rome was all-powerful two thousand years ago, when your ancestors were living in yurts on the steppe. When your father's ancestors had no written tongue of their own, and drank horse milk to survive, Rome was shaping songs and cities, codices of laws and armies the like of which made the world tremble.'

'Should we be frightened of Rome?'

Her laugh now was a little sadder. 'No, my dove. Rome now is but a shadow of what once it was. The emperor of Rome was once the most powerful man in the world. Now that is your father, the sultan. Yet the emperor of the Romans is still important, and his name, his title, carry such ancient power that men still bow to him, even though his time is clearly past.'

'So his land is gone, but even without it he is important?'

'Important enough that your father would take Constantinople if he felt he could, and end the emperor. But there are others to think about. To do so might bring your father into conflict with the Pope in Rome, and that could be a disaster.'

'Good. He's wrong anyway.'

The lady frowned in turn, now. 'What do you mean?'

'If his name is important, but the land is not, then we should take the land but keep the name. When snot-face has exploded his face in one of his sneezing fits, and I am sultan, I will go to Constantinople, and I will take it for myself. I will kick the emperor of the Romans from his palace and I shall take his place. I shall be emperor of the Romans.'

'Ha. *Kayser-i Rûm*, it would be in our tongue, I think, for they call their emperor Caesar, a little like a shah.'

Mehmet lay back with a satisfied smile. 'Yes. I shall be Kayser-i Rûm. And snot-face can be my stable boy.'

PART TWO – CONSTANTINOPLE

On November 27 of the same year, our emperor
Lord John, accompanied by the patriarch, Lord
Demetrios the despot, numerous senators, clerics,
and almost all the metropolitans and bishops,
departed for the scheduled synod. Would I that he
had never left!

George Sphrantzes, *The Fall of the Byzantine Empire* XXIII.1

4

The Question of Unification

Blachernae Palace, Constantinople

One year later: 1 November 1437

Gabriel's hand went to the hilt of the sword at his hip – a reflex only, for to draw it here would likely cause disaster.

'Threaten me again, dearest brother, and you may find you fail to wake one morning.'

'A threat for a threat?' Constantine snapped. 'Yet mine delivered like a soldier, offering the edge of a blade in the open air, while yours reeks of subterfuge and murder. How fitting for a man who spends half his time sneaking around with Turkish assassins and defaming the emperor.'

Still Gabriel's hand remained where it was. Prince or no prince, if Demetrios made a move on Constantine, Gabriel was bound to his defence. Indeed, the younger Palaiologos took a single step forward and brought up his fist angrily.

'Insult me, will you?'

'I fear you did that yourself, Demetrios. Hark, I believe I hear the emperor calling you.'

'John can wait, *forever* for all I care. I am hardly invested in this fool's errand.'

'It is the future of our empire, Demetrios, and that you cannot see this tells me just how blinkered and dangerous you are. We need the West if we are to hold back the Turks.'

'Better to hold back the *West*,' snarled Demetrios. 'Union of the Churches? Damnable talk. Heresy, pure and simple. Do you not know your histories? Do you not remember how their Pope sent his crusaders to sack and burn the great city instead of the forces of the Saracen? How the empire went into decades of exile and lost most of its territory to greedy, marauding Italian lords? And now you want to go crawling to him and tell him he is right? John is a fool.'

'John does what he can to save the empire. We have recovered the Morea, but every step we take now, we need to seek the goodwill of the sultan. Only with the support of Rome can we once more become the bulwark of God against the East. We *have* to unite the Churches. It is the only way they will help us.'

'Do you know what they say in the streets and marketplaces, Constantine? They say "Better the Turk's turban than the Pope's mitre." You want to protect the empire against the Turks? Well, most of our people would rather invite the Turks in and ask them to protect us from Rome.'

Demetrios sagged slightly, closing his eyes for a moment. 'I think it's your name, brother. Because Father named you after such a great emperor of the old times, you see yourself as him. You imagine yourself rising to preserve a dying empire and founding it anew, just as did the man who founded this great city. But the world has changed. There are no legions and consuls now, no thunderbolts of the gods. Just us, a small, crumbling empire, squeezed between the powerful worlds of the West and the Turks. We cannot rebuild what was lost. In time we will either serve the Pope or serve the sultan, and you are determined to choose the greater evil.'

Without waiting for a response, Demetrios Palaiologos turned and strode from the room.

'Stupid,' Constantine spat once he'd gone. 'And I shouldn't let him provoke me like that. I used to be the calm one. I used to take his idiocy and his insults and let them bounce from me like slingshots from a cuirass. These days, somehow, I find it harder to be the better man.'

'You are, and always will be, the better man,' Gabriel said quietly, earning a small flash of gratitude from the prince.

'Gabriel smooths over your rougher edges, though,' noted Sphrantzes, where he lounged in a chair in the corner.

'Oh?'

'Oh, you are the better man, of course you are, but you are also not the man you were. You *have* changed, Constantine. It started that day in Patras, when you lost Theodora. We noticed the change in you straight away, but I think we all saw it as part of your mourning, and that eventually you would recover. Yet you haven't. Not entirely.'

Constantine turned and took a step towards him, his face creasing into irritation. Sphrantzes held up his hands. 'I will always tell you the truth, Constantine, and you know that. I will never sweeten it for you. You are different. Darker. Less forgiving. Don't get me wrong, you've not followed Theodore on his spiral of misery and fury, but I do worry that the future may hold precisely that unless you change once more. We, the empire entire, need that shining prince of the Palaiologoi who walked the walls of the city when the Turks came.'

The prince stopped, sighed, scrubbed his head with the palm of his hand.

'Can a man change willingly? Can a man pull himself out of a darkness that enshrouds his soul, George?'

'You know what you need, Constantine? You need a wife.'

'Hardly. You've just been telling me that my wife was what *caused* this.'

'*Losing* your wife was what caused this. And you are a prince of the Romans. Moreover, John has vouchsafed time and again that you are his chosen heir. He is on his third wife, and still no children, Constantine. You know what that means. The succession will pass sideways, not down, and both he and your sainted mother favour you. You need a wife, and with her you need children. What use rebuilding the empire if you cannot secure a way to control it? Without an heir you would have to designate Theodore, Demetrios or Thomas as your heir. One is dangerous, another untrustworthy and the last unready.'

Gabriel was surprised when Constantine, silent and thoughtful, turned to look at him. The prince said nothing, but there was a question in his eyes.

'Sphrantzes is right, I think,' Gabriel said, hoping his opinion really was being sought.

'Oh?'

'But not just a wife. You need the *right* wife. A woman who sees things the way you do, who can work towards goals with you. A strong woman.'

Constantine gave an odd chuckle. 'Here I am with a politician and a soldier. Where else would a man go for advice on his love life.' He took a deep breath and straightened. 'All right, George, I accept your notion. I need to recover my humour and light, and perhaps someone by my side can make that easier. And no one knows me better than you, George. My match with Theodora was happy accident, the Lord at work, but the Lord cannot be relied upon to find me a wife every time, so this time I shall rely upon you. Go and find me a wife.'

Sphrantzes frowned. 'There are people who do such things, Constantine. Professional matchmakers. You will need me concentrating on things here in the coming days, not messing around with hopeful fathers, painted beauties and clinking dowries.'

'You are a talented man, George. I'm sure you can do both.'

Before Sphrantzes could argue any further, a small collection of pages, musicians and courtiers flurried into the room, backwards, trying to announce the emperor's approach but failing to do so in time as John Palaiologos marched into the room at speed, waving them out of the way.

'There is a time and a place for pomp and ceremony,' the emperor told the most senior of his people drily, 'but this is not it. These are my brothers in my own palace. Go away.'

Unhappy at being dismissed so, the collection of desperate servants retreated into the door from which they'd entered, which John then shut with his own divinely regal hands before turning to the others.

'God in Heaven, Constantine, but it takes ten times longer to do anything when the court follows you around. Remember that when your turn comes.'

The emperor's younger brother laughed. 'The burdens of empire are many and various, are they not, Your Imperial Majesty.'

'Shut up. Have you seen Demetrios? He was supposed to provide me with a list of his retinue this morning. The Venetian captains are requesting passenger lists right down to the last servant. Something to do with having adequate supplies on board, I think.'

'Follow the swearing and the bad smell, and you'll find him,' Constantine grumbled.

'Rather unkind, my brother.'

'He's a fool. Worse than that. He may well be dangerous. Possibly even more dangerous than the Turks. Why in God's name are you taking him with you? It's like taking a whore into a convent. Mark my words, he will work against you in Italy. He will undermine everything you try to build. If you come away from the council without a deal of union, it will be his doing. He would rather sink a knife in all our backs than see an alliance with the Pope.'

The emperor rolled his eyes. 'Try not to over-dramatise, Constantine. He disagrees with us, and he is an angry man by nature, but he is also our brother, and whether we agree with him or not, he believes what he does is for the good of the empire.'

'Leave him here. It's the only way.'

'No, Constantine. He goes with me. You don't know him as I do, and you can't work him the way I can. You've gone your own way so much these past years, while I've been with him since the day he came back from Hungary. Better I have him where I can see him and put an end to any of his mischief, than I leave him here with you. In the city, he would have the chance to work against you.'

'I could stop him.'

'No you couldn't, Constantine. You'll learn this in the coming weeks. There is a view that being an emperor is like it was in the times of men like Nero – all parties and banquets and music and fornication. Silk pillows and velvet robes. It is so far removed from that. It is a world of constant requests and pleas, of oily courtiers and needling ambassadors. From the moment I wake to the moment exhaustion takes me, my world is one of difficult decisions, political balancing acts, subtle control and preventing disasters. All this will be yours as regent. You will not have time to pay attention to men like Demetrios. You will be lucky even to use the latrine without an attendant feeding you paperwork as you shit.'

Gabriel couldn't help chuckling at that, which drew the attention of all the other three men.

'I still think you should leave him,' Constantine said, turning back to his brother.

'Noted. Now where is he?'

'He marched off that way. Only a short while ago, too. You'll find him easily enough.'

The emperor nodded, and followed the directions, leaving the room without his entourage. Alone once more, apart from Gabriel, Sphrantzes sighed. 'Of course, the best way to deal with Demetrios would be to assign him to some godforsaken *appanage*, perhaps of Imbros island or somewhere equally unimportant. Or maybe send him off as the imperial ambassador to Trebizond. Somewhere he could do little damage.'

Constantine shook his head. 'No. John is right about one thing: Demetrios needs to be somewhere one of us can keep an eye on him.'

Gabriel nodded. Funny how every time they overcame a foe, the Lord saw fit to produce a new one, and sometimes from among allies.

Rarely had one room in the city played host to such a collection of political and military skill. Senior generals, ambassadors and courtiers sat around the chamber, each of them carefully selected for their ability and their loyalty to the emperor and his regent. Even then, Gabriel and four of his men stood around the periphery, just in case.

'Are we sure?' Constantine asked quietly. 'I will not commit unless we are absolutely certain we are the target.'

'Who else, lord?' one of the generals shrugged.

'Mark this, Achilleos, but we cannot afford to commit militarily without being absolutely certain. If the sultan actually has other plans, and we meet him with brandished weapons, we may well trigger the end of our world.'

'But, lord, if he means to crush the empire, then not standing against him will only hasten that end.'

A sense of gloomy and tense agreement floated across the room. What Sphrantzes had noted at Edirne during his last visit had been confirmed now by four different sources. The military build-up at the sultan's capital was not only certain, but appeared to have increased continually, to the point that the last report to come to the city suggested what could only be described as an invasion force.

'If I am to commit militarily, we have to be absolutely certain. We cannot afford to be wrong.'

'Lord,' said another of the generals, leaning forward, 'the army is gathered to the south-east of Edirne, a mile from the city, astride the road to Constantinople.'

'That proves nothing,' the regent said, shaking his head. 'Edirne is in a horseshoe of rough peaks. Only the south-east has sufficient flat and open land to host a large force. No matter where they are bound, they would be mustered there.'

'We are unaware of any other power the sultan is sufficiently in conflict with to require such an army, lord,' one of the ambassadors noted.

'Again, inconclusive. He is not currently in such conflict with us, either, and there are plenty of potential targets. The new voivod of Wallachia, Vlad Dracul, is engaged in a very tense set of negotiations with the sultan, which constantly threaten to erupt into full-scale war, and the despot of Serbia walks a very fine line, paying tribute to prevent a full invasion. Even Trebizond itself is not entirely without threat, despite being at the far end of the sea. No, again, motive is blurred.'

It was Sphrantzes who spoke then. 'Though it is not conclusive, the presence of a small unit bearing the colours of Torno Tocco lends a great deal of weight to the notion that their target is us. Torno has no known enmity with any other power at this time, and we all know how much he would like to remove the regent from the world of men.'

Constantine sat for a while digesting this, then leaned forward.

'Tell me, how is the mood of the people? Demetrios seemed to think the majority would welcome the Turks, given our current engagement with the Pope in Ferrara.'

One of the court's senior administrators cleared his throat. 'The move for union is not universally popular, lord, for sure, but I think we need not fear popular unrest. The sacking of the city by crusaders will ever sit badly with the people, but the memory of the Turks' own attempt to do the same just sixteen years ago is considerably fresher. The tidings that a Turkish army is on the approach will, I am certain, galvanise the people into defending their land.'

Constantine nodded. 'That last time, I was impressed with how every soul in the city seemed to lend whatever hand they could to the city's defence. Should Murad come with his army, it will take that same strength of body, and of will, to stand against them.'

'That and a miracle,' Gabriel said, then flinched. He'd not meant to say it aloud, but the room went silent, and every pair of eyes turned to him, some turning away again at the sight – those who did not know him.

'It seems I omitted an advisor from my council,' the prince said, his face betraying nothing. 'Go on, master Catalan.'

Gabriel shivered. He didn't like addressing groups, especially of men like this. 'I was simply thinking back, my prince, to the last time. The city fought valiantly, without doubt, yet it is my opinion that it would still not have been enough. The city would still have fallen had it not been for the miraculous appearance of the Theotokos on the walls.'

'My mother, you mean.'

'Quite, sir. In the end it was she, and the Mother of God she was mistaken for, who broke their spirit and ended the siege, not force of arms.'

'Then we are very lucky she still walks the walls on occasion, eh, Gabriel?' He smiled. 'But I take your point. If the city is to defend itself, it cannot rely upon the paltry handful of men we had last time. We need an army of sufficient strength to hold the walls for a full season or more. If Murad does come, we need to protect Constantinople until the emperor has concluded his negotiations and the Catholic nations have agreed to come to our aid. I fear it is time to start increasing our military readiness regardless of the sultan's current intentions, for if we do deal with the Pope, Murad will be most put out. Perhaps even put out enough to nullify all our agreements.'

'Maintaining a standing army is expensive, lord,' one of the councillors said, 'and the city cannot bear much more in the way of taxation.'

'We have always worked on a promissory system with most of the nations who supply mercenaries. Our standing with them is good, for we always pay up.'

'Because after the fact, half of them are dead, so they come half price,' Sphrantzes noted with his usual dry humour.

'We will offer generous financial terms to all our allies, on the basis of repayment once the emperor returns and negotiations are concluded. That way, the Pope and his rich Italian cronies can pay for it.'

This raised smiles and a few laughs, which soon died away. The very real threat of a Turkish assault was not a laughing matter, after all.

'And George?'

'Lord?'

'Send out three letters. Two to Thomas and Theodore, commanding them to have their armies ready for war, and to move them to their main port cities ready for embarkation at short notice.'

'They're going to love that,' Sphrantzes noted. 'They may even refuse.'

'I don't think so. They might be angry, but my command right now carries the authority of the emperor. Neither of them would defy that. The third letter I want you to deliver to the Venetian ambassador, asking to contract ships for the ferrying of armies from the Morea. Oh, and send a fast courier boat to Ferrara, with one of our best ambassadors, to see my brother and help him persuade the Pope to send warships and men to our aid, ahead of any agreement.'

One of the military minds frowned. 'It is possible, lord, that even if the sultan has no designs on the city, when he gets word of our military build-up, he will start to have them.'

'And it is also a worrying possibility,' another general added, 'that stripping the Morea of its men will simply lead to its invasion by its various hostile neighbours.'

'Both valid concerns.' Constantine nodded. 'But George here has ample experience downplaying our moves with the sultan, and manufacturing very plausible excuses. We have to be prepared, and if he does not come, I am content that we can keep him sweet. As for the Morea, the armies will remain there until we are sure they are needed. At that point, the Morea's safety is our lesser concern in favour of the city itself. Logic dictates this.'

He leaned back and yawned. 'I do believe that's all we need for now. With luck, our agents in Edirne and the scouts in the region will swiftly supply us with confirmation of Murad's plans one way or the other. Thank you, gentlemen.'

With that, Constantine rose, received the bows and praise of the crowd, and left the room, Gabriel and the Ianitzaroi gathering around him. They left the Danubios palace and strolled out through the warm evening air into the massive courtyard with its playful burbling fountain, colourful flower beds and neatly manicured lawns, and followed the portico around the edge, heading for the Bertha palace ahead.

'Will the Turks come?' the prince said suddenly, quietly.

Gabriel looked about, but there were only he and the five other Ianitzaroi, so he shrugged with the assumption Constantine was talking to him.

'I cannot be sure, of course, but I don't think so. Not yet.'

'Not yet?'

'At the moment the sultan has troublesome neighbours to the north, but as you noted earlier, they are constantly in flux. All it will take is for those conflicts to resolve sufficiently to be ignored, and Murad would then be at liberty to start wars elsewhere. I do not think he will turn on us while he still has such an advantage over the empire and can be content that Rome is a vassal state in all but name. That may change, depending upon the results of the emperor's council with the Pope. To see the empire allied with the Catholic states will be troubling to him. It will set off a major alarm.'

Constantine nodded. 'It will take us four months, perhaps five, to pull all our forces together into place, so we will have to pray he does not move before then. It would take anything from ten days upwards for that army at Edirne to reach us, and if he has heavy cannon, longer than that. If he manages to neutralise our scouts and spies, we might not get warning until he is over halfway. Timing could be tight if he *does* decide to move.'

Gabriel frowned. Something was nagging at him – an itch in the back of his mind. Something Constantine had just said. He ran back over the points of the conversation, and found nothing, until he recalled walking along the portico before the conversation began.

Five men.

He turned, his hand going to the hilt of his sword, eyes darting from face to face. In the council chamber there had been four, and *he'd* only *assigned* four. His gaze was just alighting on an unfamiliar face wearing armour very similar to the others, when the man realised he'd been discovered, and started to run.

'Stay with the prince,' Gabriel shouted at his men, as he sped off after the stranger. The man had a slight head start, and was fast. Lithe and fit, he raced through the ornate archway in the portico side and out of the courtyard, alongside the south wall of the Bertha palace.

Gabriel could feel his heart pounding, hear the blood pumping in his ears. He was a fit man, strong and with good stamina, and even fast, when it came to a fight. But he would never be a runner. He just didn't have that kind of frame. That was why he knew he was going to lose the man. The stranger was fast. The Bertha palace was a massive building, and this northern elevation a high affair, the walkway framed on the far side by the thirty-foot drop of one of the three terraces in the palace, and Gabriel made sure not to come too close, in case of a slip.

He was going to lose the stranger. The moment the man got round the corner, he would be among the next set of gardens and the bathhouse, with plenty of places to hide or slip through. And despite the fact that he was, in theory, trapped within the confines of the Blachernae palace complex, the Blachernae was immense, with a hundred or more places a man could hide out for a day and a night. Moreover, he had somehow got into the palace, so it seemed ridiculous to assume he could not also get out.

Then fate intervened. It so happened that a pair of the palace guards strolled around the far corner of the Bertha, chatting quietly, then stopped in surprise as they saw two men running their way, both armed and armoured.

'Stop him,' Gabriel bellowed, pointing at the man he chased. The two guards drew their swords, and the running man skidded to a halt on the terrace. His head snapped this way and that. He was caught. The unscalable wall of the Bertha palace to one side and a vertical drop to another flagged walkway on the other, two guards ahead and the commander of the Ianitzaroi behind. He looked around, desperately, but there was no way out.

'This doesn't have to hurt,' Gabriel said, slowing, drawing his sword, but holding up the other hand, palm out. 'We just need to ask a few questions.'

But the man was not going to be fooled by such words. For a moment he hefted his own sword, looking this way and that, but clearly decided fighting his way out was unlikely. Then he ran. Gabriel started to move again as the man jogged over to the Bertha wall, then turned and ran for the terrace. Despite being older and slower, Gabriel almost caught him. In fact, the fingers of his free hand brushed the tip of the man's elbow just as he sailed out into the open air. He fell without a word, and there came a dull thud moments later.

Gabriel arrived at the edge at the same time as the two guards, looking down. He half expected the man to have made some miraculous acrobat's landing and then run on along the second terrace and to freedom. But no. Somehow the man had twisted as he fell. Judging by the state of his arms, he'd gone head first and in desperation put out his hands at the last moment. It hadn't saved him. All it had done was shatter both arms all the way up and then smash his head open like an overripe cantaloupe.

'One thing's for certain.' He sighed. 'He's not going to answer any questions now.'

Constantine and the others caught up with him a few moments later. 'You got him?'

'Sort of. He thought he could save himself, but it turns out he's not as good a diver as he was a runner. Stay here,' he added, then pointed at his men. 'Keep him safe.'

With that Gabriel ran past the palace, and past whence the guards had come, then past the baths and towards the city walls at the western edge of the complex. There, he reached the wide stairway that led down to the next terrace, and followed it. Off to the north, he could see the Golden Horn twinkling in the moonlight. His attention, though, was on the shape on the ground. He jogged over. Despite its broken state, he had the horrible feeling that if he wasn't fast, it might get up and walk away, or some accomplice might appear and steal it away.

No one did, and it did not move. Reaching it, he turned the body over with the toe of his boot and looked it up and down. He crouched for a better examination.

'Anything useful?' the prince called from the terrace above.

Gabriel shook his head and looked up. 'He looks quite miscellaneous. Not a Turk, I don't think, but not Italian either. Maybe from the local area, or as far afield as Serbia or Hungary. Maybe even the Morea, but I'd bet against it. His sword is too ordinary to give anything away. The dagger he has, again, I might say was Serbian or Hungarian.' He rifled through the man's purse. 'Not much money, most of it imperial, alongside a few Turkish and Greek coins. The man could be from almost anywhere. Nothing incriminating on him…'

He paused, and lifted the man's hand. The ring on his finger looked familiar.

'Assassin?' the prince called.

Gabriel pursed his lips. 'Could be,' he replied, still trying to place the ring. 'He must have been waiting outside the Danubios in the dark and slipped in among us as we walked away. I noticed quite by accident that instead of six of us there were suddenly seven. Could be that I made him before he drew his sword.'

He rose from the body and rolled his shoulders. 'Or a spy. Seems convenient that he was prepared to take his chance just after an important meeting, rather than when you were less protected. He might have been supposed to walk with us until he'd heard something useful, then slip away again. Makes me wonder how many times he's done just that in the city without being caught. How many times has he sent useful information back to his master before now?'

'And we will never know who his master is.'

The ring. Where had he seen it before? It struck him in a single image, of a dark chamber. Was it the one he'd taken from the German imposter at Patras? Yes, it was very reminiscent of that, though he could not say for certain. If it was, then it hinted very solidly at Torno's involvement, and certainly it would not be the Epirot's first attempt at subterfuge and wiles. He contemplated telling Constantine, but kept his peace. He could not be sure, and certainly couldn't prove it, and would telling the prince change anything?

'Quite,' he answered with a sigh. 'Given that this is Constantinople, I wouldn't even limit the list to enemies. In my service to your father, half a dozen times spies were caught who were working for other nobles or members of the imperial house. Besides, it would be a lot easier for a man with a legitimate reason to be here to achieve such closeness than a man sent by an enemy far away.'

'Demetrios?' The prince sighed.

'As good a guess as any. Or maybe Theodore. Or any number of nobles who aren't your relations, but could find swift advancement with the right information. Of course, we cannot *rule out* foreign agents. Karaca Pasha, I think, owes you enough for something like this. And God alone knows Torno is not above such activity.'

'I wonder if it might be time for an overhaul of our security arrangements?'

'Perhaps, though I doubt it will stop things like this happening.' Gabriel punched his fist into his palm in irritation.

'It just occurred to me that I shouldn't have shouted the alarm. I should have kept going. I could have had him followed, and we could even have started feeding him misinformation. Sadly that ship has now sailed... out over a cliff, in fact.'

'Come on back up, Gabriel. I think we should sit and drink wine while I pen a letter to my brother the emperor.'

Constantinople

Eighteen months later: 1 February 1440

'Our city seems prepared for war, dear brother?'

Constantine bowed his head to the emperor. 'As close as possible, yes. It has been a somewhat nervous time in your absence. For months we feared that Murad was coming for us with his army, given the build-up of forces facing us at Edirne and the knowledge that the sultan was not going to be pleased at our overtures to the Pope. When news came that his army had actually moved on Serbia to take Semendria, and was in the end nothing to do with us, we all heaved a sigh of relief. In the aftermath of that tense time, George and I decided that if war with the Turks is likely enough that we fear it just in watching an army build, then perhaps it was time to do the same.'

'You are aware we cannot afford a full standing army, Constantine. Otherwise we'd have already had one for some time.'

'I am aware, John, that you have been swanning around Italy courting lords with so much wealth they veritably drip gold. Once upon a time *we* were Rome, and the world trembled at our name. Now we are the desperate scions of that empire, and we tremble in turn at a new Rome. But since all seems to have gone well, I will propose that part of the help these Italian lords offer us could be financial aid in keeping our city defended? Perhaps the new Rome can help the old Rome in becoming the bulwark of the East once again.'

John sagged back in the chair. 'You seem to think everything is so easy and cut and dried, but this is like marriage negotiations, Constantine. Both sides want to gain as much as possible while giving away as little as they can. How do you think the Italians *became* that people who drip with gold?'

'Are you saying it was not a success?'

'It was a *qualified* success, I would say. Yes, we have agreed terms with all appropriate parties that will see the two Churches unified, but I had to give rather more concessions than I hoped to make it happen, and the powers of Italy are edgy about committing too much to our support until we have shown them our willingness to abide by the new agreement.'

'Our willingness to be their servants, you mean?' spat Demetrios from the corner. 'To bow and scrape before the lowliest of their Popish priests, to put away a thousand years of the true Church's glory in a dark cupboard and replace them with Latin rites?'

'You exaggerate.'

'Hardly. I was *there*, brother. I heard it all – how we will become a poor cousin of the Romish Church, how we must be willing to let their rites walk all over ours, how the Patriarch will have no more power than one of the Pope's cardinals. I warned you what they would want, and we've agreed to it, regardless.'

With a sigh, John turned back to Constantine. 'Demetrios emphasises the most negative points, but he is correct in one thing – we may have bent our back too much, and the load will be heavy. The people of this city and the wider empire already distrust the Catholics, and when they hear what will be required to bring the Churches into alignment, there will be trouble all over. We need to counter that from the very beginning in every way we can. The Patriarch remains in Italy for now with his entourage, fine-tuning the details of the agreement, but we need the most respected men of the Church across this whole city to begin preaching the sense and right of this new union – men the people will listen to and will follow.'

'There are few such men who will do so, lord.' Sphrantzes sighed from where he sat. 'Odd ones, perhaps, but many of the more senior clerics will refuse to do such a thing. In fact, I think you will find they will be harder to placate than the ordinary citizens. I suspect we will find it far more difficult to implement this union in Constantinople than it was to agree it in the first place in Italy.'

'At least that will not concern *us* for a while, eh, George?' Constantine said, and a smile broke out finally, across his usually so-serious face.

The emperor frowned. 'Oh? And why is that?'

'Well, I presume that with your return, my regency is at an end, and I am free to devote some time to other things?'

'Yes, I no longer need you as regent, but I have tasks for you yet, brother.'

'Perhaps you would let them wait for a while? George here has found me a bride, and one he *approves* of. It's taken some time, for it seems few women meet his approval criteria.'

John grinned at Sphrantzes, who rolled his eyes. 'I myself have married within this time, Constantine, and I have far fewer criteria for my own spouse than I have for yours. *I* can marry for love and have no concerns beyond that. *You* are a prince of the Palaiologoi, and so there is more at stake for you.'

'Listen to your friend.' The emperor smiled at Constantine. 'He talks much sense. Who is this woman who will soon be my sister-in-law, George?'

'She is Aikaterine Gattilusio, my emperor,' Sphrantzes said, 'daughter of the lord of Mytilene.'

'Of this woman I have heard, Constantine. Genoese, yes? Her mother fought back a Turkish raid with sword in hand, an impressive woman. Aikaterine is said to be a marvel. Be very careful with her, for our family has poor luck with brides.'

Gabriel's gaze darted to Demetrios in time to see his lip curl. It was true. The emperor himself was on his third wife, still without issue, and the other brothers – Constantine, Theodore and Demetrios – had all lost their spouses, the latter only mere months before, while he was still in Italy.

'Unfortunately,' the emperor went on, 'I cannot spare you to run off on romantic liaisons at the moment, Constantine, even for legendary warrior women. Perhaps as the months pass there will be an opportunity, but for now the Sublime Porte reels from our alliance with Rome, and there will be a great deal of work to do to prevent the Turks taking sufficient exception to annihilate us before the Italians send any real help. And with the act of union passing, the city will be troubled and will need every steady hand on the tiller until the worst passes. And while I am hale and hearty, it is never a bad thing to have a ready successor to hand. So no, I am afraid you cannot go off paddling on the beaches of Lesbos with your new love. Send George to secure everything ready, and you can go when you can be spared.'

Constantine shot a look at his friend, and Sphrantzes gave him an encouraging nod.

'Very well, John, I will do whatever you ask.'

'As will I,' muttered Demetrios, though the look on his face might have suggested otherwise.

'Good. Then let us all sit down and discuss what is to be done. Father always said that what the empire needs these days is less of an emperor and more of an administrator. I'm sure between the three of us we can adequately fill that role.'

'Then I suspect I will be best served leaving you to it, while I plan a trip to Lesbos.' Sphrantzes smiled, rising and bowing to the brothers each in turn. The emperor dismissed him with a friendly nod and a brief gesture, then beckoned to the other two princes before marching over to a table already filled with documents and maps. Gabriel remained standing by the door, looking at the emperor's own chief bodyguard, who was standing with a professionally blank expression at the far end of the room. It took a moment for Constantine to notice his guard, and then dismiss him with a gesture.

'Go and find something to keep yourself busy, Gabriel. I shall come to no harm here.'

That, the Ianitzaroi suspected, was not guaranteed. Demetrios might be every bit as much a threat as the Turks or the Italians. Still, with the emperor's guard in the vicinity there was little danger for now, and he had been dismissed by Constantine. Gabriel nodded and turned, leaving the room. On the way through the palace, he found Gaspar and Manuel sitting and playing dice, and waved at them. 'Unless you're tied to the chair, I'm buying the drinks.'

True to form, Manuel was upright before Gabriel had drawn another breath, and Gaspar close behind, putting away his lucky dice. They left the building and made their way through the Blachernae grounds and out into the streets of Constantinople, enjoying the crisp, cool February air after the cloying atmosphere of the palace itself. All around the city, the evidence of the triumphal return of the emperor was to be seen. Bunting and garlands adorned buildings, flowers in evidence everywhere, including petals blowing around the street itself, petals that had been cast as a carpet for the emperor to ride across as he'd re-entered the city in glory that afternoon.

There were ports in the city itself, of course, both on the Propontine coast and in the Golden Horn inlet, and the emperor and his entourage could have landed there and made a short trip back to the palace. But instead it was at the harbour of the Hebdomon, outside the city walls, that the imperial party had disembarked. The triumphal route of ancient emperors passed through the Golden Gate on the Via Egnatia, along the Mese, through every forum in the city, and ended at the *milion*, near the circus and outside the ancient imperial palace and the Hagia Sophia. Of course, the great palace of the original Constantine was little more than a ruin with some overgrown gardens these days, and the circus had not seen a chariot in an age of Methuselah, the emperors these days favouring the Blachernae palace out by the northern walls. There had not been a triumphal procession in many years, but Demetrios had been in contact by courier and arranged the arrival with Constantine, and had then taken a swift ship home ahead of his brother to plan it all. The triumphal John VIII had entered the city like a Roman emperor of old, through the great Golden Gate, and followed along the mese to the old centre. There, however, it had turned, and taken the other mese road that brought them back across the length of the city once more, and to the region of the Blachernae. As such, most of the city had seen the emperor's journey, and had a chance to throw petals and marvel.

The bunting now hung limp, the garlands fading, the petals scooped up in swirls by the wind, and the crowds of cheering citizens gone about their business. The emperor was in his palace once more, planning, and the city was rapidly returning to normal.

'Almost like it never happened, eh?' Gaspar grumbled as he kicked a beer jug out of his path, to roll into an alleyway.

'Few things make me want to drink too much, more than watching this city lose heart, you know? Years of worry and fear, and they almost break the treasury on a grand celebration of imperial success, but mere hours after its passing, Constantinople is back to being a self-involved, angry, fearful and despairing place.'

Gaspar frowned. 'I don't know about *despairing*, boss?'

'Can you not feel the air around us? Feels like resentment and abandonment. Like a building that was burned and then left for decades to slowly collapse. Makes me want to shiver, that feeling.'

'That's because you're not wearing beer armour.'

Gabriel made a strange squawking noise as his giant ourghos grabbed him and turned him, propelling the commander towards a doorway. The 'House of Golden Pillars' was one of few places Gabriel felt truly calm. There were half a dozen taverns around the city that habitually catered for soldiers, but only this one, nearest the palace, was used to seeing the marred face of the Ianitzaroi commander walk in through the door, and he was a regular enough visitor that it was rare for even a customer to gasp when looking at him.

'Gabe, darlin', what can I get ya?' Maria called as she laid eyes upon him. 'Wine? Chian?'

'Beer, Maria, and keep it coming until I can see sprites and faeries wherever I look.'

'You've got it, darlin'.'

She chuckled, and turned her impressive bosom to the beer casks behind her as Gabriel and his two senior men played 'sword, shield, horse' to see who would go to wait at the bar for the drinks. Having lost, as usual, Gabriel strode across to the far end of the establishment while Manuel and Gaspar secured a table by the simple expedient of standing uncomfortably close to some regular soldiers and glaring at them until they eventually rose and left.

Smiling at his friends, Gabriel turned and waited as Maria located three glasses that came passably close to being see-through, and began to fill them from the cask. His attention wandered as he waited, and, at raised voices, alighted upon two men standing at the far end of the bar.

'Don't you remember the siege?' one snapped angrily. 'The fucking Turks were hitting us with cannon and arrows and swords and fire and everything they could. That Murad bastard would burn the city to the ground just to own the ashes.'

'You're drunk, Valens. When the Turks came last time, I seem to remember you hiding in the shitter most of the time.'

'The Turks will burn and peel us all, Michael, you shit.'

'No, Valens, they won't. We've been allies now for twenty years, and they've never turned on us in all that time. They hold to their word, which is more than the fucking Catholics will. Show me a popish priest and I'll show you a treacherous prick in a pointy hat. At least with the Turks we know where we stand. I would open the Golden Gate and throw rose petals for

Murad himself if it meant keeping Rome's cardinals out of the city.'

Gabriel slid along the bar towards the pair, his eyes picking out the knives strapped to their belts. Off-duty soldiers? In here, that was most likely, but whoever they were, they were drunk and angry. As he moved, other patrons were noticing the raised voices and moved away from the bar. Even Maria stopped pouring beer for a moment, waiting.

'You can take your fucking sultan and stick him up your well-abused arse, Michael.'

The first knife came out.

'And you can piss off to Rome and suck your Pope's cock, because no one here is going to bow to the bastard.'

Gabriel was close now. Perhaps he shouldn't interfere? After all, this would be far from an isolated incident. Little arguments like this had been cropping up across the city ever since the emperor left for Italy, and they'd only got worse and more frequent in recent days. Stopping one such drunken fight was like trying to plug a colander with a pin.

'Fucking emperor and his fucking Romish alliances,' the drunken soldier spat, and the knife came up, glinting in the lamplight. The man was inebriated, and angry, but not yet quite enough so to start something he wasn't certain about, and the knife wavered, not quite threatening.

'If you don't put that away,' Gabriel said quietly but firmly from a few paces along the bar, 'I might have to find a new sheath for it, if you get my drift.'

'You another Turk lover are you?' the man snarled, and then focused on Gabriel finally, and blanched at what he saw. The knife drooped a little.

'Good lad. No one needs to fight in here. Whether you're pro-union or not, everyone in here's a citizen of the empire and a follower of the Patriarch, eh? Plenty of enemies to fight out there without turning on our own.'

'*You* don't sound like a native,' the other drunken man said, turning to Gabriel and recoiling even as his hand went to his own knife.

'Served the emperors all my working life and seen off plenty of sieges, my friend, both by Turks and Italians. Now why don't you two forget your little spat and go your separate ways. I'll even buy you a drink each.'

'Thanks,' slurred the one called Michael, 'but my appetite's spoiled now thanks to this Pope-loving fuck.'

Just as things had almost defused, the argument exploded, and, before Gabriel could even respond, the one called Valens slashed out with his knife. The blade drew a jagged red line across Michael's forearm, where he leaned on the bar, and the injured drunk roared with a mix of pain and fury. The wounded arm came round sharply, gripping a heavy wooden tankard, and slammed it into Valens' face. The knife-wielder was sent spinning, and Gabriel had the momentary hope that the blow had ended the fight, but he was wrong.

As he reached across and grabbed the mug-wielding arm, gripping it tight, he watched the other fighter, drunk, pained, and now a little dazed, stagger into a big Bulgar mercenary, whose drink tipped, spilling all over another man. In the space of a heartbeat, the bar erupted into a full-blown melee. Gabriel snarled, his noble attempt at keeping the peace so swiftly thrown aside, and in irritation he reached out and grasped the head of the man whose arm he was gripping, slamming it down against the bar with a deep wooden clonk. The body went limp in his hands and he let the brawler fall in a heap.

He turned and looked about. The brawl had spread to cover most of the clientele already, and he leaned sharply backwards as a bottle came from nowhere and whipped past his nose to shatter on the far wall. Two small puddles of calm seemed to exist amid the chaos. Over to the right, half a dozen soldiers sat still fully armed and armoured, having clearly just come off duty, and no one had yet had the guts to make a move on them, for six sober and tired men with sharp blades might be a dangerous proposition. The other small world of quiet was a table not far from the door, where Gaspar and Manuel sat, feet up, waiting. As Gabriel's gaze reached them, Manuel mimed drinking and then pointed at the bar.

With a snorted laugh, Gabriel turned back amid the chaos, to discover that Maria had clearly seen the motion too, and was pouring the beer. She passed the three mugs over and sighed. 'I'll run a tab and you can settle up later, if the place is still standing. Shout when you need me, I'll be staying out of the way in the back room.'

Gabriel nodded his thanks, gathered up the three glasses in a delicate juggling act, and then turned, trying to identify a safe path through the chaos. For a good minute, he weaved among the combatants as they merrily battered one another, until he reached his friends. Just as he arrived, a half-conscious man with a broken nose slammed backwards across the table, where Manuel and Gaspar simply put their feet out and pushed him away until he slid back off the board and onto the floor. Gabriel put the glasses down in a rare spot that wasn't already covered in spilt beer or smears of blood, and then sidled around another fight before sinking into a third chair beside the others. The three of them grasped their glasses and lifted, drinking slowly, appreciating the flavour as they watched the world around them devolve into a private and petty war.

'This is going to happen a lot in the coming months,' Gabriel noted sourly.

'As long as it stays as bar brawls and doesn't turn into a mob,' Gaspar replied. 'This city riots all too easily.'

'True enough.'

A figure lurched backwards towards their table from a heavy punch to the jaw, turned, ready to lay a blow on the person behind him, then focused on his would-be victim. Gaspar gave him a nasty smile, pushing away his glass with his stump of a left arm as he bunched his right hand into a fist the size of a cannonball. Muscles in his arm moved around like flotsam in a current. The lurching man wisely decided Gaspar might not be an enemy after all, and stepped away. The ourghos retrieved his drink.

'The emperor is going to have to do something,' Gaspar sighed. 'As it stands, the city is not going to accept papal control, even if the Patriarch is nominally still the head of our Church. I've listened in the streets. No one is prepared for it.'

'If they don't,' Gabriel replied, 'then the alliance with Rome will fail, and we'll lose their support. The people cannot see the danger. They do not stand and look down the barrel of the Turkish gun, and it has been near twenty years since Murad last came for us. A whole generation of imperial citizens doesn't remember having to fight off the Turks from our very walls. They see an enemy in the West, who burned our city four centuries ago, but don't see one in the sultan who tried to do the same only yesterday.'

Manuel sucked down a mouthful of beer and frowned. 'I dunno. I think the Pope's like a poor whore.'

This had Gaspar and Gabriel both turn to him with arched eyebrows.

'This I want to hear. Go on.'

'Well, a poor whore really needs the money, so she'll do just about anything even for the promise of a few coppers. A well-off whore wants to see the money up front.'

'You've lost me,' Gaspar said, grabbing a passing combatant with his good arm, letting him go, slapping him hard, and sending him flying away again.

'Well, the Pope wants to control the imperial Church. He's a poor whore. He'll do what the emperor wants, just on the understanding that it will happen. He doesn't need to see the effects of union up front, just to know that it will happen.'

'God in Heaven,' Gaspar hissed. 'Insight from Manuel. Who'd have thought it?'

Gabriel nodded. 'He might be right, in his weird way. The people will probably never truly accept the union, but as long as it's officially in place, perhaps the Pope will help us anyway. As long as the troubles can be kept on a small scale.' He turned to Manuel. 'A pearl of wisdom there, my friend.'

The banner-man shrugged as he used a boot to push away a pair of fighters. 'What can I say? I spend a lot of time with poor whores.'

They laughed, and there they stayed for the night, drinking and watching the fights, praying that it did not bode ill for the city in general.

One year later: 16 April 1441

'Our family should take lessons from you, George.' Constantine grinned as he slapped Sphrantzes on the back, the nobleman's ostentatious gold accoutrements, worn for the occasion, jingling in response.

'Oh?'

'Seven wives between the five of us,' the prince chuckled, 'and of all those marriages, only two daughters to show for it? Whereas you, George? You've been married three years with two sons and a daughter to bounce upon your knee. And I don't know where you found the time, since you've spent half that time abroad and most of the rest with me. You must never sleep.'

Gabriel grinned as he walked behind the pair, out of the church's narthex and into the sunny courtyard.

'Just a few short months, my friend.' Sphrantzes laughed. 'July, I reckon, and we'll head to Mytilene and get you married. Aikaterine can't wait, believe me.'

'That is only if things are settled here,' the prince replied, his expression darkening.

That was a sobering thought. The brawl Gabriel and his companions had sat through that night in the bar near the palace had been but one of a rash of such conflicts that had broken out, and things had only become worse. As the imperial

157

brothers had attempted to bring the more leading lights of the Church on side, all they had met was increased resistance from the Orthodox clergy, refusing to preach union to an already restive flock. Though the fights had begun to tail off after a while, the city had settled into a sort of sullen denial. The union of the Churches was no closer to acceptance in Constantinople than it had ever been, despite the agreements made in Ferrara, and given that failure and refusal, the assistance the West was proffering in return had never been further away.

John had finally, these past few days, made the decision that he would have to leave the matter of the union in the hands of the few churchmen and philosophers who accepted it, and move on to deal with various other problems that had arisen. As such, Constantine was going to be freed to travel and marry before returning to the Morea, where Turahan Bey kept finding loopholes in agreements to move the border of his Sanjak of Tırhala gradually further into imperial-controlled Athens. Similarly, Demetrios had been sent to rule Mesembria as despot, guarding Constantinople's northern approach from the neighbouring Turkish provinces. There had been no suggestion of conflict from the Sublime Porte, but everyone knew how the sultan would be viewing the Church union and where that might lead.

There was no doubt that Demetrios was pleased to leave. He had despised every moment of trying to make the act of union work in the city, given that he was personally more set against it than almost anyone, and he had used a number of unkind words about his brothers as he left to take up his appointment.

'I hear that Demetrios is remarrying,' Sphrantzes said, as though plucking the subject of the absent brother straight from Gabriel's thoughts.

'Yes,' the prince replied. 'Indeed, even though he and I are hardly the most convivial of companions, I received an invitation to attend the wedding.'

'Surprising, but perhaps welcome, all things considered. When do you go?'

Constantine shrugged. 'I don't. I've missed it. It's today, up in Mesembria.'

Sphrantzes stopped sharply. 'What? Why aren't you there? He might see this as a snub, and your relationship won't take too many more knocks.'

The prince replied with an easy smile. 'I received two invitations for the same day – Demetrios' wedding, and your daughter's baptism. I could hardly turn you down when I am her godfather, could I? Besides, you are one of my oldest friends, while Demetrios and I are only linked by sour blood.'

'I do appreciate it,' Sphrantzes sighed, 'but if you had warned me, I would have changed the date. I do hope that this does not widen your rift much further.'

'Must you two talk about politics even on such a day as this?' Helene, Sphratzes' wife, scolded the pair as she came alongside them, her nurse following on bearing the new baby girl, ahead of the servant pushing the two boys along in a small carriage. She deliberately did not register Gabriel, which was something he was plenty used to. Indeed, he had kept safely hidden at the back in the church so that his marred face did not cause a stir during the ceremony.

'I am truly sorry, Helene –' the prince smiled – 'and I am equally sorry that I shall have to take your husband away again soon. I will need his company at my forthcoming marriage, and then undoubtedly his diplomatic talents in dealing with the Morea and the Turks. He may be away for some months.' He turned a mischievous look on Sphrantzes. 'So you'd best get started on the next baby swiftly, eh, George?'

5

Consolidation

Mytilene, island of Lesbos

21 August 1441

It had been a strange and uncomfortable summer.

Gabriel glanced across at Constantine and his new wife, trying not to look as though he was paying particular attention, though he doubted anyone would notice anyway, with him sitting in the shade of a large chestnut tree. That the prince kept looking away from Aikaterine seemed to have escaped everyone's notice, including Constantine himself.

As predicted, it had been July by the time they left the city, and Gabriel had noticed a change in the prince the moment the ship departed. As long as he had been in Constantinople, dealing with the problem of the church union, with potential Turkish aggression, with Demetrios' constant barbs and arguments, and with all the other issues the city experienced, Constantine had been able to shelve thoughts of what was to come. None of them had realised he was doing that until he no longer was, and even then it seemed to be only Gabriel who had noticed.

Once they'd set sail, and there was nothing else to concern Constantine other than his forthcoming nuptials, his offhand levity on the subject slowly faded, to be replaced by a pensive and uncertain air. Oh, he masked it well, laughing and smiling with everything but his eyes, but Gabriel could see it, perhaps precisely because Gabriel had never experienced anything like love or companionship, and never would. It gave him an almost uniquely objective viewpoint.

Still, he had kept his peace, and they had reached Lesbos in late July, being met at the port in Mytilene by the entourage of Dorino Gattilusio, Lord of Lesbos. It had been a great state occasion, and though Gabriel and his Ianitzaroi had been armed and present, he'd not had them ready for any real trouble. It was to be a happy occasion, after all.

Gattilusio was an impressive man, and Gabriel formed an instantly positive opinion of him. Tall and broad, his colouring said that though he might be Genoese by blood, he was a born and bred son of the East, and his Greek was that of a native. He had an easy and welcoming way, but there was ever that something about him that told Gabriel the Lord of Lesbos was a man of the sword, and would never shrink from drawing it if required. Indeed, the man had earned renown in the Genoese–Venetian war, and was even now already at odds with other nations for having married his daughter to the exiled despot of Trebizond.

Everything had been good-natured and pleasant as they were led from the harbour through the ancient streets of the town, the populace cheering their arrival from a safe distance, held back by Gattilusio's men. They had climbed the slopes of the low hill on the headland to the castle that was the Lord of Lesbos's home, and there Gabriel had realised just how powerful Gattilusio must be, for the place was an immense fortification with powerful walls, well guarded and strategically sited. The army of Lesbos was strong and numerous, with the ratio of military to square mile vastly greater than the empire. Sphrantzes had taken into account not only the lady herself and the dowry that would come with her, but also the advantages of marrying into a powerful lordship with a history of successful warfare and strong allies.

They had passed through the lower fortress and into the upper one – if anything, even more defensive – and there they had finally met Aikaterine Gattilusio, standing beside her mother and surrounded by their servants and guards. The mother was, if anything, even more impressive than her husband. She was strikingly handsome and elegant, and one might easily mistake her for a fainting lady of the court, yet the moment Gabriel had set eyes on her, he knew her for a warrior to match her husband. Even if he had not caught the steel in her eyes, he noted the sword-wound scar on her forearm that had almost been successfully hidden by the sleeve, but not quite.

Then there was Aikaterine herself. She was a younger echo of her mother. There was no sign of the warrior about her, probably because there had never yet been a call for it, but Gabriel was certain that should the time come, she would be just as at home with sword in hand as her parents.

And if there was any doubt as to her mind and wit, it evaporated the moment she opened her mouth.

'Ah, you're that one,' she said, without a sign of an opening greeting. 'Thanks be to God, eh, Mother?'

Constantine had frowned in puzzlement. 'I beg your pardon?'

As her mother gave an odd smile, Aikaterine chuckled. 'We visited your great city a few years ago, and I saw a painting on the wall of all six of you with your father, though I suspect it was already quite old, as Thomas was little more than a toddler. The day George Sphrantzes first came to put your suit to Father, I prayed so hard to the Lord Almighty that you weren't the one who looked like a sick duck.'

Gabriel had almost exploded, then, stifling his laughter and disguising it with a cough, as Constantine frowned. 'Duck?'

'Theodore,' Sphrantzes said, with a wicked smile. 'Tell me you can't see it.'

Constantine blinked. 'Good God, yes. How peculiar.'

They had been invited into the great keep at the highest point of the castle, which was well appointed and stately, and they had all been given their own rooms – the noblemen, at least. The Ianitzaroi were barracked in a good building in the upper castle, just a couple of men at a time on duty, though Gabriel was given his own chamber close to that of Constantine.

Gabriel, having been aware of the prince's strangely disconnected sense throughout the journey, watched the introductions and the first few days intently, wondering whether meeting the glorious lady of Mytilene in person might change him.

It didn't.

Constantine was polite, generous, smiled and laughed at all the right times, even joked and talked of the future with his intended family, and his easy manner might have fooled everyone else, including the prince himself, but it did not fool Gabriel. A soldier learned to read a man's eyes, for within them lay intent and warning, and throughout those meetings all Gabriel saw in his master's eyes was distance. Constantine's body was there, but his mind was not.

And it did not change as the days wore on with the preparations for the wedding. Gabriel forced himself to silence, though part of him felt he needed to confront his master and open up this Pandora's box. The world of both parties, both Roman and Genoese, drifted steadily towards matrimony with a woman who seemingly thought the world of her husband, yet a man who played a part while not truly recognising she was even there.

It came to a head for Gabriel the night before the wedding, when Constantine made the most appalling faux pas he could possibly have done, and only got away with it by pure chance.

The conversation around the noisy and busy table at dinner that evening turned to the relative strengths and weaknesses of Genoese, Venetian and Imperial ships. Several of those present had seen and experienced all three in use, and Constantine had at one point gestured at his betrothed and spoken the worst words possible.

'I don't know. Perhaps Theodora does?'

Gabriel had felt the floor fall away beneath him, his veins ice as he heard it. It confirmed exactly what he had suspected from the very outset. It was not that Constantine did not appreciate his betrothed. It was not that he did not love her. It was simply a case that he had still not let go of his first wife. She was in his heart and in his head, and while her memory still gripped the prince, he was unable to open himself again. It was a terrifying thought that perhaps Constantine would never again have lightness of heart.

The prince was incredibly lucky that at the very moment he almost ruined everything, the conversation became very loud and two men laughed, so that the man he was talking to completely missed the mistake, and asked Constantine to repeat it, which he did, but this time with the correct name.

The prince's gaze darted this way and that as he realised what he'd done, and as it fell upon Gabriel, who was looking at him, he flinched.

That night, most of the occupants had retreated to their chambers early, determined to be well rested before the day of the wedding arrived, but Gabriel, unable to sleep, had found himself on the battlements of the keep, looking out across the rippling waters of the Aegean, the moonlight flickering silver across miles of black. As he breathed in the heady scent of night-blooming jasmine, mixed with the salt tang of the sea, Constantine suddenly appeared next to him, leaning on the battlements.

'Only you noticed.'

'Luckily,' Gabriel replied, without turning. A bat screeched somewhere nearby, and both men were silent for a long moment in its wake. Then:

'I meant nothing by it. It was an accident. More habit than intent.'

'It was your heart, instead of your mind, using your mouth.'

A short silence.

'She is a remarkable woman,' the prince said, finally.

'She is. You should consider yourself lucky.'

'I do.'

'But you should also call it off.'

Constantine turned then, looking closely at Gabriel. 'That would be foolish. Also not possible at this point.'

'"Foolish" is labouring on in a union that is doomed from the outset, Constantine. I think we've all come to the conclusion that no matter what was agreed in Ferrara, the great city is never going to accept the union, and therefore the West is never going to come. To keep trying is wasting the time we have.'

'I thought we were talking about my marriage,' the prince said.

'We are. It was an analogy.'

'The problem, Gabriel, is not with her. It is with me. I just cannot seem to let myself accept her. I know Theodora… Maddalena… has gone, and I will never see her again. I know that I only ever knew her for a matter of months. But she had crawled inside my skin, and it seems she is still there now. I don't want it like this, but I do not know how to get rid of her.'

Gabriel sighed. He was not the person to talk to about such things. Every relationship he'd had with a woman had involved the exchange of coins, after all. But he knew a disaster approaching when he saw it.

'You should speak with your mother about that. The empress is shrewd and wise, and if anyone could help you there, it is her. But the fact remains that walking into that church tomorrow and accepting the marriage crowns from the priest is simply tying you into something you cannot deal with.'

Silence had fallen again, and when Gabriel turned a few moments later, the prince was gone.

He half expected a commotion in the morning, and Constantine to have called off the wedding. He was both surprised and a little disappointed when everything went ahead as planned.

He watched Constantine throughout the morning, and then through the great ceremony in the castle's ornate church, and once more the prince wore that mask of contentment, and not once in hours of activity did his gaze meet Gabriel's. It was not the first wedding Gabriel had attended, of course, in many years of serving the Palaiologoi and the Byzantine court, but it was certainly one of the most lavish, the rich Lord of Lesbos having spared no expense on his daughter and the prince who would be her husband. Gabriel committed to staying sober throughout the affair, allowing all but himself and the two men on duty to get drunk and enjoy the festivities. In fact, Gaspar announced that he would stay sober and allow his commander to celebrate, but Gabriel turned him down, knowing that he didn't feel particularly celebratory anyway.

The days that followed were among the most troublesome in Gabriel's life. He felt perfectly fine knee deep in entrails and bones, wading through a fearsome enemy, and quite comfortable in the sort of complete solitude that drives most men to despair, but this was something he did not know how to deal with. A perfectly fine and happy world, with the glory of a new couple, a rejoicing family and all their islanders, no direct threat, and all perfectly jovial. Except that underneath, Gabriel knew that it wasn't, and the only person he could talk to about it seemed in no great rush to speak of it again.

It was as September came about and the weather began that subtle shift that word arrived from the capital. Turahan Bey was gathering forces both across the Gulf of Lepanto from the Morea, and along the frontier with the Duchy of Athens. He continued to pick away at the borders, but there was a growing fear that worse was to come. In the Morea, Theodore simply brushed it aside, claiming it would come to nothing, and remained in Mystras with his forces, far from any danger or use. Thomas was more concerned, and closer to the action, but he was also young, inexperienced and weaker in arms. The emperor commanded Constantine to travel to the Morea with all haste to take up its defence against any potential Turkish move.

Constantine, of course, obeyed with alacrity. He explained the situation to the Lord of Lesbos, and Dorino Gattilusio, himself no novice in the world of politics and warfare, granted the prince four of his fastest ships to sail to the Morea. Constantine said a quiet farewell to Aikaterine in the halls of Mytilene that afternoon. Gabriel felt awkward standing and listening, particularly given that he had more insight into the meeting than anyone else. The prince was sailing into an uncertain situation, with the potential to turn into a desperate defence of Greek lands from an angry Turkish bey, and while they had been married mere days, Constantine could not in good conscience put the lady in such peril.

It was so perfectly reasonable. Even her father accepted it as the act of a gentleman. Only Gabriel and the prince himself knew the real reason she had been left in Mytilene as they sailed away.

'This is only an end to it if you die on a Turkish sword,' Gabriel murmured as they stood at the ship's rail, watching Lesbos fade into the distance.

'We live in uncertain times, Gabriel. I will tackle obstacles as they present themselves. Right now, that obstacle is Turahan Bey.'

'And for reference, I'd like you not to try and get yourself spitted on a Turkish blade, since you pay my wages for keeping you alive.'

And that brought the first *genuine* laugh Gabriel had heard since they'd left the capital.

Korinthos

June 1442

'It is time to rebuild the Hexamilion,' Thomas Palaiologos said, slapping his palm on the table. He leaned back, his firm gaze on his brother.

'No. Not yet,' the older man said, busily examining the map.

'Constantine, if we hope to hold the Morea and the Turks are truly coming, which they seem to be, we cannot hold the Duchy of Athens, but with the manned wall, we might keep them out of the Morea.'

Constantine took a deep breath. 'Thomas, as much of this is about politics as about warfare, and when politics is the issue, nine tenths of that is about what can be *seen* to be there, not what is *really* there.'

'I don't understand.'

'I know, dear brother. At the moment, we are still officially allied with the Turks. We are, in fact, little more than a vassal state. Though it pains me, we must be careful that everything we do aligns with what the sultan expects. With our strength as it is, and his as it is, if Murad decides we have turned on him, he could crush us with little difficulty. We had been hoping by now to have Catholic crusader steel strengthening our defences, but without the people accepting the union, that may never happen, so we are still beholden to the Turks. Years ago, just along the coast, I looked the Turkish ambassador in the eye, and I told him that we would man the border but not rebuild the wall. They had taken offence that we'd previously done so, if you remember, and demolished it. Currently we walk a very fine line with the Turks, since our overtures in Italy, and rebuilding the wall might just be the spark that ignites the powder magazine. No. We gather, and we prepare, but we do not provoke.'

'And then, when he comes – which he will?'

'I still hope to calm all tensions with politicking, Thomas. Murad is a strong and conquering sultan, but currently his steel is being brought to bear against Serbia and Wallachia, and we are considered an ally. Let the Serbs and Wallachs appeal to Italy for aid, and we will take our peace and use it. And the direct threat here, Turahan Bey, is a very reasonable man. Both George and I have spent plenty of time speaking to him. He can always be persuaded to listen to sense.'

'And yet their armies build across the region.'

Gabriel nodded quietly in the corner. Everything he saw suggested a major Turkish offensive on the rise, and this one would not trouble the Serbs or Wallachs.

'All things in time. Patience, Thomas. Play the game.'

The youngest of the Palaiologoi gave an exasperated splutter and straightened, striding from the room with a final few expletives that a noble prince should not know. The door clicked shut behind him, leaving the prince alone with Gabriel.

'I handled him wrong, and I *keep* doing that. In some ways he's right, of course, but left to his own devices, he would start a war in trying to prevent one.' Constantine turned to Gabriel. 'Do you think he knows about the plan?'

Gabriel shook his head. 'If he did, there would have been far angrier words.'

The prince nodded, then looked back down at his maps. Gabriel slumped a little. He was missing Sphrantzes. When the effusive ambassador was around, Constantine asked his old friend all the most difficult questions, and Sphrantzes usually had a sensible answer. Without him, often Constantine turned to Gabriel, whose grasp of international politics was mostly based on where to stick a sword.

'I wish George would send word,' the prince sighed.

Sphrantzes had departed in October, only weeks after their return to the Morea, and had been gone for five months without word. The plan was simple. Constantine did not trust Demetrios, but he knew him to be a good commander of men. He trusted Theodore and Thomas to preserve the empire's peace, but neither was a good commander. To put the right man in the right place, Constantine felt he needed to be appointed once more up in Mesembria, on the capital's doorstep, where he could rush to its defence when required, but which was currently in the grasp of Demetrios. If he and his brother could swap, he would be close to the capital for its defence, but also as John's heir if required, while Demetrios would take the martial role in the Morea. He would give the region the military strength it required, while Thomas and Theodore could keep him from dangerous behaviour. It was a clever idea, although it required the agreement of both Demetrios and the emperor. They had not told Thomas or Theodore, in case it caused argument.

Sphrantzes had been sent to negotiate the swap, but in five months he should have either succeeded or failed, and been back. Instead, he seemed to have vanished without trace.

'Gabriel, where do we look for support? Where do we find strength? We have retaken the Morea, and indeed, we now have the Duchy of Athens. The empire is larger than it has been in generations, but where do we go next? What do we do next?'

Gabriel sighed. 'I don't know. I'm a soldier, not a strategist. You need a general.' He jabbed his finger at the map. 'The rest of Greek lands, all the way up to Serbia and Wallachia, is now part of Turahan Bey's *sanjak*. Any attempt to annex anything more on the mainland will start a war with the Turks. So that leaves the islands. Perhaps, with your new father-in-law's support, you may be able to annex a few islands at a time, and rebuild there? Perhaps an overture to him to become part of the empire himself on Lesbos? Offer him a despotate?'

'I think he's too bright for that. He's strong, so why sell himself to a weaker neighbour. No, I shall not involve him.'

'You can fool yourself, Constantine, but not me. That has nothing to do with Dorino Gattilusio, and everything to do with his daughter. You will have to see her again, you know? She's your wife.'

'Gabriel, leave the subject alone.'

The Catalan sighed. 'All right. But there is no easy path now. Every step forward is going to be tiny and fraught with difficulties.'

'I know. I wonder if, when I get control of Mesembria, I can come to some arrangement with the sultan to divide up Wallachia? If we lend him a hand in taking it from this bloodthirsty Dracul fellow?'

'Selling out a neighbour? That's dark.'

'The Wallachs have never helped us in our struggles with the Turks, so I see no trouble in our siding with their enemy. Anyway, it's a dream and nothing more. Murad doesn't need our help and isn't in the habit of giving things away. The solution was always going to be union with Rome. Our empire used to be East and West, Constantinople and Rome. Only together do we really have the strength to hold the Cross high across Europe, but that path has ended, Gabriel. Our people will not accept it. There are some days I fear we are our own worst enemy.'

Gabriel lapsed into silence and stood as usual, glowering in the shadows, while Constantine went over all his documents again and again, always referring to the regional map, as if perhaps a short break might make things change, or help him find something he had missed. In fact, it was probably about time for the evening meal – or so Gabriel's stomach was telling him – when there came a polite knock at the door. Constantine called for entry, and the servant outside admitted a weary and travel-worn man.

'My lord, I have dispatches from Athens and beyond,' the man announced, head bowed as he slowly moved into the room.

Constantine waved at him. 'Leave them on the table and go and sort yourself out. You need rest, and a bath, for certain.'

The messenger shuffled across to the desk and placed the various sealed packets there reverently, head bowed at all times, trying not to come too close to the prince, especially with his horrifying, disfigured bodyguard standing close by. Once he was out of the door, and it closed with a click, Constantine spent some time going over his documents once again before finally turning his attention to the post. Nine missives. There had perhaps been delays and a backing up of the post.

The first he opened, read, and tossed across the table to his pile of discarded paperwork, without even blinking or saying a word. The second and third held little more interest, but the fourth earned a twitch and a grunt. 'Turahan Bey has annexed

Libadostro. Seems there is some ancient clause about it being subject to Thebes, and since the bey's banner currently flutters over Thebes, arguing the point will be difficult. Certainly not worth the trouble it would bring. Try to make sure that Thomas doesn't hear about this, or he'll be calling for a crusade to liberate the place.'

Gabriel nodded, silently, in the gloom, like some shadowy sentinel.

The fifth letter was opened with a snap.

'Better news, though not enough. Despite not being able to start rebuilding the Hexamilion yet, Thomas is correct that if they come, Athens will fall and we can't hold it. I've set what merchants and ships I can find to start bringing in supplies and stockpiling them at various positions across the isthmus. When the time does come to rebuild, I want it to be a quick and simple job. The first load of stone has arrived and is being ferried into place not far from here. A small step forward, but a welcome one.'

Once again, Gabriel acknowledged the news with just a nod, waiting, silent, shadowed, as the sixth letter was opened. He felt an odd chill run through him as he recalled his religious schooling in the palace so many years ago, with the Revelation of Saint John the Divine, and the opening of the seven seals that heralded the end of days. Despite himself, he found he was gritting his teeth.

'Another reminder from Theodore,' Constantine grumbled, 'that he is to be considered the senior despot in the region, and so any decision I make should at least be given his nod before being put into place.' He snorted, then cast that document into the brazier that burned nearby. 'Unfortunate that that one never reached us, eh?'

Seven and eight: the passing of seven allowed Gabriel to heave a sigh of relief and stop fretting over Armageddon. 'Two rather verbose appeals,' the prince said, having opened the pair and tossed them across to the pile. 'Local noblemen suggesting that in return for the peril they incur in supporting the empire against the Turks, they should receive a handsome stipend and a grandiose title. I rather think that being close to the border, they might be better seeking support rather than trying to extort gifts from us. I shall have very verbose refusals drafted in return.'

Gabriel gave a dark chortle at that, remaining silent otherwise, apart from the rumbling of his stomach. When *was* dinner?

Across the room, Constantine opened the last letter, sealed as it was with the imperial seal, slid out the document, and read it. Gabriel tensed, straightening, at the look that fell across the prince's face. 'What is it?'

Constantine held up a hand to shush him, and then ran his gaze down the document once more, slowly, before lowering it with a deep exhalation of breath.

'I am recalled, Gabriel.'

There was more to it than that, clearly. 'Mesembria?'

'The capital. Trouble has arisen. George Sphrantzes visited the emperor with some success, then went to secure Demetrios' agreement, and there everything has rather fallen apart. George is back in the city now, having met with my brother's army up in Mesembria.'

'Army?'

'It seems Demetrios has had enough of his brothers running the empire, and believes it's his turn. He's sold himself to the sultan as some sort of pro-Turk emperor, promising no connection to the Pope and vassalage to the Sublime Porte if Murad helps put him on the throne.'

Gabriel blinked. He'd always known Demetrios to be a dark horse, but to actually ally with the Turks and persuade them to invade the empire? 'Never.'

'Demetrios was still a boy when they last came. He doesn't remember the blood and the desperation like we do. John says Demetrios has his own army formed of anti-union imperial units and mercenaries, along with a sizeable Turkish contingent. George saw them all at Mesembria, and raced back to warn the emperor, who wants me there to take control of the defence. Me and my entire court, including my wife.'

Gabriel nodded. 'It should be done. You and the emperor together are strong. Alone, you are half that. With much of Murad's strength still bearing down on Serbia, he cannot bring all his forces to bear on the capital, and the army you gathered there. My feeling is that it will be token support rather than a proper invasion force. Constantinople may hold back an attack, but it will be better with you leading it. Shall I ride to the port and find a fast ship?'

Constantine nodded, but chewed his lip. 'What of Aikaterine, though?'

Gabriel shrugged. 'She may be better where she is, Constantine, safe with her father.'

'But John expects me to return with her. Perhaps it would look better for the people of the city if I returned married and calm, rather than alone and panicked, with my new wife exiled on an island? A sort of vote of confidence in our survival? It would take a day longer – no, more – to return via Lesbos. And given Aikaterine's Catholic faith, it may help a little for the people of the city to see the Church union in effect among their ruling family.'

He straightened. 'Have two messages delivered. One to the port, securing fast ships and an escort for us, the other to the garrison down at the isthmus. I want every man that can be spared on board a transport and heading for Constantinople as soon as possible. I will catch up with them when I have collected Aikaterine, but we must take as much help as we can. And while you do that, I shall find Thomas and explain. He will be the shield that protects the Morea when we leave, for Theodore is too far away and too uninterested. This will be a test for my brother. Let us hope he lives up to it, for if the Turks are content to march on Constantinople, they cannot be assumed not to have designs here too.'

Gabriel nodded. 'But I think they work within your politicking. To the wider world they are not invading the empire, but supporting a prince of Rome against his brothers. Murad and his beys are clever. If it all goes wrong, they can still claim to have been acting in the empire's interest.'

'*I* will act in the empire's interest when I get my hands on Demetrios, by roasting him alive in the bronze bull of the Forum Tauri. The devious little bastard. Go. Arrange the ships and the men. We leave for Constantinople via Lesbos in the morning.'

6

A Lion Caged

North of Lesbos, Aegean Sea

July 1442

'How long to Imbros?'

The ship's captain turned to his passengers. 'Two hours, maybe a little more, lord. We have favourable winds for north-ward sailing.'

Constantine nodded and turned, tense, to watch the waves as they raced for their next destination. Behind him, Aika-terine Gattilusio stood with a carefully blank expression. It made Gabriel wince as he caught sight of her. She was regal, impressive, beautiful, seemingly serene, but it was all still forced.

They had reached Mytilene yesterday, and the Lord of Lesbos had greeted them warmly. There they stopped over only the single night before setting off once more with the prince's wife aboard. Their reunion had been almost a repeat of the previous visit, with Constantine playing every bit the attentive and charming husband to Aikaterine and the gracious son-in-law to the lord of the island, and yet his eyes betraying a lack of true engagement. Gabriel fretted throughout the night.

It was not Gabriel's strength, relationships, and yet he was watching this one carefully. It mattered not to him what the other Palaiologos brothers went through with their wives, but Constantine affected him directly. He had watched Theodore slide rapidly from simply being a difficult and contrary character

177

to being downright trouble – dark, careless, selfish, and very possibly mad. All through the loss of his wife. And Gabriel would never have thought Constantine might go through similar, he being the bright and positive man who'd stood proud on the walls of the capital all those years ago. But Sphrantzes had already issued the fear that if the prince did not manage to get over his loss, he might slowly spiral down the same pit.

Aikaterine was supposed to be the panacea, the way to prevent that, yet it didn't seem to be working. If anything, the prince was just becoming distant and hollow, playing the role without that vim and power he used to have.

The Lord of Lesbos was clearly ignorant of any of this, and if he thought anything at all off about his visiting son-in-law, he would reasonably put it down to the tautness of his nerves, knowing that an enemy was about to besiege his favourite brother in their home city.

Gabriel had been the only one who knew different, or so he'd thought.

Then they had put to sea and he'd had the chance to observe the new princess away from her father's influence. It had taken less than an hour for him to come to the conclusion that Aikaterine was entirely aware of how her husband felt, and was simply playing a role, the same as he was, with mask in place, but that she was better at it, and had hidden it from everyone until now.

By noon on the journey from Lesbos to their overnight layover at Imbros, Gabriel was beginning to find it unbearable. It made his very bones itch to see. For another two hours he'd endured the horribly polite and nice conversations, the occasional touches that had been forced by both sides, and all through it he had repeated a mantra.

I will not get involved.

In the end, though, the mantra was not enough, and he knew that if he didn't do something, he was going to explode. He approached the door to the rear rooms, grateful that these

Genoese sailing ships had far better accommodation than the open Byzantine galleys. Inside, there were three cabins, one of which had been put aside for the imperial couple to relax in, despite the fact that they slept ashore each night. He marched towards that one, spotting Manuel and two of the Ianitzaroi in the shadowed corridor and jerking a thumb over his shoulder.

'Out.'

They departed, and he checked all three rooms for occupants. Finding them empty, he returned to the exterior door, and then marched over to the prince and princess.

'We need to talk. Come with me.'

He turned and made for the door, and after only a moment, realised only one set of footsteps accompanied him. He paused and turned. 'You too, my lady, if you would?'

She frowned, and then followed without a word. Manuel was still chatting with the others on the deck, near the door, and Gabriel gestured to him. 'No one comes in until we come out.'

The banner-man nodded, and so Gabriel led the couple inside and to their cabin.

Once they were all within, he closed the door behind them and pointed to the bed. 'Sit.'

Aikaterine was clearly not used to Gabriel yet and, unsure what was happening, simply crossed without a word, still frowning, and sat. Constantine turned a puzzled look on him.

'Remember who you're speaking to, Gabriel.'

'Sit,' he said again and, with a disapproving look, the prince joined his wife, the pair of them looking up at him, confused.

'What's my job?'

'You are the head of my bodyguard, of course.'

'Yes. And it's my job to protect you. I never thought I'd have to say this, but I only recently realised that this also means protecting you from yourself.'

'Gabriel?'

'I'm sorry for this,' he said, this time looking at Aikaterine, then turned back to the prince. 'You loved Theodora. I know this. We all do. And so you should. She was your wife. And though she is gone, it is only right to remember her fondly and with respect. Everyone would agree with that. But it has been thirteen years, Constantine. *Thirteen*. No woman should maintain such a grip on your heart that long in death. I know you cannot control such things, my prince, but you have to let go. You *have* to. Aikaterine Gattilusio deserves so much more than a polite mask. She deserves the truth. She needs to know why you wear that mask, although I think she already does. But now that it is in the open, you can *drop* the mask. Be straight. Honest. Be you.'

The prince's face had paled throughout that, but Gabriel had not finished. He turned to the princess. 'Yes, I have confirmed what you already knew or suspected. It is true, though it is not the prince's fault. He can't help it. But your playing the same role, wearing a similar mask, is not helping. The prince needs help to get past this, and that help can only come from you. And you need to be open and honest, the same as him. I've watched you both, and I am far from a professional matchmaker, but I see in both of you the possibility of something so much better. Sphrantzes made this match, and he is the cleverest man I know. He understood that you two could be good. But to do that, you need to start by being honest. Neither of you wants it to be like this, so both of you need to work together to put it right.'

The princess stared at him in surprise.

Gabriel stood there for a count of ten, waiting for arguments. When none came, he put his hands on his hips. 'Good. You both understand. I think you have a lot to talk about, and watching this awful dance for the past few hours has given me a headache. I'm going out for air. Join me when you're ready.'

He left them to it, then, marching out and closing the door. On deck, he told Manuel to keep others out until the prince and princess returned.

Back at the rail, Gabriel found he was trembling. He was not used to displays like that, and he was very acutely aware that he'd just overstepped the mark by a clear mile and could easily find himself unemployed by morning, or even under arrest. But it had needed doing.

He pinched the bridge of his nose and squeezed his eyes shut, and then relaxed and leaned on the rail, watching the sea race past.

Constantine returned mid-afternoon and joined him at the rail.

'That was rude, foolish, and downright dangerous, Gabriel. It was also clever and necessary. As such, you're off the hook on this occasion, but don't let it go to your head. I never want a repeat of that.'

Gabriel just nodded, and the prince breathed slowly for a while, the salt tang sharp and bracing. 'Aikaterine and I will be well in time, I think. For an uncultured warrior, you seem to have an uncanny understanding of such things. You were correct on all counts, of course, and we have agreed that it will take work for us to be more than strangers. Your actions shocked me, and I've known you for years. Imagine how they hit her. She may need some time before she eases, especially around you.'

And that was it. The princess returned shortly after, and the couple had a short exchange that was polite, but seemed genuine now, which was a step in the right direction, at least.

For the rest of the afternoon, Gabriel simply leaned there and watched the sea race past. It was calm and relaxing, especially now the spell here had been broken. He felt the need to appreciate that calm. That night they would reach imperial-controlled Imbros, and the next morning begin the last leg of their journey. Three further days' sailing – two if they pushed it and with the right conditions – and they'd be in Constantinople, and from that moment on, 'relaxing' was a word that would have no meaning.

The sun was now low enough on the far side of the ship that the shadows of spars and ropes and sailors moved about across the rail Gabriel leaned on, a huge shadow cast by the vessel across the waves before him. Two hours to their port. He was no sailor, but he had a strong suspicion the light would be failing long before they reached shore.

It was a clear day, and bright, even this late on, and if he squinted, he could just make out a thin smudge on the eastern horizon that would be Asia Minor, the Turkish heartland. He'd never been on that side of the water, and the idea of what might lie there was fascinating – not that he would want to satisfy his curiosity at the moment, with the Turks marching against them.

He turned, slowly, taking in the stern of the ship to either side of the cabin block, and the great line of white wake that trailed them across the water, then to the far rail. He had to scrunch his eyes up as he turned towards the sun. Another thin line on that horizon was much smaller – another island, if quite a sizeable one. He continued to turn, grateful it was away from the sun now, and he blinked as bright flashes imprinted on his retinas again and again. He looked past Constantine and his wife, past the prow and the figure of the expert captain, the open sea ahead, and then back to his own rail.

He frowned. Blinked another dozen times, hard and fast, then turned to the prow once more.

What in God's name is that?

Dots of black all across the sea ahead of them. He had just worked out what they were when the lookout, aloft, confirmed it for him.

'Ships ahead!'

Gabriel, along with Constantine and Aikaterine, hurried forward to where the captain was now making for the rail near the prow.

'Heavens, but there are a lot of them,' the captain breathed in Greek, heavily Genoese accented.

'Dozens,' Constantine agreed. 'Scores, even. Who are they?'

'I don't know, lord. Wait a few moments.'

There was a tense silence as they paused, the speedy momentum of their ship carrying them ever closer to that collection of vessels. Finally, the captain chewed his lip, then announced, 'I don't know who they are, and we won't know until we get close enough to see their colours, but I can tell you now they are low galleys, not sailing ships. No caravels or carracks there. Too flat and low in the water, too long. Could they be yours, lord? Sent out to escort you?'

Constantine shook his head. 'We have ships like that, but these days our entire navy isn't a quarter that size. Venetians?'

The captain, in turn, shook his head. 'Venetian galleys are higher and bulkier, and most of the ones in these seas have three masts. These have two.'

'Turks,' Manuel said, quietly, nearby. 'They are the sultan's ships.'

Gabriel flinched at the news. 'That cannot be good. And that they are here, now, can't be an accident. Will they have seen us?'

The captain nodded. 'The odd ship might well have missed us at this distance, but with that many? Someone will certainly have spotted us.'

'Especially with our escort,' Constantine said, and Gabriel turned to eye the two Genoese ships just to stern. Even with their help, there was no hope if they met that fleet ahead in battle.

'That must be their entire navy,' the Ianitzaroi whispered.

'Certainly a sizeable part of it.' Constantine turned to the captain again. 'What do we do? Can we get round them? Are we faster?'

'With this good breeze we are,' the man replied, 'but we'd have to cut very wide to get past them, and they would easily move to meet us. I don't see passing them as an option. We could turn about and make for Lesbos again. I'm not sure they'd pick a fight with your lordship.'

'A long sail south in the dark, chased by a Turkish fleet? Not ideal.'

Gabriel grunted. 'But if we can't get round them and the coastline is all Turkish land, what choice is there?'

'West.'

Gabriel frowned and turned. 'That's only an island.'

'So is Lesbos.'

'But Lesbos is *my father's* island,' Aikaterine put in, 'and he can help.'

'What's that island?' Constantine asked, pointing.

'That is Lemnos, my lord,' the captain answered.

'Lemnos is imperial,' Constantine said. 'It has its own strategos and a strong garrison by imperial standards. Can we make Lemnos by sunset?'

'Yes, lord,' the ship's commander said, 'but so can *they.*'

'So it is to become a race, and you already said these ships are faster.'

'With current bearings. Less so heading west, my lord.'

'So a close race, then. But a night sail and chase is worse. And heading back south only takes us further from home and our goal. Make for Lemnos, Captain, at your best speed.'

As the captain went about giving orders and the ship began to lean to port with the turn, Gabriel staggered across to the prince. 'This has to be coincidence.'

'Very uncanny, if it is.'

'All right, news of our journey will have gone ahead. As soon as we left the Morea, half the East would have learned we were on the way, but few would know we were travelling via Lesbos. That the Turks had sufficient warning to gather a fleet and come to meet us is unlikely.'

'Though not impossible,' the prince added. 'Likely the fleet was already here. The entrance to the Bosphorus is so close behind them we can almost see it. I reckon Demetrios knows I have already arranged ways to ship the Morea armies to the capital, and so he talked the sultan into blocking the sea approach. We just happen to have blundered into them. Watch what they do.'

'Why?'

'Because if they make no move, then they don't know who we are. If we're three random Genoese ships, they have no reason to stop us, but if they *are* aware I am on board, they'll turn and follow.'

As their vessel completed the turn, now ploughing slightly north of west and racing for the relative safety of Lemnos, Gabriel, Constantine and Aikaterine stood at the rail, tense, watching the Turkish fleet.

'There's your answer,' Gabriel sighed, as they saw first one, then two, then half a dozen, and finally all the other ships change angle on an intercept course. 'They know you're aboard, and it seems you're important enough that they're willing to risk attacking a Genoese ship to get to you.'

'I suspect they have orders. Demetrios will want me alive as a bargaining chip when he gets to the city. He may think John will compromise if I am at stake, and he may be right, too.'

'How strong is Lemnos?' Gabriel asked quietly.

'One of our strongest colonies. She's withstood Turkish attacks many times over the years, as well as fending off the inevitable pirates of the region. Not much in the way of ships, of course. All our fighting ships, such as they are, are gathered in the capital, but there's a fifteen-hundred-man garrison based between Kotzinos and Palaiokastron, and both those ports have strong castles with artillery that can reach out to sea.'

'So if we reach the island, they probably won't follow us onto land.'

'Exactly.'

'Then let's pray this ship is as fast as her commander claims.'

The tension climbed by the minute as their course took them slightly north of west, the huge Turkish fleet moving *south* of west to meet them, their speed seemingly sufficient for them to catch up.

'Can we make round the south coast and for Palaiokastron on the west coast?' Constantine asked the captain.

'Better not, lord. All around the centre south of the island are nasty reefs, and with us sailing into the sun, spotting them before we're torn to pieces by them is unlikely. Though it brings us closer to the Turks, at least going round the north cape and putting in at Kotzinos avoids all chance of reefs.'

Constantine nodded. 'Going to be a very close race, then. Let's hope the garrison commander's good. He's going to need his castle walls manned and artillery primed before the Turks come within range. They should have watchers with signals on the high coastal points, so he should be aware of our approach in plenty of time.'

Gabriel drummed his fingers on the rail. 'We're accepting the likelihood that they know you're aboard?'

'It's very likely, yes.'

'But they can't know aboard which ship.'

'True.'

Gabriel turned and looked at the other two vessels. The *Lucertola* was clearly the fastest among them. Having been following closely, she was now pulling alongside. The *Cristina* was still lagging behind. She was carrying the bulk of the supplies and the animals, and was, consequently, the most laden and slowest of the three.

'We split up, I reckon.'

Constantine frowned. 'What?'

'It's the game of three cups, with the ball under one, and they don't know which. In a fight, if you're against massive odds, the only way you have any hope is to split the enemy up, too. Three lots of ten to one is better than thirty to three, believe me. Give them three ships to chase rather than one fleet of three.'

'I understand your thinking, Gabriel. Elaborate.'

'We send the *Lucertola* around the south route the captain hates, with the reefs.'

'To likely die in the shallows?'

'It's possible. She will have to trust in God, or in luck, or in her crew's own skill and eyesight. But she's fast. She can stay ahead, and since she's the fastest, it's possible the enemy will think she is the one you're on. My bet is that it draws more than a third of the Turks away south, and they'll follow her straight into the reef area.'

'You have a vicious streak, Gabriel.'

'I don't like to lose. Winning means living. All right, so we assume more than a third follow her south. The rest follow the two of us. The captain said we had to round a headland to the north. He obviously knows the area, then, while the Turks probably don't. Headlands are by their very nature generally rocky. We hug the coast as close as we dare, and take the shortest possible route into the harbour at this Kotzinos. At the same time, given that the *Cristina* is the slowest of us, I reckon as we reach that headland, she turns north into open sea and goes as fast as she can.'

Constantine smiled. 'Because if she's trying to make a break for it north, past the Turkish fleet, then it will seem likely that is me, too.'

'Exactly.'

'You know they'll catch the *Cristina* long before she finds safety.'

'Then our friends on her will have to pray the Turks are bright enough to let them live in order to prevent war with Genoa.'

'You are a cold man, Gabriel.'

'My job is to keep *you* alive, not *them*. With luck, while most of the Turkish fleet are either chasing the *Cristina* north or being led onto the reefs by the *Lucertola*, we can run past the cape and into the safety of the harbour. If the signal has gone up across Lemnos, then the place should be bristling and ready for pursuit.'

'All right,' Constantine said. 'We'll play your plan out. I'll give the orders. I pray I'm always the focus of your skills, Gabriel. I'd hate to be your collateral.'

With that, the prince hurried off to speak to the captain, who would relay the orders to the other two vessels. Gabriel stood at the rail watching the Turkish ships coming ever closer, for some time, before he realised that Aikaterine Gattilusio was beside him. He did not turn to her. She seemed to have become used to his face, but he had long since learned that people were more comfortable when they *couldn't* see it.

'These are my father's ships,' she said quietly. 'My father's people. I have known some of these men all my life.'

Gabriel paused for a moment before his reply. 'I will grieve for the lost later, my lady. For now, my concern is his safety, and while you are with him, yours too. Would your father not expend every last thing he had to keep you safe?'

She gave a weird, hollow chuckle. 'You know little about Italian lords, it is clear. Most Genoese fathers would burn a city to save a son, but sacrifice little for a daughter. As it happens, my father is a rarity in that he treasures all six of his children, both boys and girls, and would sacrifice everything for any of us.'

'I had that impression from him. If your father were here, my lady, it would be he commanding two of his ships to throw themselves on the mercy of the deep to keep you alive.'

They remained there in silence for a long moment, until Constantine rejoined them. Even as the prince leaned once more on the rail, Gabriel watched the *Lucertola* make a sharp turn, align her sails to the prevailing wind, and suddenly power off at speed towards the southern edge of the approaching land mass.

Almost holding his breath, Gabriel turned and watched the Turkish fleet. It took precious moments, and for a time he thought the plan had failed, and then dozens of galleys began to turn and race off after the *Lucertola*. Less than two thirds of the Turks remained on intercept course for them.

'You clever devil.' Constantine grinned.

'The game of cups begins. Wrong cup, Sultan Murad. Choose again.'

'How long to the coast?' Constantine asked.

'Half an hour now, lord,' the captain called back.

'It is going to be far too tight for comfort,' the prince breathed.

And it was. As time slid past, every second of it heightening the tension for the passengers, they watched the rest of the Turkish fleet coming ever closer, to the point where they could now pick out details and see the Turks' colours aloft. There was a horrible possibility that they would reach the north coast first and be prepared to stop the racing Genoese.

'Jettison the cargo,' the captain shouted, suddenly. In moments, any deckhand without his own important task was finding the stored foodstuffs for extended journeys and bringing them up, tipping them over the side. Gabriel couldn't tell whether it made any noticeable difference to their speed as the last crate splashed into the water in their wake and bobbed off across the sea, but the captain seemed satisfied, so it must have helped. More noises drew his attention, and he looked up and aft to see that the crew of the *Cristina* were doing the same. He turned away in disgust as they began to lead the horses up and force them over the side, where they would certainly drown, far too far from land to swim to safety. Once all the splashing and noise had abated, he looked across and decided that the ship was moving noticeably faster.

They had done all they could. They were light, the sails were full, they had no oars, and every man aboard was praying hard for the Lord's favour this day.

The minutes continued to slide by, the coast coming ever closer, the island's details beginning to come into view. Gabriel looked away and back, and decided that it was possible now. They might just make it. He clenched his teeth. At a signal somewhere, the *Cristina* suddenly turned hard and started making directly north.

Another tense wait, and then, much to Gabriel's relief, a sizeable part of the remaining fleet turned to follow. By his estimation, as they closed on the high, craggy coastline, only a quarter of the fleet was now following. Willing the ship onwards,

Gabriel watched, white knuckles on the rail. It seemed hours, but finally, suddenly, they were closing on the rocky slopes and then began to turn, angling to round the northern cape. His heart raced as he saw the rocks in the water all along the shore ahead, and he prayed their captain was good. Turning, instead, he watched the fate of the *Cristina*.

The Turks gained on her rapidly as they cut across to intercept, and the front three vessels each brought artillery to bear. With resounding booms, the *falcons* were discharged, their shots arcing out over the water. Two fell short, but the third slammed into the *Cristina*'s hull not far from the prow and just at the waterline. Still, she raced bravely northwards, holed but intact. As she ran, though, more of the Turks closed, and shot after shot rang out. At least three hit the hull and then one miraculously snapped the mainmast, bringing down the sail. The *Cristina* drifted to a halt, and then started to lean precariously as the Turkish fleet came to surround her. The surviving Genoese vessel was too far away now to make out the details, but Gabriel could picture the crew throwing themselves into the water to avoid being trapped with the sinking ship, and the Turks would be gathering up the survivors, checking for the prince's presence with every body found.

Then the scene was gone from view, for their own ship changed angle once more, and the high aft section blocked the view. Gabriel turned and moved to the other rail, racing along the shore, seemingly dangerously close to the rocks. He swallowed nervously, and looked aft. There were the other Turks, racing to catch them, closing even now. He spun to look forward and could see the next curve as the coast followed the headland round towards the south, heading for the bay of Kotzinos.

He slammed his fist on the rail again and again, urging the ship on, praying for speed. He nearly let out a squawk of panic as they suddenly turned again, and the ship leaned perilously towards the rocks. Then they were racing past the deadly obstacles and around the corner. He'd expected to come straight into a bay, and was surprised to see the wide sea before them, the jagged coastline marching off south.

'I thought we would be at Kotzinos?' he called.

'We will,' the captain shouted. 'The headland is ten miles long, my friend. *Then* we will reach the bay.'

Gabriel fought down his nerves, which were pointing out that there was a good chance the ships following them would catch up within ten miles, and he jumped slightly as the boom of a cannon echoed out across the world. He looked sharply aft once more, half expecting a hole ripped in their hull, and was somewhat surprised to see, instead, a Turkish galley exploding in a shower of timbers and fragments. He looked up, frowning, and then grinned as he saw the smoke from the cannon shot on the top of the cliffs above them.

The defences of imperial Lemnos had gone to work.

The Turks pursuing them came on still, though a number of them slowed slightly at the realisation they were within the reach of artillery, and others veered out away from the coast a little for safety.

They raced on. The gun emplacement fired three more times at passing ships and then fell silent. Gabriel watched the northern coastline coming ever closer, and then they passed another cannon emplacement and shots began to ring out once more as they took aim at the Turkish galleys.

And then suddenly, blessedly, he saw the bay of Kotzinos reaching out like open arms, and could see the powerful walls of a castle on a rise to one side. Even as they approached he spotted cannon on those walls, and finally, aware they had lost the race, the Turks veered away and moved out to sea, out of range of the cannon.

They had reached Lemnos.

They had survived.

It had started with a simple question.

'How does one break a blockade?' Constantine mused one night as they sat in the governor's residence. 'I mean, we are all good military men, but none of us are naval strategists.'

It was a good question. Lemnos was surrounded by what seemed to be the entire Turkish fleet, stretched out in a cordon, but each vessel close enough to come to the aid of its neighbours. There was no open way in or out of the island, and they had now sat in the harbour for a week, waiting for any change.

'If we were on land, Highness,' Gaspar mused, 'I suppose I could see an equivalent. We have a handful of strong sailing ships, while they have a vast line of low galleys. If we were a group of heavy horse and they were a line of *skutatoi* forming into a shield wall, we would form up as a wedge and try to break the line with a charge.'

Constantine nodded. 'Dangerous, probably costly, and far from guaranteed success. But I agree, it's what I would do on land.'

Gabriel shook his head. 'A head-on charge is too dangerous. All it would take is one gunshot to find its target and the prince will rule from the bottom of the sea, and there will be a *lot* of Turkish guns taking aim. We are the prince's bodyguards, not his executioners.'

'Whatever we do, we will need all the vessels we can get,' Manuel put in.

And so, while plans were still proposed and discarded, orders were sent out to assemble the fleet at Lemnos. It was a pitiful sight. Over in Palaiokastron, a dozen miles away on the far side of the island, there was one military ship: a decommissioned imperial galley that had seen far better days, had been stripped of its armament, and beached years earlier. It was, however, basically seaworthy. Other than that, two merchant ships – an

Athenian and a Venetian from Crete – and a smattering of fishing vessels were all the port held. The merchants were frustrated by the blockade, but were content to sit in port and wait for it to be over, rather than running any risk. Constantine, in league with the island's strategos, arranged for the decommissioned war galley to be given a skeleton crew. There was no way to get it to Kotzinos to help, and it stood no chance against the Turks, but it might help as a distraction, or decoy, drawing their attention to the west and allowing Constantine an easier exit in the north-east.

In Kotzinos, the situation was not even that good.

Aside from the ship they had arrived on, the *Nettuno*, there was one other larger vessel in port, along with the usual small fishing boats and the like. Lorenzo Pavan, captain of the *Lorenzo*, a Venetian merchant, was not enthusiastic about their situation.

'It is my intention to leave on the morning tide,' the man told them, when they attempted to enlist him.

'Through the blockade?'

'I am a merchant, and I am Venetian, not at war with the Turks. If they wish to stop me and search for errant imperial princes, I shall invite them aboard. You have my sympathy, and my apologies, but I have my own interests to consider.'

'And if the port refuses to let you go?' Gabriel said, a touch of menace in his tone. There were cannon here, which could as easily pick off a departing ship as an arriving one.

Constantine shook his head, and when they left the *Lorenzo*, he strolled alongside the Ianitzaroi. 'I have no desire to provoke Venice, but it may prove interesting. We had considered charging the line. Perhaps we will learn something from watching Captain Pavan try to pass through the blockade.'

That was how, the following morning, they came to be standing at the viewpoint overlooking the bay, as the *Lorenzo* slipped its moorings and began to sail out towards open water. They strained to see as much detail as they could, as Pavan took his ship out of protected water and the range of the imperial guns, and made for the line of Turkish galleys. He sailed at a good, steady pace, not fast enough to resemble a charge or a threat, but at a reasonable speed for a merchant ship. He closed on the Turks, aiming for a gap between two of the vessels, and the watching Romans on the island held their breath.

If Pavan was allowed to simply sail through, then they had wasted an opportunity to get the prince out. But more likely he would be stopped, and the ship searched.

It surprised everyone when the guns started. Six of the nearest galleys discharged their artillery at the approaching Venetian merchant, without even a call or a challenge. In a heartbeat, the *Lorenzo* exploded in a shower of timbers and splinters, a mast cracked and leaning sharply. The merchant ship slewed to port, and though they were too far away to hear anything, all those watching could imagine the screams and shouts of panic aboard.

The *Lorenzo* stumbled to a halt before the blockade, now displaying her starboard side, and the Turkish gunners reloaded at leisure even as Pavan and his people were surely at the rail, shouting for mercy. Then the guns fired again, and what was left of the *Lorenzo* was smashed to pieces. As they watched, the broken ship cracked apart and began to disappear swiftly beneath the waves. They stood, silent, until the tip of the mast had vanished, and all that remained on the sea's surface was flotsam and desperate sailors, hoping to be picked up. Common sense suggested that an enemy who fired on them without warning was unlikely to save survivors.

'That was a surprise,' Constantine breathed. 'I assumed that at least they would be looking for me as a captive. They cannot have known I was not aboard, and that means they are content to see me drown.'

With that, they turned away from the unsettling scene, and returned to their lodgings.

—

The following days passed in an endless blur of plans and proposals, each seemingly more outlandish and unlikely than the last. They were one powerful ship and a small cluster of island boats against the might of the Turkish navy, and however they worked it, their chances of success seemed minimal at best.

In the end, it had been Manuel who had come up with the soundest plan of them all.

'It's a long shot,' the prince said, frowning.

'It certainly is,' Gabriel replied. 'How's the *Nettuno*?'

Manuel shrugged. 'Ready to sail, but lonelier than a eunuch in a harem.'

Aldo, the ship's captain, cleared his throat. 'I'm not worried about the *Nettuno*, lord. She'll do fine, as long as we stay out of range of their guns. We can't take the sort of pounding the *Lorenzo* took.'

'Oh, I'm aware of that, Captain.'

'It's the other ships that worry me. I've never seen it done, but I've heard about it plenty, and it's unpredictable and dangerous, even without worrying about changing winds.'

'I'm more worried about being mobbed before we can leave,' Gabriel murmured, looking out of the window and down to the harbourside. Ten men of the town garrison stood guard at the jetties, preventing the angry crowd from gaining access. As yet there had been no violence, barring a couple of half-heartedly thrown bottles and tiles that had been easily avoided. They were ordinary townsfolk, almost entirely fishermen, facing professional soldiers, but where they had started out as a small core of angry boat owners, they had gained sufficient sympathy with the rest of the town that a few others kept joining every now and then, the protest slowly forming into a mob.

It was no surprise, really, that even some of the local garrison wavered, sharing the sympathy. Constantine and his friends might be important nobles, but in a way they were just brief visitors to the island, while these ordinary folk were friends and neighbours.

And Gabriel knew they had a right to be angry.

Their boats had been taken off them.

There would be similar trouble over in Palaiokastron, too, since the prince had ordered the same thing there, and the boats from that town had been sailed here, hugging the coast all the way to stay as far from the Turks as possible. Now, Kotzinos bay was filled with a multitude of small craft, their owners in both towns demanding their return, shouting and waving things. Oh, they had been vaguely promised recompense, but Gabriel knew as well as the others that the treasury on Lemnos would be insufficient to cover all this, and the promises were little more than bare-faced lies.

'You're sure your system will work?' the prince asked.

The artillerist he was addressing blinked in surprise. 'Me, lord? No. Not at all. I am hopeful, but that's as far as it goes. Never done anything like this.'

'Fireships are as old as time,' Manuel said dismissively. 'It's a simple concept.'

'With respect,' Captain Aldo snapped in reply, 'we cannot re-create the great fireship tactics of sea warfare. Generally, they are full-sized ships, rigged out and sailed towards the enemy. All we have are small fishing boats in large numbers, and insufficient crew, given that their owners are hardly going to sail their own burning ship at a Turkish fleet. Small ships will burn much, much faster, are lighter and more prone to change direction with gusts, and therefore much harder to keep on course. We can spare no more than half a dozen men to crew them, and those men need to be able to return to the *Nettuno* in time. It is, in fact, a nightmare to organise, and at best a spear thrown in the dark.'

Constantine nodded. 'I take all those points, but I also can see no better way right now. We need to get past those Turks. By now Demetrios and his armies, along with his Turkish allies, will be at Constantinople. They'll have ravaged and burned the outskirts and now they'll be at the walls, knocking on the door.

John has the army I gathered, but they will be outnumbered still, and he needs support.'

'I am worried about the lady, sir,' Aldo added.

'Aikaterine? She will be fine. She is just a little under the weather. The sea air will probably help.'

Gabriel was less convinced. The prince's wife had not looked at all well for the past few days, her face waxy and pale, shaking a little, and constantly exhausted. Gabriel himself would not enjoy a sea voyage in that state. Still, they could hardly leave her here.

'Is that the signal?' Constantine asked, in response to the booming of a horn across the harbour.

Captain Aldo rose and crossed to the window beside Gabriel, which he opened, admitting the noise of gathered angry townsfolk. He looked this way and that and held his arm out.

'That's it. The wind is with us, and looking at the clouds, it's unlikely to change for an hour or two. We had best move fast, though, just in case.'

The men in the room gathered their things and made for the stairs, Constantine leading the way. At the bottom, the Ianitzaroi waited to escort them, Gaspar huge and impressive at their head.

'Come, gentlemen,' the prince said. 'Time to leave Lemnos.'

They strode from the governor's house out into the fortress of Kotzinos, and the dry, sizzling heat of an Aegean summer hit them as they left the cool shadows. They blinked into the bright blue, and there, before them, was the plan.

The better part of a hundred boats, almost filling the bay. At first glance it looked totally chaotic, but focusing on it revealed something beyond just anchored boats. In fact, they were not anchored at all – or at least, only a few were. They were, however, roped together in the form of a giant web of boats. The idea was that, roped together, and all with sails set, they could be guided in a single direction as a flotilla by only a few hands. The current and the wind should keep them going together, the ropes preventing them straying too far apart.

The Turks would be confused, or so they all hoped. They shouldn't be expecting fireships, certainly not in the form of a flotilla of fishing boats, and so hopefully they would let them get close before reacting. That there were so many of them – and most of them empty and unmanned – should be baffling, and that they were roped together would hopefully escape their notice until it was too late.

Every boat had been stuffed with flammable materials – sails, cloth, rope, paper, brushwood, and the like – making them potential floating infernos. So long as they made it there, and nothing went wrong.

Once they were in position, they could be ignited and cut adrift to do their work, and as the Turkish blockade burned, the *Nettuno*, coming up from behind, would pick up the sailors who'd crewed the boats, and charge for freedom between the burning hulks. It was a fiendish plan, but so laden with holes and uncertainties that no one would have bet their lives on it. In order to get the best shot at it they could, they had needed to wait for the tide to be right, and for the wind to be sufficiently strong and from the right direction. Everything had been in place ready for a swift departure, the *Nettuno* loaded and prepared, crew and passengers on board.

And that was why now, when the signal had been given, the group wasted no time. As they descended the slope in the castle grounds towards the harbour gate, the artillerist led two of the Ianitzaroi over to the castle's workshop, from whose chimneys great coils of black smoke rose. Moments later they reappeared and rejoined the party at the rear, carrying ceramic pots with great care by their rope handles, careful to keep them away from their bodies. Gabriel could see the shimmer around the pots from the heat they gave off.

Then they were through the castle gates and out into the harbour. The crowd of angry citizens erupted into a roar now, and the garrison men struggled to hold them back as Constantine and his people crossed the dock and made for the jetties. The majority made for the *Nettuno*, of course, where sailors were already preparing to get underway, men standing and waiting to cast off the ropes. The artillerist and his companions moved to the central jetty, where the pots were lowered, the Ianitzaroi leaving them with some relief and returning to the ship. At the jetty, nine men joined the artillerist now, three for each of three boats, and took up a ceramic pot each, before moving to their boats. As soon as they climbed aboard, another signal was given, and the fleet set sail.

The web of small boats was guided now, as the anchors were raised, by three vessels, one on the far left, one far right and one at the centre rear. As soon as the lines were untied and the anchors raised, the entire flotilla of small craft moved off at a surprising speed, carried north by a combination of strong wind and tidal current. There was a certain amount of worryingly random movement as boats bumped into one another or veered away until the ropes connecting them went taut.

It was fascinating to watch, and Gabriel's gaze followed them as they moved out ahead, making for open sea with only a minimum of human guidance. Once they were far enough ahead that he could only just see what was happening among them, Captain Aldo put out a call. The *Nettuno*'s tethers were let loose, the sail unfurled and the anchor raised. The ship raced out into the water in the wake of the flotilla.

Gabriel saw problems immediately. In a matter of heartbeats they were gaining on the boats, the huge sail of the *Nettuno* giving them much greater speed, and he was grateful for the knowledge and skills of Aldo and his sailors as they swiftly adjusted the sails until they had slowed sufficiently to keep pace with the boats, some way to the rear.

Back aft, Constantine stood with the captain, while his wife lay sweating and unwell in the cabin inside. Gabriel moved to the prow, close to the bowsprit, where the salt spray came in waves, making him blink, cooling the unbearable Greek summer heat. He peered between the gusts as best he could, trying to keep track of everything.

The Turkish cordon was not moving, that line of galleys remaining resolutely in place, watching the strange, empty flotilla closing on them, probably unaware even of the crews in the three most peripheral boats, wondering what on earth was going on.

The disaster occurred while they were still some distance from the Turks. Gabriel had no idea how it happened, but suddenly the boat to the far right of the flotilla exploded in a fireball of golden red. He'd never seen a fireball go up quite so spectacularly. That boat was, of course, packed with kindling, and everything was so parched and dry that it was easily combustible, but also those three men had a ceramic pot of burning coals from the forge. There had clearly been a spillage of some sort, and the result had been catastrophic. There was little hope for the three-man crew. Indeed, he only saw one figure move, and that was because it was flailing and screaming, completely ablaze as it tumbled into the water.

Everything happened at once, then. Aware that the surprise was already out, the crews of the other two boats used the metal scoops that had come from the workshop to carefully pull out blazing coals. These they cast at other boats, which slowly took flame and began to burn. Already the accidental blaze on the first boat had caught adjacent vessels, partly from sparks and burning debris floating on the breeze, but also as the fire raced along the ropes holding them together. In moments the flotilla began to burn.

It was too soon, and Gabriel could see that.

Had they managed to get considerably closer before the fires lit, the fireships could have been devastating. Having begun to burn too soon, they were no great danger. The Turkish galleys backed water out of the way, extending their line and easily curving away from the approaching blaze. The Theotokos was willing to give them a small consolation, apparently, as one of the Turkish galleys struggled with its movement, and had only managed to turn side-on before the blazing flotilla reached it.

They could count a victory over one ship. Captain Aldo bellowed out commands, and the *Nettuno* slowed and began to turn. He'd not waited for Constantine's orders, for it was clear the plan had failed. In the end, all they had achieved was one enemy vessel aflame, and the gap they'd created filled with their own blazing flotilla. There was no way through without charging straight into the galleys or trying to sail through the middle of the inferno.

A few of the nearer Turkish vessels let out a hopeful cannon shot as the *Nettuno* turned, but Aldo had been sharp and had brought them to a halt the moment he realised, turning them fast outside the enemy's gun range. They tarried there only long enough to pick up the six surviving men from the flotilla, who'd dived from their boats once their task was complete and swum with all haste for the *Nettuno*. Now, they were already on their way back to the harbour, slowly, labouring against the wind. They did not fear pursuit, though. The Turks would not be able to go any faster and would not catch up, and right now, they were more concerned with keeping away from the blaze.

As Gabriel leaned on the rail and watched their open prison glide slowly back towards them, he sighed. What would the next idea be? Would they become increasingly desperate and dangerous as the prince felt the pressing need to be in the capital weigh on him more and more? As if he had called the man, Constantine was suddenly beside him.

'God was not watching over us today.'

'Personally, I'll take it,' Gabriel replied.

'Really?'

'We just made an attempt to break out, and we only lost three men. Pavan lost a whole crew.'

'We also lost around ninety fishing boats.'

'Last time we lost a Venetian ship. Face it, my prince, this was a long shot to begin with. We should not be surprised it failed, but rather we should be grateful we survived it. We lost three men. They lost a galley.'

'True. But I need to get off Lemnos, Gabriel.'

'I know the emperor called you, and I know there will be a need for good men back in Constantinople, but in the grand scheme, your brother still has the army and he knows what he's doing. Trust him.'

There was a moment's silence, and then Constantine turned to him. 'It's not just that, Gabriel.'

'Oh?'

'Aikaterine is with child.'

Gabriel blinked. 'She…? Really?'

'The town doctor confirmed it. She is carrying my heir, Gabriel. But she's ill. She'll get over it, of course, but I worry she will lose the child in the process, and that, my friend, terrifies me. I asked the doctor what he could do, and he was very apologetic and said he would do whatever he could, but he did not sound confident. Gabriel, in the capital there are the best medics and surgeons in the world, plus the most holy relics and artifacts. Here, I fear for the child, but I am sure if we can get her back to Constantinople, there is sufficient skill and knowledge there to help.'

Gabriel nodded. Now he understood why the prince, normally not one to throw men away so easily, had pinned much on such a far-fetched plan. Desperation had already begun to claw at Constantine.

He tried to think of something soothing and supportive to say, but came up empty. In truth, he was still trying to work out how it had happened… not in a physical, sweaty, bouncing up and down way, but in so far as the couple had never yet seemed to be close enough to be intimate.

They stood side by side in silence as the bay slid past, the castle and harbour approaching, and Gabriel tapped his lip. 'How long overdue do we have to be before someone questions it?'

The prince frowned. 'Our failure to arrive in the city will already have been questioned, but there's little my brother can do to help with Demetrios and the Turks camped outside the walls and the Turkish fleet between us.'

Gabriel shook his head. 'I wasn't thinking of Constantinople. We've been here a month now, and the night we arrived, we were expected at Imbros. Given how close they are, they have to be aware of the Turkish fleet. Surely over a month they will have seen the fleet, noted our disappearance, and connected the two?'

'And done what, precisely?'

'Well, I presume they would send word to the city, for a start.'

'And as I said, my brother's a little too busy to help right now.'

'But they will also know we were travelling with your wife, in her father's ships. Surely that means they will also have sent word to Dorino Gattilusio, back at Mytilene?'

'Yes, I would be surprised if they hadn't.'

'And if I read the man right, he would not leave his daughter to languish in the grip of the Turks?'

'No, I suppose not. But since it's been a month, if he were sending help, I would have expected it by now. Besides, he's a powerful lord, but this has to be the whole Turkish fleet. What could he do?'

'I don't know,' Gabriel admitted as the *Nettuno* slid in alongside the jetty, a sullen, unhappy populace awaiting them, 'but at least it gives me a little heart to think there may be someone on the other side of the blockade trying to work out how to get us out.'

Palaiokastron

Late August 1442

'What is the matter with that family?' Manuel grumbled as he cut a slice of cheese and nibbled the edge, making sure it was still viable after sitting on the sunny windowsill for the day. He shrugged, accepting the slightly damp rubberiness, and began to eat.

Gabriel glared at his banner-man. 'Don't forget that he pays your wage. Have a care, Manuel.'

'*You* pay my wage, boss. He pays yours.'

'And he's a prince of the empire. Politeness is part of your job description.'

'Since when?'

'Since you started working for royalty, same as the rest of us.'

'All I mean is...' The standard-bearer sighed, put down his cheese and took a swig of wine, swilling it for a moment before swallowing. 'Well, the other brothers... I mean, the emperor is clearly clever and straight-minded. Just what's needed. But even he can't pick a wife. Three barren ones in a row?'

No one would voice the possibility that it was John himself unable to sire a child, of course. There was a moment's uncomfortable silence.

'Then there's Andronikos. Never married and died young. And Theodore. Lost his wife and went out of his mind, so far out that he can see the back of his own head. One daughter, gone to the king of Cyprus. And Demetrios? Also on his third wife with no children. Then there's Thomas with one daughter. And then our boss. Second wife now, and she don't sound too good, and it's looking like—'

'Don't you dare say it,' Gabriel cautioned, holding up a finger. 'Tempt fate and I personally will cut you a second arsehole.'

'Well, either there's something wrong with the family, or they are *really* bad at picking wives.'

Gabriel silenced him with another glare. Manuel often had a big mouth, and no idea how to not use it. But the problem was that he was only voicing what they all thought. Six siblings, with ten wives between them, and only two daughters to show for it? Compare that with Antoni, the youngest of the Ianitzaroi, who had been only too glad to leave the city for the Morea, having got the third of his three simultaneous girlfriends pregnant. It was not a good record for an imperial family.

And Manuel was also right on another count. It did not look good for the prince. Aikaterine had been ill now for weeks, and far from improvement, she was looking worse by the day. Gabriel had seen the look before. Men who'd been wounded and then left in the hospital to hopefully recover, but who had picked up an illness instead that brought sweat and fever, and a sickly-sweet smell. Then one morning, you'd drop in to wish them well and they'd be lying there on their backs, staring at the ceiling with glassy eyes. She had that look now.

The doctor in Kotzinos had tried everything he knew, but he was little more than a village healer, really, with a pack of bandages and a few tinctures to remove headaches. Constantine had begun to fear genuinely for the future, and had sought any help. It was said that at the church of Agia Triada in Palaiokastron, there were monks who knew the healing arts, and so the prince had removed his wife to the far side of the island, for a time taking his attention away from the task of breaking the blockade, worrying that Aikaterine would not live to board another ship.

The monks in Palaiokastron had been no more hopeful than the doctor in Kotzinos, really, but there were at least more possibilities here. A few miles inland there were hot springs, associated with healing since the days of many gods, and at first the monks directed her there. When she showed no improvement over three days there, she was given a very specific diet, as Gabriel well knew, having been given the task of rounding up the ingredients on a daily basis. The monks had given her a bed in the monastery, and had spent days and nights plying her with potions and tinctures, herbs and compounds. One had tentatively raised the possibility of bleeding her, but Constantine had refused that, and others had agreed with him.

And everything they did seemed to make no difference. Aikaterine simply slid into a daily decline.

'You're wanted, sir,' a monk called, gesturing at Gabriel, who, tense and fearing the worst, followed the man to the princess's chamber. The smell hit him at the door. That same smell of wound rot from a hundred friends in a hundred hospitals over the years. It did not encourage him. But at least she was still with them. As he entered, Aikaterine lay in sweat-soaked sheets in her nightdress, pale and waxy, hair soaked, eyes pink. But there was still that wit and brightness in them. Ill she might be; delusional she was not.

'Go,' she said to the prince, who looked pleadingly at her, but then rose and left, with just a glance at Gabriel and no words.

The door shut. Gabriel was alone with one of the most important women in the world.

'You are a good man, Gabriel Casals.'

He blinked. Where did she learn his name? He never used it, and as far as he was aware, even Constantine had only ever known him as 'Gabriel Black-eye'.

'Don't tell anyone that. It would kill my reputation.' He tried to give her an encouraging smile, though he was aware that at best he could manage a horrifying grimace. Oddly, she smiled back.

'I've not known you long, and that is a shame. I think there is a lot to you that most people miss. But then I've not known my husband for long, either, and without you, I doubt I'd have known him for the man he is.'

She paused, wincing, tensing, and then coughing.

'You should not speak. You need to rest.'

'No, Gabriel. That time has passed.'

'Don't say that.'

'Heavens, man, but I can even see it in your expression. You know I'm dying. I know I'm dying. Constantine knows I'm dying, and so do all the priests and monks, and yet everyone denies it, and everyone tries to give me encouraging little lies. I sent for you, specifically because I thought you would *not* lie to me.'

He closed his eyes for a moment, then opened them, and was surprised to find them brimming a little.

'All right. Yes, I think you are dying. But like everyone else I have to hope I'm wrong, and to fight for every day. You are more important than you know.'

'Not true. I know how important I am. More than the daughter of a lord and the wife of a prince. I am the only thing bringing him out of that miasma he sank into, and I am his hope for an heir. I know that. I also know that he is about to be crushed. I have days at most, Gabriel. More likely hours. And then he is going to go through it all again. Perhaps it would have been better if you hadn't dragged us into that cabin on the ship and healed the rift. He would not have felt such loss as he will now, because he will lose me soon, and the child, too. I think it's a boy, but he's only weeks old, so it's hard to tell. I asked the priests how young a child can be born and still live, but they are of a unified belief that my son is too early to survive. He will never be born, and he will die inside me.'

'You are the mistress of cheerful conversation,' Gabriel snorted, attempting to lighten the mood, and cursing himself for it.

'I am talking straight, Gabriel. I will die very soon, and the child will die with me. Perhaps if we were in Constantinople, his brother John would be the comfort Constantine will need. I know he dotes on John alone of his siblings. But we will not reach Constantinople. We will be here, and I will die here. And the only man on this island who may be able to stop his descent into despair is you. I charge you now with doing that. When the time comes, find a way to divert him, to stop him wallowing. He is a great man, and the world will need him. His empire will need him. He cannot spiral into darkness the way his brother has. Will you do that?'

'I don't know how.'

'Then work it out. Find a way. But do it quickly. You do not have long.'

'I... I am sorry, my lady.'

'You have no reason to be. You have been his friend when he needed one, and now you have been mine. Go with God, Gabriel, for it is possible that this is the last time we shall speak.'

He left the room feeling as hollow and broken as he had ever felt. He was extremely grateful that Constantine had gone to the latrine briefly and they did not meet at that time. Instead, he hurried back to the room where his men waited.

'Gaspar?'

'Yes?'

'You were married. You lost a child. How did you cope with it?'

'I joined the army.'

'That's not the answer I was hoping for.'

The ourghos shrugged his massive shoulders. 'I spent a month crying. I spent nights at the graveside. I went to church and blasphemed, calling God a bastard for what he did. I drank enough that most men would probably have died. Then your predecessor, Enric, found me in the gutter. He was doing a tour of the Catalan neighbourhood, looking for recruits. He dragged me up, sobered me, and made me a soldier. In all probability he saved my life, because that is the only way to overcome such grief. To have so much on your plate that you have neither the time to think, nor the energy to cry. And after a while it dulls. It never goes away, and every time I break a head, I'm cursing God a little. But it becomes manageable.'

Gabriel frowned. 'Lord, but I never thought I'd hear such depth. You and Manuel still find ways to surprise me.'

'Yeah, well, likewise. Let's not tell anyone, and go back to sticking pointy steel into bad men, eh?'

The rest of the evening passed with a sullen and worried atmosphere, and Gabriel almost entirely failed to sleep. Rising in the middle of the night, sick of lying staring into the dark, he wandered across to the desk by the window. On it lay Manuel's books, and he perused them for a moment. The standard-bearer was the only real reader of the unit. Most of them didn't know how, and those who could, like Gabriel, rarely had the time, but Manuel was an oddity. There was a persistent rumour that he'd actually taken holy orders many years before, and had been a monk for a while, though there were other explanations for the expansive bald spot, of course. But certainly he read. And whenever they found somewhere with books, he gave away one or two from his stock and bought new.

Procopius' history of the Roman wars. The epistles of Ignatius. The *Agricola* of Tacitus.

Gabriel frowned. Nothing better to do than read. But what? Not Ignatius. Church writers were always boring and a bit too snobby. He toyed with Procopius, but in the end he was not sure that what he needed to read right now was about Roman wars that went wrong. In the end, he grabbed the *Agricola* and made his way down to the communal room, which was empty at this time of night, and lit a lamp and poured himself a drink.

An hour later, engrossed, he was gaining a new appreciation for one of Rome's most famous generals when the words on the page suddenly hit him:

'In his grief, he found solace in war.'

Agricola, it seemed, had lost a son. The solution was right there.

Gabriel finished reading for the night, and then finally put the book back and managed a couple of hours' sleep before the morning and sunrise.

—

It was that afternoon that the world changed. He knew immediately what had happened when an anguished cry rang out across the building, and by the time he got to Aikaterine's room, there was quite a gathering in the corridor outside. Priests, monks, soldiers and servants, all anxious and ready to do what they could.

'Go away,' Gabriel told them. 'All of you. Go.'

There was some argument for a moment, but the Ianitzaroi among them knew better than to argue with their commander, and helped usher the others out, until Gabriel was alone in the corridor. He could hear nothing from the room as he leaned close to the door. He wasn't sure how best to go about this, and in the end, rather than knocking, he simply pushed the door open and walked in.

As he'd expected, Aikaterine was in the bed, still and grey, and Constantine was kneeling on the floor by her side. He turned at the interruption, and his eyes narrowed.

'You made me care, Gabriel. Until then, I didn't.'

'And now I will make you care about something else, Constantine.'

The prince's eyes blazed for a moment, but Gabriel shook his head. 'No. This is not my fault, and nor is it hers, nor even God's. Horrible things happen. I am the living proof of that. She is gone, and with her the child, and I know that is a terrible thing to bear, especially when you've been through it before. But she was a fighter, Constantine, and a noblewoman. She knew what needed to be done, and would not shrink from it.'

'You would have me not even grieve?'

'Grief is a luxury. You are a prince of Rome, and your brother, the emperor, is under siege. Earlier this month, you told me we *had* to break the blockade and get to the capital. We still do. She can be buried in this place, exalted and loved. But we have work to do.'

'She put you up to this. Yesterday. That was what she wanted.'

'Yes. And she was right. You can do nothing for her now but remember her fondly. You lost a child, but you are a prince of Rome. Every citizen in the empire is your child, and unless we can get out of here, you might lose them all.'

From the appalling look on Constantine's face, Gabriel worried for a moment that he'd gone too far. Then the prince rose and turned.

'We are going to leave Lemnos today, Gabriel.'
'That's quite soon.'
'I have an idea.'

Kotzinos

Late August 1442

'What the fuck is he doing?'

'I think that's quite obvious,' Gabriel replied to the artillerist, as a group of Ianitzaroi rumbled past with a cart that held three more barrels.

'But he hasn't asked for one of the guns. Mind you, that might be better for me, since the last time you took two guns, you lost both of them.'

Gabriel turned, treating the man to a full view of his ravaged features. True to form, the artillerist looked away, unable to meet his eyes. 'Just let him do what he needs to do. He is a prince of Rome, and we are just soldiers.'

But as he watched the activity, Gabriel was not entirely sure what was happening, either. The barrels were being gathered on the dock, but without guns. So far, nine barrels of extremely expensive gunpowder were all waiting, with three more on the way down the slope. That was most of the stock in the fortress, and to take any more would be to leave the defences danger-ously short. Another six barrels were coming from various gun emplacements nearby. Shortly, there would be enough gunpowder on that dock to leave a crater the size of the Hagia Sophia should someone accidentally drop a cinder. He trembled at the thought.

He'd once seen a magazine explosion, and if anyone had thought that gun detonating near them on the ship in the Echinades to be a disaster, it was nothing compared to that. Up in Mesembria, under the old emperor, one of the coastal fortifications had caught the stray spark from a torch that had stupidly been positioned too close to the window. There had been three barrels of gunpowder in the ancient turret, and Gabriel had looked up from his evening meal at the bang, in time to see thousand-year-old masonry hurled half a mile out to sea, while nearby buildings were demolished and anything combustible caught fire. One explosion, from one spark, had destroyed an entire coastal station, with just three barrels of powder. Gabriel had felt the heat on his face at the time, but had been grateful he'd been far enough away not to be properly hurt.

The dock currently held three times as many barrels, and shortly: *four* times. And when the rest arrived there would probably be enough to seriously reduce the size of Lemnos.

'I hope he knows what he's doing,' he murmured under his breath, quietly enough that the artillerist would not be able to hear.

Down on the dock, Constantine was animated. He had not stopped moving since the moment they arrived back in Kotzinos, probably because he did not want to allow himself time to think. Gabriel had set him on this course, for good or for ill. But what that course *was* was now starting to worry him. He watched the three barrels trundling down to the port and then being stacked beside the others. It was late afternoon. They had maybe three hours of light left, so whatever Constantine was up to, he had better do it fast. The prince had maintained throughout the journey back across the island that they would leave Lemnos that day, and that he had the only idea that might work.

Enough gunpowder to blow Lemnos high enough to see Jesus on his throne...

'Manuel? There's someone cooking fish down there. Go and stop them.'

'But they're on the far side of the harbour. Quarter of a mile from the barrels.'

'One spark on a breath of wind, Manuel. Go and stop them.'

Gabriel stood there while the standard-bearer hurried down the slope and ran along the harbour side until he reached the sailors, whereupon he threw and kicked sand across the fire, ruining the meal but extinguishing the flames.

Better safe than sorry.

Over the next hour, the other six barrels arrived from various directions and were added to the growing pile on the dock. Eighteen barrels of gunpowder. Gabriel was far enough up the hill, within the castle walls, that he couldn't hear even shouting down on the dock, and the people down there were like ants. Yet if that lot went up, half this hill would go, and Gabriel with it.

He did not like guns.

Still, intrigued, he watched as the full collection of barrels sat there, and Constantine started to issue new orders to the various sailors. In a way, Gabriel had half expected the next move, but had told himself it wasn't going to happen, for it was clearly crazy.

The sailors began to collect the barrels of gunpowder, rather gingerly, and manhandle them along the jetty to the *Nettuno*, where she wallowed quietly in the bay. Gabriel winced a couple of times as they struggled and almost dropped their first load, despite the fact that there was no flame nearby to trigger a disaster. It was still nerve-racking, regardless. By the time the first barrel was aboard, the second and third were on their way. The first was carried to the prow, and there settled into place.

There was little doubt about the prince's plan now. The *Nettuno* was being turned into one massive floating explosive. Gabriel tried to picture the damage a ship loaded with eighteen barrels of gunpowder could do, and even recalling that coastal emplacement years ago was frightening. This would be six times that size. If it detonated anywhere near the blockade, there was little doubt that it would take half a dozen ships with it, and the wave it created would likely capsize several more. It would be catastrophic.

Which raised two important questions for Gabriel. Firstly, how would they take advantage of the gap it left if they had blown their only sailing ship to pieces, and secondly, who was going to be the fool ordered to light it. The answer to the latter worried him, as it was precisely the sort of job Constantine reserved for him, and the prince was currently not in the most stable frame of mind. Gabriel had prevented him from wallowing by giving him a task, but he was now rather worried about how Constantine was going about that task.

He eyed the harbour for a moment, but there was no help there. There were three other vessels, none of which he would trust on the open waves outside the bay, and certainly not as far as Imbros, for they were the ones too small and rickety even to have been part of the fireship fleet.

There was one glaring answer, and he hated the very idea, but when one of his men came running up the hill with a summons from the prince, it seemed inevitable. He followed his man back down to the harbour with a sense of foreboding, watching as the last barrels were heaved down the jetty and aboard the *Nettuno*. He found himself trembling slightly as he trod the damp boards of the jetty down to the boarding ramp.

Climbing aboard, he spotted Constantine standing perilously close to those barrels in the prow of the ship, directing the sailors as they dragged the last two into place. Gabriel strode across, and was somewhat surprised as the lines were cast off behind him and the ramp brought aboard. He'd by now resigned himself to the fact that Constantine intended to sail the floating bomb out there himself, but he'd not realised they were leaving immediately. He'd not had time to pray for his fate or go to the latrine, to avoid the very real possibility of soiling himself in the action.

Ropes were brought and used to secure the pile of barrels, so that the rocking of the ship on the waves did not see them unsettled and rolling around. Once they were solidly in place, another sailor came forward with a bucket and brush, and under the supervision of the prince himself, began to paint across the front face of the barrels.

Gabriel, intrigued, edged closer to the explosive heap, still worrying about its presence, and moved to the prow even as the ship began to slide slowly across the harbour. He turned to look at the pile of barrels.

BARUTLAR

He looked across at Constantine. 'I'm not sure the Turks will need a label to identify it. It's unlikely to be barrels of wine.'

'I just want it to be clear.'

'Do you really expect the Turks to believe you would detonate it? They have to know you're not insane.'

'But the problem is if they do not move out of the way, I fully intend to do so.'

'You would kill all of us, and everyone within a quarter of a mile.'

The prince did not reply, but Gabriel caught his expression as he turned, and felt a hollow worry that the man truly did not care. He would do just that if needed. Perhaps taking Tacitus' suggestion and throwing him into the war to occupy him might have been a dangerous idea.

The *Nettuno* slipped from the arms of the harbour and out onto the open sea with ease, the tide gentle and the weather good. Already Gabriel could see the Turkish fleet out in the water, black blots in a line across the horizon. He had perhaps a quarter of an hour before they were close enough for trouble. His gaze swept the ship, but came up with nothing encouraging. There were places aboard where a man could hide from enemy fire, but not from what the prince had planned. If those barrels went up, there would be nothing left of the *Nettuno* larger than a man's hand.

His stomach lurched as he saw a man appear across the deck, carrying a blazing torch, which he handed to Constantine before scurrying away. He shut his eyes tight. *Is the man mad?*

Of course, there was now the very real possibility that the answer to that was yes, given that Constantine seemed to be following the same dark spiral as his brother Theodore had in his grief.

'Don't get any closer,' Gabriel called, but the prince ignored him, and stepped closer to the pile of barrels. Gabriel was shaking now. Fear was not unknown to him, and even though he would count himself among the bravest of men on the battlefield, moments like this still threatened to unman him.

'What is he doing?' Gaspar breathed nearby, his tone filled with nerves.

'Delivering an ultimatum.'

'Does he really need to stand so close? What if the ship lurches and he drops it? Or even just a spark?'

'I know. But I think I know his mind. The only way the Turks could stop the explosion would be to put an arrow in him, but now they can't. If they shoot him and he falls, the powder will go up anyway. He's made himself an impossible target. Essentially, there is nothing they can do. Of course, they may call his bluff, suspecting that he would not go through with it.'

'Which is true, of course.'

When Gabriel failed to answer, Gaspar turned a frown on him. 'It's true, yes?'

'Who can say? When we buried Aikaterine in Palaiokastron, I suspect we buried a part of his soul with her. All we can do is pray, and pray hard.'

Gaspar retreated, twitching, to speak to Manuel, who was staring at the gunpowder in horror, and had been doing so ever since they boarded. Gabriel sighed, and walked forward. It made him nervous coming closer to the barrels, but when he allowed logic to rule, he knew that it mattered not where he was on the ship. If the powder went up, he'd be dead anyway. Turning, he made a few gestures and, white-faced, Gaspar sourced another torch and brought it forward, the brand starting to blaze as he walked. He handed it very carefully – and very gingerly – to Gabriel, who looked across at Constantine. The prince nodded.

He had obviously already briefed the ship's new captain, for Aldo was turning the *Nettuno* slightly now, angling for one of the vessels. The Turk dead ahead was a particularly large galley, bearing the usual red crescent banner, but also the three crescents of a fleet commander. An important ship, and, given that they all knew the prince to be in Kotzinos, probably the flagship of the entire fleet. A game of brinkmanship had begun.

As they sped towards the Turkish fleet, the *Nettuno* picked up pace. Gabriel felt panic hovering at the edge of his nerves with every spark the wind plucked from the brand in his hand. In truth, a spark was unlikely to cause an explosion even if it landed on the barrels, for they were sealed, and regardless, the wind was carrying sparks back across the deck, far from the barrels. But should the entire brand fall, there would be enough residual powder floating around to set the whole lot off.

Gabriel did not like this bluff.

As they sailed directly for the flagship, the Turks responded, a dozen of the closest ships beginning to pull in and forward, joining the flagship in an attempt to intercept the *Nettuno* – something that would play to Constantine's advantage shortly. Every heartbeat now ranked among the most tense in Gabriel's life, as the ships ahead grew, each now moving towards them. He watched the flagship, for which Aldo continually adjusted, keeping them on a collision course, and tried to spy details in their prow, in the sure knowledge that as soon as he could do so, they would similarly be able to see what was happening aboard the *Nettuno*.

Closer and closer. Heartbeat by heartbeat. More detail every moment.

Then someone aboard the *kadirga* ahead raised an alarm. Whether they'd identified what the barrels were already, or perhaps someone had sharp enough eyesight to read the painted slogan, they were suddenly aware of the bomb floating their way – and judging by the instant reaction, they also realised just how big the explosion would be. A din of shouting arose from the ship, and men started to run around the deck in a panic. The flagship started to turn, picking up speed as rapidly as it could, and the motion echoed down the line as every ship bellowed a warning to their neighbours. They were scattering to get out of the *Nettuno*'s way, and not a missile flew, neither arrow nor cannon shot, for fear of setting off the small mountain of explosives and destroying a sizeable part of the Turkish fleet.

'Keep on him,' Constantine called, holding his blazing torch right over the barrels. Captain Aldo obeyed the command, though Gabriel could only imagine his reluctance to do so. The *Nettuno* slowly angled to port, maintaining their collision course with the flagship.

'What are you doing?' Gabriel asked, breathlessly. 'He's getting out of the way.'

'Just making sure.'

The Ianitzaroi commander stared at his prince. *Is he actually crazed enough to go through with it?*

The crew of the Turkish flagship were in a true panic now, watching a bomb bear down on them, and conflicting commands rang out, the ship floundering. The *Nettuno* came closer and closer, and Gabriel began to shake.

Then Constantine called for starboard, and Aldo heaved on his wheel. Gabriel lurched with the sudden leaning of the ship, and almost fell into the barrels, still holding his torch. The moment of panic passed as he righted himself and stepped away. He looked up.

They had turned just in time. Any longer and a collision would have been inevitable. The *Nettuno* raced alongside the Turkish ship, close enough for Gabriel to see the horror on the faces of the sailors as they passed, and then, in a matter of moments, they were past.

They were outside the Turkish blockade for the first time in weeks of imprisonment.

'All speed, Aldo. For Imbros, and then home.'

The crew began to run around making adjustments to lines and sails, getting the most out of the wind, and Gabriel stepped away from the barrels, looking back. The Turks would not catch them. They had been racing south to intercept, and had turned to east and west to get out of the way, but by the time they were facing north again and picking up speed, the *Nettuno* would be far ahead and racing away, out of cannon shot.

They'd done it.

Still, Constantine stood there for a time with his torch held over the gunpowder. Finally, when the Turkish fleet were little more than black blobs on the horizon once more, and Lemnos just a hazy strip beyond them, the prince stepped to the rail and cast his torch into the sea, where it extinguished and bobbed away in the surf. Gabriel followed suit, heaving a huge sigh of relief. Moments later, at Constantine's command, the sailors began untying the ropes and carefully, one by one, rolling the barrels away from the heap and tipping them over the side.

Gabriel only started to breathe normally as the last of the eighteen barrels went over and bobbed away across the sea, adding to the jetsam in their wake. Around them, the crew of the *Nettuno* gave a loud cheer, almost enough to be heard back among the Turks. Constantine slumped, as though the strength had gone out of him, and staggered over to a crate, where he sank to the timber and sat, trembling.

Gabriel walked over to him.

'For a moment, I wondered if you'd do it anyway.'

There was a pause, only for a heartbeat. 'You think me a madman? No, Gabriel. I had to look as though I was prepared to do it, in order to convince them.'

But Gabriel was less sure. That pause had been telling. Still, they were out and safe, and bound for the capital at last, and all the gunpowder had gone.

'I presume we are not stopping at Imbros?'

The prince shook his head. 'I'll not risk them sailing north and trapping us again. Now we're out, we need to stay ahead of them and get home. We'll pause at Imbros only long enough to change ship and resupply, and then head straight out and overnight at sea now until we reach Constantinople. I have no intention of being held up again.'

'Good.'

Because now that they were out and making for home, the prince would have time to reflect on his loss, and the sooner they reached the capital and the disaster awaiting them, the better.

7

City in Foment

Constantinople

Autumn 1442

The sound of waves and creaking timbers, gulls and busy sailors.

'Nothing,' Constantine said, standing at the port rail, voice taut. 'Where *are* they all?'

'A very good question,' Gabriel replied, as his gaze swept across the shore. 'And one to which I have no satisfactory answer.'

The ship ploughed on along the Propontine coastline, approaching the city proper, with its massive walls and guarded harbours. For a mile and more of suburban land, they had seen the signs of the war's aftermath, but no sign of the enemy itself. Whole areas of the settlements outside the walls had been ravaged and burned, and there was what appeared to be a massive abandoned campsite close to the shore, just outside of bowshot of the ramparts.

Of a besieging army: no sign.

Still uncertain as to what it was they were seeing – or, more correctly, *not* seeing – they gripped the rail and watched the city slide past. Nothing seemed untoward; life was going on as normal, though there was more than one possible explanation for that. Indeed, the most likely one was that Demetrios and his Turkish allies had taken the walls with little difficulty, swamped the city, and that Constantine's bitter, dangerous brother was

221

now seated on the throne, with John wallowing in a dungeon. In truth, the ordinary citizens of Constantinople would not notice much difference, and would simply be grateful the siege was over.

They raced past the Eleutherian harbour, once the heart of Byzantine sea trade, but long since silted up and given over to farmland, enclosed by walls that had been blocked up to form a solid defensive line, and ahead lay the Kontoskalion, a smaller affair, but busy and lively. Ships of half a dozen nationalities were docked there as they entered the harbour mouth, further evidence that the war was over and the city settled.

Gabriel braced himself as their ship slid towards the jetty, slowed, and finally settled with a bump against the timbers. The ramp was run out, the cables were tied, and all was made ready. A small party of administrators and courtiers stood on the harbourside with their servants and guides, the path across to them having been cleared of people and clutter. The tension and worry that the city would not welcome them disappeared as they alighted, and George Sphrantzes stepped out of the crowd and to the fore.

'A good sign,' Gabriel noted.

The prince just nodded. If Demetrios ruled now, it was unlikely Constantine's great friend would be so easy and free.

'My lord, it is a balm to see you again,' the scholar said as they reached the end of the jetty.

'I am surprised, George. I had thought to arrive and find the city invested by the Turks. Their navy did its best to stop me getting here.'

'It was a difficult thing,' Sphrantzes admitted, turning and walking alongside Constantine as they made their way to the waiting carriage. 'Your brother was determined to wrest the city from the emperor, though I fear the Turks were involved only on an opportunistic basis. I don't think either was prepared to meet a reasonable standing force protecting the city. The Turks thought us to be poorly manned, and Demetrios expected the city to open up to him. Neither was true. In the end, the sultan pulled his support out and left your brother to it on his own. I gather there is pressing trouble from Hungary and Wallachia, and the Sublime Porte needs to concentrate elsewhere for now. A crusade may be in the wind.'

'So, the city was essentially saved by lack of effort.'

'Something like that. Now tell me of your own time, Constantine. I have not seen you in Methuselah's age.'

Gabriel and his men found horses at the harbour stables and mounted, riding alongside the carriage as it rolled through the streets on its way to the Blachernae and the main imperial residence. Nothing looked amiss, which was a strange feeling when he'd been expecting a desperate city filled with misery and hardship. Moreover, he wasn't sure what enforced peace and quiet might do to the prince in his current state.

He and the others dismounted as the carriage came to a halt in the courtyard of the Palatium Imperatorum on the northern fringe of the Blachernae.

'…and your brother has been based here, rather than in the main Blachernae ever since,' Sphrantzes finished, stepping out of the carriage. 'The damage to the Blachernae walls is minimal, though, and should be repaired within the year.'

Constantine led the way now, striding into the palace, as guards and attendants bowed their heads in respect with his passing. Gabriel left the other Ianitzaroi outside and joined the two noblemen as they moved through the palace until they entered the *aula* of state, where John sat poring over documents, with two clerks handing them to him and taking them away when complete. The emperor looked up as they entered.

'Ah, excellent. It will be good to have a little help, brother. And George here has been of precious little use since he heard you were approaching, for he was too excitable, like a puppy whose master was coming home.'

Sphrantzes had the grace to look a little embarrassed at that, but it was Constantine who spoke next. 'It would appear you did not need me after all, John.'

'In truth, you had already done much to help. It was the force you had assembled as regent, bolstered by the units you sent from the Morea, who kept the enemy from the walls. We lost many men, though Demetrios and the sultan lost more. Lucky, in a way, since I struggled to find funds in the treasury to pay even the survivors. I need the taxes from the Morea and the tribute from Athens with some urgency.'

Constantine nodded. 'But we have weathered the storm, and now Murad must turn elsewhere, for the king of Hungary looks ravenously to his lands. We should send someone to the Sublime Porte. It may be that we need to strike a new deal with them, and perhaps we may get a better one. Though I am running to the end of my patience with the Turks right now. As for Demetrios?'

The emperor pushed away the documents he'd stopped checking and leaned back. 'He is in the Anemas dungeon, though I was thinking to commute his sentence and put him under house arrest in the palace.'

Constantine's face darkened. 'House arrest? He should be flayed and burned for what he did.'

'Constantine, he is our *brother*.'

'He is a usurper, a traitor, and entirely untrustworthy. I would run him through myself, but for the fear that his corrupt blood would rot my blade. Put him in the bronze ox and light the fires, John.'

The emperor fixed Constantine with a hard look. 'No. He is our brother, and though we might not agree with him, he is a man who holds the good of the city high in his mind. It is his staunch belief in the failure of the act of union that brought us to this, after all. No, Constantine, he will be held for a time, until he is willing to take a solid oath. We will have use for him yet.'

'Then do not put him anywhere near me, for should we meet alone, only one of us will leave, mark my words.'

The emperor frowned. 'Where is your clemency, Constantine? Your compassion?'

'Save compassion for church, John. Emperors do not have such luxuries.'

The emperor sighed. 'I am rapidly running out of brothers, now, apparently. Demetrios was the despot of Mesembria, but he has lost that position. Theodore still maintains Mystras, and Thomas is settled in the Morea with him. That just leaves us. I want you to take Mesembria, and all the lands north and west of the city, as your despotate, including Selymbria.'

Constantine shook his head. 'My place is in the Morea now.'

'It wasn't a request, Constantine. Damn you, but you *wanted* Mesembria not long ago, and now you *refuse*?'

'Give it to someone else. Recall Theodore or Thomas.'

'Theodore has precedence in the Morea. I will not order him away. His wife is buried there. And Thomas is too young for such a critical post. If Murad decides to come again, Mesembria will be the first line of defence.'

'You have a hundred hungry courtiers, some of whom can hold a sword.'

'No.'

'Find someone else, John.'

'I say again, no, Constantine. Do not make me order you. We have never had that relationship, and I do not want to start now.'

'Give it to Demetrios if you think you can trust the weasel.'

'That's *enough*, Constantine. You are despot of Mesembria. I give you two days in the city to put things in order, and then I expect you to take up your posting.'

For a moment, it looked as though the prince might argue, but instead, he simply turned his back on the emperor and walked away.

'That had better be mute acceptance,' John snapped at his retreating back.

Gabriel looked across at Sphrantzes. 'I had best go with him.'

'Me too, I think.'

The two men made their polite farewells to the emperor and backed from the room, before turning and following Constantine's trail. He would be heading for the exit, though he was obviously walking fast, angry.

'What has happened to him?' Sphrantzes breathed as they hurried in the prince's wake.

'Aikaterine. She died on Lemnos.'

'God above, no. I had not heard.'

'She was with child.'

'Oh my word. And it has broken him?'

'If not, then it has come very close. You remember what he was like before? When he lost Theodora? How he would stand and face down arrows, or walk into the enemy's arms, heedless of the danger? Well, that is back, and far worse. He invites death as though it is a friend. And his lightness has gone. I thought to distract him with action, but I worry that to throw him into war now is to invite death all the more. Yet when he is not fighting, he wallows in despair. The journey from Imbros has been one of the most terrible times I have had. I simply do not know what to do. How to end it. He is becoming Theodore.'

'That must be stopped. I, too, am unsure of how to press him. I fear finding him a third wife may heap further sorrow on him, yet war may not be the answer, as you say. There will be a solution, and I wonder if the empress, his mother, may not hold it. She is without a doubt the most shrewd woman I have ever known.'

They reached the main door, and Gabriel saw Constantine climbing into a saddle, the Ianitzaroi around him.

'One other thing,' Sphrantzes said, grasping Gabriel's shoulder as he made to follow. 'It may change things with the prince, or it may not, but it should be noted anyway. Among the sultan's forces last month was a unit of Westerners bearing the arms of the Tocco. I never saw Torno himself, but I do not doubt he was there, by the Turkish commander's side.'

'That man's end is coming,' Gabriel said quietly. 'And soon.'

'And the emperor is not well, Gabriel. Not an illness, per se, but exhaustion and hopelessness, I think. He is permanently tired, and struggles with the weight of the crown. I do not think he needs Constantine in Mesembria to guard the city approaches, but to be on hand for support. The prince is, of course, the only one he ever trusted like that.'

'Sounds to me like he puts unrealistic trust in Demetrios, too.'

'That is a cauldron of trouble I'd rather not stir.'

Selymbria

Winter 1442

'The news from the city is worse, week by week,' Constantine spat, casting the dispatches across the desk to where Sphrantzes sat, working through lists.

'Oh?'

'Demetrios was released at the end of last month, against all my counsel.'

'I remember.'

'Well, now he's in prison again. Back in the Anemas tower. Seems he's been building another plot in the city. Details are vague, but if I read between the lines, I might think that Theodore has been stirring things, making overtures to Demetrios.'

'That bodes badly for the peace. Demetrios can clearly not be trusted, and Theodore has had no time for either you or John ever since you were made regent. Could it be that now Theodore sees himself as the next emperor?'

Constantine snorted. 'He always has. But he will not snatch the throne from John as Demetrios tried. His belief in the Lord's plan and divine right is unshakeable, and he would not stand against a God-given emperor, ever. But John is tired, and not a young man now, and he has no heir. And since we became a

227

little more distant, I am not sure he sees me as his successor any more. It may be that Theodore is simply lining up for when the time comes and making sure he has Demetrios' support.'

'And what of Thomas?'

'He would back me, always, but he also holds far less authority and power than the rest of us. If John settles upon Theodore – and he *is* the senior brother – then there are no legal grounds to oppose him. As things stand, I would be very surprised if Theodore is not the next emperor.'

'Then that needs to change,' Sphrantzes said, leaning forward.

'What?'

'If John goes to God and joins Andronikos in Heaven, then there are four of you left. Demetrios would hand the empire to the Turks in return for the title of bey, and that must not happen. And Theodore would turn away from all our allies, Turk and Catholic alike, for he cannot abide any but the Patriarch's Church. We would be small and powerless and friendless. It would be a huge step towards the empire's end. Thomas, as you say, has not enough authority or power to challenge anyone. That leaves you.'

'What makes you think I want it?'

Sphrantzes frowned. 'You were not averse to the idea when he made you regent.'

'And I had my taste of power. Besides, for all its vaunted value, the city and its crown are little more than pretty symbols these days.'

Even Gabriel started at that, frowning. That did not sound like Constantine Palaiologos.

'You don't believe that,' Sphrantzes said quietly.

'The true power in the empire, such as it is, now lies in the Morea, George. It is defensible, surrounded by sea, and with only a land approach that can be guarded by the Hexamilion. It is a land of growth and of wealth, while the city here is a shrinking, impoverished jewel, surrounded entirely by the

Turks. You heard John when we came back. He drained the treasury saving the city, and the only thing that was going to save him was the taxes from the Morea and the tribute from Athens. Here, we are just caretakers of the shroud for a dying city.'

'Surely you cannot believe that?' George breathed. 'The city has weathered every disaster and come through triumphant. Even decades of control by the Franks, with your forebears in exile, and yet we still took it back. The city is important, and so is the crown.'

'Hmph.'

Sphrantzes looked across at Gabriel, who shrugged. He had no idea how to tackle this. Sorrow and anger were hard enough to counter, but defeat? That was something he couldn't work with. No soldier could. Gabriel stepped forward, clearing his throat. If an appeal to Constantine's ambitions didn't work, perhaps one to his duty would.

'Once, two decades ago, when you were a young man, and I a less old one, we stood on the ramparts of that city and faced an army the likes of which we'd never seen, with weapons that could tear apart stone like parchment. You remember?'

'I do.'

'That day you fought for the city, even when you didn't need to. When you probably shouldn't have. And I remember you shouting at the people, urging them on. That Constantine, the one I stood beside that day, thought the city important. Worth fighting for. I am Catalan by blood, and mercenary by trade. I could serve anyone, work anywhere, but Constantinople and the empire are all I've ever known, and your family all I've ever served.'

'Gabriel, I...'

'A soldier takes oaths, Constantine. I took mine to your father, and then to your brother, and finally to you. And an oath is an important thing. It defines duty. I have a duty to protect you. But you are the son of an emperor, and on occasion the chosen heir of one, too.'

'I'm tired of this, Gabriel.'

'I don't give a shit.'

The prince blinked in surprise, but Gabriel levelled a finger at him. 'You are a son of the Palaiologoi, and that means you have a duty to the empire – to your *people*, just as I have a duty to you. You can be tired, or angry, or sad, or weak, but it matters not how you feel in your heart. Duty means you hammer a plank over that weakness and you stand up and fight anyway. Demetrios may be dangerous and cunning, but even he knows that.'

Constantine sagged. 'What would you have me do?'

'Fight. Fight for the empire.'

'Fight who?'

It was Sphrantzes who answered now, leaning forward. 'It is said that the Pope calls for a crusade. This winter. He will issue a bull, and the West will come for the Turks. For a generation now we have had to mollify and please the Sublime Porte with everything we do. They ratify all imperial decisions, define all our policies. If ever we had a chance to be free of Turkish power, it will be when the West marches to war. Think of it, Constantine. An empire free of influence once more, with the Turks pushed safely back across the Bosphorus.'

Constantine sat in the silence that followed, his expression unreadable.

Finally, he looked up at Gabriel. 'You humble me. Not an easy thing to do.'

Gabriel couldn't think of anything to say to that.

'Of course,' the prince went on, 'if we want to help the Pope when he comes, this is not the place to do it. We would be marching directly into the sultan's heartland. Better we build up the walls and the garrisons here, but we begin the campaign elsewhere.'

'The Morea again?'

The prince nodded. 'John doesn't need us in Selymbria now. Theodore wants to stand as heir? Then let him come and protect the city with John, and we can join Thomas in the Morea once again. In a decade we have taken a shattered, small province and rebuilt it to cover the Morea entire. Perhaps we can do better.'

Sphrantzes frowned. 'I'm not sure I like the idea of putting Theodore so close to the throne, Constantine.'

'It is a matter of expediency, George. Here, I can do little but challenge the sultan's heartland, while Theodore is content to sit in his mountains and present no challenge to the Turks in the Morea. On the other hand, he could sit in Selymbria and dream of the throne, while in the Morea, I could take the sword to the Greek mainland and start to rebuild an empire.'

'So I presume you would like me to pen letters to Theodore and propose an exchange?'

'Do it.'

Across the room, Gabriel breathed a silent sigh of relief. He still wasn't sure that war was the best focus to keep the prince's mind off his sorrow, but it did seem to be the only thing that worked. And at least in the Morea they would be free of the sort of intrigues the city was prey to.

PART THREE – EMPIRE

Constantine ... took note of the arrival of the king and of the ships at the Hellespont; he had prophesied that the total destruction of the Turks was imminent.

Doukas, *Decline and Fall of Byzantium to the Ottoman Turks*

8

To Reclaim an Empire

Korinthos

Two years later: September 1444

'You realise that if we're wrong, we are essentially declaring war on the sultan without support, lord?'

Constantine just gave a nod. John Rhosatsas huffed for a moment, then turned to him again.

'And that doesn't worry you?'

'George believes that they will listen to Cardinal Cesarini. Besides, why would the king of Hungary continue to move with his forces if he meant to honour this bedevilled pact?'

It was a good point. Perhaps not one worth wagering the future of the empire on, but well made nonetheless. The past year had been the tensest balancing act of Gabriel's life. Not that he'd had a lot of involvement in that act, other than making sure Constantine and his companions were secure throughout it. But still the tension had been tangible in the air of the Morea.

A Morea now largely controlled by Constantine.

His brother Theodore had readily agreed to the exchange of territories, taking on Mesembria, for, though it meant giving up his long-standing despotate, the notion of being so close to the throne at a time when it was beginning to look as though it might soon be empty fairly suddenly, was too good to pass up. Of course, the shifting of the two brothers' entire courts and lives from one side of the empire to the other took a number

235

of months, but by the summer of 1443, Constantine and his people were once more installed in the Morea.

That was when the balancing act truly began.

The Pope had published his bull for a crusade a few months earlier, and in the spring, at Buda, war had officially been declared on the Turks. An army of crusaders had crossed from Hungary and invaded Serbia and Bulgaria, now both Turkish territories, seizing important cities and fortresses, securing the road to Edirne and the sultan's capital. The timing was auspicious for Constantine, the crusade keeping the sultan and his beys busy and granting Constantine all the excuse he needed.

The plan had been months in the making. First Constantine's ambassadors managed to coax, beg and extort money from the many rich landowners of the Morea, citing their protection as the reason. Money began to pour into Korinthos, which Constantine now used as a base. That money was in the coffers for only days before it was shipped straight out, either paying for materials and workmen or the hiring of mercenary forces, all carried out as quietly and calmly as possible so as not to raise alarm. Materials were stockpiled every mile across the isthmus, and units were garrisoned in towns and cities, and out in the countryside, spread out so as not to create such a concentration of force as would reach the ears of the sultan or his bey.

Constantine made the first move the day the Zlatitsa Pass fell to the crusaders, signalling that the Catholics, under the command of the Hungarian king Władysław III, were almost on the doorstep of the Sublime Porte. Then, men were brought up in their hundreds and assigned sections of the isthmus. The Hexamilion, so recently demolished by the Turks, went up once more, this time higher and stronger than before, and it did so in a mere thirty days, all materials and workmen being in place ready. And while men and goods moved day and night for the construction, Byzantine garrison units manoeuvring into place to man the wall, many other forces were gradually and subtly slipped up towards the frontier, hidden among all the movement.

Sphrantzes had arrived from the capital mere days after the wall was finished, and was astonished. From that initial move, the balancing act intensified, for Constantine had already been warned against rebuilding the wall. Turahan Bey was not prepared for that to happen, and while Constantine had war with the Turks in his sights, it had to be timed and balanced carefully, and good relations needed to be maintained as long as possible.

To that end, the prince had dispatched the renowned diplomat Loukas Notaras to Turahan Bey, and to the Sublime Porte itself if necessary. He would defend the reconstruction and manning of the wall, citing the Catholic crusaders now being just three hundred miles from the Morea, and every bit as dangerous to the empire as they were to the Turks. After all, they might have recently been in talks with the Pope, but the Turks knew well enough the history of papal crusaders sacking the imperial heartland, and the bad feeling that lingered even centuries later. The Hexamilion was a level of defence for the empire, that was all, and no intended provocation to the Sublime Porte – or so Notaras would say. The bey and his master would be satisfied, Constantine was sure. Notaras could carry out such a mission almost as well as George Sphrantzes, who would have been sent himself, had he not been given another mission.

Even as Loukas poured honeyed words in the ear of the most powerful Turk outside Edirne, Sphrantzes was sent secretly to the court of the Hungarian king in Buda, making overtures to the leaders of the crusade, noting the position of Constantine and Thomas as a potential second front against the Turks. A clandestine alliance with the crusaders was possible, given that officially the two Churches were united – for all the lack of acceptance in the capital. With Władysław pushing the Turks from the north-west and Constantine from the south, it was possible they could force the sultan to retreat ever eastwards until he had to cross the Bosphorus once more. But Constantine couldn't make the next move, taking his army beyond the wall, until he knew that the crusaders had agreed, and were making serious inroads. If the Sublime Porte were to learn of Sphrantzes' embassy, Notaras would be executed in a heartbeat, and there would be war in the isthmus.

There *would* be war there, of course, eventually, but it had to be on Constantine's terms. The sultan's strength would have to be divided between there and the crusaders.

A setback had come in the summer. Sultan Murad had been content to pick away at his neighbours, but apparently had not had the stomach for a full-blown war. He had therefore begun overtures of peace with the crusaders, who, beginning to slow in their advance and feeling the pressure and ennui of a long campaign, were apparently considering accepting. Indeed, despite Cardinal Cesarini's insistence that the crusade continue – a position shared by the king of Hungary – deeds were drawn up over the summer for a ten-year guarantee of peace.

The word that the treaty had been signed on 15 August came like a hammer blow to the Byzantines, who were busy building their force behind the wall, ready to join the campaign – the first time in a century they might stand a chance of besting the Turks. Anger and frustration filled the camp for a time, then, and it seemed increasingly likely by the day that the new mercenaries would have to be let go once more, and the wall abandoned for fear of provoking Turahan Bey… until five days later, when another, secret, message arrived.

Sphrantzes, writing in carefully coded terms that only he and Constantine could unravel, cautioned the prince not to back down. He noted that though the peace had been signed, it might as well have been written on water, for eminent royalty and priests at the highest level of command in the crusade advocated a continuation of hostilities.

That could only have meant Cardinal Cesarini and Władysław of Hungary.

The weeks that followed were tense. Officially, the crusaders and their Turkish foe were now at peace, and with a written guarantee of ten years' such. Yet rumours poured in every other day. Despite the treaty, Władysław had received embassies from the Wallachian voivod Mircea, son of Vlad Dracul, who, along with the powerful János Hunyadi, was said to be on the move south, making for Turkish lands. Officially there was peace, yet the crusade seemed to be back on, regardless.

Which had brought them to this day, a bright, warm September morning at the isthmus. Mercantile traffic crossing the Hexamilion from the northern reaches of the Duchy of Athens and beyond had confirmed time and again that there was no preparation, concentration of troops or apparent alarm among the Turkish-controlled lands in the north of the duchy. Constantine's slow build-up of forces, hidden among the work, along with his placatory embassies to the bey, had apparently worked, hiding the true amassing of men at the isthmus.

'Give the order to move, Strategos,' the prince said quietly, peering into the distant north. 'Everyone knows their place in the plan. The entire army is briefed.'

Rhosatsas bowed his head as best he could with an armoured gorget bracing his neck and chin, and turned, waving to the small group of signallers. Banners were waved down behind the level of the wall, but no horns blown. The Turks might be entirely unaware of what was coming, but still, there was no need to break the silence so soon.

'Come, Gabriel. Time to join the advance.'

With that, Constantine Palaiologos, Prince of Rome, spun and ducked into the stairwell, taking the steps two at a time down all three floors until he reached the ground, where he dashed out and pulled himself up into the saddle, even as servants rushed forward to help, too late to do so. No one rushed to help Gabriel, of course, and he and the Ianitzaroi mounted professionally and massed, gathering around the prince. By the time they were moving off towards the units approaching the wall gate, Rhosatsas cantered to catch up, bowing awkwardly in the saddle to Constantine. He reached down to where his helmet – an ornate sallet – hung by a strap, and was about to lift it when he frowned, looking around.

'My lord? Your helmet?'

Constantine turned, a question in his eyes.

'We ride to war, my lord,' Rhosatsas pressed. 'One well-placed arrow...'

Constantine shrugged. 'Behelmed, I am just another soldier. Bare-headed, I am a prince of Rome. The men need to see that. Besides, a helmet is just one layer of iron. I have a dozen.' He smiled, gesturing to the Ianitzaroi around him.

'And you, Gabriel Black-eye?' the general added, gesturing to the bodyguard.

Gabriel snorted. 'And hide my lovely face from the enemy?'

Rhosatsas laughed then. 'Well, since I have no bodyguard, and my face is not ogreish, I shall avail myself of that single layer of iron.' And with that, he lifted the sallet and covered his head. As he veered off to discuss something with another officer, Gaspar pulled a little closer. 'He will be drenched in sweat in a score of heartbeats in this weather.' The big ourghos grinned.

'And you?' the prince put in, conversationally, nodding to Gaspar. 'Why no helm for you?'

Now it was time for Gabriel to laugh. 'They don't make them in his size. I suggested he adapt some horse armour, but that didn't go down too well.'

Constantine chuckled. 'I'm sure there's a large bucket, or a small barrel, somewhere in the baggage we could cut eyeholes in.' As they all laughed, he glanced across at Manuel, similarly bare-headed. 'And what of you, banner-man? No helm to save you?'

'God preserves my sorry hide, sir. Besides, it's heavy enough carrying this bloody thing,' he added, nodding at the pole carrying the unit's wyvern banner. 'I have to say,' he added, 'that I prefer serving you to your father, my prince. The old man liked me to bear his own banner as well. Two flags on one pole is a fucking nightmare.'

Again, they all chortled at this, a lightness that seemed at odds with their purpose that day. They rode in silence, then, as they passed through the Victorinus Gate and out into the countryside beyond, passing from the despotate of the Morea and into the vassal state of Athens. A mile of brown grass dotted with green shrubs spread out to the north-east to the first important position. Down by the water there, where once the Romans had begun a canal, stood a watchtower and a small settlement, controlled by the Duchy of Athens.

A gamble awaited there. Constantine had not approached Nerio of Athens concerning the campaign. The duke was acknowledged a vassal of the empire, yet his taxes went to the Turks, and it had been just too much of a risk to reveal the coming move to Nerio, lest the news leap straight from there to Turahan Bey. Now that the army was on the move, and secrecy was coming to an end, Athens needed to be approached.

Gabriel watched that tower as they closed. The alarm had clearly gone up the moment the army began to pour through the Hexamilion, and now the battlements bristled with gleaming armoured soldiers. The settlement was all aflutter, men and women at their doors, nervous, waiting to see what was coming. As they closed on the place, Gabriel noted the stable, doors wide open, with several empty stalls. He turned to Constantine and pointed at it, and the prince nodded and then reined in before the tower. No bows were visible, but there would undoubtedly be men up there with arrows nocked below the level of the battlements, ready. Gabriel's men were already close to the prince with their shields shouldered.

'Greetings,' the prince called. 'I am Constantine Palaiologos, Despot of the Morea and ally of Duke Nerio of Athens. We mean no harm here. As the armies of Władysław of Hungary and his allies march on the sultan at Edirne, so we march for the sultan's favourite bey at Tırhala. I would call upon my ally Nerio to join the cause and throw off the yoke of the Turk who takes his taxes. Send another rider after the one who just left, bearing only fraternal offers of mutual glory. Tell Nerio to gather his armies and meet me at Thebes.'

And with that, he turned, threw his arm out north-east, and the army continued that way, marching past the tower and the settlement and making for the northern edge of the duchy, where Turkish forces still maintained their hold.

'Do you think he'll come?' Gabriel mused.

Constantine nodded. 'He'll come. He is in an unenviable position, jammed between us and Turahan Bey. He bows to one of us and pays the other, and now that we are at war, he will have to choose a side. If he does not, then whoever wins will make him regret it. He cannot support the Turks, behind our advance, for he must know already that Thomas is still at the wall with a force of his own. No, he will come.'

'Let us pray that he does,' Rhosatsas called from nearby. 'And that the Pope's warriors continue on their cause.'

That, Gabriel would pray for. If Sphrantzes was wrong, and the crusaders just turned round and went home, then all the weight of the Turkish forces would come to bear on the relatively small imperial army.

It was sixty miles to Thebes, north-east around the curve of the Gulf of Lepanto and across several passes, and it was the imperial plan to hit that town – the first major Turkish stronghold – by nightfall the day after next, making it a hard march averaging twenty miles per day. But there was one obstacle before Thebes. The passes across the high ridges between here and there were largely under Athenian control and unguarded, but the Kithairon Pass, the last on the journey and just ten miles from Thebes, would be different, for it marked the edge of Turkish control. They would have to take the pass from its current occupants in order to reach Thebes, and though it undoubtedly held little more than a picket garrison, the plan called for it to be taken swiftly and without warning. Should a signal be sent, then Thebes would be prepared for the attack, but should the pass fall without such a chance, then the imperial army could be at the walls of Thebes before the local *mutesellim* could send word to his master, Turahan Bey. The greatest chance of success in this endeavour, as recognised from the start, was born from two aspects: firstly, that the Turks would be busy trying to turn back the Catholic crusaders to the north, and could therefore afford to spend little effort against the empire; and secondly, surprise and speed. The faster the imperial force could move, and the less warning their targets received, the faster they would take territory, until, hopefully, they could link up with the crusade and the Turks would be forced to fall back.

Thus it was that Gabriel felt the tension increase as they travelled, particularly with every ridge they crossed, revealing wide fertile valleys that led up to the next climb. They were moving fast. That, too, was part of the plan. By necessity much of the army was slow, with heavy infantry and the endless wagons of the supply train that rumbled along at the pace of tidal drift, but Constantine had placed most of his cavalry, as well as the light infantry, at the head of the army. It was their job to move swiftly and overcome obstacles, so that the bulk of the army could then catch them up periodically, and if they found themselves weighed down in a major siege, they could wait for the others to arrive.

The first night, they camped beside a place called Alepo-chori, a peaceful fishing village nestled below the hills on the Lepantine shore. It had been a long day and a hard slog, and the second day offered only the same, if Constantine's plan was to work. They had travelled four hours into the dark that first day, camped for six, and then risen and begun to move before dawn once more. The second day, they wound inland and, as the sun set, began the climb of the southern slopes towards the Kithairon Pass. There, they stopped once more, close to a church that had seen far better days and whose priest was long gone, so close to the Turkish border. That night they were subdued, for everyone knew what the next day meant. They had already committed and crossed the wall, but there was still time now to explain to the bey and maintain the peace. Even when they reached the pass, all was not lost. But the moment a Turk died in that pass, the gauntlet had been thrown down, and there was no turning back. The imperial army beside that of the sultan was like a goat beside a lion. If everything went wrong and the crusaders turned round, or if the duke threw his support behind the Turks, then the empire would be fighting for its life.

Gabriel slept little that night, and was wandering the camp when the scouts returned. He followed the scout officer as he was shown to the prince's tent, and there relieved the Ianitzaroi on duty of their posts and told them to get some sleep. Taking their place, Gabriel entered, to find Constantine and Rhosatsas wide awake at a table and maps. They looked up at the scout.

'Tell me.'

'Lord, there is a single outpost, with one tower, at the crest of the pass. We saw only the night-time patrol, but I would estimate not more than a dozen men in residence, and I think they will be low-quality *azab* infantry drawn from Thessaly. There is no clear method of signalling, but I would very much suspect a beacon atop the tower that we could not identify in the dark.'

'Anything else in the area?'

'Not that we saw, lord, but we did not dare come too close for fear of alerting the guards.'

Constantine nodded and dismissed the scout, then sat, drumming his fingers on the desk. 'Problematical. Even if we hit them fast, it will be hard to gain the tower-top before they can light a beacon and send word to Thebes. Neither speed nor force will win this.'

Gabriel winced. He could feel this coming like a slow hammer blow. He was waiting for it even as Constantine turned to him. 'Have my bodyguard ready for action an hour before dawn, Gabriel. We have a job.'

'Sir, you cannot put yourself in such danger.'

'We need them off guard. I can think of no better way of doing that. And before you marshal yet more arguments, don't. Just go and tell your men to be armed and in the saddle an hour before dawn.'

Gabriel, his ruined lip twitching, nodded and turned, leaving the room. There was no need to do as he'd been ordered, for the Ianitzaroi were always up and prepared by such a time, and always ready for action. Instead, he simply sat on a tree stump and kept a watch on the prince's tent until the next shift of Ianitzaroi came on, and then returned to his bunk and totally failed to sleep. A few hours later, he rose, armed and armoured himself, and then went out to meet his men. The sky was just beginning to lighten in the east, promising dawn not too far off, and Manuel frowned at him. 'You look tired.'

'I am, but I'll live. This morning brings interesting work.'

'Oh?'

'The prince is making another spirited attempt to get himself killed.'

'And us with him?'

'Yes. We're going to... No, I'll let the prince brief you. Come on.'

He led them to the stables and there they gathered their horses and led them around the tents to the prince's own. There, the two spare horses they led were given to the two soldiers on guard, and Gabriel knocked. There was no call to enter, but a moment later, Constantine emerged in the doorway, already dressed and with his sword at his side.

'Good,' he proclaimed, then sent one of the nearby servants to run and bring his horse. He then turned back to Gabriel. 'Have you briefed them?'

'With respect, *you* haven't briefed *me* yet.'

'I suppose not.' Constantine stretched. 'All right, my friends, this is what we are about to do. A garrison of some twelve Turks occupies an outpost with a tower at the crest of the pass.

We need to neutralise the entire place before they can light an assumed beacon atop the tower. Since this is unlikely with a direct assault, we need to get inside and take them by surprise. I intend to play on my value as an imperial officer, given our current peace with the Sublime Porte, and you will be, as you naturally are, my bodyguard. We will enter the place and ask to speak to the commander. While I do so, you men will subtly spread out, even to the tower. The moment I give the signal, each of you will move to take down any men within reach. One of you will remain by the gate to prevent any escape, and several of you need to get into that tower immediately and up to the top to prevent any beacon being lit. With luck, we can secure the whole place in moments, and then be at liberty to sneak up on Thebes.'

As the prince was brought his horse and mounted, Gabriel handed out further instructions, giving Gaspar control of the gate, and setting Manuel to remain close to the prince. Gabriel would take six men close to the tower and take on that respons- ibility. A score of heartbeats later, and the twenty-five of them were riding into the open even as the rest of the army was preparing to break camp and move out.

The pass lay perhaps two and a half or three miles north- east, and so the sun was just starting to gleam between the peaks, golden and warm, as the outpost came into view. A simple wooden palisade perhaps fifty feet across enclosed two buildings, judging by the roofs that rose within, and a stone tower some thirty feet high, topped with the crescent banner of the Turks, which hung limp in the still air. The scouts had been correct, for as they neared the place, Gabriel could see atop the tower an iron basket filled with timber, on a pole: a beacon waiting to be lit.

As they approached, especially with Manuel bearing the double-headed eagle banner of the Palaiologoi aloft, there was considerable activity and excitement in the outpost. Much to Gabriel's satisfaction, the gate opened in welcome, for this was seemingly an imperial embassy – a nobleman with his retinue – and no perceived threat. They rode on, moving at a steady pace, until they reached the tower, where an officer stood in the gate with one of his men. Two more were watching from a parapet walk above.

'Good day,' the prince announced, loudly and in Greek. 'I am Constantine Palaiologos, Despot of the Morea. I have business in Thebes, and ultimately in Tırhala, though our mounts are weary and dry. Perhaps we can prevail upon you for water and hay while we rest them before pressing on for Thebes?'

There was the briefest of pauses as the words were considered by the Turks, probably trying to translate some of the more complex ones, but finally the officer and his man stepped away from the gate and gestured for them to enter.

'Welcome, Despot,' the man said as they rode through the gate and into the compound. 'I am Başı Kara Kemal. Please, join us, and I will have your horses taken care of.'

Gabriel made sure not to smile, as it would be unseemly for a diplomat's guard, and kept his face lowered as often as possible, though as they passed into the heart of the place, every now and then someone would pay attention to him and flinch, then look away, clutching their blue-eye amulet and muttering wards against evil.

It was so casual. Most of the Ianitzaroi dismounted and let the Turkish soldiers lead their horses over to the stabling area, where a trough of water and a feed rail of hay awaited. They then took the opportunity to spread out, moving around the place in the manner of men long in the saddle, stamping life back into their feet. Gaspar and a chosen man sat close by the gate and immediately pulled out a pair of dice. It was all so innocuous and normal. Gabriel himself wandered over towards the tower and leaned against the wall, closing his eyes as though enjoying the play of the early morning sun on the lids. Others drifted over to join him. Constantine, with Manuel and three others beside him, engaged the officer in quiet conversation. Gabriel couldn't quite hear what they were saying, but the officer was making an almost comical attempt to nod his understanding and agreement while keeping his head bowed in respect for his visitor's rank.

Everyone had been in place for a short while when Gabriel, his eyes occasionally opening and straying to their master, saw Constantine give a small nod even as the prince's hand slowly fell to his hip.

Gabriel repeated that nod, making sure that everyone saw it, and he was beginning to move as Constantine's hand came up with the dagger in it, and plunged the blade into the officer's eye. He drove it home to the hilt as the Turk shrieked and shuddered, falling to the dirt, the blade slipping back out covered in unmentionable matter. A momentary glance around as Gabriel moved, and he saw Manuel, close to the prince, take down one of the other men, his banner dropped unceremoniously in the dust, an arm going around the Turk's upper body as the other hand came round with a blade in it, slicing through the throat in a swift single move. And even as the prince and his companions dispatched the commander and his men, over by the gate, Gaspar casually reached across and grabbed one of the guards there as he registered something was wrong, gripping his head in both hands and turning it with apparent ease so that it faced almost backwards before dropping him to the dirt. The fight was on.

As Gabriel unsheathed his sword, reached the door of the tower and kicked it open, rushing inside, he reflected upon the prince's opening move. It had been unnecessary. Manuel would have killed the man for him, and even if the prince had felt the need to deliver the kill, there were more humane ways to achieve it. Not that Gabriel would baulk at the odd eye-gouging, but it was hardly a thing one would expect from a cultured prince. That darkness that gripped Constantine's heart was still there, and even when buried, it was finding ways to make its presence known.

Inside the door, a man was busy polishing a sword. Gabriel ran past him, hurtling up the steps, leaving one of his Ianitzaroi to finish him. The second floor was empty, but as he burst out into the morning sunlight on the tower roof, there were two soldiers there, and they had seen what was happening and were ready. One had a sword out and was blocking the way to the other, who was busy flicking away with a flint and steel, trying to get the spark to catch in the tinder.

Gabriel, not the smallest of men, hit the swordsman hard, shoulder first, barging him aside. He felt the man's hastily swung blade catch him on the arm – a passing blow, but he ignored it for now. Time was of the essence. As his men followed on and dived at the swordsman, ready to finish him, Gabriel ran at the beacon attendant. Sparks leapt, the small pile of tinder bursting into flame, and Gabriel adjusted his attack as he closed. Instead of gutting the man as he'd planned, his sword slashed out to the side, slamming into the hand with the flint, knocking the burning matter to the flagged tower floor, far from the beacon above. The man yelped at the pain of the blow, flint falling away, but it did not bother him for long, as Gabriel hit him just as hard as his friend. He stumbled back two paces, then lurched, his centre of gravity too high, and tipped backwards over the parapet, disappearing with a cry and then a crunch. Gabriel walked over to the burning tinder and, just in case, ground it out with the sole of his boot until there was nothing but char marks on the stone. Then he walked to the edge and looked down even as the other soldier was dispatched behind him.

Constantine was looking up at him, standing less than two feet from what remained of the fallen man.

'Gabriel, if you're going to throw people off walls, please be aware of where you're throwing them first.'

Gabriel grinned at that as he took in the scene. The attack had been entirely unexpected, and most of the Turks had been unarmed and busy tending the horses. None of the Ianitzaroi had died, and precious few even sported injuries. Gaspar was busy beating the life out of a survivor by the gate, blocking it just in case, to prevent any unspotted survivor managing to get out and race north with news. Manuel was busy going through his victim's purse and clothing, looting merrily.

The garrison was gone.

The way to Thebes lay open before them. This was it. They were at war, and the first blow against the Turks had been struck by the prince himself.

Thebes

Late September 1444

'No one got away?' the prince asked.

The master of scouts, a grizzled Serb, shook his head. 'No, my lord. It is the standard procedure of Turahan Bey's governors to picket every town and city to a distance of a mile. We swept in from both sides and met at the northern reaches, a mile and a half from the walls, and worked our way inwards, with the Georgian light cavalry all around. We destroyed six outposts – five on the roads, and one in the eastern fields, by a river, all with between five and ten men. The cordon is now secure. No one can enter or leave Thebes, my lord.'

'Good.' Constantine squinted into the sunlight.

'The army is ready to deploy, my lord,' John Rhosatsas said quietly. 'I just need your orders.'

The prince nodded. 'This will not be a siege, John. This will be an assault. I understand the walls are fragmentary at best. The circuit was partially demolished a century ago and has never been rebuilt, so they cannot hold us out with ramparts.'

'It will mean dirty street fighting, my lord,' Strategos Kantakouzenos put in from the other side. 'Nasty work.'

'You have some advice?'

Kantakouzenos coughed uncomfortably and looked around to check who was within earshot. Only the Byzantine high

250

command and the prince's guard were within reach here. 'I am driven as much by financial restrictions as by military tactics, my prince. We need to preserve the Moreot armies as much as possible, and they constitute our heaviest infantry. They should secure the main arterial approaches, through the seven gates – or, more accurately, where the gates *used* to be – and then along the main roads to the centre, where they can seize the government buildings and perhaps the mutesellim himself. The cavalry are of little use in the city, but they can maintain the cordon to prevent flight. That means that the job of securing all the narrow streets and alleys will go to the various mercenary light infantry units, as will capturing any high points and towers and installing archers there.'

Constantine nodded. 'And then any losses in those narrow streets will limit the lightening of the imperial purse when payday comes. I understand.' He paused for a moment. 'No survivors, gentlemen.'

Rhosatsas blinked. 'Sir?'

'Every last Turk in there needs to die, as a matter of expediency. The local populace should be trustworthy enough. They are Boeotians, Greek citizens of the Duchy of Athens, who have laboured under the yoke of the Turks for less than a decade, and it will not take much for them to see this fight as liberation, freeing them from an oppressor. But we do not have sufficient forces to leave here and make sure Turkish captives behave. And if any manage to get ahead of the advance, word will spread far and wide across Thessaly, and Turahan Bey will turn his attention on us.'

Even Gabriel was shaking his head at this, but fortunately it was Rhosatsas who leapt in to respond. 'With respect, my prince, that is not a sensible plan.'

The look Constantine turned on him was bleak and dark, and reminded Gabriel of those worst times following the death of his wife. 'You have your orders, Strategos.'

Rhosatsas, to his credit, stood his ground – something rare among Byzantine officers, whose removal and punishment could be swift and brutal. 'No, my lord. If we kill the prisoners we take, we buy the security of having no Turks in our wake, but we cause three new problems. Firstly, we look far more savage than the Turkish overlord we replace, which may lose us Thebes even in the days after we win it. Secondly, Nerio of Athens is an honourable man, and he will disapprove of such an act. It may even turn him against us and send him and his men into the arms of the sultan. And thirdly, what happens if this advance falters, my lord?'

'What?'

'If reports are wrong, and the crusade has ended? If the crusade falters, even? If there is enough of a ceasefire between them and Murad that the sultan has time to bring all his might to bear against us? Notaras and Sphrantzes are wily diplomats, and yourself, my lord, you have been known to twist disasters into knots that come out as victories. If our advance falters, and the Turks become ascendant once more, if we have been just and honourable in war, there may yet be ways to mollify the sultan. If we have committed genocide against his people, though, he will not stop until the empire is no more. I beg you, Lord Constantine, to think of the future.'

Gabriel tensed, watching the difficulties of the situation made plain in the prince's expression. Finally, Constantine sagged. 'Very well, John. Once the city is ours, locate an appropriate space for use as a prison and have the captives incarcerated. They will be the responsibility of the Thebans thereafter. I cannot spare units.'

'Then I should deploy?'

'Yes. Sound the attack.'

Gabriel shivered. This would be the last surprise assault anyway, he was sure. They had swept through Attica and into Boeotia so fast they had caught the Turkish garrisons unawares, and managed to secure their gains without raising the alarm further afield. They might have managed to prevent men leaving Thebes for now, but that would buy them days

– weeks at most – and they would have to tarry for a time when they took Thebes to let Duke Nerio reach them with his men. Soon, word of the city's fall would reach the ears of Turahan Bey, and then the Turks of Thessaly would prepare for the coming war. All they could hope then was that the crusade was taking enough Turkish strength away to make this campaign feasible.

Horns blew across the field now, and Constantine and his Ianitzaroi moved position, locating a low rise that overlooked the road leading to the city's south-western gate. All around the plain that surrounded the ancient city, units were shuffling into position with *allaghia*, each of several hundred cavalry. They were thundering around the circuit, raising dust as they formed the noose around Thebes, while heavy imperial infantry moved into place on the roads, armour rattling and jingling, the clonk of shields, the thud of boots and the clang of weapons as they marched. Light infantry of the various mercenary companies fell in alongside them, ready to secure the narrow side streets as they went.

Gabriel watched the prince as the army readied. There was something about him this morning, something the Catalan was not comfortable with. Often, cracks showed in Constantine's demeanour these days, and that dark soul that had lost two wives and a child leaked out through the fissures. Most of the time, the prince managed to maintain the veneer of normality over it all, but Gabriel had a feeling that was starting to fail – that Constantine was struggling more by the day.

He didn't know what to do. He'd tried everything he could think of, and it had worked to an extent, but not totally. The prince's fingers drummed a tense tattoo on the scabbard by his side, and Gabriel could just see the clenched nature of the man's jaw from this angle, without seeing his face entirely. The man's horse pawed at the ground, and Constantine leaned forward in the saddle and whispered into the beast's ear.

Gabriel was forming a worrying thought.

'Don't do it,' he said, quietly enough for only the two of them to hear.

Constantine turned, brow creased. 'Gabriel?'

'I know what you're thinking, and it's too dangerous. Remember the triumphant entry to Patras? A few dissenting archers in a tower and you were nearly an ex-prince. And that was a supposedly *friendly* city. This isn't.'

'If you've no wish to join me, feel free to tender your resignation, Gabriel Black-eye. I have little use for a bodyguard who will not accompany me into danger.'

Gabriel ground his teeth. That wasn't the damn point. He sought some way, some reasoning he could use to persuade the prince against this course of action, but came up with nothing. In the end, he edged his horse forward to come side by side with his master. 'You know I do not fear for myself, but that I fear for you, especially when the danger is of your own causing.'

Constantine said nothing, just stared off into the distance, at the city, and the soldiers now moving in towards it. Then, finally, the prince broke the silence once more.

'I will have everything, Gabriel, or I will have nothing.'

The Ianitzaroi frowned. 'Sir?'

'This is our chance, and it may be the only one we get. As such, I am willing to wager everything on it. For centuries we have watched while the Turks chipped away at our borders, forcing them ever westwards, while the Italians and the Franks and the Spaniards carve up our once great empire for their own greed. We have watched the empire shrink and shrink and shrink, from a power that shook the world to a city trapped and surrounded by its enemies, and a small despotate in the Morea. But the Italians are changing, and their grip on Greek lands slips, and every mile they lose is a mile we regain. And as for the Turks? This is the moment. With Władysław of Hungary threatening their power on this side of the Bosphorus like no one ever before, we have the chance to expand. I will take Thessaly, and all the coastal lands round to Mesembria. I will see the empire reborn, growing and strengthening.'

He paused, and sighed.

'Or I will lose it all. Very likely that is my destiny, for God seems only to take from me, never to give. But I must try. I will put everything I have, and everything I *am*, into this. Rome will rise, or Rome will disappear, but there will be no more of Rome shaking in its boots as it kisses the feet of popes and sultans. You do not want me to ride into danger, Gabriel? I say to hell with your worries. My whole heart and my whole strength and my whole life I place on the line to beat the Turks, and nothing less. And if it *costs* me my life, then I will be with my dear Theodora once more, so even the worst outcome has a glimmer of hope for me.'

'Sphrantzes would argue. He would want you safe, to secure a future, a succession.'

The look the prince turned on Gabriel then made him flinch. 'No, Gabriel. Some men are not meant for matrimony or fatherhood, and God has made it abundantly clear that this is my fate. I shall stand alone and proud to the end now, Gabriel. And if I succeed? If I rebuild the empire? Then Thomas shall be the one to lead it.'

Gabriel nodded, though in the privacy of his head he reminded himself that John was still emperor, and that both Theodore and Demetrios were jostling for succession. It might be that Constantine rebuilt an empire only to see it snatched away from him anyway.

The Ianitzaroi commander squared his shoulders. 'All right, then. You will be part of this, right down to the blood and steel and bone? Then let's do it. What's your plan?'

'I shall ride into the city in the wake of the first wave. We shall follow the main road to the centre, and there I shall march into the governor's house and put my sword to the throat of the mutesellim and demand his surrender.'

Gabriel nodded. 'Just do me a favour and try not to sprout arrows along the route.'

'Preventing that is *your* job, Gabriel.'

And with that, the prince kicked his horse into action and began to ride down the slope. Gabriel waved to his men, and Gaspar and Manuel shouted commands and waved banners. In moments, the twenty-four Ianitzaroi were riding down the gentle gradient with their prince, armour chinking and clattering as they cantered. They reached the main road swiftly, and began to ride past the various troops marching along it, some of the Moreot heavy infantry, their commanders in plate armour of Italian design, others less well equipped – Cretans, Cypriots, Navarrese, Albanians and Venetians for the most part.

There was something oddly stirring about riding alongside this army, the largest expeditionary force the empire had assembled in living memory. Was this what the Romans had felt like in ancient days, when the world trembled at their coming?

Ahead, there finally came the sounds of conflict, and as they neared the city, Gabriel caught sight of the fighting. The walls were, indeed, ruinous. Far from forming one continuous circuit around the city, they consisted of sections of wall often only a dozen paces long, occasionally larger, but often smaller, and always crumbling and half-fallen. The gate itself, once a grand entrance to the city of Thebes, now consisted of a single tower looming over one side of the road and a shattered wall on the other. Archers were crammed in the tower-top and were loosing madly into the approaching force, who could do little about it but throw their shields up in the way in an attempt to deflect the missiles.

As the imperial party approached that position, Gabriel gave a single simple gesture with one hand, and the Ianitzaroi closed up around the prince, shields coming up and round him almost like a dome. Then the hail began. Gabriel held his own shield up, over his head, and could feel the thud and batter of missiles bouncing from it, thanking God for his mercy at one point as an arrowhead smashed through the board and stopped less than a foot from his head. He tried to take stock of what was happening, but the action and pressure and the rain of

missiles were too much. He did catch sight of the prince –
confirming Constantine lived, which was a relief – and then,
as they passed beneath the lofty gate tower, he could see a
dozen infantry smashing the door to pieces with axes. By the
time they were past, Gabriel's shield coming across behind him
now to protect his back, the soldiers were through the old,
rot-infested door, and rampaging through the tower, with war
cries in three languages. The arrows continued to clatter against
Gabriel's shield for a time, and one of his men riding just ahead
cried out in dismay as his mount took a shaft in the side and
reared, throwing him into the street as it charged away madly.

Then the imperial soldiers were atop the tower and the hail
of arrows ended, to be replaced by another, this time arcing
out in different directions and plunging into Turkish soldiers
running to prevent the incursion. They would be out of luck.
Thebes was famous as the 'City of Seven Gates', and today each
of them would host an assault like this. With no permanent
fortifications, Thebes was doomed.

Perhaps the Turks knew that, for the fight went out of them
quickly, and very visibly, as the column pushed into the city,
allied mercenaries peeling off to secure every alley, side street
and tower. The defenders rushed to hold doors or blockade
streets, but as it became almost immediately clear that nothing
was going to hold, the number of men throwing their arms in
the air and their weapons to the ground in surrender increased
exponentially.

As they rode, Gabriel did a quick headcount and noted four
of his men missing. Whether the men themselves had been
injured or killed he could not say, or whether perhaps they had
been like the unlucky rider he'd seen at the tower, unhorsed
with an arrow. Time would tell, and in truth, four was a good
number for such a fraught assault.

Thebes had left behind its glory days, when it had been a
commercial hub, the textile centre of Achaea, its trade now
diminished, its domes tarnished, walls crumbled and fallen, yet

it was still a sizeable city, capital of the district, and its houses were solid and strong. As they passed, Turks appearing here and there in small bands only to be fought back into side streets once more, the city's populace began to dare to leave their houses, emerging at their doors and windows. There was no cheering, but neither was there anger. After years of Turkish domination, they surely welcomed their liberation, but would be slow to show it until the success of the imperial army was undisputed.

Again, missiles started to come at the Ianitzaroi, as they closed on the heart of the city. A few arrows flew, as well as stones, lumps of brick or mortar, pieces of tile and the like. Figures were appearing along the rooftops and hurling down whatever they could find, the aggressors mostly Turkish soldiers, but occasionally civilians. They could be Theban natives, of course, but it was more likely they were Turks, doing their best to fight off the aggressor. Once more, the Ianitzaroi pulled close to the prince, without the need for a command, and brought their shields in to protect him. Again, Gabriel could hear the occasional cry as a missile found a gap, but fortunately none of them seemed to find Constantine, and after what seemed hours, they suddenly emerged into a massive open square.

The gubernatorial building was impossible to miss. The majority of the buildings around the square were old Theban constructions, at their heart an ancient church of very familiar imperial design, harking back to the days of Byzantine Thebes. The governor's house, though, was new – a few years old at most, constructed of white blocks and red brick and tile, a stark, yet oddly beautiful design, the hard angles of the place softened by curved recesses and domes above, and highest of all, the crescent banner of the Turks.

There had been a market on in the square, though now it was little more than abandoned stalls of produce, the owners and shoppers alike having fled potential trouble from the invading force. Even the few who remained, desperate to protect their wares, ducked away from the stalls and fled the imperial army as it flooded into the square, pouring like sudden meltwater between the rows of stalls and down the side streets. The organisation of the market, a sensible design, had left a thoroughfare through the centre in both directions, meeting in the middle, and so even as they moved into the market, the riders could still clearly see the palace directly ahead, along that wide gap.

Things had gone too easily, for Gabriel's liking. Yes, they'd faced two hails of missiles, and yes, various units would even now be bogged down securing the narrow streets of the city, but still it felt as though they'd met precious little resistance.

It was as they were halfway across the market square that the answer to that became clear. Men suddenly poured from the doorway of the palace like ants, and gathered in lines, protecting the place. They were colourful, in ornate blue and red uniforms and with immaculate turbans, though their bodies were protected with good armour, and they held blades and shields ready for war. Even as they began to form up, so another line of similar men formed all along the building's roofline, many of whom were holding bows.

'Easier to protect one house than a wall-less city,' Gabriel noted as they came to a halt, mid-square.

'Who are they?' a soldier nearby breathed in a worried tone.

'*Janissary* corps,' Gabriel replied. 'The sultan's version of us. He must prize this governor to have so many of his men here.'

Constantine shook his head. 'No. For the sultan's Janissaries to be here, there must be a courtier, a bey, perhaps, a member of the Sublime Porte in Thebes. Gabriel, you know what to do.'

Gabriel looked around. They were still accompanied by a hundred-strong unit of armoured Moreot swordsmen, as well as two smaller companies of mercenaries: a Cypriot one and a group of Venetians. He gestured to their commanders, who were looking to the prince for orders.

'You take left,' he told the mercenaries, dismounting and gesturing for the other Ianitzaroi to do the same. 'Hit them fast and hard. The quicker you get in among them, the less danger from roof missiles. Once you've overcome them, press against the wall and start to move towards the door.' He looked the other way to the Moreot regulars. 'You do the same on the right flank. I'll take the middle.' Then he turned to Constantine. 'But only if the esteemed despot will hang back out of danger. I cannot concentrate on smashing their ranks while I'm worrying about you.'

Constantine gave an odd chuckle. 'I shall do my best.'

'Manuel? Take two men with good shields and stay on the prince. Don't let him get shot.'

'Wedge?' Gaspar asked.

'Wedge.'

He looked around. The other units were still with them. 'You waiting for instructions? Go.'

As if a spell had been broken, the three units suddenly burst into life, orders shouted, men running off through the lines of stalls, left and right. It would take them no more than a minute to reach the edge of the square and be ready to close in on the flanks, and Gabriel counted the seconds off in his head. At zero, he threw his arm forth, and Manuel helpfully lifted the small horn around his neck and blew a single blast.

Leaving just three men to protect the prince, Gabriel led the rest of the Ianitzaroi forward at a run, across the square. They had to be on foot. Horseback would have made a better charge against the lines, but then they'd have to dismount within the cloud of missiles in order to get through the door.

They pounded across the flags, and as they did so, Gaspar bellowed 'Wedge!' They began to re-form, completing the manoeuvre as they emerged from the market stalls and into the open section of square before the governor's house.

The Janissaries braced themselves, weapons brandished and shields up, and it came as no surprise to Gabriel that at that moment arrows started to whip down from the roof at them. The surprise came a moment later as he looked up to see four of the men on the roof had levelled what looked like hardened tubes at them over the parapet. Then there was a small series of loud cracking noises, followed by clouds of smoke, and the Ianitzaroi next to Gabriel exploded. One moment he was running with sword ready, expression of furious battle lust across his face, the next he was a headless corpse, staggering and falling forward with the momentum even as what had once been his head spattered across the side of Gabriel's face, warm, wet, and filled with shards of bone and tooth.

'What the fuck was that?' someone shouted, echoing the thought that was going through Gabriel's head even as he blinked away the mess.

'Not sticking around to find out,' was his reply as he angled his body behind his shield, brought his sword up and back, and thundered at the men standing in front of the door. Shouts and clashes came from both sides, announcing that the attack on the flanks had begun too, though Gabriel's attention was all on the door before him now. He hit the Janissaries like a ball bowled at soft wooden pins. The Turkish elite corps were no green recruits, and they recovered well, and Gabriel even felt two cuts, one on his thigh and one on his shoulder, but there was simply no way they were going to stop the powerful momentum of the charging Ianitzaroi. In moments they were through, and Gabriel found himself standing in front of the open door. Behind him, his men began to engage properly, and he considered for a moment pausing and waiting for the other units to join him. Then there was a crack of discharged weapons above once more, and the leg of a man nearby vanished in a cloud of blood and bone fragments. In a heartbeat, Gabriel was in through the door. Whatever the interior held, it was better than being outside, in view of that.

Indeed, it was almost a relief to see a Janissary officer, sword out and ready, blocking the corridor ahead, where doors led off. Gabriel bowed his head. 'You could always surrender,' he offered.

The Janissary said nothing, but simply came on, sword swinging in the fairly restrictive space. There was going to be little room here to fight with swords, let alone with shields, and so Gabriel made his decision straight away, slipping his arm from the shield strap, such that he was gripping it with only his fist. The Turk came on, and as soon as he was close enough, the Ianitzaroi suddenly threw his shield out ahead. He'd cast it forward and down, and had it hit the Turk's shins, it would undoubtedly have felled him and left him supine. The man was quick, and reacted well, jumping over the falling shield, but unfortunately, with all his attention on the makeshift missile, he was unprepared as Gabriel suddenly lunged forth, throwing out his sword. The man wore a steel cuirass of ornate design, but that was all his armour, and the Catalan's sword point slammed into his shoulder, between the steel and the armpit, scything through blue and red uniform, swarthy flesh and muscle and gristle beneath. The blow would have been agonising, but most important, it rendered the man's sword arm useless. He cried out and fell forward, and this time it was Gabriel who jumped, leaping the falling officer and marching on into the building. Behind him, his men were now in the corridor, and the officer died moments later.

Gabriel turned into the first room, and a fierce, predatory smile crossed his face. The two principal occupants of the room were Turkish nobles. One, seated behind a desk and well dressed, was undoubtedly the mutesellim of Thebes, but the other was clearly far more important. A pasha, perhaps? Maybe even a vizier from the sultan himself.

'Good morning, gentlemen,' Gabriel said, treating them to a wide smile that distorted his face even more than usual. 'Consider yourselves prisoners, guests of Constantine Palaiologos, Prince of the Romans.'

'So that is confirmation?' Rhosatsas asked again, just to be sure.

'I don't see how it can be anything else,' the prince replied. 'George's latest letter came from halfway across Bulgar lands, and he claims to be with the Hungarian crusade, but also now with armies of Wallachs, and even far westerners. And he says that three hundred Burgundians are on their way here by ship to bolster our numbers. It appears that precisely what I had hoped for has come to pass. The crusade is on again, and now in the sultan's own gardens, and if they are sending me men, then they acknowledge our advance as part of the war. This is it, John. We are properly at war. Having spent two weeks here, the Turks must know we're coming, but they're unable to field enough men to stop us. If Władysław can keep them busy, we can retake all of Thessaly in just a few short months. God above, John, but I'd like to be there when they reach Edirne, to walk into Murad's throne room with the Hungarian king and demand the surrender of the Turks. Imagine it.'

Kantakouzenos, the general and ambassador, lounging in the corner, shook his head. 'That would not be an end to it, my lord. If Murad fell, they might abandon everything this side of the Bosphorus for a time, but there are always rival factions and arguing siblings in the Turkish court. Murad's fall would only facilitate the rise of another.'

'But another across the water, where we can keep him. And now that Nerio is here, we actually have a force to fear.'

That, at least, was true. Two days before, the Athenian duke had arrived with a hastily gathered army. He claimed that as many men again would be on the way, once they had been fully mustered, but he had already brought half of Athens, enough to seriously bolster the army. Moreover, men were even now investigating those four guns wielded on the roof, trying to work out their use, given that their previous wielders had flatly refused to reveal their secrets.

'We have delayed long enough here, waiting for Nerio,' the prince announced. 'The Burgundians can catch us up in due course. It is time to press home our attack. While the crusaders smash the north, we must take what we can for the empire. Now up into Thessaly. The mountain peoples are a law unto themselves, but they have more in common with us or with the Wallachs than they have with the Turks. They even follow the Patriarch's teachings. They will throw off the sultan's yoke with little urging, and then we can turn east and begin the push for Edirne.'

'Do you think we should consult your brother, my lord?' Rhosatsas mused.

'John is weary and busy with the machinations of our siblings. Were he here, it would be he raising the sword and proclaiming the rebirth of Rome. No. Let John hear about our success with everyone else. Have word sent to every camp – on the morrow, we ride north.'

Pindus Mountains

Late October 1444

'Who are these Vlachs?' Gaspar murmured, watching the meeting unfold beside the water.

Gabriel opened his mouth, but it was Manuel, standing leaning on his standard, who answered. 'A mix of Dacian and Thracian peoples who migrated this way from Wallachia in ancient times. Their language is still closer to Wallachian than to Greek. I believe the Turks don't really understand them.'

'I'm not surprised. Sounds like they're gargling.'

Manuel flicked his eyes skywards. 'I don't mean they don't understand the language, although they probably don't. They don't understand the Vlachs at all. But then I'm not sure anyone does. They're a law unto themselves.'

Gabriel remained silent, watching the exchange. Constantine was seated on an old broken pillar from the glory days of Greece, gesticulating as he spoke, while the leader of the Vlachs sat on a rock opposite, nodding slowly, his great shaggy fur cape rippling and tattered in the strong breeze.

This was an area Gabriel had never come to before. Not surprising, really, given that it was in nominally Turkish-controlled Thessaly, and close to the border with Tocco lands in Epirus. It had been a whirlwind of a month. The army had departed Thebes in high spirits, bolstered by the forces of Nerio of Athens. In a matter of days they had taken several strongholds and cities, initially those that could be claimed to belong to the Athenian Duchy, before moving into the fringe of Turkish Thessaly, edging on a capability of denying all-out war with the sultan. Then, the three hundred Burgundians had caught up with them, and brought with them an extra rush of confidence, for they were full of tales of victory and martial feats from the crusade in the north. They had had the occasional loss and setback, but they had refused to abide by the peace deal that had been struck with the Turks and had pressed on. Latest news had them rampaging across Bulgar lands and heading for Varna, where they could secure one of the sultan's most important ports, allowing them to ship reinforcements through the Bosphorus and directly into the lands north of Constantinople. With the increase in numbers and the new sense of confidence and hope, Constantine had decided to split his army.

Kantakouzenos had taken a force comprised of Nerio's Athenians and a similar number of mercenaries, and had been given the task of securing the south and then the Aegean coast of Thessaly. Reports were extremely positive, too. That second army had reached the border with Epirus, but with the current Tocco administration there nominally still allied to the empire and shrinking in the face of Turkish expansion, Kantakouzenos had wisely decided not to enter their territory, but to cross back to the east and move up the coast. His campaign had met with success at every turn, the general hailed as a hero, saviour and liberator, and all in the name of Constantine and the emperor.

In many ways, though, Constantine's own campaign with the other half of the army had eclipsed the general's. Racing north, they had seized strategic strongholds across central and western Thessaly from their Turkish garrisons, bringing the region under imperial control for the first time in over half a century. The sense that the empire was regaining command in the region was palpable, and the notion of linking up with the crusaders and together pushing the sultan back across the water was now beginning to look like a real possibility. The one aspect that marred the campaign a little for many was its bloodthirsty approach. Constantine had managed to convince his generals that an excessively violent advance was preferable to a careful and diplomatic one, citing the need for speed and to shock the Turks into panic and inaction. In reality, Gabriel saw it more as an outlet for that dark part of the prince that still controlled him at times. Whatever the motivation, the result had been inescapable, though. With surprisingly small losses, the army had ravaged Turkish Thessaly and wrested control from them. Of course, some of that had to be due to so much local military having already been drawn away to help face the crusaders, but still, a win was a win.

And then they had come as far as the Pindus Mountains. All that lay between them and independent, Christian Albania were the mountainous, insular Vlach peoples. For the first time in the campaign, Constantine had put aside the sword and prepared to negotiate, for these men were not Turks and not enemies, but a third party to be reasoned with. If they could ally with the Vlachs, then all the West was either imperial controlled, or governed by allies, allowing the army to move east and push the Turks from Thessaly entirely, back to Bulgar lands, where they were already fighting the crusaders. Indeed, just fifty miles or so to the south-east now lay Tırhala and the palace of Turahan Bey. Three days' march could see the armies of Rome standing in the power centre of Turkish Thessaly.

Gabriel's gaze swept across the landscape around them. The huge camp of the army, bolstered throughout the campaign by volunteers from the lands they had liberated, sat on the southern shore of the lake, carefully trying to look like an allied force just passing through, rather than an army of occupation. The lake itself, a glorious blue gem reflecting the grey-green hills and mountains around them, marched off into the distance, and a village of stone and timber cottages nestled close by beneath the slope of a high peak. His gaze reached the small gathering of Vlachs, mostly warriors in chain shirts and with heavy swords and spears, then slid to their leader, just in time to see him and Constantine rise, bow to each other, and turn to their people.

'Send a clerk down here,' the prince shouted.

Gabriel heaved a sigh of relief as, from the mass of the army, a soldier with writing equipment and a leather satchel jogged out front. If someone else was now allowed near, it was an excuse for Gabriel to go with them. Since the meeting had begun, the two leaders had agreed to meet alone, all their entourages staying out of earshot, even their guards. That had made Gabriel nervous, for the Vlach leader was clearly a powerful warrior, and if anything had gone sour, Constantine could easily have died before the Ianitzaroi reached him. As Gabriel moved over to join the clerk, Gaspar came alongside too, the pair of them intercepting the soldier and then jogging alongside until they reached the prince, who wore a weary smile.

Constantine flicked a glance at them each in turn, then he gestured to the clerk. 'Prepare to make a lengthy document by dictation, and have wax warmed for an official seal.'

As the soldier started work, Gabriel looked over to the Vlach, who was standing with arms folded and a look of approval, then back to the prince. 'Things went well, then?'

'Exceptionally so. Andrejan over there dislikes the Turks intensely, a view apparently shared by many of the Vlachs. In truth he has no great love for us, but even with the haze of half a century, he says their old folk remember imperial overlords being better. We only took taxes off them, while the Turks take their strong youths for their *devşirme* recruitment.'

'So they will join the empire?'

'Not quite. I have agreed to grant the Vlachs their independence, allowing them a state of their own between Thessaly and Albania. It has a number of advantages, not least in creating a solid neutral buffer zone should the new Albanian league start to have designs on imperial territory. And in return for their independence, they have agreed to assist our campaigns. While we turn our sights south-east, to march on Turahan Bey's capital and then link up with Kantakouzenos, the Vlachs will make war on the Turks to the north-east – a third front pushing them back. Our war picks up pace, Gabriel. If we can take Tırhala and neutralise the bey, Thessaly is ours, my friend.'

Gabriel nodded. It was good news indeed. And Turahan Bey was in their sights now.

Meteora

November 1444

Gabriel looked up, a lump in his throat. Heights had never bothered him, and he had fought atop high walls and lofty towers, climbed siege ladders, trees, and even, on one notable occasion, the north wall and dome of the Hagia Sophia back in Constantinople. But still, there were limits, and some things sent a chill up the spine of even the brave. Such was the ascent before him.

'How high do you reckon it is?'

Gaspar shrugged. 'No idea, but I suspect you're among the angels at the top.'

'One of the locals said it's over a thousand feet.'

'I believe him.'

Gabriel shivered again. The pillar of rock was perhaps a quarter of a mile across and just as far upwards. And it was neither a hill, nor a mountain, for there was no slope on any side, just craggy, rounded, grey rock reaching high into the sky, with odd ledges here and there. A fall from even the lowest edge offered only cold and very sudden death, let alone from anywhere higher up.

'How in the name of all the saints did they manage to build that?' he breathed, looking up at the small church that towered over the precipice at the edge of the rock.

'Well…' Manuel began, but Gabriel waved him into silence. It had been a rhetorical question and he wasn't prepared for a half-hour lecture on construction methods, winches and engineering. He knew damn well that the standard-bearer had been reading a recent Italian work on military engineering, and was twitching to talk about it.

However it had been done, it was an impressive feat. He wouldn't have wanted to be involved in it. He didn't even really want to think about going up there, let alone having been the first person to do so. There was no slope, and precious little angle other than vertical. No one had even begun to attempt to carve stairs into it. The only access was by ladder. A thousand feet of ladder. Worse still, the ladders were not permanent, attached to the rocks with pitons, but were created in four sections, each of which consisted of several huge ladders, much like siege ladders, tethered to one another with ropes. As the last of the sections was released to grant them access, it fell free, unfurling in sections as it came, the individual ladders bashing and clattering against the rock as the ropes holding them together creaked with the strain. The ladders were not old, Gabriel judged – not more than a few years, at least – but they had seen a lot of use and were beginning to fray and distort. It was not an encouraging sight.

'Tell me again why we must go up there?'

'Because the signal asked us to.'

Gabriel nodded at this entirely insufficient and unsatisfactory answer. He knew very well that the high command of the imperial military, and the court itself, had long since developed a code system using either mirrors or torches to convey any one of almost a hundred different one-word messages, but he had never had the need to learn the system himself. Besides, its details were a closely guarded secret, and only a handful of men in the whole army would know it.

That, he reasoned, was why Constantine was so insistent on going up there. Not because he'd been asked to do so, and not because this appeared to be a church with a priest deep in the middle of Turkish land, but because the prince would be fascinated to learn who, up here in a monastery on a stone pillar hundreds of miles within Turkish territory, was familiar with imperial code systems.

'I am not comfortable with you climbing that,' Gabriel said flatly. 'I'm not even comfortable with *me* climbing it, let alone *you*.'

'I am strong and with a good head for heights, Gabriel,' Constantine replied.

'All it takes is one slip. Let a few of the lads and me go up, while you stay down here. We can leave someone at each stage on the ledges and then pass messages up and down. Then you risk nothing.'

'No, Gabriel. This I will do myself. Although not alone, obviously,' the prince added with a dark grin.

And with that, he grasped a rung of the ladder and put his foot on the bottom. Gaspar stepped over, gripping the ladder and holding it steady. With a nod of thanks, Constantine began to climb. Despite Gaspar's enormous strength, the ladder still shook and twisted slightly as the prince climbed, tethered above by ropes as it was.

Gabriel looked around. He would not let the prince go alone, and so he and three others would go up with him. Not Gaspar. With the best will in the world, the man was strong and fearless, but with only one arm, he was not a natural climber. Manuel had left his banner with the horses and was spitting on his hands and rubbing them together in preparation, while Jordi and Esteban stood, looking nervously upwards, steeling themselves.

'Wait until I'm on the second ladder before you start,' the prince called back down, and Gabriel made non-verbal understanding noises. In truth, he had no wish to start at all, and if he had to, he would rather wait until the prince had reached the first ledge than put the weight of two men on the same roped-ladder contraption at once. He watched, sweating, as the prince negotiated the short rope join between the ladders, and then moved on to the second. Then, heart in mouth and bladder threatening to lose control, he grasped a rung.

He should have gone up first, of course. It was little use the royal bodyguard heading up there if the prince got to the top first, and died before the others arrived. But Constantine was insistent. The message had been for him alone, and he was only allowing the others to come at all on Gabriel's flat refusal to hear otherwise. Gabriel winced, and started to climb.

As he ascended, he began the longest mantra he could think of, and the only book he had read and committed to memory in sections: the *Taktika* of Leo the Wise. It was always best, when performing a by-rote operation that edged on fear, to occupy the mind with something else that kept the current situation slightly detached from the senses. There were four sections of the book he had partially memorised, and only one of them stood out sufficiently right now: surprise attacks.

> An ancient maxim, carefully observed by the more intelligent generals of old and still invariably observed and given the highest priority by our own generals, teaches us to launch attacks and raids against the enemy without causing injury to ourselves. We can achieve this if our assaults against the enemy are intelligently and carefully planned and swiftly carried out. Such assaults have been found to be effective not only against forces of equal strength but also against vastly superior ones.

Gabriel reached the top of the first ladder, his white-knuckled hands gripping the wood firmly and still trembling enough that the whole ladder shook slightly. He looked up for a moment to confirm how he would move to the next ladder, and the sight of the massive tower of rock above him, the chain of ladders twisting and shifting, and the figure of the prince, already two ladders further up, nearly sent him back down. He shook for a moment, blinking away sweat, and looked down. As he'd reached the end of the first ladder, another of the Ianitzaroi was climbing already.

Gabriel reached up and grasped the next ladder, pulling himself over the rope join.

The way the bottom and second ladders twisted in different directions as he passed the rope, with hands on one and feet on the other, threatened to dislodge him for a moment, and panic gripped him, even though he could not be more than thirty feet from the ground yet, and likely to bounce, given his frame and muscle. Only when both hands and feet were on the second ladder did it feel secure. Once again, he began his mantra, listing Leo's ruminations on the value of surprise and deception over pitched battles, and the need to vary strategies based upon conditions. Hitting the join between second and third ladder, he tried making sure to keep one hand on each ladder until his foot was high enough to reach the top rung, but the resulting contortion was extremely uncomfortable and nearly caused him to fall anyway, now a bone-breaking sixty-foot drop. He made it to the third ladder and there had to pause to remove one hand at a time and wipe the sweat from it. Looking up, he was dismayed – and quite irritated – to see that the prince was now considerably ahead of him, climbing like a lizard on a brick wall, and was already approaching the first ledge.

That irritation was what Gabriel needed, and spurred him on. Besting his own nerves, he began to climb with renewed vigour. Hand over hand, foot over foot, teeth clenched and blinking away the sweat, he ascended.

If, in the area between us and the enemy we find
a river difficult to cross, we can construct a bridge
there. Even cavalry are able to do this.

Over the rope binding and to the fourth ladder. Brief look up. Long wish he hadn't done so, but also relief that there were only two more ladders before the first ledge, where Constantine now stood, horribly close to the edge and looking down with an extremely irritating smile. Glance down, to see that Esteban and Jordi were both one ladder up, with Manuel already climbing and bringing up the rear.

Climbing the fourth ladder, moving out of logistical advice text and into the options of timing, including night attacks. By the time he had reached the warning about using good moonlight so that your force could not so easily become lost in the dark, he was crossing to the fifth ladder. He raced up this one, recalling the use of cover and the keeping of reserves, much of the fear now dulled by the removal of uncertainty. If he fell now, he would be the shape of unleavened bread when he hit, with no hope of survival.

Almost as if that thought had been a trigger, there was a shriek from below. Gabriel closed his eyes for a moment, squeezed shut, and hung there, then finally opened them and, nervously, looked down. Esteban had gone from the climb, and Gabriel could see him, a heap of humanity on the stony ground some distance below. His hands tightened on the rungs with renewed determination. Jordi and Manuel were still climbing. He returned to the task.

Sixth ladder, while considering the possibility that the supply chain may need to remain in place for the attacking force. And finally, with a sigh of relief, he clambered over to the ledge and rolled onto his back, breathing heavily for a moment.

'I had not had you pegged for an acrophobe?' Constantine noted conversationally.

'I'm not,' Gabriel replied between heaved breaths, 'but even falcons would shit themselves doing this.'

The prince laughed. 'Come on. We're a quarter of the way now.'

Gabriel glared hatefully at his master's back as Constantine sauntered across the ledge and started to climb the second set of ladders. As he slowly rose, and crawled over on his knees, Gabriel noted with some unhappiness the poor state of the iron pitons holding the thing in place. A glance down at the others, and relief that they were still there.

'Stop watching me,' Manuel shouted. 'It's making me edgy.'

Turning back, Gabriel started to climb once more, before the fear overtook him and prevented it. Once more, six thirty-foot ladders, fastened together with ropes. Once again, he resorted to Leo's advice as he climbed, and it was with a great deal of relief that he finally reached the halfway point, and found Constantine waiting, infuriatingly calm and sweatless.

'Good. Halfway.'

And with that he was gone, climbing again. Gabriel lay trembling for a moment, then forced himself up and onwards, aware that the longer he stayed here, the less inclined he would be to press on, and spending the rest of his life trapped on a ledge did not appeal.

Halfway up the third set, he made the mistake finally of looking down again. Five hundred feet was a long way, and Jordi and Manuel were small figures further back down the ladders, Gaspar little more than a dot at the bottom. The command party and the Ianitzaroi looked like ants. Gabriel nearly fell then, the height making him dizzy for a moment, and he thrust his arm through the ladder and gripped it with the other hand, hanging there until the spell passed, when he started to climb again.

The third ledge was more of a relief than ever, and he swiftly pressed on in the wake of the prince, climbing the final stage.

'"You must always investigate in detail, O General, the quality of the force of your adversaries",' he said, as he reached the top and rolled over onto rough dirt ground.

'What are you talking about?' the prince asked.

'Just talking to myself.' Gabriel gasped as he moved away from the edge and stood on shaky legs.

As the prince stood, seemingly unfazed by the climb, and hardly even out of breath, looking about with interest, Gabriel stood there and tried to stop trembling. They were still there a few minutes later when first Jordi, then Manuel, threw themselves over the ledge and onto flat ground, so close that they must have climbed that last rope ladder together. They were arguing about something as they arrived, but fell silent as they rolled out and stood.

'Fuck me, but that was a climb,' the banner-man said, breathing heavily. 'And it doesn't help when Esteban decides to take a swan dive past you, and nearly knocks you off in the process. Tit.'

Gabriel greeted that with mixed feelings. He knew that Manuel and Esteban had been friends for a long time, and the dark humour covered his sense of loss. He was floundering around for something appropriate to say when they realised they were not alone.

'I knew it was you,' a new voice called, and they all turned to see a man in a rough monk's robe, his beard and hair white, standing in the doorway of the church.

Constantine frowned, even as Gabriel's hand went instinctively to his sword hilt.

'Should I know you?' the prince murmured, suspicious.

'Probably not. Priests in the great city, even in the palace, are often overlooked. But *I* remember *you*, my boy. Indeed, I remember you that day the Turks came and your mother walked the walls and saw them off.'

An odd glimmer of recognition struck Gabriel then. The man had aged, obviously, and weathered with it, but he was definitely oddly familiar. The notion that he'd been one of the crimson–clad priests carrying the sacred icon that day was suddenly hard to ignore.

'I am Dometius, Constantine. I walked you through some of your first services and finished my time in the palace as your mother's confessor.'

Gabriel's hand fell away from his belt now, as the prince smiled. 'Heavens, Dometius, but I have not seen you for twenty years!'

'I remained at court for more than a year after your blessed father passed, making sure your mother was safe, but when she took holy orders herself, the role of her confessor seemed rather redundant, and so I sought a new challenge. There is a colony of monks here, building churches high in the clouds, close to God. This is my new court, and my new challenge. What do you think, prince of the Palaiologoi?'

'I think it is an eyrie, Dometius. And that makes you an eagle.'

The priest's gaze slipped from the prince, across the others, and then to Manuel, where it fell with what Gabriel thought was a strange look of familiarity. 'Brother,' he said, by way of greeting, earning a nod from the banner-man. Then: 'Come. I have food. Simple fare, but wholesome.'

The man turned and disappeared into his church, Constantine following. Gabriel glanced across at Manuel once they'd gone.

'Brother?'

'I am a deeply religious man,' the standard-bearer replied, eyes narrowed.

'You are a drunken, lecherous, rutting animal, Manuel. And that's being *kind*.'

'Fuck you, and fuck your mother. Which I did,' he replied, and then marched off on his own. Gabriel let him go, turning back towards the church, into which the others had gone. It seemed entirely unfeasible that this priest posed a threat to the prince, and Constantine seemed to know and trust him. It was Gabriel's sworn duty to accompany him for safety, and yet it felt like an invasion of privacy. In the end, he followed them, but hung back, and as the prince and his host stopped in a room off the side of the church, Gabriel settled in to lean against the wall outside, within reach if required, but not imposing. He was swiftly aware that he was, in fact, eavesdropping, but there was little he could do about that if he wanted to stay close enough to help, so he resigned himself to it.

There he stood, listening. He heard them discussing the food, and the scraping of chairs and the clattering of crockery. Then the monk appeared in the doorway with a bowl of some basic stew and a knowing smile. He offered it and a spoon to Gabriel, who took them gratefully, and then left again.

The conversation turned to innocuous niceties, and then to a long overdue catch-up, in which Constantine seemed to lay bare twenty years of his life in more frank detail than Gabriel would have been happy to do. The monk similarly described his last two decades, though there was rather less detail to cover. Constantine then caught him up to date on the current campaign and what it involved and meant, and why they were here, at Meteora, passing through on the way to Tırhala, just fifteen miles south-east. The monk was quiet throughout, and then explained that though the Turks ruled the region, there were still plenty of good Christians labouring under the yoke who brought offerings of both goods and of news to Meteora. Dometius was surprisingly well informed, it seemed, and was already aware of much of the political landscape.

'How do you remain safe here? Has Turahan Bey not come for you, so close to his palace? I know they can be lenient on Christians, but not ones in positions of power, either socially or geographically.'

'Ha. You saw how hard we are to reach. An army came some years ago. They besieged these perches, but the simple fact is that we have a stockpile of food in our eyries, and I even have a cow for milk and a small vegetable garden. The bey's forces ran out of strength and supplies long before we did. All I have to do is pull up the ladders.'

A thought struck Gabriel. In order to let them down, the priest must have climbed three quarters of the way down and then back up. Why had he not simply come to them and saved them the climb? That irritation nagged at him for a while, even as the prince and the monk discussed the church and its counterparts on other similar stacks nearby.

'Well, this is becoming imperial land once more,' Constantine concluded. 'You will no longer have to fear, and we shall carve you some steps.'

'How is your mother?' the priest said, suddenly.

Constantine paused. There was an uncomfortable silence. Apart from perhaps the emperor himself, Gabriel was quite convinced that this prince was his mother's favourite from the whole brood, and yet he had hardly seen her in many years, even when sojourning in the city.

'She bides, Dometius. She bides. She takes an active part in all my brother's administration, for she is brighter than all of us, and stronger than most.'

'She is. She always was. And how are *you*?'

'I… I am in high spirits. This campaign will rebuild the empire, my friend.'

There was a strange pause, and Gabriel winced. He could almost picture the monk's face.

'Lies do not befit a prince, Constantine Palaiologos.'

'I…'

'You carry a burden. I see it in you. Your heart is the size of an empire, but it is charred and black, and you carry it on your back like a weight. Tell me again about the wives you lost.'

'I would really rather not.'

'Bear in mind I was confessor to an empress. I know what I'm doing, Constantine. Tell me.'

Another unpleasant pause.

'Aikaterine Gattilusio was a remarkable woman. George knew it, and he chose well. Had I met her myself when young, I suspect we would have enjoyed romance that would make even the soppiest handmaid sick. But I was still grieving when I came to her, and she died of sickness, taking my son with her. I had been distant for a time, though some fool had succeeded in making me care for her just in time to lose her.'

There was another pause. Gabriel winced again, knowing, oddly, that both men were looking through the wall directly at him.

'She is a *symptom* of your malady, Constantine,' the monk said, 'not the cause. Both Sphrantzes in finding her for you, and the ugly one out there in making you care, did the right thing. Neither they, nor you, nor the woman herself, or even God, are to blame. Sometimes horrible things happen, and there is no reason. The cause, though… the cause is this Maddalena.'

'Theodora, as she became. She came from nowhere, the product of a political deal to secure a region. She should have meant little to me, but she came into my life like a storm, shaking everything and then clearing the air so the sun could shine anew. She was my everything, Dometius, and I lost her so quickly. I have never managed to walk past that moment, even when Aikaterine was with me. I fear I am becoming my brother Theodore.'

A snort.

'Would that you were, in one way, for rarely has a potential emperor ever been closer to God. But yes. I have heard much of the poor boy's troubles. Would you care for a gem of wisdom?'

There was yet another moment of silence, and then Constantine sighed. 'I fear you can say nothing that has not been said, but go ahead, old man.'

'Good. Pull yourself together, Constantine Palaiologos.'

If Gabriel had been drinking, he would have spat it out.

'Have a care, old man,' the prince said, an edge to his tone.

'No. Tish and fie. Rubbish. It is what you need to hear. Even thousands of years ago, our ancestors in this land knew this. The men who built the pagan oracle at Delphi carved many maxims, among which was the important phrase "Live without sorrow".

And if the pagans cannot be trusted to supply wisdom, perhaps you could pay attention to our own sacred scripture?'

'Brother Dometius…'

'"Now is your time of grief, but I will see you again and you will rejoice, and no one will take away your joy." John, sixteen: twenty-two. I suspect the "now" to which he refers was, for you, over a decade ago. Need I say more?'

'Listen—'

'All right, then. If nothing else turns your head, then it should be turned by Second Corinthians – "Godly grief produces a repentance that leads to salvation without regret, whereas worldly grief produces death." Are you in godly grief, Constantine, awaiting salvation? Or are you in worldly grief, and in nothing but a sea of death?'

Gabriel held his breath, waiting for a response, but the silence from the room was powerful, and it was the monk who spoke next.

'Corinthians is a source of much of import to you, my son. "Death is swallowed up in victory. O death, where is your victory? O death, where is your sting?" And what are you achieving now, if not victory?'

'I am disquieted by your words, Dometius.'

'Then let me hammer a nail into the crucifix of your grief, Constantine. Twenty years ago, your mother lost your father. Do you remember that time? Do you remember your mother?'

'I…'

'Because she grieved deeply. She loved your father beyond all. But she would not let the grief define her. She gave her wedding finger to God, but did she retreat to a convent to waste away? No. She remained at court, a nun with the power of an empress, and she guided your brother through his first faltering years, and God knows she still does. You have not seen her in recent years. This I know.'

'How?'

'Because if you had, this would be nothing new to you. She would have had you across her knee and given you a good hiding until you stopped moping and started behaving like a Palaiologos. Grief is good. Grief is appropriate. Grief is even *necessary*. But grief is also passing. Stop clinging to it like a drowning man, and realise that the water is only waist deep.'

There was an extended silence, then, and Gabriel suddenly heard the sound of weeping. That was enough. There was a limit to eavesdropping, and this had now become something much more private. Taking a deep breath, he walked out of the church and left them to it. It took him less than an hour to explore the whole church complex and the open ground, never coming too close to the edge. Not too far from the top of the ladder, he found another pulley, with a basket and net system attached to many, many coils of rope, and realised how things were sent up to the top from the valley below. He had a horrible feeling that the monk would suggest using it for their descent, and began to marshal his arguments against it. Much as he dreaded the return journey, the idea of bouncing down the side of the cliff in that net held greater fear still. Manuel had recovered from his momentary bad mood and was sitting in the lee of the cowshed with Jordi, playing dice, making off-colour jokes and cackling like a fishwife as he swiped away his friend's coins. Gabriel left them to it.

It was as he was sitting in the shade and contemplating the ladders that Constantine reappeared from the church. The monk was not with him, and there was something about the prince that Gabriel had not seen in years: a confidence that had long gone, a smile of determination that for once was not a mask. He almost glowed, like those haloes the emperors had in mosaics in the great city.

'Gabriel? Good. Ready yourself for a long climb. Destiny awaits.'

9 *November 1444*

'Disappointing to have missed a chance to capture one of the sultan's highest-ranking beys,' Constantine said as he dropped into the governor of Thessaly's chair and put his feet up on Turahan's desk, ankles crossed.

'Better for your men,' Gabriel noted. 'Resistance here was negligible. If Turahan Bey had been here, there would have been an army of size barring our entry to the city.'

'True.'

'More irksome are the signs of Tocco's presence.'

That had been a particular irritation. One of the better houses in the town bore the jagged blue and white of the Tocco, and though they could not definitively say which scion it had been who'd lived here until recently, Torno was the safest of bets. They had missed the man again, and this time, while they had been in the best possible position.

'Perhaps,' Constantine said, unusually dismissive of their regular enemy. 'For now, while I continue to despite the Epirot villain, it is the Turks who command my attention.'

'Understood.'

Rhosatsas came striding into the room at that moment, his plated leg armour clanking. 'Questioning soldiers and court officials gets you nowhere without time-consuming *interrogation*, but I tend to find that civilian clerks bend very easily at the slightest threat.'

'What did you learn?'

'Turahan Bey has been gone from here over a month, with the majority of his men, presumably Tocco and other allies, too. He answered the call of the sultan to join him against the Hungarian king and his crusaders. The last message he sent, he was with Murad and they were up in the north-east, on the edge of Wallachian lands.'

'Trying to stop Władysław taking Varna, I imagine. Well, then, gentlemen, I think we need to adjust our plans. I was anticipating a major struggle to take the city, and the army is getting twitchy, wanting a fight. We've not faced the Turks since before we reached the Pindus Mountains, and soldiers tend to become complacent and lax with extended periods of inactivity.'

'Where next then, my lord?' Rhosatsas mused. 'If we move north, we'll just interfere with the Vlachs in their campaigns, and south-east, Kantakouzenos will be marching to meet us by now.'

'We need to let him reach us first, I think,' the prince said. 'The next major target has to be Thessaloniki.'

'Thessaloniki is hard to hold without a massive garrison, lord,' Rhosatsas noted. 'That's why we ceded it to Venice in the first place. And they proved as much by losing it to the Turks a few years later.'

'But that is why it will not stay Turkish, too. They've ruled there for fourteen years, and the Catholics before that for eight, but the people there are still sons and daughters of the Patriarch in Constantinople, and they will welcome liberation, for certain. But we have to be prepared for a proper fight to take Thessaloniki back from Murad, and that is why we must wait for the other army to join us. Together we should be strong enough.'

Gabriel simply stood back against the wall and nodded at all of this. Grand strategies were not his thing – the movement of armies and the territories of empires. Battle, yes. Wars, no. But having sufficient troops for the task was a clear requirement, and Constantine certainly seemed to know what he was doing.

He looked at the prince. Since that day in the Meteora monastery, there was something different about him, as though a weight had been lifted from his soul. He was the old Constantine once more, or close enough, at least: the prince who had rallied a city at the walls to fight off impossible odds. It was a welcome change.

The two men on the other side of the room began to talk logistics and supply lines, Rhosatsas fetching a map and then sitting on the other side of the desk to the prince. Gabriel left them to it, content that there was no danger to Constantine in the palace. He strode out of the room, and past two of his Ianitzaroi in the corridor, protecting the prince from unwanted visitors, and out into the autumn sunshine.

The compound that surrounded the bey's palace in Tırhala was sizeable and with many buildings, and he strolled towards the Janissary barracks, where his men were currently quartered, and where he knew Mateu to be currently cooking up a pot of chicken. Out behind the barracks, Jordi and Manuel were experimenting with the four guns they'd taken from the Turks in Thebes. No one had yet hit a target smaller than a shed door, but they were getting better.

The ground was dusty and white with gravel, and Gabriel kicked up small clouds as he walked, which was why he almost trod in it before he saw it, and stopped, sharp, looking down.

The eagle was most definitely dead, its neck broken, perhaps on impact, but it had not been there long, for it was not badly damaged other than that, its wings still sticking up and out. Gabriel's heart pounded for a moment. He was not one for undue superstition, barring the usual spitting and warding of the evil eye... oh, and the cats and rats and the thirteenth falling on a Tuesday. But the clear symbolism of a glorious eagle, insignia of the Palaiologoi, lying in the dirt, dead, was hard to ignore. Out of a strange instinct, he turned, in time to see another bird – a species he did not know, but smaller and colourful – wafting up dust with its wings, crest bright and proud as it took flight and then winged its way east, across the town.

Omens. They were not the province of a soldier, but of old men with books. Gabriel could not interpret such a thing, but it was extremely hard to spin a positive angle on this. Swallowing, he pulled his scarf from round his neck and bent, scooping up the dead bird, which was large and a surprising weight, then bundled it tight and carried it away before anyone else saw it. He would live with the worry, but he was damn sure he was not going to let anyone else interpret that image.

An eagle in the dust...

20 November 1444

Gabriel ground his teeth as he stomped across the muddy compound, heading for the gate. For over a week now, everything he'd seen had felt like an omen, presaging disaster. A black cat had scurried from the governor's palace the morning after their arrival, which was a clear sign to the more superstitious. Gabriel had brushed that off, but as the days wore on, signs began to mount. For some reason, every time he saw a flock or murmuration of birds, they were always heading south, back towards the Morea. There had been a thunderstorm only yesterday and, peculiarly, it had seemed to fall purely on Tırhala, for a mile outside the city, the ground remained dry. A goat had been butchered to provide meat for the prince and his companions' evening meal, and had been found to be rotten inside even while alive.

Gabriel had never bowed excessively to superstition, but the longer this went on, the more it felt like God slapping him round the head and trying to make him listen. And he was not alone. Others were starting to see signs now, and he was extremely thankful that he'd hidden the episode with the dead eagle from everyone, for it would only have fuelled the uneasiness that seemed to settle over the city and the occupying army.

Oddly, given the past few years, the one man who seemed oblivious – or perhaps more accurately *impervious* – to such signs was Constantine himself. Despite having been dark of soul and at best pessimistic at all times, even in the face of so many signs, the prince seemed strong and positive at last.

A warning horn had been blown from the edge of the city, a particular cadence that warned of a courier approaching, and so Gabriel, along with the prince and several of his senior courtiers and officers, had hurried to the gate. Two of the Ianitzaroi stood to the sides of the portal watching, tense, as a single horseman rode down the thoroughfare towards them, fast. Lone couriers riding hard never carried good news, in Gabriel's experience, so he braced himself for what was to come.

The rider reached the gate. He dropped from the mount and let go of his reins, and the horse simply stood there, sweating, clearly exhausted from the journey as the rider fell to one knee, head bowed before the prince.

'Up,' Constantine said, not unkindly.

The man rose, his eyes finally coming up to meet them. His expression was bleak.

'What is it, man?' Rhosatsas urged.

'My lord, I bear terrible tidings from the east.'

'We presumed that,' the general sighed. 'Go on.'

'The army of Władysław is no more.'

A hammer blow hit the crowd of nobles and officers at the news. Even Gabriel, half expecting something like this for more than a week, staggered slightly at the tidings. 'More details,' the prince said, his tone flat.

'A great battle at Varna on the tenth, my lord,' the courier breathed. 'The Hungarians and Wallachians and all their allies, some twenty thousand men. They met the sultan's full force, three times that number. More than half the Pope's army was gone in just hours, and the Hungarian king himself fallen, beheaded before the sultan.'

'Survivors?' Rhosatsas pressed.

'My lord Mircea took what remained of his Wallachs back north to the mountains. The Voivod Hunyadi rallied the other survivors and fled west, heading for Hungary once more.'

'Will there be another push?' Constantine asked quietly. 'The Pope's bull still stands, and there must have been enough survivors to become the core of a second force.'

Rhosatsas, perhaps at the look on the messenger's face, shook his head. 'If the Vlachs have gone home, and Hunyadi retreats to Hungary, there will be no further push, or if there is, it will not happen until the winter is past, and the Pope and his allies can gather fresh forces. But I fear it was Władysław who kept the crusade going. It was he and his pet cardinal who defied the peace deal and pressed on. With his head on a Turkish spike, few will advocate further war. By Christ Mass there will be a peace deal struck, I think.'

An uncomfortable silence fell at this, which stretched out for some time, until finally Rhosatsas cleared his throat. 'My lord, what now?'

The prince stood for a time, cradling his chin, scratching it. 'Murad is free to turn to us, but I do not think he can crush us. He still has a huge force, but they will be weary after Varna, and he will have incurred losses. Moreover, he will now need to put strong garrisons in place in the wake of the retreating crusaders just in case we are wrong, and Hunyadi and the Pope *do* decide to renew the conflict. At best he will be able to send twenty or thirty thousand men for us.'

'That's too many,' Gabriel said. 'We can't match that.'

'We can when Kantakouzenos and the Duke of Athens arrive with the other army. We have spilled blood and burned bridges these past months to achieve what has seemed impossible for centuries. We have doubled imperial territory in Greece. I had hoped to drive the sultan out, but that clearly is not going to happen. Still, if we can rally both armies, we can hold Thessaly and face Murad here. If we can beat him resoundingly enough, we can force a settlement in which we retain control of Thessaly. It is not the rebuilt empire of which we'd talked, but it would be the greatest gain since the day we took the city back from the Latins four centuries ago. It is still something to be immensely proud of.'

'You really think we can hold Thessaly?' Rhosatsas asked.

'We will be able to soon. And I tell you this now, John, my days of fear and of pessimism are gone. We will do what we can to hold Thessaly, but if God has other plans and we cannot hold it, then I will hold what territory I may. If Thessaly falls, we will retreat to Thebes and hold Attica, and if even that is not possible, Thomas awaits us at the Hexamilion. The Morea is our heartland, remember.'

Gabriel followed the prince for the following few hours as messages were sent out, plans laid, reports gone through and consultations held with various officers and administrators. It was when they had all left, and Constantine sat alone in the room with Gabriel, that the prince leaned back in his chair and rubbed his eyes and paused at last.

'Is this all for them?' Gabriel said, quietly.

'What?'

'This show of fortitude? It's new. I'm not used to it.'

Constantine gave a strange, weary smile. 'I have decided to take my cue from my saintly mother. Faced with disaster at every turn, she rallied. She lost the love of her life, my father, and she watched the city under siege, preserved only by a miracle, or by luck. She saw vital Thessaloniki given to the Venetians and then lost to the Turks. She saw her second son die, and the others bicker and war. And faced with all of this, she married herself to God, but gripped the reins of state to help John and guide the empire through some of its darkest times. She was dowager and regent three times, Gabriel. And it is only because of her fortitude that we are here, now, having prosecuted the first successful war of conquest in half a millennium.'

Gabriel nodded. He'd always been a little in awe of the empress Helene, even when the old emperor had lived. 'She is a remarkable woman, and I suspect currently the only thing preventing your brothers from civil war in the city.'

'It would be a poor tribute to her if I were to become another Theodore, mourning my way to the grave, rigid and dark, or another Demetrios, a snake who would sell the empire to our enemies for personal gain. No. I take my cue from her. I shall not marry myself to God, though, Gabriel. I shall marry myself to the state instead, or at least *for* her, and I shall rise or fall with her. Whatever I do from this day, it is for the empire, and as long as the empire draws breath, I shall fight for her, even if it means fighting to the bitter end. In time I will have George find me another wife, but never again shall I anticipate a heart full of romance, and any future spouse will be chosen for the strength and power she adds to our dynasty.'

'Sensible. For now, we should send word of your plans to the emperor.'

Constantine nodded. 'But I need Notaras here now, as well as all my generals, and he would be my courier. George must be on his way back from Buda now. He will know the crusade has failed, and he will be racing to rejoin us. When he returns, I shall send him back to Constantinople to consult with the emperor, for he is the man I trust most. For now, we must make plans to hold Thessaly and install garrisons. I have sent word to the Vlachs that our deal holds and that we stand beside them. I need them to continue fighting in the north, lest we become surrounded.'

Gabriel leaned back against the wall. 'Then for now, we wait.'

27 November 1444

They did not have to wait for long. Word came racing from the east gate of the city, with almost a mile of warning. The army of Kantakouzenos was finally approaching. Constantine, along with Rhosatsas, Notaras, half a dozen lesser officers and his Ianitzaroi, hurried from the governor's complex to the eastern edge of the city. The air held a hint of rain, that very fine spray that was barely noticeable but presaged more, and light grey cloud had settled across the land, seemingly banishing the sun for the season. The city was subdued as they rode through the streets. There had been no grand welcome when they

289

first came, for the people of Tırhala were accustomed to their Turkish masters these days, and had greeted the arrival of the imperial army not with hope, but with guarded acceptance. But now that word had it the crusade had failed utterly and the sultan was ascendant, the mood had plummeted. Every citizen was waiting for the Turkish army to come and reassert control.

Suspicious and worried eyes watched them from windows and doors as they passed, and when they reached the gate, the men on guard there were not a great deal more optimistic.

'God in Heaven, what has happened?' Rhosatsas muttered quietly as he eyed the approaching column. For a week now, they had waited, anticipating the arrival of the general's army, a match for their own, which would double imperial forces in the city and grant them the manpower, theoretically, to control Thessaly.

They had not expected *this*.

Kantakouzenos' army looked like a defeated force. They did not so much march as trudge, their attitude weary and forlorn. No speech, no songs, no laughter, no music. Just the thud of feet and hooves, the crunch of gravel, the neighing of horses and the clonk, clang and rattle of armour and weapons. The imperial eagle banners snapped in the breeze, but even they looked limp and dejected.

'So *few*,' another of the officers breathed.

And there were. Oh, it was still an army, for sure, but compared with the massive strong force they had expected, this was a poor echo.

'That cannot be even *half* the force,' Rhosatsas noted.

And there, riding alongside, they finally caught sight of Kantakouzenos himself. He rode straight in the saddle, not sagging like most of his cavalry, and his uniform was neat and impressive, but above his sharp martial appearance, his face made a lie of it all, for he, too, bore that beaten look. Spotting the waiting officers, the general kicked his mount and cantered out ahead, gesturing to his officers as he passed. The column came to a halt two hundred paces from the gate, as Kantakouzenos reined in before them, head bowed.

'What happened?' the prince asked, quietly.

'We are betrayed, my lord. We were based at Larissa and thought to press on up the coast and secure it, placing garrisons beneath Olympos itself before returning to meet you. Then our outriders from the north met us. A Turkish army forty thousand strong marches south-west from Thessaloniki. I thought to rush and warn you, for together we might hold them, but then Nerio of Athens changed all our plans by turning on us. He has thrown in his lot with the sultan, presumably hoping to maintain his position in Attica by supporting them. I deployed to try and prevent him leaving, and we fought, but I abandoned the struggle when I realised that all I was doing was further reducing the force I could bring, so I withdrew, leaving the snake with his Turkish master, and rode for Tırhala.'

There was a horrible silence, as each man at the gate took in these tidings and ruminated upon what they meant.

'My lord, I...' Rhosatsas began, but Constantine waved a hand at him.

'Hush. I am considering the numbers.'

'Sir?' Kantakouzenos said. 'Perhaps we should be inside somewhere private? Where the men cannot hear?'

'I would *rather* they hear and understand the situation than they see us disappear inside and submit everything to their conjecture. I will not hide the truth. Forty thousand Turks. And maybe eight thousand Athenians under Nerio?'

The general nodded.

'We cannot hope to match that. Nowhere near. And to keep control of Thessaly is naught but a dream with such numbers. If we stay to face the sultan, we will lose this army along with Thessaly, and leave Thomas facing disaster when they come for him. We cannot remain in Tırhala, and must sacrifice our gains in Thessaly.'

'To Thebes?' Notaras posited.

Constantine shook his head. 'With Nerio changing sides and joining the Turks, the notion of keeping control of Athens and Attica is unlikely. He will be looking to reassert control there under Turkish authority, and the sultan will support him in that.'

'We could *submit* to the sultan,' Rhosatsas said. 'The Turks will be as tired of war as everyone. We were effectively his vassals anyway until late summer, when we broke out. To return to that situation voluntarily and save ourselves a costly war is neither cowardice nor foolishness. Perhaps it is better to survive under the Turkish flag than to die proud under our own?'

The prince shook his head. 'No. We are Romans, and I am a Palaiologos. We will fight to the death if we must to keep the eagle banner flying. It was Demetrios who claimed "better the Turkish turban than the papal mitre," not me. There may come a time for such a move, but not yet, and if it does, it will be a fiction to buy us the time to rebuild. For now, though, we fight on. We gather all the forces we can and pull back to the Hexamilion. There, we defend the Morea as an imperial land. Sadly, we will need to leave the Vlachs to their fate. Perhaps they too can strike a deal with the sultan. It may be inevitable that we submit, I acknowledge, in order to save what we can and to protect the capital's independence. But if we surrender now, we will have to accept whatever terms Murad decides upon, for he is currently in the greatest position of power in the region. Watch him spend a month or two trying to control us and the Morea, though, and his army will tire, atrophy and lose heart. Then, when he is wishing he had not come south, we may be able to strike a more favourable deal.'

'You really think we can still come out of this that well?' Rhosatsas asked.

'Murad is a pragmatic man. He will accept the most sensible path at any time. But I will wear him down so that such a path is one of easy peace. This is not over, my friends. This is only just beginning. We took a chance, based upon the actions of the Catholics, and we did not fail. In fact, we succeeded beyond all expectations. It was *they* who failed *us*. The empire has lost wars before and come back seemingly from the grave to stand proud again, for that is our fate. We are the bastion of God against the East. And I will fight when I can, and bow my head when I have to, to preserve the empire and allow us to fight another day.'

He turned and put his hands on his hips. 'Let this be known throughout the army. We are not beaten. In fact, we are *un-beaten*. We have fought across Attica and Thessaly and won every engagement. And we are neither routing nor fleeing. This is not a retreat by a lost force, but an ordered withdrawal from a territory too large for us to hold without the traitor's forces. We do not run. We move like an army, south to the isthmus, where Thomas awaits us with the rest of the army. We will defend the Hexamilion, and even if that falls, we will make the Morea so expensive to hold that Murad will offer terms. Now send word to every unit. Officers to a briefing at the palace one hour before sunset, and the army prepares to break camp at dawn. Tomorrow we march for Korinthos.'

9

A Wall at the Edge of the World

Korinthos

Early 1445

'We lost another unit this morning. Venetians,' Rhosatsas sighed.

Constantine shrugged. 'They were never very happy that our Thessalian conquests impinged on Venetian lands anyway. And being mercenaries, they are another unit we do not have to pay.'

'Soon we will have saved lots of money, because we will have no army.'

The prince took a deep breath and scrubbed his hair with both hands. 'The threat increases by the day, and we cannot expect mercenary forces to be prepared to face certain defeat for meagre pay. It was inevitable. The latest report says that Murad remains in Thessaly, re-establishing full control there and putting the Vlachs back into place. That has bought us more time than I expected. And when he is finished there, he will move into Athens and put Nerio's house in order for him before he turns to us at the Hexamilion. Plus, I hear so many rumours – that he is having new, immense cannon cast, that he waits for Turahan Bey to join him, for the governor is on a recruiting drive, even that Murad has abdicated in favour of his son. Whatever the case, the Turkish advance against us has been delayed immensely, and that allows us time to put everything in place.'

'By "everything", I presume you mean the half-dozen soldiers we're going to have when they get here,' Rhosatsas muttered. Gabriel frowned. Somewhere along the line, the general had begun to address the prince without honorifics, and that was an odd realisation.

'We will always have the imperial Moreot garrisons. With them, we will secure the Hexamilion. I have a plan for the rest.'

'You do?'

'I am placing trusted men in charge of the Morea, John. Sphrantzes will be here in weeks, and I am putting him in command of Mystras and the surroundings. Kantakouzenos will take Korinthos here and the lands behind the wall, when we move up to the garrison posts. Laskaris will take Patras, Thomas Monemvasia, and Eudaimonoiannes will be my liaison with them all. Each will be tasked with controlling their lands and preparing for the Turks, when the wall fails. I have a list of near a hundred regional barons we can rely upon to fight back, and each will be approached and granted privileges and titles to secure their ongoing loyalty. And then that leaves our remaining mercenary friends.'

The mercenaries were now less than half the number they had been during the advance, Gabriel mused, and the three hundred Burgundians had taken their leave to return home, the crusade no longer in action.

He stood and worried about the days to come as Constantine gave his generals orders, summoning the commanders of the various mercenaries, and thus found himself in a low-ceilinged hall an hour later, with a dozen of his men, guarding the prince carefully from the two-score foreign unit commanders sitting and waiting to hear what he had to say. All were armed. Gabriel had argued against that, but it was Constantine's position that they should all be made to feel like leaders now.

'You all know the situation,' the prince said at last. 'We are in a lull. The Turks rally and dither, but we all know they must come here. They must come for the empire. But the Turks are tired of war, and even when the crusade began, Murad wanted to sue for peace. It cannot take much to force him to that again. There are tracts of the Morea that are not assigned to a noble house, thanks partly to betrayals and warfare. There are gaps to fill. That is where you come in. Many of your peers have gone, fleeing the Turks and seeking quieter futures. That you are still here tells me that you are the staunch warriors, the powerful and the strong. That deserves note, and reward, but it also gives me an idea. Here, in this room, in this hour, I offer you a deal. I will give each of you a tract of land, with resources and villages, in the Morea, for you and for your men. You will lay down your mercenary tags and become citizens... Moreots. I will gift you more than you could make in a decade as mercenaries, and with a home forever, and I will ask only one thing in return.'

'And what is that?' a bearded Cypriot murmured.

'Fight for your lands and your home. The Turks may come raiding and pressing on your land. Make them pull back. Make them wish he had not. Chastise them. Not as great armies fighting for a realm, but as homesteaders, fighting for your homes. That is what I offer. And mark my words, the Turks may now be full of vim, but soon, they will tire and wish for peace, and it is our resistance that will make that happen.'

As if to illustrate this, Constantine lifted a leather satchel from the table and upended it, watching the sealed deeds of Moreot lands fall onto the table.

Gabriel waited, breath held.

When the first mercenary captain rose to examine the documents, a small glimmer of hope rose in him. When others followed, Gabriel sagged with relief.

He liked this new Constantine – this *old* Constantine.

Varna's crushing defeat would not be the end...

In the end, they had had far longer to prepare than anyone had expected. Too long, perhaps, for the armies had begun to feel safe and secure, as though no war would come to them – and, indeed, for a time it looked as though it might not.

For months after their withdrawal from Thessaly, Turahan Bey spent time reasserting complete Turkish domination in the region, taking the opportunity to carve out pieces of Epirot territory at the expense of the Tocco family. Indeed, the alliance between that family and the empire, while still officially in place, was now a thing of dust, for the pressure the Turks had placed on Epirus had forced the current count to bow his head and accept his place as the sultan's vassal in order to keep his lands. All the Tocco siblings were now acting governors of lands they once owned, paying tribute to the sultan. It was said that Torno Tocco, the infernal and eternal enemy, had received the greatest lands, for he had been the sultan's man since the day Patras fell to the empire.

The year had been all but over by the time the Turks began to look south. Nerio's part in the imperial campaigns had not gone unnoticed, and although he was now a Turkish vassal, the new year opened with a series of punitive raids into the Duchy of Athens by the Turkish forces, including seizing a few new border lands to expand Thessaly. Nerio could do nothing but watch and mutter, and more than once Gabriel wondered whether the duke regretted not having stood with the empire.

Still the advance did not come, as spring moved into summer. The Turkish forces were largely gathered in Boeotia now, close to both Athens and the isthmus, but they simply sat there, slowly and worryingly amassing more men. George Sphrantzes, who had rejoined Constantine over the winter, explained the Turks' tardiness in coming to chastise the Morea. It was partly due to internal matters at the Sublime Porte, for the rumours had been true, it seemed. Murad had abdicated in favour of his teenage son Mehmet, perhaps due to infirmities. In fact, it was said by some that this had happened even before the battle of Varna, and that it had been the young Mehmet who had bested the crusaders. Whatever the case, perhaps the adolescent was not quite yet up to the task of governance, for the Sublime Porte had lobbied Murad to retake the throne, and he had now done so.

This muddying of the political water had been further complicated by the emperor. As soon as Constantine had reached Tırhala, John had immediately opened communications with the Sublime Porte at Edirne, offering alliances and deals. According to Sphrantzes, the emperor had even claimed Constantine's entire campaign to be an attempt to shore up the region against the possibility of Serbian and Hungarian expansion with the crusaders. He might not have managed to excuse Constantine's activity in the end, but he had made sure to secure the ongoing peace between Edirne and Constantinople, though with a huge grey area lying over the future of the Morea. In short, it was only by midsummer this year that the Turks had settled their territory, chastised Athens, returned Murad to the throne, secured deals with the emperor, and moved their forces into position. From September onwards, Constantine and his people had watched from the Hexamilion as Turkish numbers continued to grow, close by. There had been no doubt then that war was coming, and that it was coming here, and soon.

Then, three days before, the eyes and ears that Constantine still maintained in Boeotia reported the army on the move. The Turks had left the Theban plain and were moving through the passes, using half a dozen different routes, to advance on the isthmus and the Hexamilion.

There had been something of a worry for a while, as Thomas had been away with a small part of his force. His daughter was to wed the son of the despot of Serbia, and he had accompanied her to her wedding, with an additional remit to coax support and troops from the new in-laws. Unfortunately, though he attended the wedding, Thomas had cut short his trip and hurried back to the isthmus, knowing the time for war was near. He arrived with his men the morning after the Turks began to move, and, sadly, without Serbian help.

Now, as the two Palaiologos brothers stood atop the tower over the Leonidas Gate, they saw the first sign of the approach. The morning was cold and damp, and there had been an early mist that continued to cling to the lower-lying areas. Then, out of that ribbon of white that sat across the brown landscape came riders.

A small party of Turkish horsemen, lances high, each with the crescent pennant streaming. There were perhaps a dozen of them, and they rode forth almost casually, as though they had no fear of what lay ahead.

'Perhaps there will be no war after all?' Thomas mused. 'Perhaps they come to parley on behalf of the sultan.'

Constantine shook his head. 'No. They are the declaration of war. That is all.'

The riders came on, even into bowshot of the walls, and a quarter of a mile of soldiers on the defences readied themselves, archers nocking arrows ready, but Constantine waved them down. The dozen riders stopped not far from the gate, guided to the appropriate spot by Constantine's own banners hanging in the towers. As they stopped, two of their number rode out ahead, halting in front of the rest.

'In the name of Sultan Murad Han, Sovereign of the Sublime House of Osman, Sultan of Sultans, Padishah of Edirne and Bursa, Commander of the Faithful and Successor of the Prophet of the Lord, greetings.'

Constantine said nothing, but stood, watching, visible from below in his military finery.

'Though the sultan honours his alliance with the emperor of the Romans,' the man went on, 'there must be recompense for the illegal and aggressive activity of the imperial despots of the

Morea. The forces of the sultan come today. Your wall will be destroyed and your armies dispersed. The Morea will be taken and investigated with a view to its annexation by the state. You are commanded to disband your forces and quit this place, and you will be allowed to return to Constantinople unharmed. This is the word of the sultan, to honour his friend and ally, the emperor. Will you agree to these terms and abide by them?'

There was a heavy silence, then. Men all along the wall looked to Constantine, who still stood silent atop the tower. Finally, the prince reached out and leaned on the merlons of the parapet, his face set into a stony scowl.

'You, spokesman, may take this message to your master. The Morea is imperial land since time immemorial, and he has no claim upon it. I say the sultan may take his army back north and there will be peace. *I* will honour the emperor's alliance by allowing *your* forces to leave the isthmus without injury.'

The Turk frowned. He had not been expecting such defiance, clearly.

'You overreach, Prince of Romans. Do not think to defy the sultan. We know you have less than twenty thousand men. Know now that the sultan sends only a small force of sixty thousand to deal with the troublesome Morea. The wall will fall, and the Morea after. Whether you live to see this is your decision, Prince Constantine.'

Another pause. Once again, all eyes were on the prince.

'I say again, go home,' Constantine said, flat-toned. 'Out of respect for your sultan and my brother's alliance with him, I allow you to leave, and I will not cast the first stone. Any war here will be begun by you, and the consequences will be upon you. Sixty thousand men cannot take this wall held by twenty thousand. Run home while you can.'

Gabriel winced. Yes, the wall would give them a defensive advantage, but he'd still consider odds any higher than two to one to be impossible. Still, he could feel the confidence rising in the men all around him. The prince knew precisely what he was doing.

The lead rider's face contorted into a sneer. 'God is with us, heathen. I give you one last chance.'

'Remarkable,' the prince replied, 'since my bishops only this morning assured me that God is with *us*. Perhaps you are mistaken. Go now, or suffer the consequences.'

The spokesman's lip twitched; his eyes narrowed. He turned and gave a nod to the man beside him, who cast his spear down into the turf, before turning back to address Constantine. 'Then there can be no peace. War is upon you.'

'Well, if that's a declaration,' Constantine replied with a dark smile, then gave a simple signal with a flick of his finger.

Two-score men along the nearest walls and on the towers lifted their bows over the battlements and loosed arrows. The Turkish speaker, wide-eyed, did not even have time to panic, as all around him shafts thudded into his companions. In a few short heartbeats he was alone, surrounded by the bodies of men and horses, peppered with arrows.

Recovering his poise remarkably well, the Turk looked up at Constantine. 'You said you would not cast the first stone.'

'Oh, I'm sorry, my dear fellow. I presumed the spear your friend cast counted.' His demeanour hardened. 'Go to your master and tell him he may dash his men to pieces on the wall if he wishes, or he may go home in peace.'

The Turk glared at him for a moment longer through those narrowed eyes, then turned his horse and rode away at a good speed.

'Well, that went well, I think,' Constantine mused, stretching.

'You do know we are very unlikely to hold against sixty thousand, my lord?' Rhosatsas noted.

'I never expected us to be able to hold the wall forever, John. But I want these men thinking they can, and I want to make Murad pay dearly for every foot of wall he takes. When he breaks through into the Morea, I want him to leave half his forces mouldering, piled up outside the walls. With sixty thousand he could effectively seize control of the Morea. With thirty, he will find it hard to maintain a hold even on one part of it, let alone the whole island. Make sure every section commander knows the rules. Waste no man on the walls. Arrows and artillery for everything. I want to thin their ranks without meeting them face to face as long as possible.'

'Every man knows his job, my lord.'

Good.

The mist was continually receding, now, though the inclement weather looked likely to remain, for the clouds, thick and grey, presaged rain. As the watchers on the wall squinted into the distance, the Turks came. They emerged from the fading mist like a wall of humanity, marching in perfect lines, their uniforms and armour gleaming and identical, flags flying, the army stretching from the sea, almost a mile to their right, as far as the eye could see to the left – probably all six miles of the isthmus and the wall.

'God, but there are a lot of them,' someone murmured.

'There are,' Constantine agreed, 'but there are also a lot of us, and they are only Turks, while we are Romans.'

Laughs broke out here and there at the prince's statement, but they soon died away, like all forced bravado. Rank after rank after rank of infantry came from the tattered white mist, and now, behind them, they could see the cavalry coming on high-stepping horses. They stood for a good hour, then, just watching the army arrive. Thousand upon thousand of the heavy infantry, rank upon rank of cavalry. A multitude of archers, gathered into units hundreds strong, placed intermittently among the infantry.

'They clearly plan to hit the whole wall at once,' Rhosatsas said.

'That will be very costly for him,' Thomas replied.

'And for us,' noted the prince. 'We will not be able to concentrate our forces at all. He will keep us fighting stretched out along the line, because he knows he outnumbers us three to one. We will make him pay dearly for it, regardless.'

The enemy had moved to just outside the range of the wall-top artillery and there begun to mass as more and more soldiers arrived, a sea of humanity filling the isthmus before the wall. Gabriel looked out across the lines. It took him a while to find what he was looking for: a small group of standards higher and prouder than the others, bearing not only the crescent of the Turks, but also the personal banners of the sultan. He was not opposite Constantine, but perhaps half a mile further west, possibly positioned there to be away from the concentrated danger of the Isthmia fortress, a ten-acre walled citadel, an extension to the Hexamilion itself that held much of the supplies and support for the wall, a similar, more temporary version at the far end near Korinthos.

It had been mooted that if somehow the sultan himself fell, the Turks might lose sufficient heart to be persuaded to abandon this course. Some sultans had had little interest in the affairs of the empire, after all, but Murad was not a man known for backing down once he had cause to march forth. He was by nature a peaceful man and one who preferred the subtle work of diplomacy, but time and again he had proved that if required to step up, then step up he would. And even if Murad fell and his army lost heart, the recent abdication and brief reign of young Mehmet had proved that the army would follow the next sultan into battle with no extended period of mourning. In the end it had been decided that the fall of Murad was unlikely to avert the coming war, and given the immense effort and danger required even to try, it was not a tactically sound option.

Moving on from that flag, Gabriel scoured the army for another, a much more visible one. A blue-and-white one. Since Torno Tocco had been granted a relatively important appanage by the sultan, there was every reason to expect the bastard to be back *there*, living well in his Turkish lands, growing fat and lazy and not concerning himself with wars outside his domain. Every reason except the important one, that was. Because Torno cropped up like a bad *stavraton* at every important martial juncture, and just as Constantine – *and Gabriel* – would move mountains to get to the son of a whore, so Torno would undoubtedly be itching to finish the job and remove Constantine from the board of the great game.

No blue-and-white flag. The natural assumption was that Torno was busy governing up in Thessaly, yet Gabriel would wager his left hand that the Tocco scion and his men were here somewhere. Perhaps Murad had been sensible and put him much further along the line, far from the prince.

'Oho… What have we here?' one of the artillery commanders murmured, peering out. Gabriel followed his gaze to see two Turkish light infantry, jogging out from the lines, unarmoured, with only a stick in each hand.

'Permission to turn them into şiş kebab, my lord?' the officer asked.

'Not yet. I want to know what they're up to.'

And so they all watched from the wall-top as the two men reached a place just within artillery range, and proceeded to measure out lines, using a string tied between the two sticks. Then, when they were satisfied, they lifted the string and let go, so that it twanged down against the brown earth and dry grass. The string was clearly painted, for it left a straight white line. As they watched, the two men created two more lines from the ends of the first, marching back at right angles towards the Turkish lines. A last line, and they had a box.

'All right, Simon. Now.'

There was a one-word command, a pair of thuds – one from each tower flanking the gate – and the two men with their sticks and painted string were plucked from the ground with bolts a foot and a half long slammed through their chests, and hurled back, dying, towards their own lines.

No more came forth, but over the next hour and more, the activity was repeated, this time outside artillery range, among their own front lines. Intrigued, the imperial command watched. Once the places were marked, timber was brought forth in large quantities, and the Turks began making a literal wooden box using the white lines as a guide. And as the box rose in height, Rhosatsas mused. 'Some sort of building? A place for archers to hide inside?'

Constantine shook his head. 'No. I know what that is. Seen it before.'

And so had Gabriel. As they watched, the Turks began to bring forward barrows and carts full of earth and rubble and tip them into the box, building a ramp to it on the far side as they went. And between loads, slaves were sent up with great heavy paddles to tamp down the earth and stones into a solid base.

'What is it?' Rhosatsas asked.

'It is a gun platform for the Turkish cannon.'

'I've seen their guns in action,' the strategos replied. 'They might chip bits off the walls, but that's all.'

'Don't underestimate them, John, for not all their cannon are like that. I've seen what their big guns can do – not the cannon they use on ships or bring to battles, but siege guns the likes of which you cannot imagine. Wide enough to send a child down the barrel to clean it. I might have overestimated our own safety here. I had thought the wall sufficient to balance out our numbers. I had not accounted for Murad bringing city-killers with him. That, I fear, is why he has been so long. He's brought bronze casters with him, probably from Varna, and shipped the components all the way from Edirne or beyond. Such artillery pieces usually risk cracking or exploding with every shot, I am led to believe, so he will be making them specially, somewhere near, so as not to have to carry them across the world and risk putting strain on them. I don't know how many he can have made, but I doubt this will be the only such platform.'

Gabriel shivered. He remembered that cannon busy pounding the gate at Euripos as they stood atop it, and that had only been a small example, still enough to open the way for them. But he also remembered that one during the siege at Constantinople, when the walls had almost fallen to the monster, and surely must have done so, had not a miraculous trick saved them all.

'Shame there's no Theotokos icon to carry along this wall,' Gabriel said quietly.

'And no magnificent empress to follow it, chiding her son.' Constantine chuckled, glancing across.

'I have no idea what you're talking about,' Rhosatsas sighed, 'but personally I would rather wish for a damn great hole to open up and swallow half the Turks.'

'Certainly a valid alternative to empresses and icons,' Gabriel muttered, 'though just as unlikely.'

'How long will these walls last against a city-killer, Gabriel?'

The Ianitzaroi frowned at the prince, for a moment wondering why he would direct such a question at his body-guard rather than the professional soldiers around him. The answer was fairly simple. Rhosatsas had never faced such a siege – not in recent years, anyway – and Sphrantzes had only been peripherally involved, even at Euripos. None of the strategists on this gate-top had seen the sultan's city-killers. Only the prince, and Gabriel and his men, who had watched that one pound the walls of Constantinople, almost into submission. Gabriel looked across at the walls. They were good and thick, solid things, with heavy protruding towers at regular intervals. But there was no forewall, no middle wall, no moat. Just one good, solid rampart. He tried to picture that thing Murad had used on the capital at work here.

'I think a day to get their ranges straight, when we'll withstand the odd shot that shakes the walls. Once they have range, the second day they will work every hour of daylight. I don't think they'll waste the shots by using night fighting, since they're hardly pressed for time. They can take as long as they want. Still, I reckon the first tower will go on the third day, and by the end of that third day, there could even be a breach. Certainly the next.'

Rhosatsas frowned. 'Surely that's just alarmist talk.'

'No. That's a solid estimate. Five days to the first breach. They won't come then, though.'

'Oh?'

Gabriel nodded. 'You know this better than me. A small breach would mean funnelling his army through the gap, which would turn it into a killing zone. Position your artillery and archers right, and you kill his men by the thousand as they enter. No, he will keep using his cannon. At least as long again. He will aim to open any breach wider and wider until it is too vast to hold. Then, after perhaps ten or eleven days, he will have a gap wide enough to commit his men, and we will be facing an army three times our size, without the wall to help any more.'

'Then we must find ways to stop his guns.'

'Not easy,' Gabriel mused. 'If you come up with a plan, I'm all ears, but it'll be a hard job.'

They watched for another hour as the terreplein was constructed, the packing of the earth completed, and then the wooden floor for the gun nailed into place.

'Shame the rain's stopped,' Gaspar sighed. 'A good torrential downpour while they're trying to build that thing, and the earth they're working with would be soup.'

Gabriel nodded, said nothing. They couldn't change the weather, and it was dry and mild, for mid-winter.

'If the timbers were destroyed, that packed earth would just collapse outwards,' Rhosatsas mused.

'First you'd have to get to it.'

The strategos gave Gabriel a weird smile. 'I have a trick I might use, something I've done before with enemy artillery. Give me a quarter of an hour.'

And so they watched for another fifteen minutes as the platform was made ready, until the general reappeared with a small unit of men. Gabriel put the plan together in an instant as he looked down at them. A dozen archers, each with a quiver holding just four arrows. That meant bulky arrows, and the presence of men with torches alongside them meant fire-arrows. Of course, it would take far too long for fire-arrows to burn an earth-packed timber mound, so Rhosatsas must have thought of that. An accelerant of some sort, presumably.

'They still have to get close enough, of course,' Gabriel called down. In reply, Rhosatsas called another unit over: men carrying wicker shields eight feet high and six across.

'It *might* work,' Constantine conceded from close by.

'A small chance. And if it does, they wait for it to go out, then build another, and the next time, they're ready for the trick. Costs them nothing but a little timber and a couple of days.'

'Never forget the knock to morale, Gabriel. Anything that makes them worry is worth the chance.' He leaned over the wall-top. 'Good luck, John.'

The strategos touched his forelock in response, and moments later, the gate was opened. Naturally, Rhosatsas himself stayed at the wall, watched his men go, and then began to climb the tower as the gates were shut again. It was just as he reached the top and joined the others, watching, that his team moved into range of the enemy. Almost the very moment they crossed some invisible line, the Turks began to attack. Missiles came arcing over in their dozens. The men with the wicker shields rushed ahead, the archers scurrying behind them, and only when the archers' leader gave a signal did they stop. Even from this distance, Gabriel could see the arrows thudding into the shields in their scores, and then their hundreds. First one shield-bearer fell, then another, but by then the imperial archers were at work. They drew back their shafts and two of their number hurried between them with torches, igniting the arrows.

Strain, aim, release. Twelve arrows whipped out between the shields, their path easy to follow from the streak of fire and the black smoke trail they left. Almost all the missiles were true, and Gabriel prepared himself to eat his words. With each hit, there came a small explosion, sending what should have been a small fire into a true conflagration.

'Oil?'

Rhosatsas nodded. 'A small glass vial tied to each arrow, right next to the flammable wadding. In ages past we might have used Greek fire. Would that there were any alive who knew how to create such a thing.'

Gabriel nodded, rather absently, his attention on the terre-plein. The strategos had been right, and his plan had been a good one. Where fire-arrows would not have done enough damage, combined with the oil, the timbers were alight on all three faces they could hit. At a command, the defenders began to pull back. They lost another two shields, and three of the archers, to Turkish missiles before they were back out of range and running for the wall, but the job had been done. The gun emplacement blazed out of control, and even though the Turks threw bucket after bucket of water on it, they could not stop the inferno. By nightfall, a couple of hours later, the ruined timber edifice was still glowing, despite the timber faces and floor having collapsed and burned, and the packed earth burst free to run down to the ground once more.

'Well done, John.'

'They will rebuild it, of course, and the same thing will not work again,' Gabriel said.

'But damage has been done to their morale, while spirit has been put into our own. And it buys us another day or more. Messages are now going out to all my people across the Morea. When the wall falls...'

'*If* the wall falls,' Rhosatsas added.

'Then the whole of the Morea is waiting to make the Turks wish they'd never crossed the isthmus. And yes, perhaps the wall will hold. There are always miracles, of course.'

'I would love to be able to hear the conversation in the sultan's tent tonight.' Sphrantzes grinned.

'I fear not everyone over there will retain their commission past the morning.' Thomas laughed.

Gabriel almost jumped as he realised that Constantine was suddenly next to him, leaning on the wall. The man seemed to be able to move up to you unnoticed, on feet lighter than a cat. 'What troubles you, Gabriel? You are unusually quiet.'

'I am *always* quiet,' he replied, flatly. 'But as it happens, I am wondering where the Tocco animal is.'

'Yes, I scanned for his flag when they arrived. And I, too, would love to meet him again. I still owe him for hanging my people at Patras, not to mention other crimes,' he added, fingers going up to the scar on his neck. 'He will be here somewhere, of that I am sure. Out to the west, across the isthmus. Perhaps, when dawn comes round, we might seek him out?'

'I would appreciate that very much.'

'Good. Then we shall do that. Every part of this wall is as valuable as the next, and I would like to see what we're up against.'

'Then why not go now? We can fight in the morning, but four or five miles' stroll before bed might be just the thing.'

An answering grin from Constantine was all he needed, and a few minutes later they were gathered on the tower-top with half a dozen of the Ianitzaroi accompanying them. The enemy might be out of missile range, but Constantine seemed to have regained something of his old self, just when they really needed that prince, and Gabriel was damned if he was going to let something happen to him now.

The Hexamilion, as the name suggested, was six miles long, sealing off the isthmus – and therefore the whole Morea – from the mainland. It was twenty feet high, and with almost two hundred towers, spaced roughly every hundred-and-fifty to two hundred feet. Nine gates across its length, with a controlling fortress in the east, and a lesser 'mirror' one to the west. It was possible to use the wall to walk from coast to coast across the isthmus without ever descending to ground level.

A heartening sight was the depot in place every five towers, which held ammunition, arms, medical facilities, bunk rooms for rotated serving units, and even cook rooms and storehouses. The wall was well planned and well provisioned, more than ever in its two-thousand-year existence. More heartening still was the attitude of the troops and their commanders, all of whom were in high spirits.

Less heartening were the terrepleins. The one they had burned near the Isthmian fortress was far from alone. There were, in fact, five such platforms being constructed, roughly each mile along the wall. Constantine passed on the suggestion of repeating Rhosatsas' plan to them all, or execute any other plan they could come up with, to destroy the platforms and delay the deployment of guns.

It was at the fourth mile that they found Torno Tocco. The blue and white of the Tocco family stood clear and proud, so different from the crimson of the Turkish banners that even at night it stood out.

'That,' Constantine said, coming to a halt, 'is what we want. I fear the wall must fall, and many Turkish boots will cross it to tread upon the throats of the Morea. We will make them pay for it, in time, but for now, I tell you this – it is my vow that Torno Tocco will not cross this wall alive.'

Gabriel could only nod at that, and suddenly he was hungry for morning to come.

4 December 1446

The dawn brought a hive of activity on both sides.

Even as the pale sun broke free of the hills across the isthmus, the Turks were moving their artillery into position. Safely beyond the range of the Roman weapons – largely tower-mounted catapults and bolt-throwers – Turkish engineers were bringing forth their own armament, and it was clear at first sight that the least of their weapons could outstrip the greatest of the Roman ones.

'They're incredible,' Thomas breathed. The younger Palaiologos had arrived before dawn with many of the senior officers, and now watched, wide-eyed.

Sphrantzes nodded. 'Sadly, while we stagnate, the sultan moves on. Centuries ago we had weapons that launched fire that could not be extinguished, and even burned upon water. We had weapons that were the envy of the world, and the cleverest engineers to be found anywhere. When we lost Asia Minor, we lost the resources for such beastly weapons, and in time, we forgot how to make them. Now our weapons of war are the same ones our ancestors used to hold the Goths across the river. The Turks, on the other hand, are learning all the time. Forty years ago, they had never even heard of cannon, and their catapults were poor copies of ours. Now they have counterweight trebuchets, and cannon of ever-growing strength and variety, engineered by geniuses from Albania and Serbia and Varna, and so on. The more lands and peoples they take, the more they discover, and the stronger they become.'

Gabriel watched, tense, as the machines were settled into place. The trebuchets were enormous, sufficient on their own to bring down towers and walls in good time. Between and around them were installed smaller catapults, bolt-throwers, then small cannon, medium cannon, and finally, as they watched, the first of five city-killers was moved into position.

It was not as large as the one Gabriel remembered from the siege of Constantinople when he was a younger man, or possibly time had magnified that beast in his memory, but still it was big enough to put the future of the Hexamilion in serious doubt. A muzzle, he reckoned, around a foot to a foot and a half across. The ammunition was being brought up in carts, stone balls that took a team of men and ropes and pulleys to stack. Indeed, eighteen oxen pulled the cannon into position, with some hundred or so men helping and guiding it.

Gabriel's gaze strayed from that monster across to the gathering of blue-and-white flags not far away.

'How will we single out Tocco?'

Constantine scratched his chin. 'He would be foolish to come out ahead of their lines before the wall is breached. In fact, almost certainly the sultan has already issued a blanket command that no one moves out of position until the order to advance comes from high up. So Tocco is unlikely to come to us. But equally, we cannot go to him. To advance into range of their archers and anti-personnel artillery would be foolish in the extreme, and I suspect there is not enough honour in that shell of a man to accept a straight fight.'

'So how do we get to him?'

'We make him come to us.'

Gabriel frowned and scratched his head. 'You just said he wouldn't do that.'

'Not willingly, or straight away. But the man is arrogant, and hot-tempered. And clearly not averse to disobeying orders if it suits him. I intend to goad him.'

'How?'

The prince turned to the commander of artillery on the tower-top behind him. 'What's the maximum range of your ballistae?'

The man tapped his lip and moved to the parapet, looking out. 'Effective range is roughly where that bush with the bare branch is, my lord. See, some hundred yards short of their cannon.'

'And your catapults?'

'A mite further than that, lord. Perhaps half as far again towards the enemy. Still sadly not enough to reach them.'

'What would it take for you to put a shot into the blue-and-white force over there?'

'Begging your pardon, my lord, but a bloody miracle is the answer to that.'

'What happens when you overwind your torsion weapons?'

There was a dubious pause. 'Well, my lord, one of two things. Either the shot range is increased, though accuracy falls, or the whole machine fails to cope with the pressure and explodes, probably killing everyone within at least ten feet.'

'A pretty even chance, you'd say?'

The artillerist stared. 'Never tested it enough to count, lord.'

'Today's the day. Use the catapult on the next tower. It's closer to Tocco's men anyway. Have all but the essential crew clear the tower. Ready the weapon, and have your men overwind it sufficient, in their opinion, to reach the tents in blue and white.'

'Sir, it'll probably kill them all, and it's very unlikely to work.'

'Indulge me, Commander.'

The officer scurried away, heading for the stairs to cross the gate and climb the next tower, and once he was out of sight and earshot, Thomas cleared his throat. 'This is not a wise course, brother.'

'Engineers are very precious about their machines, Thomas. It is my notion that they deliberately play it safe, and that those weapons can be tightened considerably before they present a danger.'

Still, they all watched, tense and silent, as the officer climbed the next tower and spoke with the crew. From here, the exchange that followed was not quite audible, but the gesticulating made it quite clear what they were saying, and Gabriel could have predicted it anyway. Eventually, half the crew, and all other personnel, left the tower, along with the officer, and the three remaining men went to work.

The machine was brought to its standard tension, and the stone cautiously placed into the arm. Then, slowly and carefully, and with the crew doing their best to hide behind one another, the torsion was tightened again – a full turn. Even a tower away, Gabriel heard the ominous creak, now that the world was silent, watching. Another turn, and a horrible ligneous groan. 'Another,' called the officer, wincing. The arm was turned once more; every spectator braced himself, jaw clenched, eyes narrowed, waiting for the disaster.

The machine was loosed.

The bang as the arm hit the crossbar was impressive, and the great stone, as large as a man's head, hurtled aloft across the open ground. The three turns had just been enough. The stone fell short of the lines of blue-and-white-clad men, let alone the tents that were the nominal target, but the result was horrendous, nonetheless. The rounded boulder hit the hard-packed ground and bounced. The angle was just enough that it caught the front rank of Tocco's soldiers at waist height. Two men disappeared in a cloud of blood, bone shards and unmentionable matter, while half a dozen more were thrown aside or knocked back, limbs torn free by the heavy shot. A ploughed furrow through the field of men stood as horrific testimony to the shot, a gouge six ranks deep, carpeted with limbs and bodies.

'Dear God in Heaven,' Thomas breathed.

'Another turn,' Constantine said.

The artillery officer swallowed nervously, then turned and repeated the command across to the other tower. Gabriel couldn't hear the response from the men there, but he could guess what they were muttering to one another. The process was repeated, and Gabriel divided his attention between the worrying sounds of the tortured catapult, as it was pushed ever further past its optimal tension, and the Tocco ranks, where officers were now bellowing and marching around, while the men tried hard to back away out of range, despite there being rank upon rank of men behind them.

The machine reached the previous level, and Gabriel could see the artillerists praying and crossing themselves, with two extended fingers and two folded, as they gripped the handles and gave one more turn. The sound that came from the machine was reminiscent of a tortured animal, and it made Gabriel wince.

Then it loosed. Another head-sized boulder whipped out as the arm hammered loudly home. This time it took the head off a man several rows back, pulverised the top half of the next few ranks, and rolled to a halt out of sight, at the rear of the blue-and-white lines.

'Another,' Constantine called.

Now, the officer too was praying as he turned and made the call. Gabriel turned back to the enemy. There, now, was a figure in gleaming armour and blue and white, on horseback, behind the others, but waving his arms madly. That had to be Torno Tocco.

For a moment, Gabriel wondered whether they might be obsessing a little too much on a man who was, in the grand scheme of this fight, just an underling. But as the moments passed, he listed the man's transgressions time and again, from the murder of innocent citizens, to the attempts on the prince's life in Patras, to changing allegiance repeatedly to ever set himself against the empire, even back to that chase at the Echinades, and, though they'd not been present for it, marching with the Turks in support of Demetrios and trying to storm Constantinople itself. No, Tocco deserved what was coming to him, and Gabriel would happily deliver it.

The shot of the overwound catapult was announced with the thud of arm against beam, and the rock sailed out, though this time, Gabriel failed to see it strike. Though the missile flew, the arm smashing into the crossbar cracked it, and the beam started to bend with ominous creaks. Gabriel could hear the shouts of panic from the crew, and he watched as the machine groaned and creaked and splintered. The three men dived for the stairwell. The first two made it into cover before the entire machine exploded. The third took the full force of flying timbers that plucked him from his feet and sent him shrieking over the parapet to his death.

Indrawn breaths drew Gabriel's attention to the enemy ranks once more, and he tried to ascertain where the stone had landed. It did not take long. One of the Tocco command tents had gone, and men nearby were lying scattered around the ground. Torno himself, still astride his horse, yelling and gesticulating, was only just outside the area of destruction. The men atop the tower watched, breath held, as a Turkish officer rode up to the Epirot, and an angry exchange ensued. Time passed, and finally, it seemed the Turk had the best of the argument. Torno gave an exasperated expression, throwing his hands in the air, and turned, riding away between the tents.

'It would appear that we cannot goad him into an attack,' Sphrantzes said quietly.

'Yes. The sultan has him on a short leash today. All there is now, then, is to wait for him to come to us in due course, which he must eventually do, though it will be when the wall is breached.'

'Then if we cannot concentrate on your vendetta with Tocco,' Thomas said, 'what do we do?'

'My dear brother,' Constantine said, 'we make them pay for every shot they take. We delay the inevitable, so that they suffer hardships and difficulties. We hit them when we can, how we can, and we abrade their forces until the day they have too few to control us.'

He turned to the others and folded his arms. 'The first concern, I think, is removing the threat of their city-killers. I want plans as to how to remove that cannon from the game. Thoughts, gentlemen?'

'We could overwind some more artillery and try to hit it,' Thomas said.

Though they all mused on this for a moment, eventually Constantine shook his head. 'We cannot afford to lose the weapons, and we've seen the end result. I am loath to do that again. It was a single chance. Besides, trying to target one cannon with such a weapon is a far harder task than trying to hit a whole swathe of troops.'

'If we cannot hit it from a distance,' Rhosatsas said, 'then we are going to have to go to it directly, for all the danger that entails.'

'It is,' Constantine agreed, 'more or less suicide to do so.'

'We would have to ask for volunteers,' Thomas said.

'No,' Constantine replied. 'This is an army, and men are called upon to do what they must.' Gabriel waited, hands clenched, for the call, but for once it did not seem that this disaster was coming his way. 'This is a job for a few horsemen only, and the fastest we can find. I have a plan.'

Thus it was that Gabriel found himself still standing with the officers in the mid-morning, and watching the sally force gathered at the gate ready. The Turks had already begun pounding towers all along the walls with their catapults and with the smaller cannon that were swift to load and discharge. The city-killer, on the other hand, was taking some work to prepare. Firstly, it had arrived in two pieces, and the barrel had to be joined together with massive, riveted iron bands. Then it had to be secured in place, so that it did not roll or recoil with the detonation of its firing. Indeed, even as the party of horsemen preparing to neutralise the thing readied themselves to ride out, the Turkish crew began moving the great stone ball with the use of a crane and forty men. Soon it would be ready to fire.

At the prince's signal, the gate below opened – just one leaf, and with no great fanfare – and the six horsemen rode out: four riders with shields and swords, and two with buckets, upon whom the plan relied. They emerged into the open, brave men all, and rode towards the enemy at a good pace. Had the wall-top artillery the range, they would have provided covering shots, but there was nothing anyone could do but watch and hope. As the men rode closer and closer to the enemy lines, they picked up speed until they were at full gallop, a pace that would quickly exhaust the horses. The four men with shields advanced in a line, the two with buckets following on, partly protected by their companions.

Then the enemy missiles began. Archers loosed at will, and crossbows began to thud. The six men came closer and closer to the cannon, and for a moment it seemed they would make it with ease and without damage. Then the first horseman fell, arrows thudding into his mount, which reared and fell to the side, the others racing on past him. It was the steel arrow from a great bolt-thrower that took the next, the blow powerful enough to rip straight through his shield and bury itself in his midriff.

Still they rode. The enemy were coming out to meet them now, sensing true danger. The riders bore down on the cannon, and a third shield-man fell, missiles thudding into horse and rider in numbers. The other three rode on. Then Turkish *sipahi* horse intercepted them. The last of the swordsmen went down to a series of blows, while a sipahi plucked a bucket-carrier out of the saddle with his lance, hurling him away across the ground to land roughly and then die in agony.

One rider ploughed on amid the hail of missiles, his companions having diverted the attention of the enemy horse. Gabriel held his breath as the man neared the great cannon, into which the stone ball had now been loaded. A stray arrow thudded into the rider's leg, but he ignored it and pressed on. He reached the cannon alive, by some miracle, and Gabriel sent up a prayer – one among many at that moment – as the horsemen rose in the saddle, even with the shaft jutting from his thigh, and threw the bucket of half-congealed concrete at the muzzle of the gun.

It missed.

In truth, the man would have had to be incredibly lucky to hit it, for atop the terreplein the gun's muzzle was a good twelve feet from the ground. The concrete slopped across the gun's base and the wooden platform below it, and a moment later, the bucket man breathed his last on the end of a Turkish lance.

If anyone had laboured under the false impression that the plan might have succeeded, they were disabused of that notion a moment later, as the cannon loosed its first shot with a sound like the world being torn in half. Gabriel almost threw himself to the tower floor as the great rock came directly at him, but at the last moment, it dropped, and the shot struck the wall beside the gate tower just four or five feet from the ground.

The shudder of the shot was felt all along the walls and up all the towers, and Gabriel found himself dragged back through a quarter of a century to that day on the walls of Constantinople, when the sultan's great gun had thundered and battered the walls. The city defences had held, that time, for many days, and on the very verge of failure, the battle had been won and the siege lifted. But those walls were the best in the world – defences unmatched throughout every nation and across all of history. These were not.

As the shuddering stopped and the cloud of dust began to settle, Gabriel staggered over to the parapet and looked down. A crack had opened up, almost a foot wide, black and ominous, between the wall and the tower. That was not a good sign. And that had only been the first shot, and a mis-aimed mistake.

'It'll be a while before it can be fired again,' Rhosatsas noted, pointing. The Turks were busy throwing buckets of water over the gun, cooling the metal.

'Foolish,' Sphrantzes noted.

'Oh?'

'Hot metal cooled too quickly is wont to crack.'

But the hope that the Turks' poor understanding of their weapon might lead to its destruction was clearly unfounded, for moments later, an officer came over, waving his hands and stopping the cooling process.

'Still, it will be hours before the second shot.'

Thomas drummed fingers on the wall-top. 'Perhaps a second attempt with concrete?'

His brother shook his head. 'It was a valiant plan, but I've no wish to lose another six riders repeating a guaranteed failure. I'm afraid we are now simply going to have to withstand. With luck, those great cannon will destroy themselves before they can destroy the walls. All we need to do is wear down their army by attrition. Soon enough the weather will change, and winter is an ally to all besieged folk.'

In the end, such hopes were clearly in vain. For the following three days, the Turkish artillery continued to pound the walls and towers and gates of the Hexamilion, and in all that time only one of the five great city-killers suffered a problem. The westernmost, near Korinthos, badly overheated after one shot, and though the Turks were careful with their slow cooling, trying to preserve it, still the next shot blew the barrel apart – an unseen crack the problem – and killed the entire crew and dozens of men nearby.

It was a small thing, though, in the grand scheme. One great cannon down, but the other four continued their work, as did all the other artillery. By the end of that day, Constantine had ordered all but essential personnel from the tops of walls and towers, for men were beginning to die in droves as the shots demolished battlements, sending stone debris in every direction and removing what little cover they already had. The imperial artillery had taken hits numerous times, and many pieces were now little more than kindling, having never had a chance to loose a shot at the enemy.

The mood among the men had plummeted, and the previous night there had been a meeting of the senior officers, courtiers and nobles to work through any possible change and any possible plan to prevent what now seemed inevitable.

Finally, Constantine had sat back and sighed. 'All we can do, then, is wait for them to decide they have battered us enough and storm the walls, and then meet them and attempt to make them regret it. I had hoped to be in a better position by now, but all we can do is work with what the Lord gives us.'

And that had been that.

This morning was one of signs. Gabriel had seen several that a superstitious man would label an 'omen', but the main sign was one no one could argue with. That morning, the barrage paused, and great fires were lit all along the isthmus in the Turkish camps.

'What is this?' Thomas had asked, voicing a question many held.

It was Sphrantzes who replied. 'The ritual purifications. The Turk has to purify himself before battle if at all possible. It is a long ritual, and usually lasts three days. You realise what that means?'

'It means we have three days until they come for the wall,' Constantine clarified, just in case. 'On the morning of the tenth they will come, probably with first light. We have little in the way of protection on the walls now, but we can keep men in the towers until they are needed to repulse fights. Is there anywhere in full breach?'

Rhosatsas nodded. 'Only a *small* breach, but yes. The sultan himself has had his artillery concentrating on the central section, and some of the wall has fallen close to the gate. For now, it's a little narrow for comfort, but with a little work it will open wide.'

'And the cannon will start again shortly. Despite the purification, the artillery will continue to work for three days, pulverising the Hexamilion until it is little more than a garden wall.' The prince sighed. 'We are going to lose much of the Moreot garrison on the tenth, and we have to choose whether to make a stand and fight with every man available, or to cut our losses and send some of the forces away to places like Mystras and Patras to wait out the war.'

'Losing any men now will make the fight that much briefer,' Rhosatsas said.

'But will allow us a chance to rebuild in time,' Thomas argued.

Constantine stood for a time, drumming his fingers on what was left of the battlements. 'All right. Have every officer go through his squad. Men with children under the age of six, or whose wives are expecting children, are to be given the option of being transferred out to the city garrisons in the Morea, where they can join our mercenary friends in making the entire peninsula a nightmare for any Turk attempting control. Any man without children or wife, or whose children are grown enough to survive the loss of a father, will stand with us and fight. George? It is time you left.'

'I will do no such—'

'I appointed you to rule Mystras and to take control there for when the Turks come. You will be of greater value there than dying meaninglessly on this wall. Go, George. I shall make it an imperial command if I must.'

Sphrantzes sagged with a nod.

'Other than that, we wait for them to come, and we fight. We fight like the Roman lions we are, even in the face of impossible odds. Any man who runs, I will find in the afterlife and tear off his angel wings.'

This raised a dark chuckle from some.

'All right. Everyone off this tower-top before the guns start again.' As the officers filed out, Constantine gestured to Gabriel. He wandered over as the tower emptied, and the prince waited until they were alone.

'I intend to survive this, Gabriel.'

'Good. There was a time when you wouldn't have tried.'

'Those days are past. I will survive this. I need you to divide your men, though. I need your Ianitzaroi to protect Thomas. We Palaiologoi all seemed doomed to fall without issue, but Thomas is young, has a good wife, good children, and is happy and, to an odd extent, innocent. I want him to survive even if I do not. He may well be the future of the empire.'

Gabriel nodded. 'And what of the tenth, when it comes?'

'When that happens, we are going to stay right here, for the first man who will come for this gate will be Torno Tocco, and I stand by my word. He will not cross this wall alive.'

Gabriel escorted the prince down into the protection of the tower, delivered him to three of the Ianitzaroi for safe keeping, and then strode down the stairs and out behind the wall to find the bunk room assigned to the bodyguard. As he walked in,

Manuel was busy leading the men in prayer, and Gabriel waited by the door, head bowed respectfully, until the small service ended and the men rose and went about their business.

'Rare to see you down with the men,' the standard-bearer drawled. 'Run out of wine with the officers?'

'You're a funny man, Manuel.'

'So funny three wives have left me so far. Ritual preparation for the Turks?'

A nod.

'Three days, then.'

Another nod.

'We'll have our work cut out to protect the prince on the tenth, you realise?'

'I've been thinking about that. The Turks will be looking to take any noble or officer prisoner. They've got the whole isthmus covered, but there's one thing they've missed.'

'Oh?'

'The sea. The Gulf of Lepanto is largely controlled by imperial and Venetian ships. The Turks have very little sea power there. Korinthos is a good port and there are many ships in the harbour. Better still, the cannon at that end has destroyed itself, and the western end of the walls, near Korinthos, are the best surviving stretch, and will be the last to fall. The prince intends to face and to kill Torno Tocco.'

'He could die. That's stupid.'

'That's why I won't let him. I'll do it myself on his behalf. But Tocco is no fool and is a noted warrior, so if I fall, I need you ready to take charge – you and Gaspar.'

'And save the prince?'

'Save Constantine, and Thomas too. And Rhosatsas, if you can. And any other major officer. Get them behind the walls, away from missiles, and hurry them to Korinthos. Have a dozen horses rested and ready, saddled from dawn on the tenth. The moment the walls are taken, make sure the Palaiologoi and any other officer you can find makes it to the port and gets on board a ship. Where they go after that will be the prince's decision, though I favour back to Constantinople.'

'You'll do it yourself.'

'Of course I will. The Epirot has yet to be born who can best me with a sword. But still, just in case, that's your job. You can do that?'

'Of course.'

'In the meantime, I want half the Ianitzaroi assigned to Despot Thomas and the other half to Constantine.'

Leaving the others to it, Gabriel strolled away and went to sit in the shade of a tree, close to a horse trough. How had it come to this? Mere months ago, they had been building the empire anew, and now they were waiting for the hammer blow that would shatter it once more. Of course, the answer to that was men. *Men* had failed them. Men had failed them at every turn: Theodore by failing to support his brothers; Demetrios by actively seeking to usurp them; Nerio of Athens by throwing in his lot with the sultan; Władysław of Hungary by overreaching at Varna; Torno Tocco at every damn turn. In truth, even Gabriel could not think how Constantine could have improved on what he had done. Had he not suffered failure after failure at the hands of men he should have been able to trust, the empire might even now be ascendant once more.

It was not.

The Hexamilion was going to fall, and they were all aware of it now. This war was over and the conquests they had made lost once more. But Constantine had been right. What was important now was forcing a peace, preserving the Morea and what he could of imperial power. He could not save the Morea by holding the wall, so he would have to save it by making the whole peninsula too hard to hold.

But one thing was certain: Torno Tocco was not going to live to see it.

7 December 1446, evening

'You realise, Turahan, that you have committed us to a war in the winter?'

The governor, head lowered, nodded. 'Yes, Majesty. But we will take the wall in days, and then we are free to ravage the Morea.'

'That will be all we can do, Turahan. I will have to send my men to every town and village and put the fear of God into every living Moreot soul. You know we cannot hold it for any length of time, with winter coming, my health in decline, and with the Wallachs and Hungarians regrouping. I will need the bulk of the army in the north. I wish we had not come. John Palaiologos offered us full peace. We should have taken it. I wonder if Constantine would accept that olive branch yet?'

'Majesty, surely you would not offer peace on the eve of victory?'

'Victory is an elusive thing, Turahan. They will call it victory when the wall falls, but all that marks is the opening of a new, and much worse, campaign.' Murad sighed. 'I will be grateful when all this is over.'

10 December 1446

The end began with an innocent-sounding horn calling out across the Turkish camp. In truth, it had started days before and never let up, for though the army of the sultan had spent three days in ritual cleansing before the battle, this had apparently not applied to the artillery, which had continued to pound the Hexamilion throughout that time.

Three main weaknesses had been identified by this morning, where the artillery had concentrated: an area around the gate into the Isthmia fortress had been turned into little more than rubble; the central gate had gone, including both flanking towers; finally, a stretch of wall between two towers, just to the east of where Constantine and his commanders were observing, was low enough now for men to clamber over.

Gabriel looked back down from the tower in the predawn half-light as that delicate cadence rang out.

They had done all they could.

The manpower of the wall had thinned out by half, all those men who could be spared dispatched to bolster imperial garrisons at places like Mystras, Patras, Akova and Monemvasia. Those men who remained at the Hexamilion were under no illusion. This day would hold defeat. For most of them it would mean death or captivity, and there had been plenty of horror stories about what the Turks did with their captives. Death might be preferable.

There really was no way to hold the wall for longer than an hour or two, and the notion of simply abandoning it and moving back to fight a guerilla-style war in the hinterland had been mooted. In the end, despite the clear problem with the plan, it had been decided to stay and make a fight of it. Simply retreating in the face of the Turks would send a message to the sultan that the empire was frightened and weak, and would bolster their desire to annex the Morea, and that was the one thing Constantine was determined to avoid. They would hold the wall for as long as they could, stand defiant, and take as many Turks as possible with them, reducing the sultan's likelihood of having sufficient a force thereafter to hold the Morea.

Every man knew what was at stake, and it both surprised and impressed Gabriel how few desertions there had been over the past three days. Just as the Turkish bombardment had opened up those great gaps, so the Roman army had been plugging them as best they could, with anything they could find.

Gabriel looked across now to the nearby breach, roughly blocked with carts, barrels, beams, grain sacks and anything that could be swiftly procured and piled up. More carts had been wheeled up behind to create a makeshift fighting platform. Then up to the tower-tops. Few pieces of artillery remained, and though the archers had taken up their positions atop the remaining walls and towers, there were precious few remaining sections of battlement to take shelter behind, so when the missiles came at them, they would have to retreat or die loosing shafts into the approaching enemy.

Constantine had never expected to hold the wall against such a force as Murad brought. Had there been just a few bombards and pieces of field artillery, the Hexamilion would have held for months before a breach, and the enemy would have suffered huge losses in the process. No one had expected those city-killers to be brought in, and they had changed everything. The wall might as well have been made of paper.

'Here they come,' someone called, drawing Gabriel's attention once more to the front.

The Turkish force was surging forward. Though it was hard to make out too much detail, the sun still hovering below the eastern horizon, the sense of an immense mass of men on the move was there, like a carpet of ants in the gloom.

Another glance back. Many of the Ianitzaroi stood behind the gate, with the small corral of nine horses, plus the unit's own mounts, ready to whisk away the officers the moment there was no other option. Gabriel had ridden out the day before to Korinthos and had there secured a Venetian merchant ship's services. He had offered a princely sum, and paid half up front, even that part being far more than such a voyage would usually cost. The merchant had been retained to take whatever survivors he could hold, depart as fast as possible, and leave the entire battle zone in record time. The ship would be ready even now, stripped of anything that would slow it or weigh it down, prepared to depart.

Constantine had agreed to the plan readily, on the condition that Thomas was brought to the ship too, though the younger brother had decided not to sail to the capital. He would stay in the Morea and supervise the seeing off of any attempted Turkish occupation. They would travel all the way round the Morea, and then disembark at Monemvasia, somewhere the sultan would never expect the brothers to relocate.

The assault began with drums. Interspersed among the massed forces of the sultan, musicians began to hammer drums so large they were mounted on carts. The rhythmic boom was soon joined by horns of half a dozen different styles, then pipes, and even lutes, creating a complex melody that was at one and the same time charming and stirring. And as that exotic sound wove across the landscape, so the sun suddenly put in a sliver of an appearance over the eastern hills, and the spearpoints and helmets of the vast army glowed and twinkled like a thousand thousand suns. Gabriel knew the Turks. Nothing they did was by chance. The assault had been so planned to make use of the sunrise, making the army an awe-inspiring sight, particularly with that melody flowing across them. Along the wall, many a man would now be evacuating his bladder or bowels at the spectacle.

'Hold steady,' Constantine called, and his officers spread that sentiment.

Another glance behind. Further back, beyond where the Ianitzaroi waited with the horses, a man with an imperial banner stood, watching the tower-top carefully, preparing for his only job – one of the most important there was, today. He would give the signal when the first breach truly opened, sending word all along the wall that the Hexamilion had fallen.

Men readied themselves.

The sun was rising swiftly now, and every moment made the approaching army that little bit more visible, as they neared the wall. Then the light caught the blue-and-white standards of Torno Tocco, and Gabriel glanced across to see the prince concentrating on them. Retribution was most certainly at hand.

'Archers, artillery… ready.'

And then, as the Turkish forces crossed an unmarked line in their approach, the command was given, and every remaining weapon on the towers loosed, as did every archer. Hundreds of arrows arced out, along with stones and iron bolts, and for a moment it looked quite impressive and gave heart to each man on the wall. Turks fell all along the front line, having marched within range, while the stones from the catapults ploughed into their ranks and sent whole flurries of men into a chaos of corpses and dismemberment.

But then the Turkish response came.

Even as the men atop the walls nocked their second arrow or reloaded their weapons and began to wind, the enemy ranks stopped, the soldiers stepping to the side as archers hurried out front, and in mere heartbeats, a full front of archers faced the wall, as far as the eye could see in both directions. Gabriel tensed, aware of what was coming, for he had seen Turkish archers in battle. Each had a thumb ring to effectively draw the string, and each had three extra arrows expertly jammed between the fingers of their draw hand. As they moved out front, they dropped to a knee, drew and loosed, and even as the first arrow left the bow, the second dropped from the archer's grip into line, was drawn back and released, then the third, and then the fourth, all so swiftly that the first arrow had only just struck by the time the fourth left the bow.

The flurry of missiles was truly horrifying to behold, and deadly accurate, the cloud of shafts thick enough to blot out the new-risen sun as it arced up over the battlements and fell like the wrath of God.

The results were devastating. Fully half the archers and artillerists on the wall had failed to get into any sort of cover or to throw themselves to the ground in desperate hope. Perhaps a dozen, maybe even a score, managed to get a second arrow out before they were felled by shafts in their hundreds, plunging into flesh all along the Hexamilion.

Gabriel breathed a sigh of relief as his own defences proved adequate. He'd had three great wicker shields six feet wide and eight feet high, backed with leather and wood, placed on the tower-top behind what was left of the battlements, and as the archers loosed, three of the Ianitzaroi rose with the shields, creating a temporary shelter for the officers. Here and there, along the wall, similar shields would have been put in place, but they'd simply had neither the time nor the manpower to create them in sufficient numbers to line the wall.

Even as those men who had survived the cloud of arrows rose, shaking, to look out, a new section of the Turkish army emerged. The archers remained in place, spaced apart just enough to allow a single man between them, and the Turks came on, again, carrying siege ladders. Gabriel watched as those great timber lengths were hurried out front, and then the men carrying them began to run, the archers dropping away in their wake to allow infantry forward, and the army was on the march again.

The few remaining archers and artillerists on the tower-tops began to loose as they could, though it was of little effect against such numbers, and seemed to make no difference to the advance.

Gabriel looked up. Constantine's personal banner, the double-headed eagle of the Palaiologoi, stood proud above them in the morning sunlight, an invitation to anyone who desired the prince's head, but specifically levelled at one adversary.

The first scaling ladder hit the parapet of the wall nearby. The towers themselves were too high for such work, but the walls were lower and within reach. The defenders there hung back and waited as more and more ladders hit the stonework. Still, they left them for many heartbeats, waiting for the signal from an officer. When it was given, the commander having waited until the attackers had climbed halfway up, the defenders moved forward with pitchforks and pushed, heaving the ladders back out away from the walls until they reached the vertical and then toppled backwards. The Turks fell away with shrieks into the crowds below, but now the archers were back in commission. Behind both the ladder-men and the infantry that followed to climb them, the archers were in the open, nocking and releasing. Here and there, a misplaced arrow took one of their own, but the numbers were small and the losses negligible for the sultan, for many arrows found a home in the men with the forks; fewer and fewer defenders were there pushing the ladders away. And each time a ladder disappeared, another was returned.

Here and there, groups of men were heaving boulders to the parapet and dropping them, not only killing the men who climbed the ladders, but often breaking the rungs as they went and rendering them useless. But it was too little. The damage the defenders were doing was little more than a gnat bite to the Turkish ladder-men, and more and more ladders appeared.

Gabriel peered out. At least the remaining archers and artillery were working well. They were loosing and then dropping out of sight repeatedly, and because of the throng into which they shot, they could hardly fail, every missile finding a target.

He turned to the breach. There was a different story going on. The generals had concentrated defenders there, knowing it for a true weak spot, and it was only the hardiness and bravery of those men atop their makeshift fighting platform that had prevented the Turks from already being inside the walls. They fought hard as infantry poured up the rubble and launched attacks over and over again. They would fall eventually, of course. If they held for an hour, it would be noteworthy – a thing to remember.

The Turkish archers were no longer loosing massive clouds of arrows at the walls, for fear of injuring their own, but individually they still shot as targets of opportunity presented themselves, every Roman they could put down a step closer to taking the wall.

Another glance back at the horses. The Ianitzaroi had to have the princes at those animals before enough Turks crossed the breach to threaten their chance of escape.

It was not long before the first Turk managed to reach the top of a ladder and throw himself over onto the wall-top. He was run through the moment he arrived, skewered with a Roman blade, but even as he died with a groan, two more were pulling themselves up onto the wall. Another imperial soldier staggered back, guts sliding out of a gash across his midriff as he desperately tried to hold them in, eyes wide. Between that scene and the tower where they stood, an imperial officer, bellowing and waving his sword, took an arrow in the face and was thrown from the parapet.

The wall was falling.

'We have to move inside,' Gabriel said. 'Now.'

'No,' Constantine replied, still looking out around those big shields to the Turks.

'If they secure the door into this tower, then we'll be trapped up here. We need to be down a floor in order to be able to leave.'

'And I can see Tocco himself. He and his men are trying to push forward, to reach the front, for he can see my banner. I cannot leave without facing him.'

'Then most likely you will not leave at all.'

'There is time. We hold until I see Tocco himself climbing. *Then* I will descend a floor.'

Gabriel fretted. Now, he walked over to the western edge of the tower and concentrated on what was happening on the wall-top. The door to the tower had been closed and barred, and a score of men were working to try and push the Turks back off the wall. He could now see the men in blue and white approaching the bottom of the nearest ladders, and one of them, on horseback and armoured in gleaming steel, was forcing his way through. Tocco was as adamant about fighting Constantine as the prince was about staying to face him.

Gabriel turned. Constantine had a determined, hungry look. Close by, Thomas looked drawn and worried. Gaspar, Manuel, and six Ianitzaroi were gathered behind those wicker shields, all waiting on Gabriel's order to move.

That was when it happened. Despite the wicker shields, occasional shots were making it through the defences, and suddenly a black-fletched shaft thudded into Constantine's forearm. He cried out, looking down, then gripped the shaft and pulled it free with his other hand, casting it to the wall-top as blood welled up and gouted from the wound. Manuel ran over, pulling out a scarf and wrapping it around the arm, tying it tight.

'Damn them,' Constantine hissed, 'but that is the most blood they will get out of me.'

'It's not bad,' Manuel reassured him. 'Not enough to see you off the field.'

'He needs to be off the field, anyway,' Gabriel said, then turned to Constantine. 'You need to leave, my lord.'

'What?' Constantine looked slightly glazed, perhaps suppressing the pain in his arm.

'The wall to the west is swarming with Turks, and shortly they will start battering the tower door down. When it gives, they will be in the tower below us, and we'll be trapped. The wall to the far side, the breach, is close to falling. When it does, the enemy will pour through the gap, and one of the first things they will do is surround this tower, kill my men, and take the horses. In two entirely different ways, we are about to be trapped and captured. I need you to go down to the horses now and be ready.'

Thomas made to argue for a moment, but his roving gaze took in everything Gabriel had mentioned, and finally he nodded.

'Gaspar? I need you and the others to get the prince downstairs, along with his brother.'

The big ourghos looked over at the prince, who was cradling his damaged arm, but still peering intently out into the fighting. 'He won't go.'

'Carry him if you have to. Even knock him out if you must, though be careful not to damage him. Do what you must to get him downstairs.'

Gaspar nodded. 'And you?'

'I'm going to kill a man, then follow on. Make sure my horse is ready.'

Another nod, and Gabriel stepped in front of the prince, blocking his view of the fight and attracting his attention. 'You have to go.'

'No.'

'It is the job of your Ianitzaroi to protect you. To save your life. You have to let us do our job.'

'I will face Tocco.'

'No you won't. You *can't*, not with your arm like that. Instead, you will be downstairs on a horse. I will kill him for you.'

'I...'

'Years ago, at Patras, you were content to let me go for him in your stead. You have to do the same now. Regardless of the Epirot, you are too important to the Morea, the empire and the throne to die here for the sake of retribution. Go. Be a despot. Be a strategos. Be a Palaiologos. Regroup, rebuild and fight on. But not here.'

Gabriel drew his sword, and the prince looked him square in the eye for some time, and then finally nodded, and relented with a sigh. Moments later, they were on the stairs, descending to the tower's top room. Six soldiers stood around the door to the wall-walk, weapons out, and the beam across the door was already shaking in response to a series of loud bangs. The Turks were coming in – and soon.

'Go,' Gabriel said to the others, pointing at the stairs down, and Gaspar led the others to it. Constantine paused for a moment, meeting Gabriel's gaze.

'Do not sacrifice yourself,' the prince said. 'There will always be another time.'

'Not for Tocco. You vowed he would not cross the wall, and I will hold that vow for you.'

The gaze lingered for a moment, and then the prince was gone with the others, racing for safety. Gabriel turned. He was determined, but he was also no fool. He needed to be sure he could still get out, and so he backed across the room until he was standing in front of the stairs down.

A minute passed, perhaps more, and then the latest bang on the tower door was accompanied by an almighty cracking noise. The six men by the door readied themselves. When the locking beam broke, it exploded inwards, the door hammering back against the stonework, revealing men in blue and white out in the bright sunlight, where they squinted into the gloomy interior.

Gabriel stood still. For a strange moment, no one moved. The soldiers inside were braced, waiting to defend, and no one out there was over-eager to be the first one in the room. Then someone outside shouted a muffled order, and they came. The soldiers barrelled in through the doorway and were met by the six imperial men inside, the struggle tough and hard-fought.

A warrior squeezed past them and came at Gabriel. As the man ran for him, the Ianitzaroi ducked to the side at the last moment, dropping, and swinging a scything blow at the back of the man's legs as he stumbled past in surprise. The blade cut the hamstrings of his knees, and his momentum carried him on into the staircase, where he disappeared, tumbling downwards with a series of thuds and screams. Gabriel rose once more and faced the doorway.

Just beyond the ongoing scuffle, he could see his prey. Oddly, he realised that though he had faced Torno Tocco and his companions time and again over the years, he'd never actually seen the man's face. The two times he'd stood over his fallen adversary and looked him in the eye, it had turned out not to be Torno, but some foil standing in for him.

The man had a hateful face. Just to look at him was to despise him. He had a mouth that was given a natural sneer, a nose just too short and pointy, so that he seemed to be looking down it at you, and a thin moustache that was impossibly neat. Of course, in truth, he was probably not half that bad, but Gabriel's mind was painting him with everything he loathed, exaggerating the worst features.

One thing was sure. This time, it was actually him. He had no reason not to be here, and he knew that the sultan – and therefore he, too – was going to achieve victory today.

'Where is Palaiologos?' the man demanded, stepping out of the sunlight and into the gloomy room. The imperial soldiers were still fighting to hold the Tocco soldiers back, but two were down already, and they were struggling sufficiently that Torno simply stepped past them, more of his men coming in with him.

'I'm afraid you missed him,' Gabriel replied conversationally. 'Perhaps I can take you to him? Your head, anyway.'

'I remember you. Hard to forget anyone that hideous. His protector. I shall enjoy gutting you on the way to him, but we must be fast. I will be the one to bring Prince Constantine's head to the sultan.'

'You are mistaken.' Gabriel swished his sword back and forth a couple of times. He wore trousers and a tunic, and his sole concession to war had been a cuirass that covered his chest and back. Torno, on the other hand, wore shoulder plates and armour down to the elbows, his thighs similarly protected to the knees. He had no shield, but he too had a sword out, a match for that in Gabriel's hand, and he too tested it as he approached.

The Catalan took a moment to weigh up his opponent. The only vulnerable parts were his forearms and shins, and his head. Clearly Torno would concentrate on defending those, so Gabriel would have to feint somehow and trick him. His eyes picked out those of Torno, who was clever enough not to give anything away with them. Then he was close, and the Epirot's sword lanced out, surprisingly quickly. Gabriel sidestepped it, just in time, and brought his own sword round in a swing aimed for the man's sword arm. Tocco was fast enough to pull back and get his own weapon in the way, using it to turn aside Gabriel's blade. They separated, breathing heavily, testing the blades again.

'You're good.'

Gabriel nodded. 'Plenty of practice.'

'But are you fast?'

In a blur, Tocco leapt to one side and swung with a backhand blow. It would be enough to catch most men off guard, but Gabriel had noticed the change in the way his feet were braced – a telltale sign of what he was about to do. As the swing came, Gabriel was safely aside and his own sword was there again, blocking it.

'You are.' The man nodded, stepping back again. 'Well, well.'

'I can tell you one thing I'm not,' Gabriel replied as he took a swing for Torno's face, only to have it knocked away again.

'And what is that?'

Following up on that swing for the head, Gabriel spun, bringing the sword round again. But even as his opponent swiftly parried the blow, Gabriel's heavy boot came down hard on Torno's foot.

'A gentleman.' Gabriel grinned as the other man gasped and staggered back, wincing at the pain of what had to be several broken bones.

'You oaf,' Torno snarled, and lunged. Gabriel tried to sidestep it in order to have his own counterattack, but was rather taken by surprise as Torno moved with him, during the strike, impressively fast. Instead, they met, the Epirot hitting him hard with a shoulder. Had he not reacted instantly, Gabriel would have fallen, likely at his enemy's mercy, but in the event, his free hand came out and grabbed the top of Torno's breastplate. Even as Gabriel toppled backwards onto the stairs, his surprised opponent came with him.

As they fell, Gabriel made sure to keep his head up so that it did not clonk on a stone step and rob him of his consciousness. Unfortunately, his sword hit the wall and was knocked from his fingers. As he tumbled again, falling further down the stairs, still holding tight to Torno, he noted that the Epirot's sword had also gone in the fall. Down they went, step by step, rolling, tumbling, sometimes one on top, sometimes the other, each concentrating largely on not breaking his head. The tower room with its dying struggle was lost to sight, though the two men had enough to concentrate on right now, anyway.

Even as Gabriel fumbled at his belt during the constant descent, struggling to free his dagger from its sheath, he spotted Torno doing the same. The Epirot's free hand was now gripping Gabriel by the throat, and so both continued to roll painfully down the stairs, one hand gripping the opponent, the other fumbling for a blade, and nothing to stop their fall.

Gabriel's dagger came out, and he tried to find a way to stab Torno with it, though as they tumbled and fell there was little room for an orchestrated blow. And then the Epirot's knife was out too, and the daggers met between them with a metallic scraping noise, first of blade on blade, and then of blade on cuirass.

Now it was all a blur. Breathless, aching in every inch of their bodies, heads bruised and semi-concussed despite all their attempts, both men fell, bounced, and rolled the last few steps until they reached the floor of the tower's middle level. They continued to roll for a moment, their grips torn from each other, separating as they slowed.

Gabriel gave a yelp and looked down to see Torno's dagger jutting from his left forearm, wedged between the two bones, blood flowing free. His gaze picked out the soldier he'd hamstrung nearby, dead still and head at an awkward angle where the neck had broken in the fall. Then he saw the Epirot.

Torno Tocco lay perfectly still, Gabriel's knife driven upwards into his neck beneath the chin, pushed in so hard completely by accident during the fall that the point must have torn through his brain and now touched the inside of his skull.

He was well and truly dead.

Gabriel shuffled over, groaning, and pulled the coloured scarf from the man's belt, yanking it free, then turned, and very slowly and carefully rose to his feet. He was as woozy as a twenty-drink bar-tab night, and absolutely everything ached. He would have dawdled, recovered for a moment, but he could hear the shouting of the Tocco men as they started to descend the stairs. He pulled himself together and barrelled into the last stairwell, which he descended gracelessly, bouncing off the walls and taking the steps two at a time, tears streaming down his face at the impressive pain in his arm. He almost fell several times, and was immensely grateful when he reached the ground and staggered out across the room to the door. Flinging it open with his useable hand, he bumbled out into the open and looked about.

For a moment, he felt panic, that the whole defence had fallen and that the Turk were through the breach and in command. Then he realised that while that was almost the case, and certainly would be within the hour, as yet only a few small groups had made it through.

Clearly at least one had moved to intercept the escape. Three Ianitzaroi lay dead near the horses, and several animals had broken free and skittered away from the fight. A fair number of Turkish infantry lay dead alongside his men, and every imperial there, from the bodyguard to Constantine himself, and even Thomas, was holding bared blades stained pink. All were spattered with blood, and several men sported wounds. Mercifully, both the Palaiologos brothers seemed unharmed, and as Gabriel staggered over towards them, where Gaspar was helping the prince into the saddle, they noticed the guard captain coming their way.

'Bloody hell,' Manuel said, looking at him. 'You're going to be uglier than ever!'

Gabriel ignored him as he gripped the hilt of the knife through his arm and pulled it free with a massive gout of blood. He turned and proffered it to the prince, who was looking at Gabriel's arm and then back down at his own similar wound. 'Souvenir.'

Constantine took it, frowning, as Gabriel wound the blue-and-white Tocco scarf around his arm several times, tight, and then tied it off with his teeth.

'He's dead then?' Gaspar noted.

'Yes. But a lot of his men aren't, and they're right behind me,' Gabriel said, putting a foot in the stirrup and using his good arm to mount, awkwardly.

'Time to move,' Manuel urged, looking over his shoulder to where another large unit of Turks had spilled over the crumbled defences and were looking this way and that, suddenly spotting the men and horses. Over at the tower, two men in Tocco colours burst from the doorway, pointing and shouting.

No one needed any encouragement. In moments, the two Palaiologoi, along with three senior officers and the rest of Gabriel's Ianitzaroi, were kicking their horses into speed, cantering and then galloping away from the fallen Hexamilion and making for Korinthos.

As the enormous defensive system on which they'd staked so much, and which had fallen so quickly, slid past them in their desperate ride, Gabriel found himself wondering whether the prince had underestimated everything. Whether the Morea would now fall entire, and this might be the last time any of them walked on Greek soil.

Then he shook off his thoughts, bent low over the horse's mane, and rode for his life.

Epilogue

Monemvasia

June 1447

'His Excellency, Karaca Pasha,' the announcer called.

Constantine glanced across at Gabriel, who straightened. There was a fine balance to be struck here between contrite acceptance and defiant aloofness. There was no doubt in anyone's mind that the Turks had to be appeased, but Constantine was still determined to do so in a manner befitting the scion of two thousand years of Roman empire. Besides, he disliked Karaca Pasha almost as much as he'd hated Tocco, and making the man uncomfortable would be a thing of joy. Thus Gabriel had eschewed his usual background position for a place front and centre, close to the prince, where his ruined features would be impossible to ignore. Not only would the pasha be face to face with him throughout, but he would also remember Gabriel from their previous two meetings.

The tall, thin and angular pasha swept into the room with his customary sense of superiority and walked down the aisle until he was directly in front of Constantine. Gabriel almost smiled. It was like a face-off before a fight.

The Turk was accompanied by half a dozen brightly attired officials, a scribe or two, an imam, two men who could only be generals of some sort, and a score of Janissaries in their armour and uniform, weapons sheathed but in evidence. It was a delegation meant to impress with an image of power and control.

Constantine met it with an equally impressive group. George Sphrantzes, Loukas Notaras, Kantakouzenos, John Rhosatsas and Thomas Palaiologos all stood with him, the absolute cream of imperial command over the past years and campaigns, and half the court lurked around the edges, while the martial aspect was provided by Gabriel and his men, all armed and looking ready for war.

The air was frosty despite the heat, and fair crackled with dangerous energy.

'Greetings, Prince of the Romans.'

'Karaca Pasha.'

There was an uncomfortable pause.

'Our dominance in the Morea can no longer be doubted,' the Turk announced. 'We control all, and I am here to accept your submission.'

Flat. Direct. Mistaken…

'On the contrary, my dear Karaca Pasha,' Constantine replied with the sort of smile one usually saw on a snake. 'Reports state that despite the work of Turahan Bey and the Sultan Murad in butchering whole communities in order to impose Turkish control, this policy of brutality has failed utterly. All it has done is to make the people of the Morea ever more resistant. And while you may bluster all you like, I am also keenly aware that neither the sultan, nor his favourite bey, have any interest in remaining in the Morea. In fact, I'm fairly sure that Murad has already left, and that Turahan Bey is preparing to pull out his forces.'

'We have ravaged and controlled all.'

'A laughable overstatement, my dear pasha. Turahan spent months bogged down at Mystras, where the noble George Sphrantzes —' a nod to his friend here — 'kept you all safely outside the city. Indeed, I understand that the attrition among the bey's army constituted the greatest loss of Turkish power since Varna. And the sultan himself failed to take Patras, where the honourable Laskaris continues to rule in our name. In fact, what you did was to wander around the Morea, failing to secure any important site, murdering villagers to put the fear of God into the region, while slowly your power waned until it became clear you would have to leave.'

'Watch your tongue, Palaiologos. You are not the strong one here.'

'I disagree. However, I do recognise that Sultan Murad offers me a solution. We have sufficient strength to cause difficulties for your army in the Morea, but I also know that should Murad decide that we are truly enemies, he could gather such a force as to wipe the Morea from the map forever. Of course, he doesn't want to do that, because he needs his army in the north. But I note his power, and I have already written up my letters to him accepting his overlordship and offering fealty. I acknowledge that the despotate of the Morea needs to consult with Murad over any critical policy decision at this time. I accept that Turahan Bey is his representative in the region, and that the borders as currently drawn will not be crossed again. I even accept his demand that the Hexamilion never be rebuilt. All this I will bow to. However, while I accept Murad's authority, and therefore that of Turahan Bey, I note that you are a relatively minor pasha, in the presence of a prince of the Romans. As such, you are my inferior in absolutely every way, Karaca Pasha, and I mean *every* way.'

The oddly angular Turk's face was slowly turning a faintly purple colour. He opened his mouth to bluster, but Constantine levelled a finger at him.

'You will treat me with the deference deserved by my blood and rank, the same as I would for Murad and Turahan. Now, if you have nothing of any true import to say, other than overstating your importance, my secretary will supply you with all the documents you need to deliver to the sultan, and this audience is over.'

Again, the ruddy-faced Turk opened his mouth, ready to speak. Gabriel, knowing what was required of him, took two steps forward, dropping his hand to the pommel of his sword meaningfully, while he gave the Turk a totally humourless smile.

Karaca Pasha shivered, looking at Gabriel's face, meeting his dead black eyes for only a moment, before looking away in discomfort. He murmured something quietly in Turkish and turned, storming from the room, his companions hurrying after him. As he walked away, Constantine called to his secretary. 'Please deliver all our missives to the pasha before he departs Monemvasia.'

Moments later, the Turk was gone, and the doors of the room closed.

'That was dangerous,' Sphrantzes muttered.

'He oversteps, and he's a monumental rectum.' Constantine grinned. 'Few things recently have given me joy, but watching that man squirm is definitely one of them.'

'He could go straight back to the sultan and Turahan and complain.'

'They would ignore him if he did, but he won't anyway. Both of them are sick to death of the Morea after this half-year of trouble, and are only too happy to be leaving it back under my control. Yes, I have to bow my head to Murad for now, and even pay him taxes, but that will not be forever. It is a temporary measure. John has secured the capital's ongoing safety with Turkish support, while it is said that János Hunyadi already stirs the pot to restart the crusade. Hunyadi is a warrior of old mettle, and it is possible he could succeed where Władysław failed. The future is far from written yet, George. Now, we take what time we have to rebuild. The Morea has been ravaged, but it is still wealthy, the harvest has been good, and with the foolish decision of the sultan to press his boot down on Greek necks, they are more loyal to Constantinople than ever. We will strengthen the Morea once more, carefully, without the Hexamilion.'

'Have you given thought to a wife yet?' Sphrantzes asked carefully.

Gabriel noted a slight twitch in Constantine's face at the comment. He had recovered much of his old self since that day at Meteora, but there was still an element of sadness he could not lose. 'This is not a discussion to be held in front of the whole court and half the military, George.'

He gestured to the door at the side, and strode over to it. The senior generals followed, and Gabriel and two of his men joined them, the rest moving to guard the door.

Inside the antechamber, Constantine slipped into a chair and poured himself a glass of pomegranate juice. Taking a sip, he sighed.

'Tell me again, George.'

'Theodora Megale Komnene, daughter of the emperor of Trebizond, who is said to fair glow with beauty and whose eyes are crystal blue, and Irina, a cousin of the king of Georgia, whose image has been compared favourably even to Helen of Troy.'

'Very nice superlatives, George. The simple fact, though, is that I am not concerned with their looks. Indeed, they can resemble a horse for all I care, as long as they fit the bill in other ways. The question is what they can offer the empire in terms of a dowry. Money and soldiers, ships and land. These are the things we need, not love, for there can be no more of that. I fear that neither of your candidates can offer enough to make it worth the match. Georgia is a shadow of her old self these days, ravaged by the riders from the steppe and constantly at war with herself, and Trebizond is almost a lost outpost of the empire, clinging on to independence desperately. We need strength, George.'

Sphrantzes sighed. 'The problem is that we do not have much to offer them *ourselves*, Constantine, and so only others in need are seeking a match. There may be somewhere to go in Wallachia, for I understand that the old Vlad Dracul is facing overthrow by Hunyadi, and destruction by Murad. But then, once again, he will not bring what you want to the table.'

Constantine nodded and sipped once more, leaning back. 'I thought never to have a wife again, and I care not for a lover, but if I marry, it will be for strength. Go east, George. Visit your friends and learn what they can offer. I will send overtures west. Venice, Serbia, the other Italian states. Someone who can supply us with an army, a navy, chests of gold, and alliances with the Western powers.'

He straightened. 'For now, we rebuild.'

Monemvasia

10 December 1447

Autumn slowly came around and spun into winter, and though things remained quiet and uneventful in the Morea, everything changed in the wider world. In August, Sphrantzes had gone east to find a suitable bride for the prince, while other notables had gone west with the same goal. Thomas, despot of the Morea, had travelled to Constantinople with Constantine's blessing, to make plans for the future of Greece and to consult with the emperor.

Within weeks of the two men's departure, word came that Theodore Palaiologos, that great pious despot, elder brother of Constantine, had passed away. With John reputedly ailing more every day, his gout insufferable, and leaving much of the administration to their mother and trusted notables of the court, that left only Constantine, Demetrios and Thomas.

Then, in October came the most earth-shaking news of all. The emperor had succumbed to his illnesses, and passed on. The court at Monemvasia immediately burst into lively anticipation. Who had John named in his will as his successor? Once, it would have been guaranteed to be Constantine, but he and his brother had been a little estranged for a time, and the prince's campaigns in Thessaly while the emperor was trying to maintain relations with the sultan had only made that worse. Demetrios was considered a poor choice in many ways for having already tried to pull off a coup against his brothers, but then his own role in smoothing over relations with the sultan had been a large part of the political security for the capital, and so he might look quite attractive as a proposition at the moment. And then there was Thomas, no longer the green young man of their early days in the Morea, but a solid, dependable prince with a good reputation, liked by all. Perhaps most critically, Thomas was in the city when the emperor died.

Constantine fretted. He would have liked nothing more than to travel there straight away and secure what he could, but the Morea required his attention for now. Several nobles were attempting to secede following the Turkish withdrawal, Nerio of Athens was making opportunistic moves at the isthmus, and most critically of all, Constantine was awaiting replies from Venice and Taranto concerning potential marriages, alliances and offers of support, and those messages would come here, not to the capital. As such, he decided he would have to await news on what John had favoured, what his mother supported, and whom the court preferred.

And so time passed in Monemvasia, tense and expectant.

'A ship from the capital, my lord,' one of the local officers announced, standing in the doorway.

Constantine looked up, sharply. In moments, he was hurrying through the palace and out through the gatehouse, his entourage trying desperately to keep up with him, as Gabriel and his Ianitzaroi kept pace, some moving ahead to clear the way. The town's streets, down from the fortress to the seafront, were vertiginous, and it took concentration to prevent taking a tumble as they descended in haste to where they could all see the impressive Venetian ship docking, the double-headed eagle of the imperial house fluttering atop every mast. By the time they reached the waterline, already fighting for breath, the ship had docked and the ramp been run out, and men were disembarking.

It was not difficult to spot the deputation as they came around the dockside towards the imperial party. Ianitzaroi spread out to secure the area for the prince, who came to a halt close to the water, his court settling in behind him, heaving in breaths. The nobleman approaching was Markos Palaiologos Iagros, one of the most influential luminaries in the capital, and a man who would have been a prime player in the choice of a successor. Gabriel found he was almost holding his breath. If the choice had settled upon Constantine, surely he would have been summoned to the capital? This had more the look of a deputation sent to inform him of another's selection… but…

The many courtiers and servants accompanying the noble came to a halt behind him. Iagros bowed his head.

'My lord despot.'

Constantine met this with a bow of his own. 'Lord Iagros. I am honoured by your presence.'

The nobleman's face had been unreadable, tense, but suddenly it broke into a wide smile. 'Likewise, my prince. I bear news of great import. Though there was no settled provision of a successor in your brother's last records, your vaunted and saintly mother has pressed your case relentlessly to all. It took little to talk the council into such a decision, and Despot Thomas was wholeheartedly in support. Your brother the lord Demetrios was less pleased, though in due course he has accepted the decision and sends his congratulations. You are chosen successor of John Palaiologos.'

Gabriel almost exploded with relief. Constantine managed to retain his regal composure, though Gabriel could almost see how he wanted to be away, somewhere a little more private, to make his true feelings known.

'You are here to summon me to the city?'

Iagros shook his head. 'Thomas explained the necessity for your presence here. It has been agreed by the court and the Patriarch himself that a coronation and investiture can be legitimately held at Mystras, and so all those whose attendance at such an event is expected will be travelling here over the next month in preparation. I'm afraid your friend Sphrantzes will not be among them, for even now he travels to the Sublime Porte to secure the acceptance and support of Sultan Murad for your succession.'

The nobleman, still smiling, stepped back and bowed once more, deeper this time.

'Congratulations, Majesty.'

Gabriel himself broke out into a rare smile. After a few years of trouble and uncertainty, things seemed to be coming together once more. The Morea was back in imperial hands and thriving, a new push of the crusade in the north might be in the offing, marriage and alliances were on the horizon, the Turks had settled in acceptance of the situation, and Murad would have no reason not to favour Constantine.

Things were recovering.

The empire would go on.

Historical Note

> Much-lamentable Corinth, what great destruction
> did you witness, when the Turks destroyed the
> Hexamilion; the entire world was filled with arms
> and bows, gold-feathered arrows, and decorated
> swords. Heads, arms, and bodies stretched over the
> plain. Ill-fated Corinth, how great a destruction
> did you witness, as well as you, manly emperor.

> Anonymous poet

Clearly, when someone is interested enough to pick up a book on a character, even if they have to read the blurb first, they are going to make certain assumptions about the book's general plot. This is rarely more true than any novel about Constantine XI and the city of Constantinople. Even the series title (Last Emperor of Rome) tells the reader what is likely to happen. And at the start of a book series, it is not uncommon for an author to frame the entire series by starting at the end and casting the whole work as a flashback. Thus, when a reader picks up this book and begins to read it, since they are immediately launched into a Turkish siege of Constantinople, I suspect many will imagine this is the last days of the empire, and the fall of the city.

Of course, you've now read the book, and so you know otherwise. In fact, of the thirty-six(!) sieges that have threatened the walls of Constantinople – of which fewer than a third could claim success – the last five were all prosecuted by the Ottomans. They had attempted to break the great eastern bastion of

Christendom in 1391, 1394, 1411 and 1422 before the city finally fell to Mehmet the Conqueror in 1453. In looking to tell the story of the life of the very last real emperor of Rome, telling the story of the second-to-last siege is unavoidable, since that is the first moment in which Constantine sees action and the time he begins to shine as a character.

We are immensely lucky to have a first-hand account of the siege from the pen of the historian John Kananos, a Byzantine writer of the time. Kananos gives a great deal of detail in his colourful account of the siege, much of which I have used or paraphrased in my own telling. There is no need to delve into too much detail, but Kananos attributes the saving of the city (as per my own version) to the use of the icon of the Virgin Mary that was the city's most sacred object, which tourists came to see, and which was brought out in times of peril, and then to the empress's appearance on the walls and the Turks mistaking her for a vision of the Mother of God. Fairly fanciful stuff, of course, and though I've followed it here, being the main written account, it is not hard to believe that in actual fact the siege was lifted so that Murad could return across the Bosphorus and put his own house in order, with the full intention to return and finish the job some time.

The Turkish obsession with Constantinople went far beyond politics and geography. Yes, their expansion had brought them into conflict with the empire in time, and they had gradually abraded imperial lands, even through earth-shaking wars at times, until they had reduced the empire to a small strip of land around the city and some territory in Greece, but it was not this that was necessarily the driving force for the sultans. In some ways, it was jealousy mixed with reverence that drove the need to have the holy city of Constantinople. Don't forget that the Turks, as Muslims, believed in many of the same legends, characters and tenets as the Orthodox folk of Constantinople; that their emperor was ordained by God made his position something of a challenge to the sultans. There is a strong suggestion that when the end came in 1453, Mehmet did not see himself as the conqueror that history names him, and the destroyer the Greeks remember, but more as a successor. He saw himself as taking over from the Byzantine emperors, rather than removing them.

Anyway, I digress from the plot of the first book in this series. On to the characters. Most of the personalities in this book are real, but I have created a cast of soldiers to be my protagonists, based upon vague references to a military unit. Rome has a long history of foreign service as imperial bodyguards. Emperors from Augustus to Nero had a Batavian Guard, Constantine the Great had plenty of Germans around him, and students of Byzantine history will know of the Varangians, a guard initially of Scandinavian and Rus Vikings, then later Saxon Britons, who protected the emperor in Byzantium.

The Varangians were long gone by this time. Even in their homelands Vikings had become a thing of legend, with the last even vague suggestion of Varangians serving in the city in the siege of 1204 during the Fourth Crusade — and yes, I've written about that too. In fact, you could read my *Wolves of Odin: Bear of Byzantium* to see the imperial guard in 1041, and then *Templar: City of God* to see them in 1204! But the simple fact is that all the more famous Byzantine military units had gone by the early fifteenth century. All we have left is names, a few fragments and vague clues. One of them — and in fact the only one that could be considered to be an imperial bodyguard — is the *Ianitzaroi*, which I have used for this book. They appear referenced in only one work, and because of that, in only one brief period, and there is sadly no real information about them. Their name, as you undoubtedly spotted, sounds a lot like Janissary, the bodyguard of the Ottoman sultan, though it is generally assumed that it was the Byzantine unit that led to the development of the Ottoman equivalent, and not the other way around.

The writer Gregoras tells us that the emperor John VI formed a bodyguard from 500 former Catalan sailors who had remained in the city, and it is suggested that this is the basis for the unit. E. Zachariadou asserts the belief that the name *Ianitzaroi* is a Greek corruption of an extant word already in use in Western Europe, variously heard as *janizzarie, janizzeri, janua, genetari, giannetario, janizzeri* and *janitor*. This word is presumed to originate in the Berber tribe called the Zanata, who had supplied light cavalry as guards in Spain, settling in Catalunya. Catalans are noted, as you are now aware, as being involved in imperial affairs throughout this period, and so this connection is far from impossible. That they might be from an originally Islamic tribe and almost certainly converted to Catholicism in Spain does not mean they should still be that in 1422. Just as Constantine's wife in the Morea converts to Orthodoxy and takes on a Greek name, so it could be considered normal for foreigners in the service of the emperor to convert. This certainly seems to have been the case for the Varangians.

Thus were born my protagonists. Gabriel (a good Catalan name, along with Gaspar and Manuel) are Ianitzaroi: Catalan mercenaries of Berber heritage who for three generations have served the Byzantine emperors. Oh, and incidentally, the condition in Gabriel's eyes is a known phenomenon, by the name of *aniridia*. He is by far the ugliest lead character I have ever written, and probably the least friendly. I love him.

The scope of this novel is in some ways so far beyond anything I have written before, in that even during the planning stages I knew a hard decision needed to be made. Either the trilogy was going to expand to cover ten to fifteen books, or I was going to have to find a way to streamline it. Hence the *Star Wars*-style scene-setting pages here and there. I imagined them in yellow lettering disappearing into the darkness of space as they appeared, before a Star Destroyer showed up and blew Constantinople to smithereens. I hope this has worked for you. It has allowed me to skip years of politics at a time, and Byzantine politics is one of the most convoluted things in world history. (In a deputation to Italy to discuss unification of the

Churches, it took twenty days to arrange the seating plan!) This is the problem sometimes with carving up a story into chunks. Book 2 will cover only a few short years, and Book 3 just the one great cataclysmic event, but that meant that Book 1 needed to cover everything that made Constantine who he was by the time he took the throne. Phew. It has to get easier from here on...

So we move on to the Battle of the Echinades. This battle is renowned as the last true naval action of the Byzantine Empire. It took place, as noted, around that set of islands in north-west Greece. Though I have nodded to all the detail in the single account of the battle, the action I have described is based on one specific part of the battle. Torno Tocco is known to have fled after reaching Lefkas, while another cousin was captured. Laskaris was the man in charge of the battle. Constantine is not mentioned as being part of it at all. Perhaps in truth he remained at Glarentza, making the tea for his brother, but it suited my plot to have him present, and his involvement is far from impossible.

I have referenced a cannon on the Byzantine ship. The world had changed by this point from the late Roman world of dromons and catapults, and cannon were definitely being used aboard ship, but these ships were still galleys, long before men'o'war with their gundecks. The technology was still relatively new, and what that might mean aboard a galley led to the scene of the exploding gun. The guns would have been falcons at this time, smaller cannon, before the development of the falconet later in the century.

I'm not sure there need be much said about the entire affair of Patras. It is more or less lifted from the history books, with Gabriel and friends shoehorned into the timeline. The texts tell us more or less what happened, including the episode with Constantine being unhorsed before the walls and saved as George Sphrantzes was dragged inside as a prisoner, including that ridiculous (but true!) scene where Sphrantzes finds out the intentions of Malatesta and the Turks by getting them all drunk in an inn and copying their letters. All should be good. My only 'mea culpa' throughout the campaign is the inclusion of Torno Tocco.

Quite simply, I wanted an antagonist I could drag through the book and make part of everything bad that happened. If I could have made him responsible for the deaths of Constantine's wives, I would have considered it. Tocco certainly had a martial career. After the death of Carlo I, the man against whom Constantine had campaigned at Glarentza, the succession passed to his nephew, Carlo II. Unfortunately, this kicked off a family feud and semi-civil war. We are not told where Torno fits into the mess (and attempting to follow the family at this time is a true lesson in chaos), but the Turkish general Sinan became involved, and ended up taking control of Ioannina from the family in 1430, expanding Turkish power in the Balkans, and reducing the remaining Italian power. We are told that Carlo II maintained his rule (with Ottoman vassalage), but the various sons opposing him ended up serving as Ottoman puppets. Torno (also Turno) Tocco's fate is unrecorded, and so I have pulled him into subsequent events.

You may be surprised to hear of the Hexamilion. In truth, it was never particularly effective. Covering the six miles of the Isthmus of Corinth and therefore effectively sealing off the Peloponnese (six miles being the base for its name), the wall was built, destroyed and rebuilt many times, and never really held anyone out. In some ways it was more important as a symbol than as a true defence. Few parts of the wall are now visible, though fragments have been unearthed during excavations.

One of the main themes of this first novel is the attempts at unifying the Catholic and Orthodox Churches. Quite simply, it was never going to happen, but the tantalising possibility of it working led the last few generations of the Palaiologoi to cling to it as the only great hope to save the shrinking empire from the Turks. The older emperor Manuel II (I have never referred to him by name in the text to prevent confusion with Gabriel's third in command) had pursued the possibility, and so did John. Even Constantine believed it was the hope for the empire. And as happens in this book, despite everything, a deal of union was agreed. All terms were settled, and the emperor returned to Constantinople, where it quickly became apparent that no matter what the emperor or the Patriarch said, the people and the clergy of the empire were never going to accept the terms.

Moreover, the attempts at union offended the Turks, and drove them a little closer to conflict. Thus, while Constantine was regent, Sphrantzes tells us how they feared a Turkish attack in the emperor's absence, and were relieved when the army marched on Serbian Semendria (modern-day Smederevo) instead. That they might throw in their lot with the treacherous Demetrios when he turned on his brothers and attempted to wrest power from them by force can hardly be a surprise, given that he promoted himself as the pro-Turkish, anti-papal option. That Demetrios was let off so easily remains, for me, one of the failings of John and Constantine.

I note strongly the ill luck the Palaiologos brothers had with wives. In fact, in the end it was only Thomas who managed to sire a serious family, and that too late to make much of a difference to the dynasty. Constantine certainly seems to have fallen for Maddalena Tocco, and was bereft following her untimely death. His second marriage we know little about. Sphrantzes, our main source, only really tells us that they were married on Lesbos; Constantine left her there and went back to the Morea, then picked her back up on the way to the capital before being trapped on Lemnos with her, where she died, and miscarried their child. That he did not take her with him to the Morea so soon after their wedding suggested to me something wrong with the relationship, yet the existence of an unborn child at her death suggests that it was overcome. I have attempted to give this sequence a reason. I hope it holds.

We know little about the Ottoman blockade that holds Constantine up for around a month from Sphrantzes' account, other than he eventually gets past it, only to arrive at the capital and find he's missed all the action. I have attempted to gloss over this rather unexciting and flat lack of event by building more into the blockade, while having it as Constantine's initiative when regent that gifts his brother a sufficient army to throw back Demetrios and the Turks.

Khalkokondyles, in his account, makes a different claim: that the Turkish admiral landed troops and besieged Constantine at Kotzinos, demolished the city walls with cannon, but was unable to take the city and eventually just left. This sequence of events seems odd. That the whole Turkish fleet could demolish the walls but then not take the city is strange, and given that we are told that Aikaterine was ill and buried at Palaiokastron on the far side of the island, a city siege seems unlikely. I have therefore plumped for limiting the Turkish action to a naval blockade.

For the sea actions here, I'm grateful to Simon Elliott for introducing me to naval wargaming, which I used to map out each plan so that it worked. The various actions Constantine takes against the Turkish blockade are my own creation, given the lack of detail. Both attempted direct attacks with blockade runners and the use of fireships are tried and tested naval tactics. Though the idea of turning a vessel into a floating bomb is mine, it is inspired by the story of the Confederate submarine, the *Hunley*, which was used to break the blockade of Charleston harbour in 1864, sinking the *Housatonic* with a torpedo attached to the front of the vessel by a spar. The damage done by detonating powder magazines can be atrocious, as can be witnessed in the shattered remains of the powder tower at Heidelberg castle, or in the story of the Nea Ekklasia at Constantinople, used by the Ottomans as a powder magazine and struck by lightning in 1490, leaving no trace of the building or the surrounding area.

And so Constantine returned to the capital once again, only to find that he was too late, and that the usurper and his Turkish allies had been beaten back. The Turks had left, and Demetrios was in custody. It remains a ridiculous fact that he was neither executed nor exiled, but was in fact released shortly thereafter to go out and start causing trouble again. There are several reasons why Constantine might have wanted to return to the Morea over staying in the city, but bad feeling between him and the emperor is one of the most likely. I have glossed over much of the politicking around this, and moved on to the action in the Morea, not because it is not interesting, but rather because it would considerably slow the pace of this book, when what was coming was so exciting.

In his account, Sphrantzes oddly makes no mention at all of any campaign in Thessaly, which is staggering, considering the import of the war. He merely mentions the Hexamilion being rebuilt and his various journeys to see kings and other dignitaries. Khalkokondyles, on the other hand, does talk of it. He gives, in fact, history's only account:

> While he was repairing the wall at the Isthmus, he seized from the sultan the land outside the Morea, annexed Boeotia, made the city of Thebes his own, and seized the entire Boeotia. The tyrant of Athens made a pact with him and promised to pay tribute to him. The Wallachians who inhabit Mount Pindos speak the Dacian language and resemble the Dacians by the Ister came and gave themselves up to him; they began to campaign against the Turks who had settled in Thessaly and received a lord from the ruler of the Moreots. Leodorikion, the small town in Lokris, settled by the city of Phanarion near Pindos, received its lord from the sultan [...] When Constantine finished the repairs of the Isthmus wall, he sent an army against these territories of the sultan, raided the region, and maintained a state of war.

Thus we have surprisingly little information about the campaign, even given that account. I have done what I could to flesh it out and tell the tale a little more fully. The garrison in the pass is my own invention, though such a garrison makes perfect sense, and that pass would be the most direct route to Thebes from the isthmus.

We have no information on the fall of Thebes, and the presence of Janissaries is my own conceit. The corps had already been in existence for the better part of a century, and were often armed with bows. It was, however, during the reign of Murad II that they started to arm with guns, and by the time he passed away, only six years later, guns were their standard weapon. As such, it seems reasonable to put at least a few guns in their hands in 1444. We know that the invasion of Thessaly came in two prongs, led by Constantine and by Kantakouzenos, that the latter was so successful that towns were renamed after him, and that Constantine made it as far as the Pindus range in northern Greece, securing the support of the Vlach peoples. What happened between this successful push and the sudden collapse of it all in the wake of the crusade's failure, we have in no detail. Between the Pindus and Tırhala lay the Meteora monasteries, which had managed to stay oddly untouched despite Turkish overlordship. Though the surviving monasteries these days are generally reachable by steps, they were not in 1444, and we know only that they were reached by ladders and ropes, which protected them from Turkish raids. Dometius is a real character, though that he was Helene Dragaš' confessor is my own invention in order to tie threads of this story together.

And there is where the dream of imperial rebirth dies, sadly.

Władysław and his crusaders met a sticky end at Varna, and the campaign against the Turks ended there and then. It took some time for Murad and Turahan Bey to come for Constantine, despite the clear provocation that the prince had taken half of Thessaly off them for a while. He spent some time ravaging Athens and putting Nerio in his place, then came for the isthmus. He is known to have used artillery at the wall, and it is this – something the Byzantines seriously lacked – which changed everything. Constantine clearly planned on holding the wall, at least for a while, since he garrisoned it so strongly. That it fell in a matter of days can only be down to the immense damage the cannon did. There is no direct evidence that any big 'city-killer' cannon was used, but given the speed with which the wall was destroyed, it seems highly likely, plus that would have been another explanation for why it took Murad so long to begin the war. Also, the securing of Varna would give Murad access to engineers and resources that could build such monsters.

Though we have yet to see the Turk's biggest cannon, designed by Orban and deployed in 1453, there were still immense cannon used earlier than that, and examples survive to this day, including the so-called fifteenth-century 'Dardanelles Gun', now held at Fort Nelson in Portsmouth.

The wall fell quickly and with immense losses to the imperial forces. There are a few accounts, which I have used where possible to give life and colour to my story, but what happened to Constantine is not given in detail. We know that he escaped to Laconia, and that Thomas also survived. Which brings us almost to the end. I have given Torno Tocco a nicely fitting demise. And from there, it is really mostly a matter of mopping up. The following year saw some of the most important events in the last century of the Byzantine world.

Murad and Turahan Bey ravaged the Morea, with some recorded viciousness, yet they failed to take control of the important cities of Patras and Mystras, and though they compelled Constantine to accept the position of a Turkish vassal, they left soon after, and little had changed in the long run in the Morea. Constantine began the search for a new wife who could bring him political and military advantage, and then two of the brothers died in quick succession. Reading into the various sources, it is clear that Demetrios hurried to the capital upon the death of John, and immediately began a campaign to succeed, but finding Thomas in the city, he was prevented from doing so easily, and with Helene Dragaš already favouring Constantine, along with many of the court, the selection was simple. Constantine was the only brother not in the capital when he was chosen as successor.

Thus we have followed his life from his first engagement to his succession as emperor, outliving three older brothers, prosecuting the last expansion of imperial territory in Byzantine history, the last Byzantine sea battle, witnessing the failure of a crusade, and the rise and fall of the fortunes of the Morea.

We shall return to his tale in the second volume, with our protagonist no longer prince of the Romans, but now Constantine XI Palaiologos, emperor of Rome.

Thank you for reading, I hope you enjoyed our journey, and see you soon.

Simon Turney
June 2025